THE TAKEN ONE

A FALCON FALLS SECURITY NOVEL

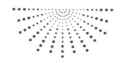

BRITTNEY SAHIN

Chief Editor: Michelle Fewer

Editor: Ashley Bauman

Proofreader: Judy Zweifel, Judy's Proofreading

Cover Design: LJ, Mayhem Cover Creations

Image License (front/back): Alejandro Caracuel

Ebook ISBN: 9781947717350

Paperback ISBN: 9798386618636

❀ Created with Vellum

This book is for a special person.

*It's for **you.***

It's for you on the days when you may want to give up.
Don't.

It's for you on the days that it feels like there is no light at the end of the tunnel.
There will be.

And it's for you on the days that are amazing and bright. On the days your dreams come true.

MUSIC PLAYLIST

Spotify

Most of these songs are paired with chapters based on the beat/vibe of the music. Enjoy!

Hope (feat. Winona Oak) - Parker remix - The Chainsmokers *(prologue)*

Last Night - Morgan Wallen *(playing at the bar in chapter 1)*

On My Way - Kate Linn *(chapters 3-4)*

OUT OUT (feat. Charli XCX & Saweetie) - Joel Corry, Jax Jones *(first half of chapter 7)*

Feels Great (feat. Fetty Wap & CVBZ) - Cheat Codes *(second half of chapter 7)*

Roller Coaster - Luke Bryan *(chapter 11)*

On Tonight - Chase Rice *(chapter 17)*

Calm Down (feat. Selena Gomez) - Rema, Selena Gomez *(chapter 20)*

Darkside - Alan Walker, Au/Ra, Tomine Harket *(chapters 32-33)*

No Time Soon - Jordan Davis *(chapter 35)*

A Little Bit Dangerous - CRMNL *(chapter 34)*

Ciao Adios - Anne-Marie *(chapter 37)*

Wannabe - Dylan Schneider *(chapter 39)*

Going, Going, Gone - Luke Combs (*chapter 40*)

Love You Anyway - Luke Combs (*chapter 41*)

My Person - Brandon Ray *(chapter 42)*

PROLOGUE

SUMMER 2010 - THIRTEEN YEARS AGO -
WASHINGTON, D.C.

She leaves tomorrow. And now of all days, I find out that . . . Gray allowed the thought to circle down the drain, remembering he was at a bar to numb the pain, not aggravate it.

But the second glass of whiskey had yet to ease the band of discomfort stretching tight in his stomach. The pain reminded him of his days as a teenager in Dallas, when he'd belly flop into his pool, trying to prepare himself for becoming a SEAL.

Not that he wound up going that route, but thanks to his stupidity, he could outswim most men in his battalion. *Well, I could swim. Now I have to learn how to do that all over again too.*

"And you don't think there's a chance Tessa didn't make the connection?" Jack asked.

Gray looked over at his best friend sitting beside him. They were at a whiskey bar in Brightwood, a neighborhood in the northwest part of D.C., not far from Walter Reed Army Medical Center. He'd spent most of his summer in rehab there after his accident almost four months ago. "You're not serious, right?"

"I guess I can see why she wouldn't want you to know," Jack said with a shrug. "Conflict of interest." He raised his glass to his lips, his eyes moving to the wall of whiskey behind the bar. "And not for nothing, but when I couldn't get through to you, she did."

Gray grumbled, thinking about the first time he'd met Tessa. Two months ago, his physical therapist, Terrance, had introduced her as a "PT hopeful," there to shadow him and learn from the best. And yeah, Terrance was one of the best. *I'm walking because of him. And, well, because of Tessa too.*

When Gray had first set eyes on her, he'd grunted and demanded she work with someone else. He didn't need some gorgeous young woman with big brown eyes pitying him. She had too much pep in her step, while he was lucky to take three steps without pausing for a deep breath. Hell, the woman even drew hearts around her name on her temporary ID badge.

No, he'd decided on the spot it'd be a piss-poor idea to work with her. He may not have been a Navy man, but he inherited his "sailor's mouth" from his father. One that he could use freely around Terrance, a veteran himself, but not around Tessa. Her sweet, innocent ears wouldn't be able to handle his daily string of *fucks* when he tried to stand or walk. Not to mention his strong Texan mother would have his ass if she heard him talk like that around a woman. And he doubted he'd be able to bite his tongue and not curse when shit got hard. Because it HAD been hard. Every hour of every day since his accident in April.

"I asked her flat out," Gray finally revealed, thinking back

2

to when he first noticed Tessa's name badge when they'd met. "I said, and I quote, 'Please tell me God doesn't hate me that much, and you're not related to THAT Sloane. You're not *his* daughter, are you?'"

Jack set down his glass and swiveled on the seat to face Gray, resting his forearm on the bar top. "Well, in her defense, you told her not to tell you."

The slight twitch of his friend's lips had Gray tipping his head, eyes moving to the ceiling as he released a harsh breath. He was doing his best to ignore the pain creeping up on him, this time in his leg.

"I remember Sloane mentioning he had kids," Jack continued, "but—"

"Well, Tessa's not a kid. She's twenty-one." Gray dropped his attention to his whiskey glass, debating a third. "*Barely* twenty-one," he added, frustrated at that fact.

"That's not *that* young. Besides, you're only twenty-eight." Jack chuckled. "It's not like you're her old man's age."

She was still too young for him. Not that anything had happened between them. But over the summer, he'd nearly crossed the line more times than he'd like to admit. Tessa didn't work for the hospital, so the doctor-patient lines were a bit blurry. And since she was only in D.C. for her shadowing hours, they'd decided to hang out after hours, even though she drove him crazy ninety-nine percent of the time.

But she was leaving tomorrow. Heading to Boston for grad school to start her life. *And I'm going . . . where?*

Forever and a day ago, he'd known where he was going.

To the Army.

Jack had given him the idea to change course and not follow in his father's footsteps in becoming a sailor. And his

3

father had almost punched Jack in the face after Gray's accident.

"He'd still have two feet if he'd joined the Navy, like he should've, instead of listening to you," his father had barked at Jack while by Gray's hospital bed. There'd been tears in his eyes that day and Gray couldn't help but wonder . . . had he ever witnessed his father cry before then?

He knew his father didn't truly blame Jack for what happened. He just wanted a targeted enemy. Someone he could unleash hell upon. And Jack had been willing to take the verbal beating if it'd make Gray's father feel better.

Gray swung his attention back toward his friend, doing the math in his head again. *Twenty-eight minus twenty-one . . . fuck.* Every time he analyzed it, the numbers kept coming out ass backward. Sure, he was only seven years older, but his body felt more like that difference was closer to fourteen. "So, what's your point?"

"I actually forgot my point." He smirked. "But what I do know is on the days when your family and friends couldn't be there for you, *she* was. Terrance is great and all, but if I'm being honest, Tessa motivated you in ways he couldn't." He lifted his brows a few times, his insinuation not lost on Gray. "So, maybe don't be mad at her for withholding the truth about her father. You needed her. I'm glad she didn't retreat when you tried to get her to quit on you."

And he'd tried damn hard to get her to bow out too. That first month with her, he'd been a total asshole eight out of seven days a week. But Tessa, with her bubbly personality, and adorable klutziness, dug her heels in and refused to leave.

Not that he'd ever seen her in heels. Occasionally, his imagination would run wild with images of her naked, wearing only blue stilettos that matched her ridiculous blueberry-scented lip balm. He hadn't even known scented lip balms were a thing until her. But the number of times he'd nearly kissed her to see if her lips tasted the way they smelled had been one too many.

"It's not like my lips are blue. They just smell like blueberries." She'd brushed off his complaint after he'd grunted his frustration with her choice in lip wear. He wasn't angry with her; he'd really just been pissed he couldn't stop staring at her mouth during their PT sessions. *"And what do you have against blueberries anyway?"* she'd asked while waving an arm around in an overly dramatic but adorable way.

"And why do you like them so much?" he'd growled back during one of his less-than-stellar assholery days. He'd been angry with her because she kept giving him the will to live when he'd been content to "just survive" in a foggy state of misery.

"Maybe don't even mention the fact you know when you go to say goodbye?" Jack interrupted his memories, snagging him back to the present issue: Tessa had lied.

"Who says I'm still going to see her?" Gray sloshed the liquid around in his glass before finishing his drink.

Jack shot him a smug look. "Oh, I don't know, because you're not a dick. And we're at a bar two blocks from where she's been living this summer."

"First of all, I am a dick. Second, we're here because"— Gray lifted his now-empty glass—"this is one of the few bars that never fails to carry Buffalo Trace. We're *not* here because she's down the street packing, preparing to leave me."

Jack's mouth rounded into a smartass O, and Gray lowered his head, realizing his Freudian slip.

"Don't say it," Gray warned, his free hand going to his

leg, hating the throb there. Would he ever get used to what happened?

"Listen, I've known you for almost two decades, and there's not a chance in hell you'll let Tessa leave without seeing her off."

"Yeah, and what makes you say that?" Gray set down the glass and went for his wallet, deciding against a third round, but Jack beat him to it, paying the check first.

"Because Tessa's the *only* woman you've never compared to your West Point ex-girlfriend. And you've dated *a lot* of women since her. You don't have the Romeo call sign for nothing, man." He grinned. "That lack of comparison has to mean something, don't you think?"

Sydney? Why in the hell was he bringing up her? "Tessa's a friend. Maybe not even that. She was just babysitting me at the clinic for her hours. We just . . . got to know each other during that time. She likes to talk. In fact, she never shuts up. That's the only reason I know every detail about the woman." He cursed. "Except that her father's the colonel." *Was* his colonel. *I'm out now.* "She left that part out."

Jack tossed back the rest of his whiskey and set his hands on the mahogany bar top. "The woman drives you nuts because you like her."

"Yeah, that makes no sense." He shifted his ass around on the seat, holding the counter for support, then adjusted his leg in preparation to stand, still not used to the prosthesis. At least he'd been able to ditch the crutch.

He tried to tell himself one day he'd forget it was there, and he'd just be . . . himself, but he had no clue when that day would come.

"So, if she's a glorified babysitter, why'd you ask her to hang out these last few weeks? And why are you so upset about her old man?"

"Did you drive all the way here just to irritate the hell out of me?"

"Abso-fucking-lutely." Jack winked.

Gray rolled his eyes and tossed a quick look around the bar. An old habit, but he always liked to clock everyone in the room. He never knew if someone might turn into an enemy. The place was pretty dead since it wasn't even seventeen hundred hours yet, and most people were still at work.

His gaze landed on a woman sitting alone at a nearby table. Her eyes were focused on his jeans as if she knew something was off.

While the specially designed pants fit over the prosthesis, they didn't hide the awkward bulk from the socket; a dead giveaway he was different. But he hated the scared looks he got from kids (and hell, adults too) while wearing shorts, so he regularly opted for pants.

"Let them call you a machine. A robot. Don't hide the leg. Different is interesting. Hell, maybe you can get more chicks with that thing. Some sympathy fucks," his childhood friend, Dale, had told him last month when visiting.

"Thanks, but I don't want or need anyone's sympathy. Fucks included," Gray had grumbled back.

Gray did his best to push away the emotions trying to choke him and fixed his attention back on Jack. What had they been talking about? *Right. Tessa.*

"So, tell me. Why, oh why, did you choose to spend more time than necessary with her?" Jack pressed.

"I was hungry one night," Gray offered up a bullshit excuse. "Thought she might be too. So we ate." He clutched his thigh, hating the pain below the knee that wasn't there and only in his head. *Fuck phantom pain.*

"And that turned into an every-night ritual with you two, followed by her—"

"Forcing me to walk around places." *Like Blockbuster.* The woman acted as though she could never decide whether to watch a romantic comedy or a horror film. There was never an in-between with her.

Was she indecisive? Sure. But he knew she liked to push him to his limits, believing him capable of giving her more than he did back at the hospital. So, laps around the store three times a week to choose a movie had become part of her routine for him. Not that she ever admitted it.

"My advice is to forget what you learned about her father and go see her. She's officially done with her PT shadow hours, and is no longer off-limits, so maybe now is the time you test out your third leg." Jack stood and offered his arm to help Gray rise, but he stubbornly resisted and managed himself.

"I'm not sleeping with Tessa." Instead, he would just continue to have fantasies about pinning her to every surface of his temporary D.C. digs. Fantasies where she wore only stilettos and matching blueberry lip balm. *Or was it ChapStick?* Whatever it was called, he'd visualized kissing it free from her lips, then sinking his mouth between her thighs and kissing her there as well.

"But you want to," Jack, the know-it-all, commented.

"Have you heard nothing I've said?"

"No, but I was listening to your obnoxiously loud internal monologue." Jack elbowed him. "I mean, fuck, turn down the volume on those thoughts if you don't want me hearing them."

"Screw you." *Not that you're wrong.* Gray started to walk but faltered, slamming his hand onto a nearby high-top table to balance himself. *Shit.* He inhaled through his nose and gave himself a second before freeing the breath to try walking again.

"But seriously, I know what you want. Or should I say *who* you want?" Jack tapped Gray's back twice once they were on the street, and the harsh August sunlight had them both grabbing their shades. "So, I'm heading to the hotel to call my wife so she can yell at me again because it's always something these days, and you're going to Tessa's."

"Things still not good with Jill?"

"She wants me to quit, you know that. Do the civilian-life thing. Try real estate if you can believe that." He leaned against the building, folding his arms. "Can you imagine me selling houses? I know how to breach properties. Blow shit up. Kill people if I have to. But have an open house, smile, and talk about square footage and school districts with random people? Hell no."

The idea *was* comical. But historically, what Jill wanted, Jill got.

"Is she worried what happened to me will happen to you?"

"I'm only ten years in. I'm not done. I didn't bust my ass to get the Girl Scout hat," Jack began in a teasing voice, "just to get out now."

Army Special Forces. AKA, the Green Berets. America's quiet professionals. Unconventional warfare to get shit done for the military. That'd been Gray's life too. *And now I'm on disability. I'm done.*

"Shit, I'm sorry, man. I shouldn't have said that," Jack apologized. "I know you'd operate another twenty years if you could."

"Look, I'm lucky to be alive, right? I'm fine. I'll figure something out." Maybe those lines were a bit rehearsed, but he'd quickly realized his family and friends worried too much about him when he said anything dark. They'd poke and prod with concern if he didn't act optimistic. Of course there'd been some bad days. Weeks, really. But he had Tessa reminding him at every turn he was a fighter, so he did his best to be one. Even on the days he wanted to give up.

"Well, I'm planning to swing by your place in the morning before I head out. I'm spinning back up for an unknown amount of time." Jack reached for his shoulder, ignoring a few people passing them on the street. "But if you're not there because you've opted for a sleepover with Tessa, consider this my goodbye, just in case."

"Not going to lie, I'm jealous you're operating. There. I said it." Gray set his back to the building, needing the support. He wasn't used to standing in one place for too long. "Charlie Company just got back from a five-month deployment. So I know you're not attaching with them. What's the op?"

Jack's focus moved to the ground between them, and he smoothed a hand over his beard. A beard was often viewed as a status symbol in special operations since most soldiers had to be clean-cut. "I have orders not to tell you until after the mission is complete." His shoulders fell with the obvious weight he was holding, and now Gray knew why his best friend had popped in for the impromptu visit. "But fuck it."

Gray's heart jumped into his throat, and he nearly lost his balance. Thank God for the brick wall behind him. "You're going after them, aren't you?"

Jack slowly looked up. "The Agency secured actionable intelligence. We have a location for their base of operation in the Helmand Province. And I'm going to kill them for what they did to you. Every last one of them."

"Is that why the colonel randomly showed up today? He hasn't shown his face to me since TK."

TK, or Tarinkot, had been the base in southern Afghanistan with the closest level-one trauma center to his accident. From what Gray was told, the medevac pilots barely had time to land their Black Hawk before being called away to try and save another wounded warrior.

Gray had watched the news all summer, and it was being dubbed by the media as one of the deadliest years for special operations in Afghanistan. Of course, Gray had witnessed it firsthand, so it wasn't new information to him.

"He should've visited you sooner." Jack shook his head. "All I know is we'll get justice."

"I don't care about me. I care about the Rangers who died that day. Get vengeance for them. For their families." He removed his glasses to look his friend in the eyes.

Jack shoved his shades into his hair as he promised, "You have my word."

THIRTY MINUTES LATER, GRAY STOOD OUTSIDE TESSA'S place, staring at the number 3 on the blue door of her temporary home. Even her door was blue. Of course, it would be. She was the sunshine to his gloomy skies. *And the reason for my blue balls.*

But Jack had been right, and he couldn't let her leave without saying goodbye. He just couldn't decide if he planned to share the fact the colonel visited him today.

"My daughter worked here this summer. Shadowing a PT," Colonel Sloane had mentioned in their conversation, and then Terrance spoke up and shared that Tessa had worked with Gray.

And Gray's world had flipped upside down. He'd actually lost his balance and fallen, and Terrance and the colonel had helped him sit.

"Of all the PTs she could've matched with, she wound up

with yours? God sure hates me, huh?" Sloane had said once realization struck.

"Yeah, my thoughts exactly," Gray had responded. Whatever Sloane had planned to say after that, it never came. He doubted it would've been an apology. Sloane commanded a brigade of over four thousand men. He had to make tough calls. But in Gray's mind, he'd made the wrong call in April.

Gray let go of a heavy breath, preparing himself to knock, but the door swung open before he had a chance, and he found himself facing Colonel Sloane.

Murphy's Law: anything that can go wrong will go wrong. The guys on Gray's team had their top-ten rules they'd dubbed **Murphy's Laws of Combat**, hanging up at their last FOB, forward operating base. And all ten popped to mind at the sight of the colonel before him.

"Shit," Gray mumbled, the thought meant to stay trapped behind the walls of his mind.

Sloane held the door open with his palm, his green eyes landing tightly on Gray, a gruff breath falling from his lips. The colonel resembled the actor, Liam Neeson, and when the movie *Taken* came out in 2008, every guy on base referred to the colonel by the movie character's name when talking shit about him. Even though Sloane was American born and devoid of a foreign accent, he would forever be "Bryan Mills" in Gray's mind.

"What are you doing here?" Sloane asked as Tessa appeared, ducking under his arm.

Wearing a plain pink scoop-neck tee partially tucked into a pair of frayed jean shorts, Gray did his best not to allow his focus to wander to her long, tanned legs. *Shit, how do I explain this?*

"Right," the colonel blurted out, letting go of the door, but Gray caught it, stopping it from closing. "I'm leaving, and he's walking me out." He kissed Tessa on the cheek, then added, "I'll be gone for at least two months. I'll check up on you in Boston when I get back." And with that, he stepped into the hall with Gray, tipping his head as a directive for Gray to follow him.

Tessa bit her lip, lacking any gloss tonight, as her brows slanted over her apologetic brown eyes. He nodded, unsure what for, then proceeded to follow the colonel down the hall and into the parking lot.

"You mind telling me what you're doing here? Her shadowing your PT is one thing; you feeling friendly enough to visit my daughter after hours is quite another." His palm hit the sleek black frame of the SUV, his eyes catching Gray's in the window's reflection.

"I don't see how that's your business." He was no longer under his command, so why not speak his mind?

That had Sloane about-facing, turning quickly toward him. "What you do with my daughter is sure as fuck my business, son."

"I'm not your son. Not your anything for that matter. Not anymore," he attacked back, hoping he could remain standing without grabbing hold of his leg as pain shot down his thigh. Not that he'd regularly worked with the colonel given how high up Sloane was in the chain of command, but still . . .

Sloane cupped his mouth, eyes surrendering to the sky as if resisting the impulse to pull rank on him, knowing it damn well no longer mattered.

"Stay away from my daughter, Gray." The finger-pointing came next. Right to his chest. "Do I make myself clear?"

Crystal fucking clear, Gray kept his sarcastic comment to himself. Number three on **Murphy's Laws of Combat** back at his last FOB: *If the enemy is in range, so are you.* And right now, that enemy was Tessa's dear old dad. "*Lima Charlie*," he said, military parlance for loud and clear.

"Boy, it's like you woke up today and thought, today is a good day to . . ."

Gray interrupted the colonel's borderline snarl, "To die?" He cocked his head, forgetting the pain in his leg, and he felt Tessa watching them between the blinds. Sloane must've realized the same because he backed up, removing his finger from his chest. "I did die. For thirty seconds that day," he reminded him. "But you know that, right? Read the report." His hands tensed at his sides as he tried not to walk through the messed-up events of his team's mission from that day during his last deployment.

But as much as he tried to resist, the memories were like a bright, hot flash of light in his head. They made it hard to see straight. To see the man before him.

"You blame me for what happened?" Sloane scoffed. "You're kidding me, right?" He shook his head.

His words knocked Gray back to the present. "My captain sure as hell didn't tell us to stand down, but I know his orders came from above. From you." Gray jutted out his chin. "We could've made it. We could've saved those men. We were the closest element to them and already in the air. You ordered my men to stand down and leave them there to die."

"You *wouldn't* have made it in time, and we would've been burying more bodies had we given you the green light to assist. And believe me, I've had words with our point man at the Agency for the bad intel he gave us. I'll have to live with the fact those Rangers were ever out there in the first place because of it." Another pointed finger. "But my decision to turn your ass back around—"

"Caused our helicopter to get shot down." Gray gripped

his leg. "Had we kept moving forward, maybe I wouldn't have a prosthesis?" And he still believed those men may not have died, and that was what haunted him the most. Gray had attempted to convince the pilot to ignore orders, but the pilot never had a chance to defy them. They took a hit and went down. "But you know what really pisses me off? You were willing to risk sending a Black Hawk to medevac me to safety as if my life mattered more than those Rangers on the ground."

The colonel, who'd only recently earned that rank before Gray's last deployment, shot him a dark look as if he'd been insulted and wanted his pound of flesh.

"My life wasn't more valuable than theirs just because the government spent more money on my training." Gray angled his head. "I also can't help but wonder if it's because of my father that our bird was ordered to turn around in the first place."

"Your father is a rear admiral. We all know he'll wind up as close to the White House as he can get one day," Sloane bit back. "But my decision had nothing to do with your father's rank. Trust me." Sloane lowered his arm to his side. "I'm done with this conversation. And you need to move on and forget what happened."

Move on? Was he kidding? "I can barely fucking move." A dark, angry laugh left his lips.

Sloane jerked a thumb toward the apartment. "Which is exactly why you need to leave my daughter alone. She's young. Has her whole life ahead of her. The last thing she needs is a man in uniform taking a wrecking ball to her life the way . . ."

Let me guess, like you did to your ex-wife's life? But he managed to keep that thought locked up as well. "Sir, there's not a damn thing you can do to stop me from going back in that building when you drive away," he said as "lima charlie" as possible. "Also, she's only a *friend.*"

"Took me all of two seconds to see the way she looked at you to know you're full of shit." He slammed his hands to his hips, still in uniform, probably since he'd visited Walter Reed earlier. That place could often feel like a fish tank with the glass walls and constant barrage of celebrities, not to mention the brass like Sloane, walking through looking at the patients.

Gray replayed the colonel's words, allowing them to sink in. *Wait, how'd she look at me?* "I came to get her off." *Shit.* "*See* her off. To say goodbye." Sloane didn't deserve the truth, but he went ahead and gave it to him anyway. "Tessa's a grown woman. She can be friends with whoever she wants."

"No way will you *just* be friends. You'll draw her in, then ruin her life." Sloane opened his door and slid into the driver's seat before fixing Gray with one last stare. "If you don't want to hurt her, stay away from her." And with that, he slammed the door of his vehicle, the conversation over. Gray waited for him to leave and went inside to confront the woman who really did drive him nuts.

As he'd expected, Tessa was waiting for him in the doorway. The distraught look on her face was the last thing he wanted to see. "I'm so sorry." Her words were soft. A breeze carrying her whisper to him.

"Can I come in?" He set a hand on the wall outside her door, needing the support.

Her brows lifted. "You still want to?"

Gray nodded and quietly followed her in. He only made it as far as the foyer before he had to catch the wall at his side for a break.

"You should sit," she urged, her eyes going to his leg.

"I'm good," he croaked out the lie. A lie for so many

reasons. Because Jack was right. He did have feelings for Tessa that went beyond friendship. But Sloane was also right. He'd ruin this woman's life if he followed through with them. "I'm only going to be a second." It was easier to stay standing than sitting just to get back up.

"I wanted to tell you so many times." She tucked her brownish-blonde hair behind her ears, revealing the small diamond studs that her mother had given her for her birthday —a fact he knew because she really had told him *almost* everything.

"You lied to me on day one, Tessa. I asked you." His voice was hoarse after his confrontation with her father.

Her eyes fell to the distressed floors. "You would've made me work with someone other than Terrance."

"Yeah, you're right." He waited for her eyes to meet his again. Three long seconds later, she met his gaze, a frown on her full lips. "But you should've told me and taken that risk."

Tessa took a hesitant step closer, and when her finger met his chest, it was much more vulnerable and sincere than the angry stab of her father's touch. "You needed me. I saw it in your eyes. And look at you now." Her wobbly lip was going to be his undoing. "You've made so much progress, and I'm so proud of you, Gray. And you should be too. But, if you have to hate me, then hate me. It's worth it."

"You think I could ever hate you?" He covered her hand over his heart with his own. "The woman who ate with me every single night these last three weeks? The woman who researched and took explicit notes on how I could have sex without hurting myself when the time came . . . only to throw them away, too embarrassed to hand them over?"

Her eyes widened in horror. "You saw those?"

"A crumpled piece of paper in the trash may have caught my eye. More specifically, the words 'Sex Life How-To

Cheat Sheet.'" He couldn't help but smile at the memory. "The research wasn't needed, but it was cute. Sweet even." *It also made me hard as a rock.* Because he'd envisioned attempting those tips and tricks with Tessa.

"Oh." She chewed on her lip. A habit of hers he noticed more and more. "Does that mean you've, um, tested . . ."

Gray laughed, forgetting all about her father, and he lightly squeezed her hand. "Tell me when I would've tested it out? If I'm not at the hospital, I'm with you."

"Not always. Not at night." A shy red moved up her slender neck and to her cheeks. God, the brush of freckles beneath her eyes and over her nose added to her sweet innocence somehow.

He pushed away from the wall, letting go of her hand. "No, not at night. You're right." He captured her cheek with his rough palm, and she leaned into him as if she might turn her lips and kiss the inside of his hand. "But I can assure you I've spent every night alone. Well, unless you consider the memories from the helo crash as keeping me company."

A soft exhale left her bare lips, and she rolled her tongue along the seam.

Can I do that? "I'm, um, here to say goodbye and wish you luck. And to thank you for being stubborn and not quitting on me when I tried to get you to." He hated what he would say next, but it had to be done. "You're leaving tomorrow, and you've got three years left to finish the three-plus-three thing you're doing to get your degree, and—"

"You don't want me in your life?" She stepped back as if preparing to turn and flee, but she tripped over a shoe near the door.

He wasn't all that quick on his feet given his situation, but he was used to her constantly tripping around him, and he reached out and caught her, preventing her from falling. He nearly bit a hole in his cheek trying not to drop to the ground as he held her upright, his arm across her midsection.

"I'm such a klutz." She righted herself, and he let go of her and set his back to the wall.

"It's better this way," he said, his tone as broken as he felt. "I can't stay in your life. I'll ruin it one way or another."

"Not even as my friend?" Her saddened expression had him nearly faltering.

"I can't be your friend, and you know that." The idea of her dating someone else had the walls closing in on him just thinking about it. "I have to let you go."

"My father's words, right?" She crossed her arms, a dare in her eyes to defy the colonel's orders. He could see it written there. Her soft, always happy look was gone at the mention of her father. "He thinks he knows what's best for me, but he doesn't." She shook her head. "Do you know he arranged my shadow hours at Walter Reed?"

"How could I know that when you never told me he was your father?" he grunted in frustration.

She shot him an apologetic look before sharing, "Dad hoped once I came down here, saw the reality of what I'd be doing, I'd change my mind about who I wanted to work with. He wants me away from the military. Far, far away. But he was wrong. It's *all* I want to do. So, his plan backfired."

And he doesn't want you dating a man in uniform, either. Especially not a man like me. "This isn't about your father. I'm not good for you. Too old. Too jaded. Too everything." He found the energy to shove away from the wall and stand without support. "This is one thing I'm asking you not to argue with me about. Please."

Tears welled in her eyes, and she looked away as if embarrassed by her reaction.

He reached for her arm, but she resisted. "I guess I should

go," he relented. Hating himself more than ever, he turned and went for the door.

"I want it to be with me. I—I want you to test things out . . . with me before you go," she blurted, stopping him in his tracks.

He set a trembling hand to the doorframe as he replayed her words.

"If you really haven't been with anyone since the accident . . . let your first time be with me. I, um, I know that sounds super line-crossy, but it's what I want. So, if you want it too, then turn around."

A few deep breaths later, he slowly faced her. How could he not when he knew having her in his arms, even for a brief time, would be as close to Heaven as he'd ever get? Because he'd seen Hell the day he died, not the pearly white gates.

Tessa stepped his way, locking eyes with him as she added in an unwavering tone, "Walk away tomorrow, Gray." She offered her hand. "And stay with me tonight."

CHAPTER ONE

FALL 2023 - PRESENT DAY - WASHINGTON, D.C.

"I THINK THE BRIDE-TO-BE IS ABOUT TO BECOME A RUNAWAY one," Naomi, Tessa's best friend, said while elbowing her in the ribs at the crowded bar.

"What makes you say that?" Tessa asked without looking at Naomi. She was too distracted by a group of women tucked away at a back booth. One of the women looked familiar, but she couldn't quite place how she knew her.

"Umm," Naomi began, "because you're wearing her bridal sash, and she's taking shots from some hottie at the bar."

Tessa fidgeted with the white and pink "BRIDE" sash hanging across her chest. Jenny had shoved it over her head a few minutes ago on her way to the bar.

"She's just tipsy. She doesn't have cold feet." She looked around for Jenny, finding her at the horseshoe-shaped bar at the center of the place. *And no, she shouldn't have a guy taking shots from her breasts.* "Yeah, we better move in."

But before she could stop her friend from any potential

oops-moments, a man in a backward ball cap walked through the front door, causing her to stop dead in her tracks.

Is that . . .? No, it can't be. Can it?

Tessa stumbled, bumping into a few other girls in the bridal party to get a better view. Her breath hitched as he turned her direction, scanning the room.

It *was* him.

It'd been thirteen years and two months since she'd seen him in the flesh. Not that she'd been counting. And now there he was, less than five feet from her, causing her mind to become a discombobulated mess.

"Grayson Chandler, is that you?" The words slipped free from her lips, and her eyes widened in shock. She hadn't meant to say anything, let alone say it loud enough for him to hear over the blaring music.

But he clocked her a breath later. The second their eyes locked, he took a step back, knocking into the guy next to him. "Sloane?" he mouthed, equally stunned to see her.

At least he remembers me. Tessa's brows slanted as she looked at the guy beside Gray, assuming he was a friend. Instead of going with a normal conversation starter as she should've, she walked closer and asked, "He always address everyone by their last name?"

Gray pointed to the sash across her chest. "I guess that won't be your last name for much longer." He peered at his friend while tipping his head toward the door. "Nice to see you, Sloane. Congrats."

The quick retreat was a punch to the stomach, and her abs were already sore from the brutal workout Naomi had dragged her to earlier. Her best friend was about to head to Jamaica and insisted Tessa get bikini-ready with her, even though she had no plans to wear a two-piece until next summer.

She barely heard Gray's friend, or whoever he was to Gray, excuse himself as she began to mindlessly remove the sash. *Wait, what just happened?*

Naomi joined her again. "Who in the world was that?"

"Did you avert a potential disaster?" Tessa asked instead, searching for the bride-to-be.

"Yeah." Naomi took the bride sash from Tessa. "But why do you look like you've seen a ghost when the two men you were chatting with were very much alive? Hot men, might I add. And I know I'm taken, but I can appreciate two fine men when I see them."

Fine men? Yeah, Gray was still . . . "That was Grayson Chandler," she finally confessed. "Gray."

Naomi snatched Tessa's arm, demanding her attention. "Whoa, hold up. Gray, as in Gray-Gray?"

Tessa nodded, wondering if the stunned state would ever end. "Yeah, Gray-Gray," she whispered, her stomach turning. "And damn, forty looks good on him." Well, he'd be forty-one now, right?

Thirteen years later, the man still managed to wreak havoc on her. Were those butterflies in her stomach compelling her to want to puke?

"I'm going outside. Maybe he's still there," she decided. "Wait here, okay?"

"Maybe don't go?" Naomi frowned, her light brown eyes meeting hers.

"I'll be fine," she promised, and Naomi released her, but it was more than likely to stop Jenny from doing something out of character again. Before Tessa could chicken out, she went for the door and swung it open, catching sight of Gray and his friend standing near the entrance. Her heart climbed, landing square in her throat as she croaked out a small, "You're still here."

Gray removed his ball cap and ran his fingers through his tousled brown hair, a similar shade to her own. It was shorter on the sides and thicker on top. A messy look that she doubted was only from his hat, and the man rocked it.

"Yeah, I . . ." Gray began, avoiding eye contact. When he didn't continue, she realized he was focused on her neon blue stilettos, and he probably found them as obnoxious as she did.

The maid of honor had insisted the women all wear them to match the neon blue bridal tops. *Two hundred bucks for shoes I'll never wear again.*

Gray slowly dragged his gaze up the length of her body, and her skin prickled with awareness. Finally making eye contact, he said in an oddly flat voice, "You look the same." It was like his world wasn't as rocked as hers at their chance meeting.

"I'll give you two some space," his friend said in an uneasy voice, but Gray held up a hand.

"No, stay," Gray gritted out, a sharp change from how he'd just spoken. He put his hat back on, forward-facing this time, shielding his eyes a little.

"Uh, okay," his friend said, shrugging.

"And you look . . ." Tessa trailed off as she focused on his strong chest muscles stretching out his army-green long-sleeved shirt. Then she worked her way down his jeaned legs that showed off his muscular thighs, and—

"I had osseointegration surgery a few years ago in Australia," he interrupted her thoughts. "No more socket. I can even wear regular jeans." He patted the side of his leg. And was he smirking at her? "I guess you noticed." *Was it that obvious I was checking him out?*

She *hadn't* noticed, probably because she'd been too shocked he was standing there in the first place. But now a million questions raced through her mind.

He had to learn how to walk again with an osseointegrated prosthesis. And why did it hurt that he hadn't reached out to her for help after his surgery? "Are you happy?" she whispered. "Sorry, not like, are you happy in general," she babbled while talking with her hands. "I mean, with the surgery?" *Well, this is going swimmingly.* "Well, of course, I'm curious if you're happy in general too." *Oh just stop talking.*

"The surgery was life changing." He angled his head, eyes intensely focused on her as if he wanted to say more but was intentionally holding back.

Some things never change.

"So yes, I'm happy with the surgery."

"Good." She smiled, waiting to see if he'd answer the happy-in-general question, but he kept quiet. "Well, I've heard great things about that surgery." The procedure was revolutionary. A titanium rod was implanted into the bone of the residual limb to attach the prosthesis, eliminating the need for a socket and liner. "The surgery is still kind of new here."

"Yeah, that's why I went to Melbourne to get it done." Clearing his throat, he took her by surprise and asked, "So, are *you* happy?"

I thought I was until five minutes ago. Now seeing you . . .

Pages of memories flipped uncontrollably in her mind as she considered how to answer. The memory of Gray pinning her against the wall in her foyer that night she asked him to stay. The second their mouths had touched, and he'd lost all control, devouring her every breath as his tongue twined with hers in a beautiful dance. He'd deftly unbuttoned her jean shorts without losing her mouth. Slid his hand beneath her shorts and cupped her pussy over her panties. And the moment he'd touched her bare, discovering how wet he'd made her, he'd nearly bit her lip as she'd moaned in ecstasy.

"Tessa?" Gray prompted.

She pulled herself free from the past and blurted, "Happy? Sure." God, she almost snorted in her attempt to not be such a nervous mess. "Why wouldn't I be?"

"I'm Jesse McAdams, by the way."

She could kiss him for saving her from whatever insanity might have fallen from her mouth next. Stepping forward to offer her palm, her heel caught in a sidewalk crack, and she tripped.

Gray was at her side in a heartbeat, catching her. He had a hand on her back and another at her breastbone, keeping her from an awkward and embarrassing face plant.

"I'm still a klutz," she murmured, arching back to look up at him. There wasn't enough light outside to make out the beautiful shade of his eyes, but she'd never forget the light green color. Or the heat and humor in them when he claimed she drove him nuts.

"I can see that." Gray swallowed, and he was close enough for her to see his Adam's apple roll. "You good if I let you go? Won't fall on me, will you?" The dark, husky rasp of his tone had her wanting to plead that he never let her go.

She smacked her lips together, hating they were nearly bone dry. Sadly, she'd forgotten to stick a tube of her favorite ChapStick in her pocket for tonight. "I'm good," she lied.

In a matter of seconds, this man managed to stir up feelings she had long ago suppressed. How was that possible?

His hand wandered a few inches up from her lower back before he freed her from his semi-possessive hold. A moment that would live rent-free in her head for, at the very least, the next few days.

She smoothed her palms over her tee, pushing away wrinkles not actually there, then offered her palm to Jesse as originally planned before Mr. Chivalrous saved her from connecting with the pavement. "*Tessa* Sloane."

"Ah, so you do have a first name," Jesse said with a smile, his joke most likely meant to break what felt like third-wheel ice.

"I do. A middle one too." *A middle one, Tessa? Really?* Thank God there wasn't great light, so no one saw the blush she was most likely sporting.

"Where are you working now?" Gray asked, taking her by surprise. She'd half expected him to bolt and be halfway to Delaware the minute he let go of her.

"Oh, um. I was working at the new Walter Reed in Bethesda. Well, not new anymore, right? It's been over a decade since they shut down the place you, um . . ." *Why am I stumbling through this?* "But last year, my best friend and I opened a private practice on the D.C.–Virginia border. Still veteran-focused."

"Your dad must *love* that," Gray remarked, his tone tight. Tense. *Was he still upset?* Memories of the lie about who her father was resurfaced, along with his anger about it too. But he stayed that night, and she thought he'd forgiven her. Maybe she'd been wrong.

"He's accepted once I make up my mind, there's no turning back."

"You sure you don't want me to leave so you two can catch up?" Jesse hiked a thumb over his shoulder.

"No," Gray and Tessa snapped simultaneously. Jesse tossed his hands in the air in mock surrender and took two cautious steps away from them.

"My dad retired, and he's off the grid right now with his new girlfriend. He went to the Philippines for vacation last summer and fell in love with a woman in Manila. She's far too good for him in my opinion, but they'll probably marry.

Making this his fourth wedding. Hopefully his last, but I'm not holding my breath. Oh, and your dad is the Secretary of Defense now, that's awesome. Congrats to him. My dad always said your father would end up near the White House . . ." *I'm oversharing. And rambling. Just stop. Stop now.*

Gray frowned. Not a fan of her info dump?

"And what are you doing now?" After Gray had left that morning thirteen years ago, they'd emailed a few times, but then one day, he stopped responding to her messages. Eventually, she gave up trying, realizing he'd decided to move on.

Gray looked at Jesse as if sending him a silent request to answer instead. Jesse nodded and said, "We work in private security. Company is called Falcon Falls Security." He held up a hand. "And before you ask, the name is because our headquarters is near Bushkill Falls in Pennsylvania, and we saw a falcon one day and . . ." His words trailed off as he smirked and did a one-shoulder shrug instead of finishing.

"I was running a security place in California up until about a year ago, then I partnered up with another guy," Gray offered, his hands lingering near his pockets as if he was torn between hiding them or going for that mad dash away from her.

"Oh, with Jack London?" She remembered Gray's best friend from back then; he'd been at his side as much as possible whenever he wasn't operating. "Or was it that other operator friend of yours who visited you a few times? What was his name?" She snapped her fingers when it came to her. "Chip?" *No, that's not it.* "Dale?"

"It's Dale, but he's not my partner." He scratched his jaw. "But, uh, Jack started working with me after he left the Army." A strange pause followed as if there was more he was

28

considering divulging. "But no, the guy I partnered with has deep pockets, so he can help fund us."

Cryptic as always. Gray had never been an open book, so she wasn't about to press him for more information now. She, on the other hand, had always been open. Well, mostly open. There'd been two things she'd withheld from him back in the day, her father's occupation being the first.

The moment she'd set eyes on Gray at Walter Reed, she'd put two and two together, realizing he was the Green Beret who'd had a below-the-knee amputation due to a failed mission in Afghanistan. It was a mission she'd assumed her father had overseen since Gray had asked if she was THAT Sloane. When he'd questioned her, she'd panicked and lied.

"Well, we should probably go now." Gray choked out the words like they'd been physically painful to say—a sharp contrast for a man with such a powerful and commanding presence.

And there it is. What I expected. Running.

"Wait, um, where are you living now? Pennsylvania?" she blurted in a silly attempt to keep him from bolting.

"Ironically, none of us actually live near our headquarters," Jesse spoke up when Gray remained silent. She redirected her focus to the only one willing to answer her. "I'm in Alabama, not that you asked. And this guy finally sold his place in Cali, and I think you're moving here, right?"

That had her attention. Heat snaked up her neck and around to the tips of her ears. *Live in the same city as Gray? Potentially bump, well, fall, into him again?* "Oh?" She pointed at the sidewalk. "Like, here-here?"

"I don't know." His tone echoed the uncertainty in his answer. "Maybe not." He cleared his throat. "Like I said earlier, it was good to see you, Tessa. Congrats on the private practice. That's . . . I'm happy for you." He paused. "And congratulations on the other thing."

Other thing? Ohhh. Engagement? No.

But just like that . . . he left before she had a chance to ramble away about how wrong he was on that last part.

Jesse shot a puzzled look at Tessa before facing the direction Gray had gone. "What about Rory and the others?" he called after him.

But Gray kept walking. And walking damn well. It was a nice sight, even if he was anxious to get the hell away from her.

"Rory? She, um, his girlfriend?" Tessa asked, hoping Jesse didn't hear the tremble in her tone.

"No, Rory's my sister." Jesse faced her, seemingly giving up on chasing after Gray. "And his sister, Natasha, is also inside." He hooked his thumbs in his front pockets. "We were checking in on them."

Natasha? The blonde in the back booth. That's why she looked so familiar. She'd visited Gray in the hospital a few times, but Gray had been a pain in the ass, sending almost everyone away. *"No pity parties, please,"* he used to say.

"Does he always take off like this?" *I shouldn't worry about him. He's not my friend. Not my patient. He's just . . .*

"Honestly, I've never seen him react to anyone that way." A smile ghosted his lips. "Might have something to do with the fact you're getting married though."

"Married?" Tessa shook her head at the memory. "Ohh, but I'm . . ." Her words trailed off at the sight of a pretty blonde exiting the bar, her eyes riveted on Jesse.

"Jesse, why am I not surprised to see you?" The woman smiled and slammed her arms over her chest in disapproval. "Go on, give me some silly excuse why you're here."

"Shit." Jesse lifted his hands in a prayer position. "Coincidence?"

"Liar." The woman looked over at Tessa. "My brother's paranoid. Can't let a girl go out for a night on the town without worrying some creep will bother her." She frowned as if disturbed by something else. "And I'm not sure who you are, but he's married. Baby on the way. So find someone else to hit on."

"Rory," Jesse snapped. "You know I'd never put myself in a position to be alone with a woman like that."

"Newsflash, you *are* alone with a woman. And she's beautiful."

"I know Gray," Tessa blurted the truth. "He was here a moment ago but took off."

The woman's shoulders relaxed, and she freed her arms from across her chest. "Shit, sorry." She looked down the street as if wondering why Gray had left.

Jesse pivoted his focus back on Tessa. "You have a phone on you?"

"Umm, yeah." Tessa grabbed it from her back pocket. All she had on her tonight was her ID, credit card, and phone. With her luck, she'd forget a purse if she brought one and wind up dealing with identity theft the next day. "Why?"

"Yeah, why?" Rory shot out, clearly in overprotective-sister mode, which Tessa found rather endearing. She must've also been close to her brother's wife. And she seemed to have her friend's back the way Tessa knew Naomi would.

"Because I want you to save Gray's number. He's unlisted. But if you ever get the urge to talk to him, or find yourself needing help for whatever reason, you can call him." He rattled off the digits before she had a chance to question whether it was a bad idea for her to have access to a man who was still capable of making her heart do an uncomfortable tap dance.

"Why would you think he'd want me to call him?" she asked, considering Gray had taken off.

Jesse smiled. "Like I said, I've never seen him react to anyone like that before. So, I'm thinking you're special."

CHAPTER TWO

"HEY, MR. WHITLOCK, THIS IS TESSA," SHE BEGAN AFTER her call went to voicemail, "I'm just checking in since you missed your appointment today. Please call me on my after-hours cell so I know you're okay." She ended the call, tempted to phone her patient again. He never missed his appointments.

Whit, as he preferred her to call him, was one of her favorite clients. He was a sweetheart who liked to indulge her sweet tooth. He brought her a donut on Tuesdays and dark chocolate Raisinets on Saturdays.

She sensed Whit's sessions were less about hip pain from his Army days and more about his need for companionship. He'd admitted his wife had died the year prior, and at sixty-three, he was now living alone.

After one more attempt to get ahold of him, she swapped her work phone for her personal cell and went over to the mirror in her office. She'd added it a few months ago after the unfortunate realization she'd worked nearly an entire day with food stuck between her teeth. From then on, a quick teeth check after eating was always in order before seeing patients. But this past week, she'd been staring into the mirror for an entirely different reason.

Tessa brushed away a loose strand of her brownish-blonde hair that'd escaped her ponytail, looked herself in the eyes, and in a steady tone ordered, "Don't give in. Don't call him. Be strong. He does not want to hear from you, Tessa." This had to be her fifth time playing the "mirror, mirror on the wall, you really don't want to make that call" game in the last few days.

But Gray, and how flipping incredible he'd looked last weekend, had been running through her mind nonstop. So hard and fast, she'd burnt calories.

Thirteen years, and I still can't shake you. Why?

She set her phone on the table in front of the mirror, knowing her resolve would soon be tested like never before. With Naomi going on vacation tomorrow, the practice would close for a week. And she was forcing Tessa to take some downtime as well. They'd been going nonstop since they opened last year, with only Sundays and major holidays off.

Tessa's dad, along with her best friend's parents, had provided them with an extra business loan so they could open the Williams-Sloane Medical Center. But since they'd celebrated—well, survived—their first year in business two months ago, Tessa had reluctantly agreed to take tomorrow through next Sunday off for a staycation.

With Gray's number burning a hole in her phone, it would take everything in her not to tipsy-dial him one sad and lonely night. Because the truth was, she didn't have much of a life outside work unless Naomi was encouraging her to go out.

She held her hand near the mirror as if giving herself a high five, something she'd been doing for years when she needed a quick self-induced mood boost.

It didn't work this time.

Because she didn't want to be strong.

She wanted to give in and call Gray to see if fate had brought him back into her life. She hadn't noticed a ring on his finger, so what was holding her back?

She lowered her arm to her side but kept her eyes on the mirror, working hard to fight the memories from coming forward.

But everything in the last week had reminded her of that man. Little pockets of their conversations from the past popped up at every turn. She'd even had a few dreams about him, ones where she'd awoken in a sweat and also . . . wet.

Of course, her best friend told her if she was dreaming about someone, it was because she was on their mind too. She highly doubted Gray had given her a second thought after running for the hills.

Feeling a little overheated just thinking about him, she removed her navy-blue blazer and tossed it onto the table. With the practice closed and everyone except her and Naomi having gone home, she could finally relax.

Glancing past the strap on her silk tank top, her eyes landed on the few remaining freckles she had on her tan shoulder. At thirty-four, she'd lost the ones on her face unless she was in the sun too long.

Her father joked her freckles were all she'd inherited from his Scottish ancestry, and she'd taken after her mother's Greek and Italian side in every other way.

The only night she and Gray had made love, he'd kissed her shoulder, then traced an invisible line with his finger, connecting those freckles. They'd watched the movie *Serendipity* the week before when they'd still been in the friend zone, and she'd told him how sweet it was when the character had said her freckles looked like a constellation. So,

Gray had told her, *"I don't know much about the stars, but I'm betting you've got a galaxy here."*

She'd laughed and said, *"Real smooth, Romeo,"* knowing that'd been his call sign in the Army. Playfully swatting his muscular chest, she'd climbed on top of him for round two of lovemaking.

Their first time . . . he'd been on top. And the man hadn't needed the silly list of notes she'd made for him when it came to sex.

"Fuuuuuuck, Tessa. You're so fucking tight. You okay?" Gray had ground out when their bodies had first connected. His lips had remained parted as he'd peered down at her, holding the brunt of his weight with his forearms. *"You're not a—"*

Tessa let go of the memory when her office door opened. Naomi had her cell to her ear, and based on her frustrated breaths and the wide-eyed look she shot her, it was her parents on the call. And they were in disagreement on something.

"I'll be fine. Promise. Love you. Bye," Naomi said before chucking the phone onto the chair in front of Tessa's desk with a groan. "They can be such a pain in my ass."

"What is it now?" Tessa asked as Naomi pushed her brown hair away from her face.

"Studs or nothing?" she asked instead, showing her ears, one with a diamond stud and one without.

Naomi had changed from her typical work clothes into a pair of black pants, simple but classic black pumps, and a gold V-neck silk top. She had a pretty shimmer to her brown skin, highlighting her chest and neckline. Gold bangle bracelets adorned her left arm.

"Mmm. I'd go bare."

Naomi laughed. "That doesn't sound right," she said

while fishing something from her pocket, then produced the other earring. "And you didn't call Gray while I was arguing with my parents, did you?" Her eyes landed on Tessa's phone as she secured the second diamond in her earlobe.

Tessa's shoulders fell. "No, I'm trying to behave." *Almost failed.* "And why are you arguing with your parents?"

Naomi moved her phone so she could sit, and Tessa dropped down next to her in the other seat in front of the desk. "I finally told them I'm going away to Jamaica with Sam. You know how my dad can be. Overprotective is an understatement."

"They're in Santo Domingo for another month, right?"

Naomi's father was a well-known lawyer in Massachusetts, but he and his wife took two months off every year to spend in the Dominican Republic, where Naomi's mother was born.

"Yeah, they'll be back by Thanksgiving." Naomi frowned. "But Dad's worried about sharks on my trip. Well, *one* shark."

"So, he's still calling every guy you date that, huh?"

"Pretty much." Naomi smiled. "But Sam's different, don't you think?"

"Sam's . . . Sam, that's for sure." Tessa shrugged, unsure what to say about her best friend's boyfriend. Her mother's favorite phrase came to mind: "*If you have nothing nice to say, don't say anything at all.*" If only more people lived by that motto, the world would be so much more bearable.

"Yeah, your face doesn't lie." Naomi twirled a finger in the air, closing one eye. "I wish you'd come with us on the trip."

Tessa laughed. "Oh sure, Sam would love to have a third wheel on his romantic getaway in an overwater bungalow in Jamaica. Plus, you know I'm terrified of flying. And with my luck, the plane would go down simply because I'm on board. I'm saving lives by not flying. Trust me."

"Mmmhmm." Naomi's eyes shone bright as she shared the memory, "I remember when you dragged me on a road trip to California for your brother's wedding to avoid flying."

Tessa's brother—technically her half brother since they had different mothers—was now divorced, but Curtis had bought her a plane ticket for the wedding. The day of her flight, she'd nearly fainted from the anxiety flying caused her. So, she'd opted for a road trip instead.

"Side note, I didn't force you on that road trip. You could've flown as planned."

"Ohhhh sure. Let the girl who rescues every stray animal, and who offers rides to strangers, go cross-country alone?" She smirked. "You'd probably pick up some Dahmer-like hitchhiker because of that big ol' trusting heart of yours, and then I'd be without a best friend."

"Okay, not true." *Maybe a little.* "But you'd find a new best friend."

"Don't even start, you know you're irreplaceable. I can always find a new Sam. Not a new Tessa." She winked and stood. "But the man is having me meet his parents tonight, which is oddly suspicious before our trip tomorrow, right?"

"I'd say maybe he's going to propose, but you haven't been dating that long. No L word dropped yet." Tessa stood as well. "But he knows how much Jamaica means to you. How your face lights up when sharing childhood memories from visiting your dad's parents as a kid." The gesture was sweet of Sam, but "sweet" and "Sam" didn't really mix, so it was a curveball. He more than likely knew a guy, who knew a guy, and got a good deal for the resort, but Tessa wasn't about to say that.

"That man better not propose. My dad would lose his shit.

At least he wouldn't need to hop on a plane to come over and test Sam's swimming skills. Nope, I'd toss him into the water myself," she said with a chuckle. "I have to admit, it feels weird to close the practice for a week though."

"If anyone has an emergency, I'll come in. Just enjoy your trip. Turn your phone off and disconnect. You deserve to have some fun. Even if it's with Sam."

"That's what Sam says I should do. Shut off my phone, so my dad can't track our exact location. Good thing I didn't tell Dad where in Jamaica we're going, which of course he asked, hence the quick ending to our call."

"I hate to agree with Sam, but I do on this one." Tessa stood. "We're workaholics. You need a break."

"Fine, fine." Naomi pulled her in for a long hug. "Since I won't be seeing you until I get back, promise me you won't do anything crazy while I'm gone?"

"I feel like that request extends to calling Gray," she said when Naomi let go of her.

"The number of times I've caught you staring at that man's number in your phone, it's probably the only number aside from mine you've memorized."

"Remind me again why I shouldn't call? Because I'm tempted." *Even though I have a list of reasons why that'd be a horrible and heartbreaking idea.* "I need a kick in the ass, I guess."

Naomi's brows slanted. "That man is the OG. The original. The reason why you've had such bad luck with men. He started it all."

"I had bad luck before him, not just in my love life. I've always been a klutz. A walking disaster. And you know, anything that can go wrong when it comes to me, will."

"Isn't that called something? Murphy's something-or-another?"

"If my life had a movie title, it'd be 'The Unlucky One.' Case in point, when I finally bump into that man, he thinks I'm engaged."

"Good. Let him think that." She gave her a decisive nod, her warm brown eyes thinning for extra emphasis on her feelings for the man.

"Gray was only trying to protect me. He thought he'd hold me back, especially with our age difference and his injury. He wasn't trying to hurt me. Sex was my idea, remember? And what if we crossed paths again because we're meant to have a second chance?" *Oh my God, why am I defending the man I know will screw with my head? What is wrong with me?*

"You never really had a first chance, did you? You were working with his PT, and then you had sex. And we both know it wasn't just sex for you."

"He didn't know . . ." *Another lie I told him.*

"Just don't rewrite history and act like that man didn't break your heart. I met you in grad school a month after you two went your separate ways. So yeah, I remember your mopey-sad brown eyes like it was yesterday."

And ever since last weekend, thirteen years ago suddenly felt like it was yesterday.

"You give every guy you've dated the benefit of the doubt," Naomi went on with her lecture, one Tessa needed to hear. "When eleven out of ten don't deserve it." She lifted one shoulder. "Look at your recent history with men. John, Paul, George, and Ringo were—"

"*Beatles.* Not my exes," she responded with a laugh. "Gray's not like those jerks." *He's not, right? Maybe he is. It has been thirteen years.*

"I hate to admit it, but you two would've made for an interesting story. The colonel's daughter falls for the admiral's son. Forget a song. It could be a movie." She looked out the window. The sun had already set since they'd just entered November a few days ago. "I really gotta go. I just hate leaving you like this." She twirled a finger in the air. "All mopey-sad brown eyes two point oh."

"I'll be fine." *Hopefully.* "Nothing a little ice cream and binge-watching a series on Netflix can't fix."

"No romantic comedies. Oh, or serial killer documentaries. I swear, there's no in-between with you," she added with a smirk.

Tessa suppressed a smile, thinking back to Gray saying the same thing to her years ago. "Roger that," she teased.

Naomi reached for her arm and squeezed as she rattled off a list of things to avoid while she was gone. "And lastly, stay off your phone while walking, so you don't wind up in the Potomac." She dipped her head to catch her eyes and smiled. "Don't act like it's not possible."

"Oh my God, I fell into a river once in Boston, and you've never let me live it down."

"To save a stray puppy," she reminded her with a wink.

"Oh, like you wouldn't have done the same? Mmmhmm."

"Maybeeee."

"Okay, okay. Go." Tessa flicked her wrist. "You'll be late for dinner."

Naomi gave her another squeeze, then started for the door with her phone in hand.

"Phone off while you're there. I mean it. Go have fun."

Naomi shot her a quick look over her shoulder, and they both kissed the air as their last goodbye.

Once alone, Tessa made one more call to Mr. Whitlock, and after no answer, she sent a few emails.

Realizing it was almost seven and she'd lost track of time, she stared at her phone, debating whether to call Gray.

Reluctantly, she tucked her phone into the Michael Kors bag Naomi had gifted her last Christmas, ready to head to the store to buy a few pints of ice cream she'd need to get through the week.

As she went for her blazer, the power went out. "What the hell?"

She startled and nearly fell when the door flung open, and before she could process what was happening, a shadowed figure grabbed her and placed something over her head.

Oh my God. I'm being taken.

CHAPTER THREE

FIVE DAYS LATER - PARIS, FRANCE

GRAY REACHED FOR HIS CLUB SODA AT THE SWANKY HOTEL restaurant, wishing it was something else. Preferably with some kick to it to numb the memories he couldn't seem to shake to save his life.

Memories of Tessa Sloane from twelve days ago, and yeah, he'd been counting. He hadn't been able to stop. Like little tally marks in his head every day that had passed since he'd run into her and retreated, which was his least favorite thing to do as an operator.

"Does Beckett know your cover story has you playing the role of my wife?" he asked his "date" sitting across the table from him. The lights had been dimmed to add a romantic ambiance, but there was nothing remotely romantic about the evening. He was on what would hopefully be a quick intel-grab assignment connected to an American businessman two tables away who was currently playing footsie with someone other than his wife.

"He knows. And he's fine. Not like we're sharing a

room." Sydney pushed her steak around on her plate without stabbing a piece of the meat. "Beckett believed you when you told him you've moved on and you're happy about our engagement."

Sydney Archer also worked at Falcon Falls Security. At first, working with his former West Point girlfriend had thrown him for a loop. She was the one Jack accused Gray of comparing every woman to. Every woman except Tessa.

His path had crossed with Sydney's on an op last year, and he'd wondered if running into her years later had been a meant-to-be thing. In a way, it had. They were meant to work together and nothing more. She was now engaged to Jesse's brother-in-law, and he was genuinely happy for them both.

"Good. Just don't want it to be awkward for anyone," Gray said in a low voice, checking to ensure their target was still at his table.

Carter Dominick, the man Gray co-ran the security company with, was currently on the fifth floor of the hotel with Jack, making a copy of the businessman's hard drive. Gray and Sydney's only job: buy them time if the businessman decided to take his mistress upstairs before they were finished.

Four of their other teammates at Falcon Falls were five minutes away from their hotel, handling a separate assignment connected to their op. They planned to meet at their secure location at twenty-one hundred hours, and if everything went as planned, it'd be one of their easier assignments in the last year.

It would also more than likely be Jesse's last op of the year. He had a baby due next month, and he didn't want to be away from his wife, Ella, in case she went into labor early. Ella had given him explicit instructions to stop spinning up by Thanksgiving. That gave Jesse a few more weeks to roll around in the dirt, if need be, but Gray doubted they'd have another assignment before then.

"Don't say it. I know you just read my mind," Gray grumbled, realizing Sydney had been studying him with a mischievous look in her eyes.

Sydney smirked. "You were thinking this is an easy gig, and you know what that means . . . something's bound to go wrong now. Or, at the least, we'll wind up with a real doozy this month when it's supposed to be smooth sailing."

"'Doozy'? 'Smooth sailing'?" Gray suppressed a laugh, not used to this badass woman, who could take down an enemy target with just a bow and arrow, talking like she was on an episode of *Blue's Clues*. *Is that show still on? Hell if I know.* "Miles," Gray said at the realization, thinking about Beckett's young son.

Sydney nodded.

How could Gray forget Miles was why Sydney was working hard to swear less? Sure, she had a son back home, but he was a teenager. Once she married Beckett, she'd be adopting his kids, McKenna and Miles. Miles wasn't biologically Beckett's, but it was a long story and one that had brought Sydney and Beckett together earlier that year on an op.

"I'll never have kids. At this rate, I'll only ever be 'the favorite uncle.'"

His words had Sydney letting go of her fork to fidget with the stem of her wineglass instead. Not that she'd done more than take small sips since they were on an op. "Who says you'll be the favorite?"

"Because I'm Emory's only uncle."

His sister, Natasha, was married to one of the world's best Navy SEAL snipers, Wyatt Pierson. Wyatt also worked in private security with a bunch of other Navy SEALs. Of course, those SEALs took orders from not only Gray's father, but the President of the United States. Not that Gray was supposed to know about their off-the-books ops.

"Do you even want kids?" Sydney surprised him by asking.

"With Tessa, I do." *Fuck. Where'd that come from?* When he'd bumped into Tessa at the bar, he'd been so shocked to see her, he'd acted like a complete idiot. And seeing her wearing blue stilettos was proof the devil really did have a sick sense of humor and enjoyed torturing him. *I probably deserve it.* "Forget I said that," he rushed out at the sight of Sydney sitting taller. He was shocked with himself for his slip of the tongue. And honestly, what the hell?

He had to get this woman off his mind. She was becoming dangerous to his focus. He shouldn't be thinking about someone he closed the book on thirteen years ago, especially an engaged someone.

Gray leaned back in his chair, knowing Sydney wouldn't press. She wasn't the type. She was the opposite of Tessa, and neither type was "better" than the other. Just *different.*

Tessa would share her life story with a stranger on the subway. Well, that'd been her at twenty-one. Maybe she was different now?

The number of times in the past twelve days he'd nearly used his team's high-tech software to get a name for Tessa's future husband had been pathetic, to say the least.

But what if the guy was an asshole? Not good enough for her? What if he didn't have fast hands to catch her before she fell? What if he'd forced her to give up her berry-scented lip balms, which was why her lips had been bare that night?

What if . . . Stop. THIS is why you stopped emailing her back then, you idiot. You couldn't stop yourself then, and now . . .

46

"You okay, my fake husband?" Sydney shocked him by tapping into her emotional side, one she usually buried beneath layers of toughness.

"Not really," he confessed, looking around the crowded restaurant. A bunch of happy couples surrounded them. Well, maybe happy wasn't the right word. Maybe they were inwardly as miserable as he was right now?

And he wasn't just miserable. He'd been a damn mess the last twelve days. He kept trying to convince himself Tessa was on his mind because she was linked to one of the toughest years of his life. Seeing her again brought back old memories, cut open old wounds that would need to heal. That was it. Nothing more.

And maybe some guilt for walking away from her.

Hell, there was no "maybe" about it. It was there. Raw, real, and solidifying into a hard pit in his stomach.

"You, um, want to talk about something?" Another surprise from her.

"Who are you, and what have you done with my teammate?" Gray asked, returning his attention her way as a smile slid across her lips.

"I'm about to be a mother of three, that's who. Guess these kids have changed me."

"No, Beckett changed you," Gray stated. "In a good way, I mean," he added, clearing his throat.

"Maybe if you find 'the one,' she'll change you too." Sydney brought her glass to her lips, an obvious struggle for her to continue doing the feelings thing.

"Do I need changing?" Gray challenged, lifting a brow.

"I think we can all use someone in our lives to help bring out the best in us." Her eyes fell to the diamond on her finger. The wedding band next to it may have been fake, but the engagement ring was from Beckett.

Tessa saved me from the dark depths of Hell thirteen years ago. And then I ran. Took off. Fucking coward.

But it was to save her from being shackled to someone like him. Someone who'd still only felt like half a man. Now at forty-one, he was different. Most days, he even felt whole again. Physically, at least. Mentally? That was another story.

Gray gripped his thigh under the table and squeezed before tapping his ear, turning on his wireless communication device to check in with the rest of his team. "Where are we at?"

"Almost done," Jack responded. "How's our mark looking?"

Gray peeked at the businessman, getting a decent view of his face from his vantage point. "Horny. He looks horny."

Projecting much, Gray? Seeing Tessa had lit a fire in him, and he wanted nothing more than to feel the warmth of her body against his again. To taste her sweet lips, scented or bare, it didn't matter. He wanted to swirl his tongue around each soft pink nipple till they puckered. Then make her come on his tongue before filling her tight pussy with his cock.

He never had a chance to set his mouth between her thighs that night. Tessa had been shy and nervous when he'd asked to kiss her there, and he assumed no man had ever gone down on her before. As desperate as he'd been to worship her with his mouth, he'd never force a woman to do anything she wasn't comfortable with, so her one "no" was all he'd needed to hear.

Sydney swiveled in her chair to put eyes on their mark and discreetly tapped her ear. "He's not lying. The man will probably be heading your way the second he signs the check."

"Which he just requested," Gray noted at the sight,

pushing away thoughts of Tessa's moans from their one night of lovemaking. "Can you exfil in three minutes?"

"Negative. Buy us two more minutes." It was Carter that time.

"Roger that," Gray answered.

In truth, Carter really "ran the show" because his buckets of billions funded them. He'd grown on Gray ever since they began working together. It hadn't been a perfect match, and ironically, an argument at a wedding between the two of them had resulted in them joining forces.

But in time, they'd learned to trust each other. They'd both served in the Army, but Carter had been Delta Force, and Gray, like Jack, had been a Green Beret. Carter had gone on to join the Agency, but after his wife was brutally murdered, he went rogue to track down her killer.

Carter was one man you didn't want to mess with. Gray was certain if he looked up the definition of *fuck around and find out*, he'd find Carter's picture next to it. But he wasn't a bad partner to have either. Even if Gray had to rein him in from time to time.

"I have an idea. It'll ruin this guy's night," Sydney said, fiddling with the fake band on her finger.

"The you-know-his-wife trick?" Gray motioned for the check as Sydney nodded her answer.

She waited for their mark to get up from his table with his much younger date, and Gray leaned back in his seat, ready for the show.

Sydney's profile was to him as she approached the couple. The man took an uncomfortable step away from his mistress, drawing a hand over his bearded jawline as he more than likely tried to come up with some excuse about why he was with someone other than his wife.

"What's your status?" Gray asked over comms a minute later while Sydney continued to trap the man in conversation.

"We're leaving now," Jack answered. "You're good to roll out."

"Roger that," Gray said as his pocket began vibrating. No one would call his personal cell other than his teammates or sister. And his sister was also on an op. So, who in the hell was it?

Curious, he grabbed his phone from his pocket. It was an unknown number, but he recognized the country code. *Turkey?*

He let the call go to voicemail since he was undercover. Once he and Sydney were outside and on their way to their exfil spot, he brought the phone to his ear to listen to the message.

The voice and words on the other line had him nearly forgetting how to walk as the blood drained from his face.

"Gray . . .?" A pause. "This is Tessa Sloane. I—I don't know what happened, but I'm in a hospital in Istanbul, and I need your help. Can you call me back at this number? Please, I'm scared."

"What's wrong?" Sydney asked, stepping in front of him.

Gray stared at the phone, trying to wrap his head around what he'd heard. Without answering Sydney, he called the number back and waited for the operator to pick up. "Uh, *merhaba*," he began in Turkish. Aside from hello, the few other words he knew slipped free from his mind, so he switched to English, hoping the operator would understand. "I need Tessa Sloane's room, please."

"Tessa?" Sydney repeated, clearly remembering him blurting the name not that long ago in the restaurant. "Walk and talk." She nudged him in the ribs, and he did his best to move even though his body felt like dead weight.

Crazily, the only part of him willing to cooperate was his prosthesis. The rest of his flesh and bone waited for his brain to process what was happening before joining the party.

"Come on." Sydney held his arm, urging him along.

How the hell had Tessa gotten his private number? And more importantly, what in God's name was she doing in a hospital in Turkey?

"Hello?"

"Tessa?" Gray stopped walking. Her voice sounded so small on the other end of the line. So full of fear. "It's Gray. What happened? Are you okay?"

"Gray?" she choked out around what sounded like tears. "I'm so scared. I don't know how I got here. The last week is just blank in my head. I had your number, and I asked to call you."

"Um. It'll be okay." He tried to remain calm, but every nerve ending in his body was fired up. "I'm not far away. Tell me where you are exactly, and I'll come. Right now. Okay?"

"Where am I exactly?" she asked someone, and Gray assumed it was a nurse in the room providing her the information.

"I heard her," Gray said. "I have a private jet. I'm heading to the airport now," he promised, terror filling every crevice of his body.

"The nurse wants to talk to you," Tessa said.

"Hello?" a woman came onto the line.

"What happened?" Gray snapped out, the urgency of getting to her finally convincing his legs to work again.

"From what we were told, she was on the street and fell. Tumbled down into the Bosphorus in Karaköy near the ferry port. A group of fishermen happened to be there, night fishing, and they rescued her. Between the fall, bump on her head, and the shock of the cold water . . . we're assuming that's connected to her fuzzy memories. She has no recollection of what she was doing on that street, let alone in Istanbul."

The visual the nurse painted had his blood heating and his heart breaking. "Did she have anything on her? Any clues to help figure out what might have happened?" He did his best to slip into operator mode and not panic like he wanted to. The idea of that woman scared and alone in another country had him physically ill.

"I honestly don't know what to say or think," the nurse answered. "She can't even remember any other numbers aside from yours and her best friend's, but that number is going to voicemail, and she doesn't want us to leave a message."

"Not even her fiancé?" *And how'd she get my number? Why remember mine and not her fiancé's?*

"She didn't mention a fiancé, but I assumed you were her loved one since she knew your number by heart. But I'll ask when she wakes up. The morphine drip we started a few minutes ago has put her back to sleep."

"I'm on my way. Don't let her out of your sight," he rasped. "Please."

"A detective is on his way to talk with her. We'll let him know you're heading here. Can you give me your details and a number to reach you in case we need to speak before you arrive?"

"Of course. Please, keep an officer at her side until we get there."

"Why would she need protection?"

Because in my line of work . . . "Please," was all he said.

"I'll do my best." She ended the call after Gray offered her his contact information.

His mind was spinning in so many directions as he and

Sydney entered the rendezvous point to join the rest of the team.

"We need to go on another op," Gray cut straight to it at the sight of his teammates. "And this one is personal." *No smooth-sailing November.* "Tessa Sloane just called."

Jesse stepped forward, his brows lifting in shock. "Wait, she did? I gave her your number that weekend we saw her."

If Tessa was anything like he remembered, she relied on her phone for everything and didn't memorize numbers. *But why mine?*

"What's going on?" Jack asked, recognizing the name. He didn't know he'd recently bumped into Tessa.

"Tessa needs me." Gray cleared his throat, still in shock. "Us. She needs us." He squeezed his phone, eyes cutting over to his partner, Carter.

Carter nodded. No hesitation as he asked, "Where are we going?"

CHAPTER FOUR

ISTANBUL, TURKEY

"You're sure?" Relief rushed through Tessa at the detective's words. There were still so many unknowns, but at least that was one thing she didn't need to worry about.

"No signs of any kind of, um, trauma found during the doctor's exam," the detective repeated, sitting by her bed. He cleared his throat, probably uncomfortable with discussing such a thing.

Yeah, same. But also, thank God. "I just don't understand why I can't remember how I got here and what happened before I fell." Tessa rummaged through her memories, but the last five days were unreachable.

The nurse had said the detective had been at the hospital for two hours, waiting for the groggy effects of the morphine to wear off before questioning her. He'd hoped if enough time passed without the drugs in her system, she'd remember everything. No such luck.

Luck. Riiight. Because my life has been filled with that. She set a hand to her bandaged head, wincing from the pain at the mere touch. She couldn't believe it. Naomi had just been saying don't fall in a river and . . . *Wait, I remember that like it was yesterday, but the nurse said it's Thursday night. The last time I saw Naomi was Saturday at our office. And that's the last thing I remember.*

"There's no record of anyone by the name you gave us flying into Istanbul," the man said, and why'd he look so familiar?

And then it registered. "The fact I know you look identical to that actor everyone loves—John Yaman, well, spelled C-A-N—but I can't tell you how I got here is weird, right?"

He stroked his scruffy jawline. "Yeah, a little." His mouth briefly tightened. "My name is Onur. Sounds kind of like the English word for owner," he added when she'd yet to speak up. "And you can trust me. Okay?"

Trust? No, she couldn't trust herself, given her lack of memories right now, so she wasn't going to trust a stranger.

"I'll make you a deal. I'll tell you what I know, if you give it to me straight about what you remember, okay?"

Give it to you straight? There was nothing to give. Crooked or otherwise. "Sure," she managed to get out.

He offered her a small smile, then opened a pocket-sized spiral notebook, the kind she didn't think anyone used anymore. "So, the fishermen who rescued you said you pretty much rolled right into them before going into the water. They grabbed you within seconds of going in. Otherwise, the current may have carried you away." He paused to let that sink in.

Holy shit. I could have drowned.

"It was roughly a twenty-meter drop down an inclined cement slope. Presumably, you were on the street above. No safety wall or railing up top. Not uncommon. Two officers happened to be heading toward the fishermen to order them to pack up and go when you fell."

"So, if I was running away from someone, maybe that's why they didn't come down and chase after me? Because the police were there?" *But who would I be running from? And why?*

His hesitant look suggested he didn't buy into the kidnapping idea. And sure, there were quite a few plot holes to that theory, but nothing else made sense to her.

"What was I wearing?"

He gave her a curious look as if unsure why she'd ask, then checked his notebook. "Dark jeans. Black sneakers. A black long-sleeved shirt."

"No jacket? It's November. Also, the nurse said I had no ID or phone on me. I may not always have a purse with me, but I'd have something on me. A keycard to a hotel room, at least, right? And I never go anywhere without my phone." *And usually ChapStick.*

"I assume your belongings fell into the river." He scrutinized her, distrust in his deep brown eyes, even though he'd asked her to trust him. "As for your jacket, Americans seem to prefer the cold. Tourists and their love of central air and ice in their water," he challenged back.

She knew the game he was playing. She'd seen enough police shows *and* remembered them to know he was trying to throw her off. To see if she knew more than she was letting on.

"If you had been taken, there was no sign of rope burns or torture from what the doctor reported. Your bruises and cuts were all from your fall," he revealed. "Your hands weren't cuffed or tied when you were saved either. The tox report came back clean. No sign of drugs in your system."

And yeah, that was good news, but she also knew herself.

Knew she'd never be out at night in a foreign country by herself. Period.

"No cameras down where you were rescued, but I'll have my guys check in the morning to see if they can pull any footage from street level."

"Okay." She nodded. "Before waking up here, the last thing I remember is being in my office in Virginia on Saturday. Five days ago. I have no idea what happened between then and now," she repeated what she'd told him when he first arrived. Her hand trembled as the shock of her situation struck her all over again. "I'm in another country with no clue how I got here." She did her best to ignore the throbbing in her temple. "And I'm terrified of flying. Like I freeze up and faint at going in tight spaces. The only way they were able to do an MRI on me earlier was because they drugged me. I would've panicked inside that machine."

"So, perhaps you took something for the flight?"

"But you said there's no record of me flying into Istanbul." At least her brain was still quick enough to remember that detail.

He smirked. "Your memory is sharp, and yet . . . not? It's interesting."

"I'm not faking, I swear." *He's only doing his job*, she had to remind herself. "I do not fly. I just don't. I only have a passport because my father made me get it, and I used it once. I went to Mexico, but I drove. And yeah, all the way from Boston. I'm so afraid of flying that I did that."

He scribbled a few notes, then looked up at her.

"I need my brother, Curtis." She frowned. "Or my dad. He was a colonel in the Army. And my brother is . . ." *Deep undercover somewhere.*

"No luck when we tried to find a number for your brother. We can't even get a last known address."

And you won't. He's a spy.

"And whoever answered the line where your father is staying said he's backpacking with his girlfriend and gone for days. No way to reach him."

Leave it to my father to go backpacking in his sixties. Always in need of an adventure.

"What about your mother?"

Tessa's shoulders fell. "I don't want her to know. Not yet. She's overseas and busy with work, and she won't even know I'm gone. No point in worrying her right now."

"Hmm. What about close friends?"

"My best friend is in Jamaica, and I told her to turn off her phone. But I don't want to ruin her trip and worry her either. She'll hop on a plane and come here ASAP if she knows what happened." Her stomach plummeted when a horrific idea hit her. "What if she's in danger? What if she was taken too? I—I need to know she's okay. Can you check her hotel or something for me to confirm she arrived?" Her head was spinning now. It was one thing for her to be in this situation, but she couldn't handle anything happening to Naomi.

"We don't know if you were taken. And you said you don't want us to leave her a message, but—"

"No need to worry her about me. But *I* need to know she's safe. Please." She tried to sit taller, but her head was spinning, so she collapsed back onto the bed.

"I'll see what I can do," he relented, setting his notepad on his thigh. "And the nurse said you have an old friend on the way."

Old friend? Yeah, from thirteen years ago. And she only remembered his number because she'd stared at it for so long the week before she . . . *Before I what? What happened to me?* "He said he's flying here and that he isn't far. He works in private security, so maybe he can help figure out what happened?"

"Just rest for now. I'll reread the statements from the two officers and fishermen. Talk to them myself as well. And I'll also check some of the other airports to see if maybe you flew there and drove into Istanbul."

"I didn't fly," she insisted.

"Unless you took a boat, or you're about to shock me by letting me know you can walk on water—"

"Boats make me claustrophobic too. Not a chance I came here that way."

"Well, all we do know is that you were fished out of the water in one of our most historic districts, Karaköy. Sounds to me as though you're a tourist. Istanbul is known as the City of the Seven Hills. It's, well, hilly here. You were probably taking in the sights, and you tripped and fell. We just don't know how you arrived here."

"And you haven't been listening to what I'm saying," she said with a sigh, trying not to yell at the man for doing his job.

He stood and pocketed his notebook and pen.

"I feel like I blacked out and lost the last five days of my life, but I'm not crazy." *But it sounds wild.* Was it even possible to only lose specific memories? Maybe in the movies, but this was the real world. *Maybe I don't blame him for not believing me. I can barely believe it myself.*

"Let's just hope by tomorrow morning you remember. In the meantime, I have an officer posted outside your room. He'll call me when your friend shows up. I'll swing by in the morning to talk to you both and see if any of your memories are back."

"Why do I need an officer out there? Do you think I'm in danger?" She swallowed. "Or that *I am* the danger?"

"At the moment, Miss Sloane," he began, his deep brown eyes narrowing, "I think you're a tourist who has simply lost her way. But it's better to be safe than sorry."

* * *

TESSA GLANCED OVER AT THE CLOCK ON THE WALL. IT WAS one thirty in the morning. She'd woken half an hour ago, and the nurse had said Gray had called. It shouldn't be much longer till he arrived.

She'd asked the nurse to help her wash up. She didn't want to face the man with wild hair and bad breath.

The fact it was Gray coming to her rescue, of all people, was absurd. Then again, the entire situation was bizarre.

The only thing keeping her sane was the fact the detective had reassured her that during her exams, the doctors hadn't found any evidence she'd been drugged, tortured, or . . . touched inappropriately during those "lost days."

Ugh. She squeezed her eyes closed and clenched her hands into fists, hoping to somehow channel her mind into drawing forth the memories. At the sound of the door creaking, her heart skipped. She could feel his presence. How was that possible?

"Tessa." *That voice.* Her shoulders relaxed for the first time since she'd woken in the hospital.

She peeled open her eyes, and a sob escaped at the sight of Gray and a man she recognized from years ago, Jack London. So far, her long-term memory proved to be intact.

Gray quickly approached her bedside, lowered the railing, and sat beside her.

She reached for his arm and tried to sit. He leaned in and helped her up, their bodies so close she had to tip her chin to peer at him. A shuddery breath floated from her mouth before she flung her arms over his shoulders and linked her wrists behind his neck, hugging him.

"I'm so scared," she cried into his shoulder, borderline hyperventilating as he stroked her back. Never shushing her, just holding her like he'd never let go. Like he wouldn't run this time.

Thirteen years apart had time collapsing into what felt like only thirteen days. She was pretty sure he had on the same cologne he used to wear. Well, he smelled the same, at least.

And why'd he feel like home? Comfortable and safe. She tightened the hold she had on him, clinging to the sensation.

"Fuck," he said gruffly by her ear. That rough sound of despair made her feel like he still cared about her. "I'm here." His voice broke. "I got you." He held her for a few more quiet minutes until she managed to stop the tears.

She freed her arms from over his shoulders and leaned back so she could look at him. The lights were at the lowest setting, but she could clearly make out his features. He brushed the pad of his thumb along the seam of her lips, catching a tear.

"The last memory I have before waking up here was being at my office back home. I think that's all I . . ." She squeezed a lump down her throat when a flash of an unexpected memory snapped to mind.

Dressed in all black, she'd been stumbling like she'd had too much to drink. The streets had been crowded, and after bumping into too many people, she wandered away and . . . fell?

"I remember walking just before falling. But the detective told me what I was wearing, so maybe I'm creating a story in my head based on his description and confusing it with what happened. I—I just don't know."

"It's okay. We'll get you through this," Gray reassured her in a calm voice. "I'll protect you. No matter what."

And she believed him. When it came to her safety, this man would never let her down. Her heart was more than likely another story.

"The other thing I've been trying to tell the police here is that I don't fly. I'm terrified of it. I'd never go overseas, let alone by myself." She was worried she'd erupt into another sob, which wouldn't do her any good. "It makes no sense for me to be here, but why can I remember everything except the last five days?"

"Everything-everything?"

Gray shifted to the side at Jack's question, and she instinctively snatched Gray's hand. He seemed hesitant initially, but he took it and laced their fingers together.

"Everything," she whispered, her eyes cutting back and forth between the two men. Former Green Berets that now worked in private security. So, if anyone could figure out what happened, it'd be them, right? She wished her brother and dad were available but knew these two wouldn't let her down.

Jack scratched his beard, his attention moving to Gray. They both had on jeans and plain long-sleeved black shirts. Backward ball caps and dark boots finished the look. If they'd been nearby, had they been working another job? Shit, did she steal Gray away from something important?

"What do you remember?" Jack asked. He had a Ryan Reynolds thing going for him—a thought that should've been the last thing on her mind, but for some reason, those little connections she could make, even to movies, grounded her. Reminded her she still had most of her memories.

"I can remember everything else, *Jack*," she said, saying his name to prove her point. "The scar on my middle finger is from a Doberman that bit me when I was eight. And it was my stupidity to stick my hand through the fence, so I never told my parents how it happened. I didn't want the dog to get in trouble. So yeah, everything-everything." She let go of a shaky exhale and peered at Gray. "I remember the night before you took off thirteen years ago like it was yesterday. The night you took my virginity, and I—"

"I'm sorry, what?" Gray cut her off, narrowing his eyes. He gently squeezed her hand tighter as if she'd lit a worry bomb inside him, and his fuse was short.

"I think I'm gonna, um." Jack hiked a thumb over his shoulder. "I'm gonna go into the hall. Talk to the officer out there. Yeahhhh, that's what I'm going to do." He closed the door behind him, and Tessa focused back on Gray, hating she'd accidentally shared such a revelation to him now of all times.

That's my luck.

"Tessa, I asked you." Gray closed his eyes, his nostrils flaring. "When we first . . . you were so . . . and I was worried, so I asked."

"I'm so sorry. You looked so panicked when you thought I was a virgin, and I knew if you'd known beforehand, you wouldn't have slept with me. And there was no way I'd tell you after," she admitted. "The last thing I wanted was for you to stay because of some obligation because you popped my cherry."

When he opened his eyes, she tried to shrug, but damn, did that little movement have her one shoulder aching. She probably hit it hard when she fell. "Don't act like you wouldn't have second-guessed walking away that morning if you'd known you took my virginity."

"I . . ." Yup, he was speechless.

And I'm five days memoryless. "But that's not why you're

here. Not to talk about that. My point is that my memories are intact except for how I got to Turkey and what happened while I've been here."

Gray let go of her and stood. He drew his hands to his hips, giving her his profile. "I'm glad you called me because I can help. But why'd you call me instead of your fiancé?"

"Because there is no fiancé. I tried to tell you that night we ran into each other. The bride was drunk and put her sash on me. I'm not engaged. No boyfriend. Not taken at all. Well, unless you count that I was taken in the very literal sense last week, and that thought is terrifying."

Her hand started to tremble. Her lip wobbled. And Gray was back at her side within seconds, realizing she was about to reach her breaking point again.

"I wanted to tell you I'm single, but you took off and didn't give me a chance. And then Jesse's sister interrupted my attempt to tell him. But he, um, gave me your number anyway." It was all so crystal clear. But no matter how much she tried to remember anything from last week, nothing came. "And I wanted to call you so many times that I stared at your number on my phone to the point I memorized it, I guess."

"I don't know what to say." He gripped her hand, and her pulse slowed to a more normal speed. "All that matters is you're okay. I promise I'll figure out what happened."

She nodded, hoping he was right. "Can you do me a favor? I asked the detective to check, but I'd feel better if you did too." Her best friend was like a sister. Family. If anything happened to Naomi, she'd never survive that. "I won't be able to focus on anything until I know that whatever happened to me didn't also happen to my best friend. She left the office shortly before me last weekend, and I need to know she made it to her vacation safely and she's happily sipping cocktails on a beach."

He tipped his head, studying her. "What's her name? Where's she at?"

"Naomi Williams. She's at the Sandals resort in Montego Bay. Her boyfriend, Sam Hughs, checked out an overwater bungalow." She held up a hand, quickly adding, "I don't want her panicking about me."

"So, confirm she's safe but don't let her know you're here?"

Tessa nodded.

"What about your mom?"

"I'd rather not get her involved right now. But I'm sorry I'm involving you in this mess. And I promise I didn't just bump my head and forget what happened. If I'm here, it's because someone wanted me to be, but I have no clue who or why. And I know I'm a total klutz, but no way did I just trip, fall, and go into the water, like Goldie Hawn from *Overboard*. Besides, she had amnesia. I have something else, I think. And what if there's someone out there who doesn't want me ever to remember?"

"I'll keep you safe," he promised. "I'll find whoever did this to you, and I'll handle them," he added with conviction.

When he closed his eyes, and his breathing picked up, she realized there was something else on his mind. Something dark. Something he was afraid to ask.

"No," she whispered. "The doctors said no one . . . hurt me. And I may not remember the last five days, but somehow, I believe that." In her heart, mind, and body, she knew it to be true. No one hurt her. *Just stole my memories.*

Gray's eyes opened, and he surrendered to the same breath of relief she'd felt at the news earlier in the night.

She brought her free hand to his cheek, and his facial hair tickled her palm. "All I know, with absolute certainty, is that for one of the few times in my life, I'm lucky." She sniffled.

"If we hadn't bumped into each other that night, I'd be here all alone."

He shifted her hand away from his face and drew her tight to his frame, nearly crushing her. A dull, achy throb filled her chest, and another sob broke free.

"You saved me thirteen years ago, and then I walked away," Gray murmured, his breath fanning across the shell of her ear as he held her, "but I promise you . . . this time, I'm not going anywhere."

CHAPTER FIVE

"TESSA WILL BE RELIEVED TO HEAR THAT. THANK YOU FOR checking," Gray said over the phone while pacing the small waiting room. He was grateful he had the place to himself that morning so he could make his necessary phone calls in private without losing sight of Tessa's room.

At least he could tell Tessa that Naomi was safe in Jamaica when she woke up.

"Any update on tracking Tessa's last steps before she arrived in Istanbul?" he asked Mya, hoping she'd called because she had news on that front as well.

Mya Vanzetti, Sydney's best friend, split her time between Falcon Falls Security and a team of Marines specializing in dismantling human trafficking operations worldwide. She was a welcome addition to Falcon with her tracking skills, not to mention her talent at getting people to talk and turning them into sources and assets.

"Sydney's working on that," Mya replied. "Let me hand the phone over to her."

"Hey, Gray," Sydney said a few seconds later. "You okay?"

"Been better." He swallowed. "You learn anything?"

"Yeah. There was a power outage that lasted three and a half minutes last Saturday in the neighborhood where Tessa's private practice is located. It happened around seven at night. Reports suggest there was some power grid issue."

"Like someone hacked it, and no one wants to confess that was the cause?"

"Pretty much," Sydney confirmed. "Before her security cameras went offline, I saw footage of Tessa's business partner, Naomi Williams, leaving the office. The only car left in the parking lot afterward was Tessa's. A black Ford Explorer. And when the power came back on, her SUV was gone."

"Dammit."

"I'm working on running Tessa's face through our facial recognition software at all major transportation centers on the eastern seaboard." Thank God Sydney was not only a hell of a fighter but a computer whiz and an excellent tracker. "Her home is ten minutes away from her office. No vehicle in the driveway, but she has a garage, so it's possible her SUV is in there. We'll have the parking lots at the closest airports checked as well, just in case."

"Thank you. Seriously."

"Of course. Carter's requesting a word."

While he waited for Carter to come on the line, he looked back out at the nurses' station. It was almost zero eight hundred, and he assumed nurses and doctors would soon make their rounds.

The detective had put in a request to the hospital allowing him to show up at such a late hour the night before, and he'd stayed by Tessa's bed all night while she'd slept. She looked so fragile, and the way she'd clung to him when he'd first arrived—as if he were some savior—had thrown him for a loop. His chest had constricted, and his stomach tucked in even now at the memory of setting eyes on her in the bed.

And then she'd answered the horrible question he'd been unable to ask her.

No one hurt her.

He had every intention of destroying whoever had taken Tessa, but if they'd so much as set a hand on her . . .

He thought back to his time in the Army. Americans had a code of conduct to follow on ops when he'd been Special Forces. He'd never forget his first few missions when he'd flex-cuffed and detained prisoners, and they'd been shocked when he and his guys didn't act like savages and torture them after capture.

But Gray knew himself. He knew if anyone had hurt Tessa, he'd tear apart the code of conduct he'd lived by. Shred it without remorse. And slaughter every last son of a bitch involved.

"Hey, how are you holding up?" Carter asked, drawing Gray's focus back to the call.

"I'm not doing great," Gray admitted. "I need to get her discharged and out of here as soon as possible." The police wouldn't let her walk away without a passport and proof of legal entry, and he didn't blame them. There were too many question marks. But that also wouldn't stop him from doing what he felt was best for her safety, which was getting her away from a public place.

Unlike the malls in Istanbul, the hospital didn't have metal detectors, so at least Gray had been able to come in packing. His Glock 19 was safely tucked at the back of his jeans, hidden beneath his shirt.

"Holding up at the Four Seasons while we're in town isn't exactly ideal, but there's not an abundance of standalone properties up for grabs in the city. Especially at such short notice. I'm working on getting us a boat if we plan to stay for much longer," Carter shared.

A floating safe house? "Yeah, okay," he reluctantly agreed. "Where are we at with securing footage from her fall?"

The team had to wait until the morning to go into the area of Karaköy where Tessa had been rescued. They'd attempted to check it out overnight, but the district was a maze of small streets. Until the sun came up, the guys were just wasting their time.

"I sent Griffin and Oliver to the port where she was found. But the place is full of a bunch of historic buildings, many converted to shops, and the security systems are lacking. We can't simply hack the feeds like normal. The first place they went to still used a VCR, and the owner said it only runs during store hours. They were closed at the time of Tessa's fall. The second location's camera was a fake, just meant to deter theft."

Not an encouraging start. But he knew Griffin and Oliver wouldn't let him down.

Griffin Andrews was former Delta Force, and he'd worked with Carter before joining Falcon. And Oliver Lucas had been 82nd Airborne. Oliver had been brought into everyone's life in a wild way. Nearly losing his head. Literally.

"Griffin and Oliver had to pull back for now because the local police showed up a few minutes ago," Carter continued. "Looks like the detective sent some officers to check the surveillance cameras within a three-block radius of her fall as well. Since the store owners are less likely to talk to us, I'll tap into the local police network. Whatever they find out, we'll have access to."

"Did they get statements from those at the scene last night?"

"Yeah, there were two local police officers and a few fishermen who were there on the scene, but there's nothing helpful in the report," Carter shared the shit news.

Gray swung his attention to the elevators to see Jack stepping out, armed with two cups of coffee and a shopping bag looped around his wrist. Not his normal look.

Visiting hours had begun. At least the first person there was a friendly. "Jack just arrived. I'm guessing the detective is on his way, and maybe he'll know something. I'll touch base in a bit."

"Yeah, okay. Uh, just, um, hang in there." Carter wasn't great at sharing his emotions, but the man was trying, so Gray appreciated the effort.

Gray ended the call and pocketed his phone before accepting the coffee.

"How's Sleeping Beauty?" Jack asked, a smug look on his face. Gray knew Jack wouldn't be making jokes if Gray hadn't already told him that Tessa hadn't been hurt by whoever had her the past five days. "I know how you can wake her, by the way." He lifted his chin, his lips stretching into a smirk.

"You're a funny fucker this morning, aren't you?" Gray sipped the instant coffee. It wasn't the best cup of joe he'd ever had. He'd prefer tracking down real Turkish coffee, much stronger than what Jack had given him. But beggars couldn't be choosers, and he'd rather be close to Tessa than have good coffee.

Jack set down the bag of things Gray had requested he bring for Tessa and covered his heart over his fleece jacket. "I'm insulted. I'm a funny fucker all day, every day. It never stops." He winked.

Gray rolled his eyes. "Where's Jesse? I thought he was coming with you."

"Doing a perimeter sweep. Checking for any potential threats. He'll be our eyes and ears outside." Jack handed him a wireless comm. "Take this. You never know when we may need to hop on comms."

Gray shoved the small device into his pocket as he looked down at the black plastic shopping bag. "Everything there?"

"I asked Mya to pack for Tessa. I wasn't going to pick out Tessa's panties and bra." Jack pointed to the bag. "I did have to go to three different stores to find the candy you requested though."

"Hopefully that's still her favorite." Gray brought his eyes back up to his buddy. Based on Jack's signature devilish smile, he was about to crack a joke, so he switched back to work before he had a chance. "Maybe we need more hands on deck here? We're light on help since our thing in Paris was easy. What about flying in a few of our guys from the West Coast?"

"Or Camila and some of her crew?" Jack suggested.

Camila Hart was Carter's "not-a-sister but like-a-sister" friend. She ran a security company in South America, and she was basically Carter in female form, but with a sense of humor.

"Yeah, that'd be a brilliant idea. Because having two women I dated in the same room later today won't be bad enough. Let's add a third." Of course, he hadn't technically dated Tessa. And he'd only been on one date with Camila, not that Carter knew about it. It'd ended with an awkward kiss, followed by a handshake and an HR-like text from her the next day wishing him the best on his future endeavors.

Jack jokingly teased, "*'Romeo, Romeo, wherefore art thou Romeo?'* I mean, when else will you have three women you've kissed in the same room and not get punched?"

"Someone is gonna get punched, and it ain't me." Gray shook his head, but at least his friend had managed to unfuck his bad mood a touch.

"Maybe we hold off on calling in reinforcements until we know what's going on?" Jack sipped his coffee, switching back to operator mode with ease. "Let's see how bad shit is first. Maybe it'll be—"

"Murphy's Law," Gray cut him off. "I can feel it. Something bad is coming, and I want to be prepared for the storm, which is why we need to get her out of here."

"Yeah, okay. I'll talk to Carter and make some calls." Jack lifted his coffee to his lips. "But it seems to me that not even thirteen years apart dulled your feelings for this woman. A woman you claimed drove you nuts once upon a time ago. Why didn't you tell me you ran into her recently?"

Gray was waiting for that question to come. He just kind of assumed the virginity one would've been his first one. Hell, he was still trying to wrap his head around that fact.

The moment he'd slid inside her that night, stretching her out, he'd been concerned she'd withheld that important detail.

"Fuuuuuuck, Tessa. You're so fucking tight. You okay? You're not a . . . a virgin, right?" At that point, it wasn't like he would've pulled out and walked away. But he'd prayed to God she was just extremely tight from not having sex recently. He knew he was larger than average, but damn.

"No, of course not," he remembered Tessa answering, holding his arms as he looked down at her. *"Please, keep moving. My body will relax."* The tears at the edges of her eyes should've been enough to knock some sense into him, but he'd been so overwhelmed by his own emotions he'd struggled to think clearly.

73

She'd been so wet that it hadn't taken much movement to ease her body into taking him. And then they'd both found their rhythm, and she'd given back as much as he'd given her and then some. Her moans and breaths of ecstasy had played on repeat in his head for months afterward while he'd stroked his cock to get himself off.

"You going to answer me?" Jack waved his free hand before Gray's face, tearing him from his memories.

"Yeah." Gray rotated his neck, uncomfortable for so many reasons. "I was out with Jesse one night in D.C.," he finally answered, "and we ran into her at a bachelorette party. I mistook her for the bride-to-be. Learned earlier she's not the one getting married."

"And Jesse gave her your number anyway. Huh," Jack mused, lowering his cup to his side. "Sounds about right. His wife's hopeless romanticism is rubbing off on him. Same in Griffin's case, I suppose."

One of Falcon Falls' first cases brought Griffin and his wife, Savanna, together. Same with . . . "Damn," Gray blurted as he thought about Jesse and Ella's marriage. Then there was Sydney and Beckett. "Our ops, they have a tendency to hook people up, don't they?"

Jack smirked. "So, you're thinking you and Tessa might hook up?"

"Shut up," Gray snapped back.

"Hey, you brought it up." Jack's smile stretched. He really was the comedian on the team, and he'd always provided Gray with enough laughs over the years to offer him an abdominal workout without hitting the gym. Everyone could use a friend like that. "So, elephant in the room . . . did you really not know back then? It took you weeks to admit to me you even hooked up with her that night, but—"

"Because you were off getting justice, and I didn't need

you thinking about my sex life while on a mission," he reminded him. A mission that ended with Jack and his men successfully taking out those responsible for the helo crash and loss of Rangers on the day of Gray's accident.

Jack crumpled his empty paper cup and tossed it in the trash. "I just . . . how'd you not know? I was Jill's first," he said, referring to his ex-wife. "And well, I remember there was a noticeable—"

"Yeah, stop there." He'd never had experience with a virgin before, but he assumed Jack was right and didn't something break? *The hymnal. No, the hymen? Why am I thinking about this?* He blinked a few times, letting go of the thought. "Are we really talking about this in a hospital with Tessa down the hall with five days of memories missing?"

"I mean, if you can't talk about sex with your best friend at a hospital in a foreign country, when can you?" Jack teased.

Gray chucked his half-empty coffee cup and removed his hat, dragging an anxious hand through his hair. "When I look at that woman, I feel everything I felt at twenty-eight. But what I feel the most is guilt," he said instead of answering the virginity question.

"Guilt for walking away from her?" Jack's tone grew serious that time.

"I thought I was doing the right thing by walking away that day, but that doesn't mean I don't feel horrible about it." *Regret it.* He put his hat back on, forward this time to protect his eyes from the bright overhead lights. He was edgy, nervous, and without sleep. Not the best combination for an operator.

"Maybe this is your second chance with her?"

He shot Jack a dirty look. "I got a second chance at life,

and I know for damn certain I'm not owed one in another way." *I lost my chance at love. Game over.*

Jack reached out, gripping his shoulder. "Shut up." His lighthearted tone was to let Gray know he was full of shit. "Anyways," he went on, "you're the one who said our ops bring people together." He let go of Gray and turned toward the open doorway. "But for now, looks like you have a date with a detective, and I'd rather not be a third wheel. I'll go join Jesse." And with that, he made a beeline for the elevators, not-so-discreetly holding a hand by his face while walking past a man striding toward the nurses' station.

Jack called the elevator, then faced Gray and mock-saluted.

"Thanks for ditching me," Gray said, knowing Jack would be able to read his lips.

"You're welcome," Jack mouthed back before Gray lost sight of him in the elevator.

Gray snatched the bag and went into the hall to meet with the man he assumed to be in charge of Tessa's case. "Are you the detective?"

The man faced him, performing a quick inventory of Gray's appearance. It was as if he was assessing the threat level. Sizing him up. Doing the same, Gray noticed the detective was at least an inch taller and probably around thirty pounds heavier too. Gray squared his shoulders, feeling a ridiculous need to appear more intimidating while offering his hand.

"Chandler, right? I'm Onur." The man took Gray's extended hand, clearly deciding Gray wasn't a threat. And if he was any good at his job, he'd have already done a background check once the hospital provided his name and number last night.

"You can call me Gray."

"And has Miss Sloane talked to you? Said anything new?"

Good. Jumping right into it. I have questions too. "She doesn't remember what happened. But we haven't spoken since around zero two hundred hours. She's still asleep." Now it was his turn. "And just to confirm, her bloodwork was clean, right? No sign of abuse?" He needed to hear it again. Confirm his worst nightmares were only that, and not Tessa's reality.

"Nothing in her system aside from the morphine given to her following her fall. And they gave her an exam as well. No evidence of trauma of any kind."

Gray nodded, took a moment to remind himself how to breathe, then asked, "Have you reached her family yet?"

"Her brother and father aren't currently reachable. Aside from them, you're the only other person she wanted to make aware of her situation. She asked me to check in on her friend, and I was able to confirm she's safe, but that's about it."

"And no records of Tessa entering the country?" Gray probed.

"All I know is we have no legal record of entry. Not sure how she arrived in Turkey."

"Well, she fell near a port. Maybe she was on a boat beforehand. We should check the docks."

The detective's lips curled at the edges. "'We,' huh?"

Gray scrunched his forehead, trying to decide how he wanted to play this. He had no authority in Turkey—hell, technically, none in the U.S.—but that wouldn't stop him from investigating and running point on the case.

"On the way here, I reached out to the American Embassy and alerted them to her situation," the detective said when

Gray remained quiet. "I'm sure word will get back to her family."

Gray frowned. "My concern is who else it'll get back to." And he doubted it'd take a decent hacker long to track down which hospital Tessa was at, which made him uneasy.

"So, you agree with her, you think someone had her? And what, she escaped by falling?"

"Knowing Tessa, falling was probably an accident." His stomach banded tight at the mental image. For someone who claimed to be so unlucky, her lack of it may have been what saved her. "But her hands weren't bound? Ankles not cuffed or roped? Her injuries are more than likely just from the fall, right?"

"Right." He folded his arms over his lightweight jacket. "If someone had her, why didn't she scream before the fall? Why would they walk with her out in the open like that? And if she was running away on her own, she would've been—"

"Screaming," he finished for the detective. He considered sharing Tessa's blurry memory from just before the fall, but first, he wanted to talk to her again to see if that'd been morphine-induced or real. "Listen, I've seen a lot of wild things in my life. I think we need to consider the bump to her head is not why she lost five days of her life."

"You think someone brainwashed her? Or did something to make her forget, somehow without the use of drugs?" It was clear he wasn't buying the story.

"That's exactly what I'm saying. I just don't know how or why they did it." Before Gray could say more, the fire alarm began to wail, and his stomach dropped. "But I think we're about to find out who's after her."

CHAPTER SIX

As far as dreams went, this was top-notch. Chocolate-icing-on-vanilla-cake perfection. And she refused to wake up, to pay attention to whatever shrieking noise was trying to rob her of the intimate moment she was sharing with Gray.

She wasn't ready to leave the fantasy world where Gray was finally touching her again. Skin sliding over skin. Limbs tangling. Her body on fire.

"Tessa, it's me . . ."

"I know it's you," she murmured, battling the foggy haze as reality interrupted her reverie to pull Gray away from her.

But wait, Gray was with her, wasn't he? Not only in her head. *I'm not home, I'm . . .*

Istanbul. The hospital. Morphine. It was all coming back to her now. Well, all of it but the last five days.

She opened her eyes, slowly turning her head to focus on Gray as he removed the IV from her arm. "Is that the fire alarm?" Becoming more alert, with a bit of anxiety starting to creep in, she shifted her attention from Gray, now applying a Band-Aid where the IV had been, to the Can-Yaman-lookalike detective standing by the door.

Gray tried to help her sit, his hand sliding to her back for support. "The hospital thinks their system has been hacked. No one manually pulled the alarm. Every time they shut it down, it goes off again."

"What does that mean?" she asked, shivers coating her skin.

"Someone's creating a diversion to get to you. Chaos and panic," Gray explained, keeping his voice calm, probably so she didn't panic. "I have two teammates outside keeping watch. They'll let me know if the place has been breached, but we're short on time."

His words settled into her mind. Expanded into something harsh and ugly—the truth of her situation. She mindlessly tore at the bandage wrapped around her head and tossed it to the floor.

"I need to get you unattached from these machines." Gray's eyes fell to her chest. "You're naked under there, right?"

"I, um, assume."

"Can I reach beneath the gown to remove the wires?" He tipped his head, a sense of urgency in his eyes and tone, and yet, he was taking the time to ask permission to touch her.

"Okay." She nodded, still in shock.

"Hurry," the detective rushed out as Gray shifted the gown to the side.

Goose bumps rolled over her skin the second Gray touched her. Her abdominal muscles tightened as he skimmed her torso, searching for the wires. She stifled a gasp when his hand slid down her collarbone, his finger brushing across her nipple as he yanked a few of the leads free. *Wrong time to get turned on, Tessa.*

"I brought you clothes and shoes," he shared once freeing

the last of the wires. "You can't go running outside in that gown. Can you walk?"

"I think so. I might lose my balance though." He helped her stand, but her Jello-y legs proved as unreliable as she predicted, and she sagged against him. He circled her hips with his muscular arms, and she linked her wrists behind his neck for extra support. For a moment, with her breasts pinned against his wall of chest muscles, she'd swear they shared a heartbeat.

He dipped his chin in search of her eyes. "I got you, you good?" His hands slid around to her back, and he snatched the material together to prevent the detective from a view of her ass.

"I think I need a few minutes to get the vertigo-like feeling to stop before we go." *And to process the fact you're here holding me in your arms when I was just promising myself I wouldn't call you.*

Gray frowned. "We don't have time, I'm sorry."

Her attention landed on the detective. "I'm not changing in front of a stranger."

"Can I go in the bathroom to help you?" Gray tipped his head in question. "You're not stable on your feet."

Tessa looked over at the bathroom door, uncertain what to do. "I'd rather not show my ass to half the city."

Gray cocked a brow. "Yeah, let's not have that."

"I guess if I can let a stranger give me a shower, you can see me naked too." Her cheeks grew hot, and she quickly added, "And by stranger, I mean nurse."

A shocking smile brushed across Gray's lips. "You're going to need to let go of me so we can move, then."

"Oh, right." She pulled her arms from his shoulders as he slowly let go of her, and she reached back to pinch the gown closed.

Gray snatched a bag from the floor, then gently grabbed her by the elbow. He guided her toward the connecting bathroom while telling the detective, "You've got the door. Holler if there's a breach on the floor. I'm armed. Just FYI."

"I figured," the detective responded without facing them, eyes focused out the small glass window in the door.

Once in the bathroom, Gray locked them in as she faced the mirror. Tired brown eyes stared back at her. Pale skin was surrounded by messy shoulder-length hair. Chapped lips starved for hydration. *Ooooof.*

"Tessa," Gray prompted. "We need to hurry."

She shook her head to clear her mind, but that only made her more off-balance. "I feel like I drank an entire bottle of wine. I don't think that's the morphine."

"Probably the bump to the head from the fall."

She set her palms on the counter as she tried to steady herself, and Gray stood behind her, his focus dipping . . . *Right to my exposed ass.*

He blinked twice, reached around her, and set the bag in the sink. "Here." The word was more like a grunt, still loud enough to hear over the obnoxious alarm. "I'll face the wall. If you need help, let me know."

She nodded her okay, then rummaged through the bag, finding a black sports bra and satin panties. The gown fell to a pool at her feet, but when she bent to slip her feet through the holes of the panties, her ass bumped right into him.

"You, uh, okay?"

"I'm fine." *Just naked in a foreign country, without all of my memories, in a small bathroom with the man who broke my heart thirteen years ago.*

Putting on the bra next, she watched in the mirror as he planted his hands on the wall, curling them into fists. Was he struggling to be in this small space too? Or thinking about the last time they were in a hospital together? Thinking about his accident?

Distracted by every little thing, including the dazed and confused feeling, she admitted defeat, "Can you help? This is taking me too long. I'm sorry."

"Don't be sorry. I just don't want us to be sitting ducks." He dropped his arms and turned.

Their eyes connected as he reached around her, his hand skirting her side in the process to gather her clothes and sneakers, and that slight touch sent a tingling sensation straight down to her toes.

"Hold on to me so you don't fall," he directed while kneeling before her.

Doing as he said, she grabbed hold of his strong shoulders for support while stepping into each pant leg. When he slid the fabric up her thighs, she peered down, finding his head turned, eyes away from her panties. With efficient and nearly clinical movements, he swapped her thick hospital socks for a thinner pair, then helped her into the sneakers.

"Thank you," she said as he rose, towering over her again.

Gray gave her a tight nod as he guided her arms and slipped the long-sleeved shirt over her head. Everything took less than sixty seconds. But each movement seemed to happen in slow motion.

"You good?" He pushed some wispy hairs away from her face, the pads of his thumbs sliding over her cheeks, calming her with his gentle touch.

"I'm scared," she admitted, sucking her lower lip to resist the tremble.

"I know." His big palms went to her cheeks as he stared into her eyes. "But I won't let anything happen to you." All she could do was nod. He let go of her face, and she already missed the warmth of his comforting touch as he hollered out, "Are we clear?"

She glanced down at the bag, spotting something unexpected. *Raisinets?* But before she had a chance to say anything, Gray urged her back into the room. It took her a second to recognize the silence. The alarm had finally been killed.

"Hallway is secure," the detective said when they joined him. "My officer is helping the nurses on another floor right now. And hospital security is probably dealing with frantic patients."

Gray let go of her hand and grabbed his phone from his pocket. "One of my guys outside is calling," he said before placing the call on speakerphone.

"It's time to switch to comms," someone said without so much as a greeting. "Give me thirty seconds to connect the line. We have the car waiting for you on the south side of the hospital. Still clear out here. But firetrucks and police are en route."

"Roger that." Gray ended the call and shoved his phone in his pocket, swapping it for something small that he positioned in his ear. "We need to move now." He peered at Tessa and brushed his knuckles across her cheek. "Stay behind me, okay?" When she didn't respond, lost somewhere between fear and vulnerability, he squeezed her shoulder. "We need to go. I'd carry you, but I don't think I can protect you that way."

"I'll be okay." *Not really.* Not at all, in fact. But right now, she'd soldier on. Suck it up and go forward, a skill she'd learned from the colonel. She nodded at Gray, hoping her face didn't give away just how much she was faking the confidence in her ability to keep moving.

"I got you," Gray promised. "We need to get to the south

side. That's our extraction point."

"Take the lead so she can stay between us," the detective advised Gray, then began speaking in Turkish over the radio once they began down the eerily empty hall.

When Gray abruptly stopped, covering his ear as if listening to someone talk, she slammed into him. He spun around and held her arms, keeping her steady. "Change of plans. Police are cutting off that entry point."

"I'll tell them to let us through," the detective spoke up, sidestepping Tessa, but Gray let go of her and snatched his arm, stopping him.

"What are you doing?" The detective jerked his arm away with a quick snap.

Gray tipped his head toward the door as if worried danger lurked on the other side. "Something's off."

Aside from the obvious? Was there something else she needed to worry about now? Her lack of "Spidey-Sense" was one reason Naomi didn't trust Tessa out alone at night.

"The fire alarm is a diversion," Gray announced, leveling the detective with an uneasy glare. She didn't miss the challenge in his tone, mixed with a not-so-subtle hint of distrust as well. "It's meant to smoke us out without actual smoke. The question is, are you involved?"

Static crackled over the detective's radio and he adjusted the knob, turning down the volume.

"Why are you sweating? It's not hot in here." Gray nodded in the direction of the radio. "Who have you been communicating with?"

"Who do you think?" The detective tossed a hand toward the empty hallway. "The officer in the building."

When she took a hesitant step back, Gray pulled her safely to his side before going for his gun at his back.

Annnd you're pointing a gun at a detective. Shit, shit, shit.

She curled the fingers of her free hand inward, trying to get a grip. Panicking would not help Gray or their situation.

"This ward is empty, isn't it?" Gray asked him. "Who are you helping?"

"I'm not helping anyone but you at the moment. Before I left last night, I ordered the five other patients on this level to be transferred for their safety. Until I knew more about her situation, I didn't want to put anyone else at risk. Clearly, it was the right call. And when the alarm went off, and you first went to her room, I sent my officer to help the staff."

Gray scrutinized the detective, holding Tessa so close to him they were nearly joined at the hip. She had to assume being a Green Beret meant his "Spidey-Senses" were on point. "You're lying."

"Don't you think if I were part of this, I'd have already taken her from here?" The detective's brows dipped in over narrowed dark eyes. He had a point. "Why wait until you show up, someone I know has a military background in special operations? That makes no sense."

"We're not walking out of here together. I won't have you signaling our every move to someone," Gray said in a steady tone, keeping his weapon aimed at a man she still wasn't sure was the enemy.

But my judgment sucks.

"Fine. You want to do this your way?" The detective went for his pocket. "I'm reaching for a keycard. You'll have universal access to every door and hallway in the hospital. Take it. But if you stay with me, I can bring her to the station where we can better protect her."

Gray stepped forward, letting go of Tessa, and snatched the card from him before handing it over to her. "My team will protect her."

"You're making a mistake." He grimaced. "I'm not the

bad guy."

"I can't be sure of that." Gray lowered his weapon, and Tessa took that as a good sign. "But if I do find out you're behind any of this, I will hunt you down and kill you. I don't care who you are, got it?"

The detective looked over at Tessa and shook his head. "I was only trying to help you." His frown deepened as he turned back to face Gray. "I have your number, Mr. Chandler. I know who you are. Don't think I'll forget this." And then he turned toward the stairwell and left.

Once they were alone, Gray let go of her hand, hid his gun, then went over to a map of the hospital on the wall and followed his finger along one of the emergency exit routes. "I have an idea." He took the keycard back from her. "You okay to keep moving?"

"We don't have much choice, do we?"

He nodded, then waved the card in front of a panel in the hallway and a door electronically slid open. "Come on." They took a turn, then hurried down another empty hall before entering a stairwell.

"Stairs?" Five flights felt impossible. But they were in an employee-only stairwell, so they couldn't stand there all day. "Are *you* okay to do this?" she asked Gray, worried about him as well.

Gray's focus momentarily fell to his leg, then he looked back at her. "I can run a marathon if I have to and carry you if needed. So yeah, I'm good."

"Then I'll be good, too." *Soldier on, Tessa. Soldier on*, she could hear her father's voice in her head. Those were his favorite words for her whenever she was on the verge of quitting something, like wanting to give up dance lessons because her balance sucked to nearly dropping AP Chemistry because balancing chemical equations was also not her thing.

Stepping to her side, Gray roped her back to the present the second he wrapped an arm around her for support.

They steadily made it down the first two flights of steps before he asked, "You need a break?"

"Not if it's going to risk our lives. Let's just get this done."

He faced her and cupped her cheeks as he'd done in the bathroom. "I will not let anything happen to you. I need you to hear me." His thumbs moved in small circles, and if he stared at her like that any longer, the actual fear she was managing to block would come out in the form of tears.

She let go of a shaky breath and rasped, "Soldier on."

He blinked twice in surprise at her words, then nodded and they began to move again.

A handful of seconds passed as they rushed down the steps and finally found themselves on the first floor by the emergency exit door.

Gray quickly swiped the keycard and cracked the door to peek outside. He slowly eased it shut and shared, "Just dumpsters. But there's a cop with his back to us protecting the entrance. I'm going to need to knock him out. Stay here. Don't move."

She nodded, and he reopened the door. Catching it with her hand to keep it from slamming shut and alerting the officer, she waited for Gray to return.

He was back to her within thirty seconds, reaching for her hand to guide her outside. She faltered at the sight of the officer slouched up against the side of the building.

"It was only a chokehold maneuver. He'll be awake soon, so we need to hurry." He gently tugged her hand as they made their way to the street. "Just walk. Blend in."

Blend in? She looked at the crowds gathering by the

hospital, watching with curiosity, probably wondering what had happened.

"With the fire alarm being hacked like that, the police are on alert, and my men couldn't linger. We need to get to a new exfil spot," Gray told her as they turned down another street, the hospital now behind them.

Exfil?

"Just two more blocks. Can you walk that?"

The sky was dark, the sun blocked by clouds, which made it easier on her eyes. But her legs and body were as numb as her mind. "I just want to get out of here."

Gray looked back, his attention skating past her. His eyes narrowed as he delivered words she didn't want to hear, "We're being followed." He tapped his ear. "I have a tail. A silver four-door Renault. No view of the plate." He looked around and shared two intersecting street names, then he continued to walk in step with the foot traffic, keeping her close to his side while gently pulling her along with him. "I'm taking her across the Galata Bridge. The pedestrian walkway is crowded. The traffic is bumper to bumper. We'll try and lose them there."

Tessa shivered and brought one arm across her chest, fighting the cold as they neared the entrance to the bridge, which was more like a flat road over water.

"I'm going to lose you on comms. I'll pin-drop my location once we find a place to hide," Gray relayed to his team once they were on the bridge.

Tessa glanced back, searching for a silver Renault, but she had no clue what kind of car that even was, and there was *a lot* of traffic. "Don't tell me that's them, the ones abandoning their car in the middle of the bridge?"

Gray followed her gaze, then he tightened his grip on her hand. "Now would be a good time to run."

CHAPTER SEVEN

"THESE FUCKERS ARE RELENTLESS." GRAY KEPT A FIRM GRIP of her hand as they took another turn down a crowded pedestrian-only street. As expected, he'd lost his teammates on comms after crossing the bridge, but he trusted they'd catch up and have his six.

He hadn't been able to make out many distinguishable descriptors to provide Jesse and Jack other than the fact the two men chasing them were about six feet with trimmed beards, wearing black ball caps.

Their best chance at evading their pursuers was to find a place with enough people milling about to slow down the men's progress while he figured out a way for them to blend in.

"You doing o—" Gray's question was cut off by a scream from somewhere on the street. On instinct, he shielded Tessa with his body, searching for the source.

More screams. Shouts in Turkish. "*Silah. Silah!*"

People began to disperse in panic. And while Gray had no desire to be caught in the swell of the crowd and possibly separated from Tessa, he also knew staying put would leave him and Tessa out in the open.

Looking around, he identified an alley off to their left. "There." He tugged at her hand, trying to move her from frozen to flight. "See that dumpster," he said once they were tucked away off the street. "Hide on the other side." When she remained staring at him with wide, worried eyes, he let go of her hand and begged, "Please. Go."

"What about you?"

"I'm your cover." He waved her away, praying she'd listen, because they were more than likely short on time before being spotted. When she finally disappeared, he drew his Glock, approached the street, and positioned his back flat to the brick building. Stealing a look toward the street, Gray noted people rushing in one direction—*his* way—which meant the danger was closing in on them.

He glanced back to ensure Tessa was hidden from view, and when he took a chance to steal a look around the corner, he located their new problem. *Not* one of the men from the bridge. The man in question had a black ponytail, thick beard, and ink spiraled around his throat. His hand, currently holding a 9mm at his side, was also covered in tattoos. *Different bad guy. What in the hell is going on?*

The narrow street was nearly cleared out. Vendor stations abandoned. The smell of baked goods and black tea lingered in the air as the man kept walking. Hunting.

He wasn't pointing his weapon. No shots fired yet. But he was visibly carrying it to scare people away. *But why? Are you here for us?*

Gray ducked his head back into the alley and checked his earpiece, hoping his teammates were back in range. "Comms check. Can anyone read me?" Silence. He tried again. Nothing.

Ten seconds until he's here. Gray steadied his breathing, counted backward, and shifted in preparation to approach from the side, intending to place himself outside of the fatal funnel and remove himself from the man's scope of vision. Rather than risk hitting an innocent bystander, he decided it'd be best to disarm and fight.

He stowed his Glock and readied himself. And the second the man came into view, Gray snatched the wrist holding the weapon and positioned the barrel away while headbutting the guy.

Startled, the man tried to pull his arm free from his grasp, but Gray caught him off guard with an elbow to the side of his head. The man fired off a shot in the process, hitting the brick wall opposite them.

Outweighing Gray by at least fifty pounds of muscle, he wouldn't go down no matter how hard he hit, and it took Gray a few seconds longer than he liked to disarm him. Once the threat of the weapon was neutralized, it turned into an outright brawl.

Unfortunately, the guy was also an experienced fighter. He had hand-to-hand combat skills, and he returned everything Gray threw at him with equal force.

Hooks. Elbows to the face to get the upper hand. And then the bastard hit him with a knee to the stomach and simultaneous chop to the back. Gray nearly went down, but he was running on pure adrenaline and quickly shook it off.

As the man spat blood from his mouth, Gray kicked the discarded 9mm from reach before his enemy had a chance to retrieve it. He then returned the favor of a knee to the body, but to his groin instead. When he hunched over and groaned, Gray came down hard on his back, driving both elbows into the man's spine, knocking him to the ground.

On all fours, Gray snatched the man's ponytail and jerked

his head back, drawing his own weapon to point it at his temple. "Who are you?"

"Who I am is none of your concern," he said in an even tone as he attempted to stand. "Where's the girl?" He could hear an accent, but he hadn't spoken loud enough for it to be distinguishable. But now he knew without a doubt, he was there for Tessa.

Gray shoved the gun harder into his temple and yanked his hair, preventing him from rising. "What do you want with her?"

"It's just business. But my men are on comms. You're about to have three more armed men here. And the police from the sound of it. I'd let me go." That time he heard an accent, and it sure as hell wasn't Turkish.

Gray let go of his hair, snatched the earpiece from him and stepped on it, grinding into the pavement for good measure. "Who do you work for?" he asked again, his heart hammering so loud it competed with the wailing sirens in the distance.

"Tick. Fucking. Tock," the man barked out, his hands curling into fists on the ground. He was about to make a move, and Gray would either have to kill him or let him go.

Knowing the police would be on their asses any second, and this prick was more than likely transmitting his location to his buddies, Gray backed up. He needed to get Tessa away from there and fast. But he also needed to slow the bastard down so he couldn't easily pursue them.

He snatched the man's weapon from the ground as the guy shifted up to his knees, blood spilling from his nose that he caught with his tongue. A second later, the man made his move.

When he whipped a knife from the side of his boot and came at him, Gray discharged the firearm, double-tapping him in the chest. He heard Tessa's gasp echo in the alley as the knife clattered to the ground. Seconds later, the man went down as well.

"Tessa, you can come out." Gray whipped around to see her slowly moving into view. "More may be coming."

"Are you okay?" Her soft, terrified voice had the hairs on the back of his neck standing.

"Yes. But we need to move fast." He hid the second gun at the back of his jeans and was about to search the man, but the sound of tires screeching down the pedestrian-only road, without any accompanying sirens, confirmed his fear that the enemy had found them first. *And . . . if the enemy is in range, so are you.*

He looked around, weighing their options. Thankfully, it wasn't a tall building, and the distance between the roof and dumpster wasn't much of a stretch. "We're going to the roof."

He grabbed Tessa's hand as she stared at the body in shock. He urged her to look away and set her foot on his palm. "Focus. You've got this," he reassured her, trying to keep his tone calm when his body was in rapid-fire fight mode.

He hoisted her up a second later, never so relieved to have his new prosthesis as now. He'd never have been able to do that maneuver with his original one.

He followed her onto the lid of the dumpster and pointed to the roof. "You can do this. I've got you. Okay?" At the sound of car doors slamming shut, he growled out, "They're here. Go. Now." He gave her a boost up, and she reached for the ledge, just making it. Thank God she had upper body strength. She shifted to her stomach and scooted from sight a moment later.

He tossed a quick look down, knowing he was out of

time. More men would soon converge on their location, and he'd have to take them out so they couldn't pursue.

"Stay up there," he whispered, grabbing both 9mms while he waited for the men to show themselves.

But . . . no one came. More car doors slammed shut. *Shit.* An exchange of gunfire on the street. Doubtful that was the police. He decided to take the moment to escape. To join Tessa on the roof.

He secured the firearms at the back of his jeans, then jumped up and caught the ledge, pulling himself up to the top.

He found Tessa crouched nearby, hugging her knees to her chest. Holding a finger over his lips, he mouthed, "Get flat on your stomach." Next, he positioned himself on the cold slab, thankful it was a deck and not a pitched roof.

He army-crawled to the edge, needing to get a look at the street to see what was going on down below. The wail of sirens drew closer, and then the gunfire ceased seconds later. Either the traffic was so damn bad in this city it took forever for the officers to get there, or someone capable of hacking the hospital fire alarms was now fucking with the traffic lights to slow the police down.

Gray cautiously lifted his head and peered down. Two bodies were on the ground alongside a black BMW, unmoving. Similar clothing style and tattoos as the man he'd encountered in the alley. One of the men who'd been chasing them—bearded with a ball cap—was in the process of carting off another guy, seemingly still alive but with a bullet wound, to a nearby van, not the Renault they'd driven earlier. *What in the hell is going on?*

A second man, possibly one of the men from the bridge, had his eyes on his phone while stepping over a dead body, and then he . . . looked straight up to Gray's position. Target acquired.

When their eyes connected, Gray jerked his head back and shifted around to Tessa.

"Is that the police? Are we safe?" she asked, apparently assuming those gunshots had been from the good guys.

"I'll explain later," he rushed out. "For now, it's time to go."

* * *

TWO STREETS OVER, GRAY SPIED SEVERAL PARKED POLICE cars, their officers in pursuit of what they more than likely believed to be an active shooter situation.

"Back to blending in," he let her know, hoping she was able to continue walking after everything she'd been through. He squeezed her hand to remind her he had her six.

"Why won't you tell me what else happened while I was on the roof?" she asked as he guided her down another street, putting themselves farther away from the alley. With every turn, the streets and sidewalks buzzed with activity again, crowds of people going on with their day. A regular Friday for them.

"Because it won't help you right now. Trust me," he said, keeping his tone flat and doing his best to mask the concern in his voice.

Before she could argue, Gray abruptly stopped, and his stomach wrenched. *You've got to be kidding me.*

"What's wrong?" Tessa cried. "More of those guys? Are we running again?"

"He found us." *The guy who saw me from the street.* "We can't draw attention to ourselves. But we need to move fast and get to an even more crowded area."

He quickly navigated around a group of businessmen in

their way, then nodded toward a site that might be their best hope in losing him. "There."

"What is it?" She shot him a wide-eyed look from over her shoulder as they maneuvered around more pedestrians on the sidewalk. "A mall?"

"Kind of."

He quickly guided her through the entrance of the historic Egyptian Bazaar, a market for spices and textiles dating back hundreds of years. Red Turkish flags hung overhead, and the aromas of spices and desserts filled the air as they made quick turns inside what felt like a maze. He didn't see the man on their ass anymore, at least, but he knew he'd be there soon. He had no clue how they'd tracked him unless . . .

The hospital had my name. My phone. That's how he's doing it. He'd been in too much of a rush to get her away to think straight.

Gray slipped his hand into his pocket and powered it off. He always had an extra burner phone on him for just-in-case moments though. And unlike Tessa, he had every important number memorized for such events.

"Did we lose whoever is after us?" she asked a few minutes later as he continued to scan every shop they passed.

"I think so, but not for long." He halted at the entrance of a store free of customers. A young woman was on a stool at the back with a book in her hand, lost in whatever she was reading. *Jackpot.* "Here."

He scooped an arm around Tessa's back, pulling her to his side as she shot him another worried glance. Hopefully, he didn't have any blood on him, but he wasn't so sure. He took a few hits from that guy.

"*Merhaba*," he greeted the young woman.

When she lifted her face from her book, her eyes narrowed, and the corners of her lips turned down as if the last thing she wanted was to deal with a customer. The girl couldn't have been any older than eighteen, and when she closed her book with a reluctant sigh, he nearly smirked at her reaction.

He glanced at the cover, relieved to see an English book title. His Turkish consisted of about ten words, five of which were swears. Make that eleven: *silah*, meaning weapon. He'd never forget that one.

"Are you Americans?" A curious look crossed her face as she set aside her book and adjusted the knot of her gold silk hijab.

"Yeah, we are." He tipped his head toward Tessa. "And there's someone out there looking for her." *And maybe more.* "I'm trying to protect her, and I was wondering if you have a back room we can hide in? I know it's strange to ask, but we really do need your help."

She slipped off her stool and fingered the lapels of her jean jacket. "How do I know I can trust you?"

"You don't," Gray said, opting for the truth. "I can pay you, but I have a feeling that won't motivate you to say yes." He tossed a look back, checking the hall. Still clear.

"Please, we need your help," Tessa whispered, drawing Gray's focus back to the girl he hoped would be their savior.

The girl turned to the side and eyed the floor-to-ceiling gold curtains behind the counter. "My *baba*, my father, will be back in thirty minutes. And I know all the shop owners around me. If you hurt me, I will scream."

Gray held up his free hand. "I won't hurt you, and we don't need that long."

"Okay." She nodded, shifted the curtains aside, then motioned for them to follow her.

Once they were hidden from view, Gray let go of Tessa and looked around the dark space.

"There's a storage closet," the girl suggested while opening a partially hidden door.

Tessa stared at him wide-eyed and nervous. More than likely in shock from what went down. Unless she really was that terrified of small spaces. "There's not enough room for the both of us. Can't we just stay right here?"

"I'd rather add one more layer of protection from the bazaar." Gray went into the closet and turned to the side to fit between the rows of spices that were lined up on shelves in the narrow space. "Come in with me."

"I—I can't." Tessa balked and stepped backward, the exact opposite direction he needed her to go, nearly bumping into the girl.

"Facing your fear is the only way you can ever find out if you're capable of living without it," the young girl spoke up, taking Gray by surprise.

"I just faced a fear. More like a nightmare. The alley and those men. And oh my God, I—" Tessa clapped a hand to her mouth as if to stop her rambling.

"Please," he begged, and his shoulders relaxed as she gave him a hesitant nod and accepted his hand.

Once Tessa was inside with him, their young accomplice shut the door, leaving the cramped space in pitch black aside from a tiny beam of light beneath the door.

"I don't know if I can do this." Tessa's hands landed on his chest. "I'm claustrophobic. Maybe that fear is okay to have. Maybe it keeps me safe."

"Right now, this closet is what's going to keep you safe." He searched in the dark for her face and held her cheeks. Her teeth began chattering. "Trust me. I won't let anything happen to you."

"I know. I saw what you did out there. I mean, well, I heard it. Then saw the effect," she sputtered. "But how do you know we can trust her? What if she tells someone we're in here?"

"I'm used to making split-second decisions, and I had to go with my gut." *And that's the truth.* "I need to text my teammates and tell them what happened. I'll pin-drop our location and then hold you, okay?" He let go of her to grab his backup phone from his pocket, careful not to bump into the shelves and knock down any spices.

He held the phone at his side and quickly sent an update and instructions for his team, followed by their location.

"I don't think there's enough oxygen." Her breasts bumped his chest as she sucked in a deep, sharp breath. Her heart would claw free from her chest at the rate it was beating.

"There's oxygen." He carefully pocketed his phone. "Just focus on the sound of my voice, okay?"

"Feels like a line from a movie we may have watched together."

"Probably is," he said with a coy smile, not that she could see it.

"The way you took down that guy was unreal. I, um, may have peeked around the dumpster to check on you once or twice."

"I'm so sorry you had to be there for that and—"

"I don't understand it. Any of this. It doesn't make sense." Emotion flared in her voice, and he could hear her panic setting in. He had to calm her down somehow. He had no clue if he could get her mind off what happened, but he had to try.

"He's dead, right?"

More than just him. "Probably, but I didn't have a choice. It was him or us."

"I just . . . will you tell me what else happened there?"

"It will do the opposite of calm you down. So no, not right now." The last thing he wanted was unnecessary guilt on her shoulders about any lives taken by his hand or for her to worry about the fact the bad guys were killing each other to get to her. Talk about a plot twist he hadn't seen coming. "I'm going to hold you." *Show you I can do more with my hands than kill. I can . . . comfort? I think I can.* "Close your eyes and pretend you're somewhere else. Can you do that for me?"

"Isn't that what I used to tell you to do?" she asked, her tone somewhat lighter that time, thank God.

"Yeah." He wasted another smile in the dark at the memory of their summer together while pulling her tight against him, swallowing that last bit of space separating their bodies.

At six-two, she had to be about eight inches shorter than him, and she fit perfectly under his chin. He cradled her head and looped his other arm around her waist as she slid her hands to his back, clutching hold of him.

"The problem is, I don't think I can picture anything. I think I might faint."

Her rattling tone jarred free a memory, and he rushed out, "Naomi. She's in Jamaica at the resort. She's safe."

After a shaky exhale, she whispered, "Oh, thank God."

"See, one less thing for you to worry about." *Now, what do I say? Tell her about the time I had to hide in a coffin? Nah, that'd make for a shit story for someone with claustrophobia.* "I know you're anxious not to be pinned to my body, but—"

"The only part about today I'm comfortable with is being pinned against you."

Hell, that wasn't what he'd expected her to say. Judging by how she started squirming, she hadn't meant to share that thought either.

"We're pretty much strangers now. I shouldn't have said that. I'm so sorry."

Strangers? After that statement, kissing the adorable woman in his arms to relax her probably wasn't the best idea, so plan B. "Talk to me. Tell me something. Anything." When she kept quiet, only the heavy gulps of her sucking in air too fast breaking their silence, he tacked on, "You know, so we're not strangers anymore. Help me get to know you again. Give me some bullet points from your life." *Now I'm the one rambling. Great.* But he'd do anything to keep her calm, which would ultimately keep her safe.

His shoulders relaxed at the unexpected soft laugh rolling between them. And he hoped that was a real chuckle and not a "she's losing control" one. "How about *you* give me thirteen bullet points about yourself, one for every year we haven't seen each other?"

Shit, I stepped right into that one. But open the book on my life? There wasn't much to say. A bunch of blank pages filled with dodging real bullets.

"I'm kidding," she quickly recovered as if sensing his hesitation. She'd likely felt him physically tense up too, considering his body *was* pinned tight to her petite frame. "*But* I do have a few questions."

"I might have some answers, we'll see," he responded, thankful her trembling was subsiding.

If he could see her face, he knew she'd be tugging that plump bottom lip between her teeth as she worked up the courage to ask what was on her mind. Because he *wasn't* a stranger. Screw the passing of time. Their summer together was practically yesterday for him.

"Tessa? Cat got your tongue?"

Another light laugh from her. *Best sound of my life. Let's keep it going.* But he wasn't sure how long he could successfully get her to forget he shot someone, and that more men were after her.

"Since we're sharing body heat," she began, taking her time to answer, "I want to ensure you're single. I'd feel pretty bad about it if you're not."

Of course you'd think about that, even at a time like this. So innocent. That hasn't changed. "I'm very much single."

"And have you ever been married?" At least her teeth no longer clicked together, and her voice was less breathy.

"No."

"Engaged?"

He paused, thinking back to getting down on one knee for Sydney at West Point before deploying. *She said* . . . "No."

"You?" he decided to ask, hoping he could handle the answers. "Ever married? Engaged?"

"No." The ensuing pause was almost audible. "I have bad taste in men."

Yup, the reason for the pause. I'm one of the "men" in that statement, aren't I? "Oh." *Yeah, great follow-up, idiot.*

It wasn't hot in there, but a bead of sweat trickled down his back as he thought about the other men in her life. Had they been of the asshole variety? Did he need to pay any of them a visit?

"Are you, um, still considering moving to the D.C. area?"

He inwardly thanked her for the subject change. "My family lives around there, so I'm considering it."

"You didn't sound so certain when we bumped into each other."

Yeah, well, seeing you screwed with my head. Especially because I thought you were getting married. Because we ARE NOT strangers, Tessa. Why'd he want to have that message written across the sky for everyone to see? Put it on the jumbotron at every major sports stadium. *What is wrong with me?* "I'm feeling more inclined to move there by the second."

"Hmm." And now she was distracting him as well. Not the best idea. "You know, I saw the Raisinets in the bag at the hospital. You remembered something so insignificant about me."

"Nothing about you could ever be insignificant." Well, that sounded flirty. "I mean, how could I forget?" He chuckled, trying to shake it off. "The one time I accidentally bought you the milk chocolate ones for our movie night instead of the dark ones—your adorable little pout just about did me in." Went back to the store and corrected that mistake too.

"There's a difference between the two, I swear."

"You were as maddening back then as you were beautiful," he blurted, unable to stop himself. But his efforts to distract and calm were working, at least.

"So, I didn't drive you *that* crazy." She shifted in his arms, and he lifted his chin when she moved her head as if trying to look up at him.

"It's too dark in here to make out my eye roll. But trust me when I say it's there." She had to know she was a knockout. God, she was even more beautiful now than back then.

She freed her hands from his back and collapsed her arms between them, sliding her palms up the center of his chest to land on his pecs. And why was it that in the dark, with the spicy aromas surrounding him, he felt his senses heightening?

"What is it?" he rasped, sensing there was something else she was preparing herself to ask.

"Why does our time together thirteen years ago feel like it happened yesterday?"

And why'd he feel so relieved she felt the same way as

him? "So, you agree we're not really strangers?" His stomach muscles tightened in preparation for a verbal hit he knew wasn't coming. Tessa was a fighter, but she fought her battles differently than him. Air kisses and pep talks to his M4 rifle and Yarborough knife.

"I'm not sure if I should admit you don't feel that way to me?" she shared, and he realized something was holding her back from wanting to make that confession.

It's me. I'm what's holding her back. I walked away from her. And she hates me for it. "You can confess anything to me. What happens in the spice closet, stays in the spice closet."

She gifted him with another laugh, one not loud enough for anyone in the shop to hear, but it had his heart thundering in his ears as he drew her as close as possible. "How are you making me smile and laugh after what just happened? I don't get it."

"It's a talent. My two best skills happen to be defusing bombs and diffusing tension," he continued to tease, willing to do whatever he could to keep her from panicking. "Actually, that's a lie. I rarely defuse anything. Better to let the EOD specialists handle that stuff."

"Nice people to have in your corner."

"I'd say so." He smiled. *Again.* What was happening?

Yeah, I feel twenty-eight. No, screw that. Twenty-seven. Before the accident. Although, at that age, he'd somehow had more self-control. *Over forty and fucking hornier than in my twenties. Should be a bumper sticker.*

When a soft groan left her lips, he hated himself for allowing that sound to travel straight to his cock. Assuming that wasn't a response due to pleasure, he asked, "What's wrong? Your head?"

"I just feel like I . . ." He hated himself for doing it, but before she could finish her thought, he shushed her with his hand over her mouth.

"We're not alone," he warned at the realization someone was in the shop asking questions, and his blood pressure went through the roof. "Someone's out there." He let go of her mouth.

She began quivering again. And her small, worried breaths gained momentum and volume.

"I'm scared." The chattering of her teeth resumed, and she bumped into the shelf behind her. He freed his hand from the butt of his gun to pull her back to him before she knocked down any containers, giving away their location.

"It's okay. Just stay quiet," he whispered, but her shaking didn't stop. She needed a distraction.

"Tessa?"

"Ye-ye-yes?"

Fuck it. "Since we've established I'm not a stranger, I'm going to kiss you." He brushed the pad of his thumb up the column of her soft neck. Then along her jawline. He tipped her chin with his fist. "May I?"

"Ye-ye-yes, but they're dry."

I'll fix that. With her okay, he slanted his mouth over hers. The second they kissed, it was *his* heart that slammed against his rib cage. It was *his* head becoming dizzy.

She opened her mouth, inviting him in to taste her. And how could he say no to that? But now all he wanted to do was ravish her, which was pretty messed up given their situation.

When her panicked breaths turned into soft moans of pleasure, he gripped her hips, drawing her closer to his cock, which was growing harder by the second.

They were in danger and hiding in a spice closet in Istanbul, and yet they were making out like two high schoolers playing seven minutes in Heaven. But he didn't care. He gave himself over to the moment, too captivated by her luscious lips and the sinful sweep of her tongue meeting his.

His hands skimmed the silhouette of her body. His fingertips dragged over her skin beneath her shirt and up her back.

She molded against him. Fitting so perfectly inside that cramped space. Her claustrophobia temporarily gone. His fear that something could've happened to her in that alley sent to the wayside.

His mouth traveled across her cheek as she rolled her hips, arching into him. He kissed her temple before lowering his mouth to her ear to confess what he'd known for the last few seconds, "He's gone. We're safe."

She went stock-still against him. Bringing that slight pelvic grinding she'd been doing to a halt.

His spine went stiff, and he straightened his head while searching for his breath. And hell, his sanity too.

"Thank you for um . . . calming me down."

"Of course." What else could he say—*my pleasure*? No, because he'd sound like an asshole. *Maybe I am?* Because part of him wanted another reason to kiss her.

"You're . . ."

Hard? "Yeah, sorry." But with the lingering memory of her lips on his, it'd take some time to decompress.

"Do you always kiss women to calm them down?" The tenderness of her tone made him wonder if she was serious.

"You'd be the first."

"Oh." That little pop of sound had him wanting to swallow it with a kiss. "So, are we safe now?"

"Not yet. He could circle back." *And there could be more men looking for you.* "We'll stay here until my team gets to us so we have backup." He closed his eyes, not that he needed to in the dark, but it helped him think. "He was speaking English. Too hard for me to detect an accent," he shared, trying to push through the hazy fog of whatever in the hell just happened between them.

"So that means he's—"

"Most likely not Turkish. And neither was the guy in the alley."

"You're sure? How can you tell?"

He thought back to the man's brogue. "He had an accent. Scottish." He finally opened his eyes and reached between them, seeking her cheek to try and calm her with his touch instead of his mouth that time. Before he could think of what else to say, his phone vibrated in his pocket. He let go of her and checked his message.

> Jesse: We're outside. No sign of anyone here. And police now have that alleyway blocked off. But we've got you covered to exit in case anyone comes here.

Shit. At least he had the Scottish man's gun. With any luck, his team would somehow get IDs on *all* of the men after them that morning. "Ready to get out of here?"

Tessa arched into him, and when she murmured, "Are *you* ready?" he realized she'd confirmed he was still sporting wood.

Damn, this woman was something else. He cleared his throat and pocketed his phone. "I will be in a second." She'd more than likely hear the smile in his tone as he said, "Looks like I'm the one that needs a distraction now."

CHAPTER EIGHT

GRAY OPENED THE CURTAINS, KEEPING TESSA BEHIND HIM. Only when he'd made eye contact with Jack did he pull Tessa to his side and enter the main shop area.

"Jesse's got eyes out there," Jack said, his attention moving to the young Turkish woman now joining them.

"The English-speaking man looking for us, do you remember anything about him that might help?" Gray asked her, hoping she'd have *something* to tell them that might shed some light on what was going on. Hopefully, Jack and Jesse could fill in some of the remaining puzzle pieces and clue him in on the men from the alley.

The young girl peered at Gray and shared, "He was like you."

"You mean because he had on a ball cap? Beard?" Damn, he was hoping for more.

"No, he was an American," she said with certainty.

Considering she'd quickly pegged them earlier, he didn't doubt her. Gray exchanged a quick what-the-fuck look with Jack before focusing back on the girl, trying to mask his shock at learning Americans were also after them.

"Wear this," the girl suggested, offering a red hijab to Tessa. "It will help keep you safe out there."

"Oh, I, um." Tessa's uncertain gaze bounced back and forth between her and Gray. "Are you sure? It's not disrespectful if I wear it?"

"No." She smiled and placed the red silk over Tessa's head, then tied a knot beneath her chin. "Us women must stick together, yes?" She gave Tessa a small smile, then reached into her pocket for something. She unfurled Tessa's fingers and placed a small bracelet on her palm. "This is the Turkish evil eye." She pointed to the small blue and white eye-shaped charm attached to the white gold bracelet. "It will ward off evil. Protect you."

"Will it give me better luck?" Tessa's shoulders shrank. "I'm not so great in that department."

"You're not unlucky." Their unlikely hero eyed Gray while lifting her chin. "You have him."

"Oh, I, um, don't have him," Tessa whispered, her cheeks turning a soft pink.

Gray reached for her wrist, and in a steady tone, reassured her, "You have me." Once she nodded, he dug into his wallet and fished out two hundreds, offering them to the shopkeeper. "Take this. Please."

She shook her head and waved away the money.

"Consider it book money." He smiled and nudged the money in her direction. "Thank you," he said once she reluctantly accepted it.

With glossy eyes, Tessa smoothed her hand over the side of the scarf and added, "For everything."

The girl clenched the money, dropping her arm to her side. "You should leave before my father comes. He'll have questions."

"Of course." Gray nodded, tossing her one more grateful look before they hurried back into the main hall of the bazaar.

"You good?" Jesse asked, then nodded a hello to Tessa since it was their first time seeing each other since, well, the bar nearly two weeks ago.

"Yeah, but the woman at the shop said it was an American looking for us," Gray told him, keeping his head on a swivel in case the man backtracked looking for them. "Please tell me you have something to share that will help."

"We'll fill you in once we're all in the car." Based on the tone of Jesse's voice, he didn't have great news.

Jesse walked ahead of them, Jack just behind, and Gray remained at Tessa's side, sealing her into a protective sandwich as they made their way to the rental car, which was parallel parked nearby.

Gray quickly helped her into the backseat, relieved they were no longer out in the open. Once beside her, he removed his comm and shoved it into his pocket. When Tessa reached for the knot of her scarf, he suggested, "Maybe keep it on until we're at the hotel."

Her fingers brushed across her mouth as if she were distracting herself with thoughts of their kiss. And he'd much rather her think about that moment than remember him killing someone. He considered reaching for her hand, but he might haul her onto his lap and nestle her against him for safekeeping if he did.

Gray didn't miss the smirk on Jack's face as he peered back at him like he knew something else had gone down in that closet.

More like up. Painfully so. It'd taken a solid minute of thinking about bad shit to get his dick to go down.

With a lift of his chin, Gray directed Jack to face forward.

He didn't need comic relief right now. Fucking A, he needed an entirely different kind.

Clearing his mind except for the main issue at hand, he focused on Jesse behind the wheel. "Tell me what you know."

"Oliver and Griffin split up. We sent Griffin to check the alley and had Oliver try and locate the Renault the men ditched on the bridge. By the time Oliver got there, it'd either been towed, or there'd been a third passenger in that car who drove it away," Jesse explained, catching his eyes in the rearview mirror before pulling into traffic.

"When Griffin arrived at the pedestrian street leading to the alley, the police had everything blocked off on both ends. He couldn't access it," Jack added. "But he saw the BMW in the road. Three body bags. No van in sight."

"Wait, what?" Tessa blinked in shock.

Right, he forgot she was still clueless about that. He'd been avoiding that conversation. "While you were on the roof, the men who chased us over the bridge showed up. They got into it with the other bad guys. The Americans killed two of them, and from what I could tell, they took another alive," he rushed out the details as fast as possible. "One guy spotted me. He's the one who came to the bazaar looking for us. The American."

Her eyes widened, then dropped to her hands as her fingers curled inward. She was visibly trembling, and he wasn't sure whether to offer her his hand or hug her tight to his side.

Before he had a chance to do either, Jesse added, "Carter ordered Griffin and Oliver back to the hotel for now. Sydney will check all the local CCTV footage and pull police records from the crime scene to see what we can learn."

"Pretty sure the guy's accent was Scottish," Gray shared. "I didn't have time to check for his ID. Not even a chance to take a photo. But I took his weapon to run prints and check the serial number."

"Scottish. Americans," Jack said. "And we're in Turkey. Something doesn't add up."

"Quite a few *somethings*," Jesse remarked before changing lanes. "I'm taking a long way back to ensure no tail. Plus, there were a shit ton of accidents earlier that are still getting handled."

"So, there's more than one bad guy after me? But which bad guy group had me? Who brought me here in the first place and now wants me back?" Shock clung to Tessa's tone with fierce intensity as she asked the questions on all their minds. "Well, I suppose there's only one group left because they killed the others, right?" Her skin was going pale, the color draining from her face as everything seemed to settle in. The loss of her memories was one thing. The reality she was truly in danger was clearly another.

"I don't know what to think at this point." And while it was the truth, Gray didn't feel any better saying it. "But I think the, uh, American bad guys were the ones tracking my phone, which is how they kept finding us. But we'll figure it all out."

The backseat didn't provide much room, and when Gray's pinky finger brushed against her hand resting between them, a strange zing of electricity shot through him. Her eyes fell to their hands as if she felt the energy too.

"Why don't you rest?" Jesse suggested.

"I would, but I'm in Istanbul. I doubt I'll ever have the courage to hop on a flight and come back here on my own, so I'm going to take in as much as I can as we drive." Her tone was sweet and soft again, and Gray's heart reacted, pounding harder. "I know this isn't really a 'turn lemons into lemonade' situation. More like an entire pile of dog shit that's just shit."

She was back to her adorable rambly self, and he could listen to her talk all day long. "But yeah, either way, I'm going to take in the view while I can. And hope it erases memories I actually want to forget."

She frowned as if regretting her choice of words. She wanted to forget the men chasing her. That there were now dead bodies in the mix. But did she want to forget the kiss too?

"It's definitely shit," Jack chimed in a few seconds later. "Not the view, I mean. Istanbul is amazing. But your situation is horrible."

Gray rolled his eyes. "Thanks, Captain Obvious."

"You still have the same sense of humor you did back when we met." Tessa looked at Jack. "See, I remember *that*. Just not why I'm straddling two continents."

Straddling? He sure as hell wasn't thinking about the fact they were driving in Europe, and on the other side of the Bosphorus was Asia. No, he recalled the one and only time this woman had straddled him, riding his cock hard and fast as she'd chased her orgasm. *I took a life this morning, and I'm thinking about sex. Yeah, that's a whole new level of fucked up.*

"That's the Blue Mosque over there," Jack piped up a few minutes later, pointing toward the famous structure in the distance. Gray was fine with letting Jack play the role of Tessa's tour guide so he could sit back and try to quiet his irrational thoughts.

"You sound like a realtor trying to convince someone to move here," Jesse remarked with a chuckle after Jack went on for ten more minutes about the city's history.

"Don't remind me of that time in my life." Jack let out an obnoxious groan. "Dark days. Darker than the Army," he joked as Jesse pulled onto the Atatürk Bridge.

Gray stole a look at Tessa. Her head rested against the window, the scarf still loosely covering her hair, eyes closed. Her lips parted slightly with soft breaths. Good, she needed the sleep. "She's out. You can stop distracting her, but thank you for doing it," he told Jack in a low voice.

"Anytime," Jack returned with a quick nod before facing forward.

He looked down when Tessa's pinky grazed his again, and this time, he couldn't help himself. He tucked her small hand inside his, catching Jesse's eyes in the mirror, and damn, he knew he was fucked.

CHAPTER NINE

BEING IN A CROWDED ROOM FULL OF OPERATORS, ALL staring at her like she was holding her grandmother's favorite antique vase, worried she'd break it—and yes, maybe that happened—had Tessa feeling small. Like a kid again.

She massaged the tight knot in her chest as she scanned the eight people in the room with her, waiting for someone to break the ice so she didn't break like the metaphorical vase and begin rambling away. Pieces of her would scatter in a mess all over the fancy gold rugs beneath her sneakers.

From a hospital to the Four Seasons. What is happening to me?

"Can I get you water or anything?" Gray finally spoke up while handing over a gun to Jack.

The room had been so eerily quiet, it was like Gray had stepped on a frozen lake and everyone took a collective breath, worried the floor might fall out from under them.

Why do I make them nervous? I should be the nervous one. "No, I don't want anything, thanks." A lie, for sure. Her throat was parched, and weird tingling sensations shot down her arms and into every finger. "Am I going to be okay?" she blurted, breaking the ice. "And are you okay? You were punched and—"

"I'm a hundred percent. You don't need to worry about me." Gray stepped around her, blocking the others from view, and she was relieved to only have him before her. From what she could tell, there were no visible signs of injury from his fight earlier, and that helped her relax a bit more. "And I promise you'll be okay." He gently squeezed her arm. "I can show you to your bedroom in a second. You should rest while we figure everything out, but I thought you might want to meet everyone first." He let go of her arm, then motioned for her to sit on the couch.

Not ready to move, she remained rooted to the floor at the center of the room, feeling like a social experiment once again. "Well," she said with an awkward clap of her hands, "I already know Jesse and Jack."

"As for meeting the rest of our team," Jack began, stepping forward while pointing to a dark-haired guy sitting in an armchair, "that growly-looking guy is Griffin Andrews. He's more bark than bite."

Growly Griffin? She cemented the image of him in her head with a little name tag beneath his face so she wouldn't forget it, a strategy she used so she never forgot a patient at the clinic, even if they weren't hers.

Growly Griffin scratched his beard with his middle finger while his eyes turned Jack's way.

She could already tell she'd like the team. If only she was there for other reasons. Not that she would've flown there without a gun to her head. She shivered at the thought. *And that's a horrible picture. Because what if someone did force me here by gunpoint?*

She pushed away the shitty image, finally sat on the couch, and focused on another guy in the room. Sitting across from a pretty brunette, he sent Tessa a lopsided smile as he casually leaned back in a chair.

"That's Oliver Lucas," Jack introduced him, and judging by Gray's lack of interruption, he was happy to let him take the lead. "As long as he's not busy annoying Mya Vanzetti sitting across from him, he's damn good at hunting people down and helping us if we get hurt on an op."

"I swear, you can't take him anywhere." Oliver smirked and shot a look at the woman he'd been accused of "annoying" and added, "Or you, for that matter."

Mya flicked a dismissive hand as if swatting Oliver away. "Ignore all of these guys." She swiveled on her seat, stood, then strode toward the couch. "I was looking into your background, and I realized you were the PT who helped a friend of mine recover when he was injured. Mason Matthews ring a bell?"

"Mason," Oliver grumbled under his breath. Tessa had no clue why he didn't like Mya's friend, but she wasn't about to press.

"I worked with him years ago," Tessa said at the memory. "A Marine. But yes, I remember. No amputation, but he had reconstructive surgery on his leg, and it took him time to walk unassisted." Remembering she still had on the hijab, she untied it and set it on her lap. "And see, my memory is intact minus what happened between last Saturday night and when I woke up yesterday."

Mya turned, looking over at the last two question marks in the room. A gorgeous blonde, who could easily grace a fashion runway with her good looks, had her back to the wall, hands in her pockets while steadily observing her. At her side was a man in black slacks and a white button-down shirt, sleeves cuffed at the elbows. They looked like billionaires, not operators.

"You're the one with the deep pockets?" she asked the man, remembering what Gray had said to her nearly two weeks ago outside the bar.

"Technically, they both have deep pockets," Mya said, tipping her head in the blonde's direction. "Sydney Archer. Former Army. Daughter of a billionaire businessman."

"And that frightening-looking man is Carter Dominick," Jack said before Mya could offer the name, pulling Tessa's focus to the so-called frightening man next to Sydney. "Richer than God. Co-runs the team with Gray. Can pull stealth birds and bombers from his ass with a snap of his fingers."

"Thank you for the colorful intro, really." Carter pushed away from the wall, his dark eyes raking over her. She didn't think it was distrust there as he assessed her, but there was something about her that seemed to make him uneasy. "We're going to do our best to help you, Miss Sloane. Like most in this room, at one point in time, I worked with your father."

You know my dad? Now their unease about me makes sense. The colonel has that impact on people. "You were all in the Army?"

"I'm the only one who didn't serve," Mya answered.

"A few of us also know your brother." Carter's words stole her attention.

Know him, how? She'd only recently learned her brother was a spy. Curtis had tried to lie, then gave up and confessed he was an intelligence officer for the CIA.

"We're assuming you were taken because of your brother or father," Carter said. "Unless there's another reason you can think of?"

"Nothing else, no." Her fingertips curled into her palms,

and she focused on the bracelet the woman had gifted her. "So, you're suggesting an enemy of my dad's, or maybe even my brother's, took me?"

Carter moved to stand in front of her. "Until we can locate them, we can only speculate."

"And how do you know Curtis?" she asked him.

"I used to be with the Agency," Carter revealed, a blank look in his eyes. He turned his attention to Gray, and was that supposed to mean Gray knew Curtis too?

Tessa twisted on the couch, holding the side of her head. The dull ache from where she'd taken a hit from the fall still throbbed. "You know my brother?" *How? When?* The chaos in her mind coupled with the adrenaline from being chased was catching up with her.

Gray leaned forward and caught her arm as if sensing she might slide off the couch. "This is too much for her. She needs to rest," he snapped, his eyes shooting to Carter while he moved closer to her.

"The longer we wait, the more at risk she becomes. We're dealing with the kind of people who have the skills to take the daughter of a colonel from the country. Someone who can hack power grids, hospitals, traffic lights, and—"

"So, they did hack the traffic lights earlier?" Gray cut off Carter.

"Yeah, someone created a mess out there. Accidents all over that part of the city. My guess is they were buying themselves time before the police arrived on scene," Sydney answered instead.

"A word in private?" Carter's request sent chills up her spine.

That can't be good.

Gray cursed under his breath, then said, "Mya, can you

take Tessa to her room? I'll come check on you in a few minutes."

Tessa set aside the hijab, and Mya helped her stand. She offered Tessa her arm, and only then did Gray let go of her. She watched him leave the room with Carter, and then she looked around at the others quietly observing her. "Thank you for your help," was all she managed to get out before walking with Mya in the opposite direction Gray had gone.

"You'll be in this room for tonight." Mya shut the door and went over to the floor-to-ceiling curtains. "Open or shut?"

"As much as I love the light, it's a bit much right now."

"Agreed." Mya smiled, then drew all three sets of curtains closed. "So." She faced her as Tessa sat on the bed. "What can I do for you? How can I help?"

"Honestly, I wouldn't mind washing away the day in a shower, but I don't think I can stay on my feet any longer."

"How about a bath?" Mya was already on her way, walking past her toward the en suite before she could answer.

Tessa kicked off her sneakers, remembering when Gray had knelt before her, putting them on a mere two hours earlier. Once she removed her socks, she stood, only to fall back onto the bed, her legs like rubber.

"I'm not sure I want you in here alone." Mya studied her from the bathroom doorway. "But I don't want to invade your privacy either. What if I grab my work laptop and sit on the bed while you're in the bath?"

Work laptop? I'm your work, aren't I? Finding out what happened. How is this my life?

"I can call out to you every few minutes to ensure you haven't fallen asleep."

"That's really nice of you." Tessa found the strength to

stand, and once in the en suite, Mya helped her remove her top. "I can manage the rest. Thank you for everything."

"Holler if you need me." Mya gave her a reassuring smile, leaving the door cracked open as she walked out.

Tessa looked around the luxurious space and went over to the clawfoot tub. Mya had added bubbles, God bless her, and it was foamy and inviting. A calming lavender scent filled the air.

Exactly what I need.

Tessa peeled off her yoga pants and underwear, careful not to fall since her balance was still shit. Bra off next.

Naked, she went over to the vanity to assess the damage. A few bruises on her side. One on her ribs that was still tender to the touch. She felt around for the bump on her head. It was concealed by her thick hair, which fell over her chest, landing just shy of her nipples.

I survived. Gray is fine. Naomi is safe in Jamaica. It'll be okay. She took a few deep breaths, the last one causing a sharp, stabbing pain in her side. *Yeah, I need that bath now.*

She took her time climbing into the tub, thankful the temperature was perfect. Not scalding hot. She sank beneath the bubbles and turned off the water.

"Still good?" Mya called out.

"Yup." But there were so many things wrong about her situation, and what if she didn't want to remember what happened to her? What if it was awful?

She looked down at the only thing she still had on—the bracelet with the evil eye on it. "Luck. Protection." She sighed. "I could use that right now."

Grabbing a nearby rolled-up towel, she set it beneath her neck, then stretched out her tired legs and closed her eyes. She had to force herself to relax. To recover so she could be of help to the others trying to solve her case. She was useless in her current state. And she didn't want Gray feeling the need to hover and worry when he was one of the team leaders.

I fell into the water and called Gray. The two things Naomi instructed me not to do. It'd be laughable if the reality of her situation wasn't so damn terrifying.

She could only imagine the horrified expression Naomi would send her if she knew what had happened that morning. She'd lose her mind.

I might too if I keep replaying what I witnessed just today alone. I need a distraction.

She slid her hand to her abdomen and allowed her thoughts to travel back to that kiss with him in the closet. Remembering the heavy weight of his cock that'd pressed against her body was definitely a good distraction.

He only did that to calm me. The last thing she needed was butterflies in her stomach and hearts in her eyes when the man was only trying to protect her.

But the way he'd kissed her, leaned into her while their tongues twined, and *touched* her as her body had ached for him . . . made her wonder if it *was* something more. Or the start of it, at least.

"Tessa, you good?" Gray asked while knocking.

She opened her eyes, checking to ensure the door was still cracked open a touch. "Yeah," she whispered.

"Tessa?"

"Sorry, yes." She got her voice to work that time, and her eyes fell to the bubbles that hid her body. "You can come in if you want to talk. It's safe."

"Safe, huh? You sure?"

"I mean, I guess safe is the wrong word. My face is all

that's in view though." *Am I smiling right now? How?* "Maybe a little bit of my neck too."

"Well, damn. Not sure if I can handle that sight. Maybe it's not safe?" he teased. "But I guess I'll take my chances." The door opened fully, and she chuckled at the sight of him covering his eyes with one hand as he took a few steps in. He closed the door behind him and set his back to it. "How are you feeling? How's your head?"

"Okay, minus the memory-loss part." She drew her legs up to her chest. "You can look at me, silly."

A handsome smile met his lips, and he slowly eased his hand away to reveal those beautiful light green eyes. "You said nothing about your legs. That's a deal breaker."

She looked down at her knees skimming the surface of the water and another unexpected laugh escaped her lips. "And yet, you're still here."

He arched a brow, his attention slipping back to her face as he crossed his arms over his chest. His biceps stretched out the fabric, and she wanted to run her fingers over the ridges of abdominal muscles beneath the shirt.

"How was your conversation with that broody dude? What was his name? Carter?"

"Broody dude? That's one way to put it." Gray laughed. "And he's harmless."

She shot him her signature I-call-BS look, forgetting he probably wouldn't remember that look from thirteen years ago. Eyes narrowed. One brow comically raised. A little lift of her lips along with one shoulder popping.

"Okay, okay." He released one arm from his chest and held out his palm.

God, he had big hands. And those hands had once touched every inch of her skin. Pinched her nipples. Fingered her clit. *Stop, stop, stop.* "So, you agree he's terrifying?"

"Maybe." There was a boyish charm in his smile she found endearing. "But even I can be a bit grizzly, so I apologize in advance."

"Yeah, well, 'grizzly' saved our lives this morning. I'm okay with a little grizzle."

"That a new word?"

"I make them up as I go."

"Some things never change." His tone was borderline husky.

"I was going to say the same about you. But I'll accept your preemptive apology if you get grizzly on me." *Grizzly on me? Wow. So smooth. It's no wonder your dating life sucks.*

He tipped his head in silent thanks, but the way his eyes held hers had her pulse picking up. And when he righted his head and began to stroke his jawline, she couldn't help but wish she was the one touching him instead.

But if he was going to continue silently studying her, she'd have to be the one to speak up. "So, *is* everything okay with Broody Dude? Does your team know more than they let on in my presence?"

"Carter and I are in a bit of a disagreement on what to do next," he finally answered. "I want to get you as far away from here as possible."

Yeah, I'd like to get away too. But I want to go back home.

He pushed away from the door and gained some ground between her and the tub. His eyes skimmed along the surface of the water as if concerned the bubbles might not provide an adequate barrier. "What would you like to do?"

"I get a say?" She brought her hands to her knees, then skated her palms up and down her thighs beneath the water, waiting for him to answer.

"As long as you don't suggest something that would jeopardize your life, then yes, of course you have a say." He was at the base of the clawfoot tub now, and if he took a knee, he'd be able to slip a hand under the bubbles and circle her ankle. Smooth the pad of his thumb on the arch of her foot that was sore from the unexpected run that morning.

Her nervous swallow wasn't nearly as subtle as she'd hoped because his attention snapped to her throat, and he frowned.

"Well, I guess I should figure out what I want, then." *But wait* . . . "My legs."

"Your legs?" He cocked his head, waiting for her to continue.

Her eyes went wide. "They're smooth." She jerked upright, trying to make sense of such a small thing that suddenly felt so significant.

"Tessa, *fuck*." Gray quickly turned while covering his face, and she dropped her eyes to see her breasts above the water.

Oh my God. She dropped down all the way under, submerging her face too. *I did not just do that.* A second later, at the feel of Gray grabbing her arm, urging her to rise, she broke the surface, careful not to expose herself again.

"You okay?" he asked as if worried she might have been on the verge of drowning. *Nope, been there, done that yesterday. Just can't remember.* He let go of her and shoved his wet sleeve to his elbow.

"I'm fine," she squeaked. "You saved my life just for me to die of embarrassment though." *I can't believe I showed him my breasts.* Sure, a few bubbles were clinging to her flesh, but her nipples had been poking straight out like landing beacons for his rough palms.

"It's, um, okay." He took a few steps back and her eyes

went straight to his strong, corded forearm now exposed. He was still tan for November. Did he recently spend time somewhere warm and sunny? "What about your legs though?"

She blinked at the memory of that discovery. "My legs are smooth. You'd think if someone held me hostage, they wouldn't have given me a razor to shave, right? But there's no way my legs would feel like this if I hadn't shaved since last weekend. A day or two ago tops is probably the last time I shaved." Her stomach dropped. "Oh God, hopefully *I* shaved my legs and someone else didn't do it."

His brows tightened as he absorbed her revelation. It was important, wasn't it? Somehow, she knew that little detail mattered. "It's . . . strange, I agree." He nodded, but there was a dark, worried look that crossed his face. "I'll share that information with the team. Is there anything else you can think of that might help?"

"I'm sorry, no."

"Maybe just rest for now? Think about whether you'd like me to escort you back home and put you in protective custody there, or if you'd like to stay here a bit longer and—"

"Wait, protective custody? Like a safe house or something?" No. She had patients that depended on her. Naomi would panic. And poor Mr. Whitlock would worry if she was MIA. "That's not something I'm open to doing."

"The second your brother or father learns of your situation, they'll more than likely attempt to scoop you away from us and take control of your safety. That's not what I want. I'd rather take care of you myself," he shared. "There's a lot to think about. I just want you to rest for now. Eat something too. We can talk about everything in a bit."

"Okay, but can I ask you something? Do you know my

brother?" Carter had alluded to that fact, and she'd struggled to wrap her head around it.

He ran both hands through his hair, and then his shoulders fell as his gaze met hers. "Yeah, I know him. Our paths crossed a few years ago. In fact," he said with a surprising smile, "he even shot me."

CHAPTER TEN

Maybe that revelation was a bad idea. Because so help him, if the woman bolted upright again, he'd have his second hard-on that morning. And it'd taken all his restraint not to allow his cock to salute her when he'd set eyes on her tits the first time. He wouldn't survive a second go-around. Not a chance.

"Curtis shot you?" She was breathing hard, as if the walls were closing in on her and she was going back into panic mode. He didn't exactly need to quiet her with a kiss this time, but he did have to stamp out her worry and fast.

"Just clipped my arm. Nothing serious."

Carter's right. "Broody Dude" had given him a hell of a lecture, sensing Gray's head was off since the mission was personal. *I'm not going to be thinking clearly to make the tough calls.* He wouldn't risk her safety because he was so damn responsive to her. Simply being in the room with her, knowing only bubbles separated him from seeing her body, was testing his resolve too much.

She slid her hands over her chest to grip her shoulders,

her arms becoming shields for her nipples in case she accidentally sat up again.

"It's really not that bad." He shrugged. "I was on an op with the company I ran before Falcon, and your brother and I were hunting the same man. I got to him first. There was a case of mistaken identity, as in your brother didn't believe I was one of the good guys."

Her brows slanted harshly with regret. "I'm so sorry. He didn't tell me."

"That's the nature of clandestine work," he reminded her. "Plus, he probably didn't want to tell you he shot someone you helped teach to walk again."

She quietly studied him, and he wished he knew what was on her mind, but he couldn't get a good read on her thoughts.

"Anyways, it's fine. I've been shot quite a few times in my life. And honestly, I would've done the same in his position. We spoke afterward, and when he realized I'd once been at the old Walter Reed hospital around the time you'd spent a summer there, we put two and two together."

There was a warmth in her eyes that had his heart doing something strange. *Beating?* Nope, that was supposed to happen. So, what was this weird feeling?

"I haven't seen Curtis since then," he went on since her quietness stressed him out. She was usually the one nonstop talking. "But I have to assume there's a chance you were taken to get to him somehow. Maybe not revenge, or you wouldn't be so—"

"Intact?" she finished for him, her hands falling from her shoulders and into the water.

He nodded. "Even though your father's name is well-known, it's not often we get many targeted hits toward retired personnel. Not out of the question though. And unless you tell me he's now a spy, my gut says he's not involved."

"My dad, a spy?" Her lips twitched as if amused. "He may look like that actor who plays in all those movies, but he's not actually like him, I can assure you."

He smiled. "So, you see the physical similarity too?"

She cocked her head. "You think he doesn't know what you all used to call him on base?"

He scratched his facial hair, barely hearing a word she'd said because her nipples were dangerously close to reappearing again. *I need to warn you.* "I, uh." He walked by the tub and snatched a fluffy rolled-up towel. "How about you get out now and rest? I'll order you some food?" He bent down by the tub, and her eyes locked with his. Her dark, wet lashes fluttered a few times, and he'd swear he could swim in those beautiful brown eyes.

"Okay. But should we talk about what happened earlier? You know, the kiss?" Her soft tone had him nearly taking a knee.

"I don't know. Should we?"

"I know you did it to keep me quiet so we weren't discovered. If you're worried I'll think more of it, you um, don't have to be concerned. And the other part, well, you're human. Guys get boners and—" Her words died as she plunged back beneath the water, and he couldn't help but laugh at this adorable woman.

She was in a foreign country being hunted with no clue as to why . . . and she was throwing the word "boner" at him.

He reached beneath the water again. Guess he'd get the second sleeve wet too. His fingers skimmed her silhouette as he searched for her arm, but when his knuckles brushed across a peaked nipple, he retracted his arm and stood straight.

Tessa resurfaced, pushing wet strands of hair away from

her face, her lip wedged between her teeth as she stared at him.

He gripped the towel in his dry hand as he tried to control his breathing so he didn't look like an angry bull about to charge.

He'd given Griffin so much shit when he'd struggled to contain himself on the op with his now-wife, Savanna. *And here I am about to ask Tessa if there's room for two in that tub.*

"Sorry." She slapped a hand to her cheek, and a vision of him spanking a different cheek should NOT have popped into his fucked-up mind. But there it was. He twisted to the side and offered his arm again.

"Come for me. *To* me." He squeezed his eyes closed. "Get off." He cursed under his breath. "Get *out*."

Her soft, amused laugh rolled over his skin, hitting him right in the balls. "I'm rubbing off on you, sorry."

And I'm going to need to rub one out at this rate. "My arm. Take it," he pushed out the command, trying to regain some control.

She grabbed his arm and gently held on to him as he listened to the sloshing sound of the water. "I'm sudsy. I need to rinse off in the shower first."

Well, fuck my life. At least he kept that curse to himself that time. But his mouth wouldn't be the only thing that'd get him in trouble if he spent much more time around this woman.

Once she took the towel from him, he faced the other way, drawing his hands to his hips.

"The nurse washed my hair last night. I just need to rinse off. Twenty seconds max," she went on when he'd yet to get his voice to work.

"And if you slip and fall?"

"Then stay and just don't look." She circled him with the towel bunched in her hand above her breasts. There were bubbles in her hair and sticking all over her body.

"Roger that." He sidestepped her and went around the glass partition to turn on the water. "Need me to ask Mya to get you some clean clothes?"

She pointed to the plush hotel robe hanging on the back of the door. "That's fine for now."

He moved back around her, checking the floors to ensure they weren't wet so she wouldn't slip. "Yeah, looks thick enough." *Thick enough not to see your nipples, at least.*

"I like it thick." Her cheeks turned a soft pink. No water to duck under this time.

Of course you do. He closed his eyes and pointed toward the shower, a silent plea to get in. Any more chitchat and he'd land in blue balls purgatory. Or worse, he'd kiss that sexy mouth again.

She draped her towel over his extended arm, and he clenched his teeth. Was she punishing him for leaving thirteen years ago? Because knowing, if he parted his lids, he'd see this beautiful woman naked was pure torture.

He needed to think about all the reasons why he shouldn't allow his mind to wander to all the dirty things he wanted to do to this woman. But *instead*, he indulged in a fantasy while she showered. He considered what it'd be like to fuck her so hard her moans would be heard two suites over.

Or maybe they'd make love, soft and slow, so he could listen to every little inhalation of breath from her as he plunged in and out.

Annnnd . . . now I'm hard. Realizing he still had his arm stuck out, he lowered it and used the towel to cover his erection and thought about every exchange they'd shared since he'd first stepped into her hospital room.

He hated to admit it, but in part, she was right about them being strangers, wasn't she? Thirteen years was a lot of time and people were supposed to evolve. That was life.

But why'd she look the same? Hell, she even smelled the same. And why'd she still make his heart destroy his ribs with her laugh the way it once had?

He didn't remember feeling this way when he'd bumped into Sydney for the first time after it'd been forever and a day apart from her too.

You're different. You always have been, haven't you? At the sound of the water turning off, he released a small sigh of relief and discarded his thoughts. He needed to focus on the mission, on keeping her safe.

When she snatched the towel from him, he was forced to give her his back to hide the painful truth still evident in his jeans. "Let me know when you have on the robe."

A few seconds later, she gave him permission to open his eyes, and he did his best to get his "situation" under control to face her.

She fingered her brown hair, laying the waves over her shoulders, and he walked his focus down her body, relieved almost every inch of her was hidden behind the thick material. "Your toenails," he spoke his thoughts aloud at the sight of the nude-colored paint there. "Should they be that perfect since you've been MIA for five days?"

She stepped back so she didn't whack him in the head as she looked down, which would've been a Tessa thing to do. "They were pink last weekend, not nude." Nervous, panicky breaths followed. "Why are my legs shaved and my toenails painted nude?" Her eyes met his, wide and worried.

His instinct was to pull her tight to his chest and comfort her that way. But maybe he needed to put some distance between them? "I have no damn clue." *The theme of the day.*

"I think I need to sit."

He reached for her arm, opened the door, and guided her to the bed. Letting go of her only to peel back the comforter, he helped her onto the bed and covered her up. "I'll talk to the team and order you some food. Will you try and sleep? Your body could probably use it."

"Okay."

"Do you want me to stay?" he asked, his heart feeling heavy at the sight of her sad and defeated expression.

"I just want to know what happened to me," she whispered. "But at the same time, I'm terrified to learn the truth."

Hell if he didn't feel the same. "It'll be okay." *Hopefully.* He squeezed her hand resting on her stomach, and for some ridiculous reason, set his free hand by her shoulder and dipped in to kiss her forehead.

He took his time pressing his lips to her soft skin. Taking a second to breathe her in. Smell whatever delicious-smelling stuff she'd cleansed herself with. Or maybe it was the bubble bath?

"Gray," she murmured, an almost expectant tone in her voice. Like she was expecting him to drop his face and find her mouth next.

He eased back to find her face. Long lashes fluttered over her bourbon-brown eyes, flecks of gold and maybe even the sun, there. "Yeah?" He nearly swallowed the word back down his throat at her breathtaking beauty.

She was so sweet and incredible and didn't deserve to be running from bad guys and hiding in alleys behind dumpsters. She didn't belong in his world, one he had to admit he comfortably lived in.

Realizing they were still simply staring into each other's eyes, neither sharing their thoughts, he did his best to break the moment and push away from the bed. To focus on a mission that now centered around her. But with her free hand, she fisted his shirt, drawing him closer, stopping him from leaving.

"What is it?" He looked down at her hand holding the fabric like she was clinging to him not to save her but to kiss her. He returned his attention to her face, curious what was really on her mind. He didn't trust he was correctly reading her, not when his head was so off. "What can I do for you before I go?"

She caught her lip between her teeth. They were still so close. Him leaning in, arched over her. His hand by her body, his other one holding hers on her stomach. Their mouths inches from touching.

But then she let go of his shirt and focused on smoothing the material back in place as if worried she'd created a wrinkle. "Nothing," she whispered. "I'll sleep. That's probably what I should do."

Sleep. Right. My idea. Not kiss her again.

She rolled her head to the side, eyes closed as if fighting herself on not oversharing her thoughts. Basically, not being herself. He almost did something he rarely did and pressed for more. But when he let go of her hand and stood tall, the sounds from the other room reminded him he had a job to do.

"I'll just be outside."

She nodded without looking at him, and then he took a hesitant step away from the bed, hating the twist in his gut that told him not to leave her. But what else was he supposed to do? Get in the bed next to her? Cuddle?

He forced himself to go to the door, but instead of opening it, he set his palms to it and bowed his head, remembering their night together thirteen years ago when she'd fallen asleep wrapped up in his arms.

He hadn't slept. He'd held her. Listened to the sweet sounds she made. Kissed her bare shoulder a time or two, pressing his mouth over the freckles there. Stifled groans whenever she shimmied her ass against his crotch during her dreams. Played out all the reasons to stay the next day. Imagined what it'd look like for the two of them if he didn't walk away.

But then the sun came up, and reality washed over him. And the fear that he'd ruin her life if he stayed in it locked him in a chokehold, so he made the hardest decision of his life. And he left.

Of course, what she didn't know was that a few months later, he came after her in Boston. Only . . . he'd been too late.

CHAPTER ELEVEN

AFTER HE'D BEEN BUSY GETTING DISTRACTED AND—GOD help him, *hard*—in the suite's bedroom, Gray joined his team, busy at work in the living room.

"How is she?" Jack set his laptop aside and stood, rounding the couch to get to him.

"She's confused and scared. But tough." *And this feels awkward to say but here goes.* "She did say her legs are shaved, and she has on a different nail polish from last weekend though."

"Well, that changes things a bit." Mya's frown had Gray's stomach squeezing.

"Don't say it." Gray lifted a palm, a plea not to go there. Because fuck *there.* He knew what Mya was thinking, and he wanted Tessa, and every woman and child, as far away from *there* as possible. "I know what you're about to say, and we aren't going there," he snapped.

"But we have to consider it, whether you want to or not," Mya pressed. "I've spent years hunting human traffickers who take women for sex. It's possible she wasn't touched because they were preparing her for a sale."

Sale? Gray did his best not to fall to the ground at the picture Mya had painted. *No. Hell no.* And an entire string of *nos* waged war on his mind on repeat. "No." Gray finally shared the word numbing his mind into submission. *Not* denial. "I don't accept that. Think of another reason."

"Gray." Carter's simple use of his name commanded Gray's attention. He was on his feet, striding Gray's way as Griffin and the others fell back, becoming part of the decoration as Carter confronted him.

"I'm not wrong on this," Gray insisted. "How often are women like Tessa abducted from their place of employment? Who would go after the daughter of a colonel knowing *an army* of veterans would unleash hell on earth to find her?" And Gray knew without a doubt, her old man, as much as he drove Gray nuts, would command an entire battalion to save his daughter.

"Fine, maybe you're right," Mya relented, which allowed Gray to secure a semi-calming breath in through his nose and out through his mouth. "There must be another reason she was taken, and her appearance kept up with."

"We need to look at this differently. From another angle. Two groups chased after us today. The Americans killed those other Scots. Took one alive, presumably for questioning." Continuing to outline the facts, he went on, "One group, probably the Americans, have a skilled hacker on their team. Someone capable of some high-level shit after what we witnessed them pull off in real time today."

"Whoever was responsible for the hacks has better skills than I do." Sydney grimaced, and Gray could tell she struggled to get those words out. Hated admitting defeat. "I can't locate the source of the hack. The pricks already beat me to the punch with the CCTV footage from the crime scene. Hell, they wiped the footage of every camera within

BRITTNEY SAHIN

a two-block radius from where they gunned down the Scots."

Gray tightened his hands at his sides, unsure what to do next, but he knew punching a wall wouldn't solve their problems. "What about the footage from Karaköy where she fell?"

"That *wasn't* wiped." Griffin's tone implied that was bad news too, as did the look on his face as he hooked his thumbs in the front pockets of his khaki cargo pants. "And it also wasn't helpful. There's a clip of Tessa on the street just before she wanders near the ledge and falls. She looked, well, drunk."

"And trying to find Tessa's whereabouts before her fall is still a needle-in-a-haystack problem for our software," Sydney noted, frustration evident in her tone.

"Then get better software," Gray hissed, then shook his head in apology. When he looked up, Sydney's expression softened into understanding. She knew what it was like when a mission became personal.

"What about the footage at the bazaar? Anything on the American who followed us in there?"

"The footage wasn't erased, but there were too many guys with hats going in and out. No clear shots of faces. Probably why it wasn't touched," Mya shared that time.

"You, on the other hand, did show your face on camera," Carter added in a low voice, disappointment echoing through his tone.

"I was already a marked man," Gray reminded him. "These assholes and the detective have my information."

"I was inside the hospital too," Jack pointed out. "We both need to keep our heads down while in Istanbul."

The hospital. It was hacked. And . . .? "What if they also hacked Tessa's medical records? What if her tox report wasn't clean? She may have been drugged, which explains some of the memory issues, and whoever took her doesn't want us—or anyone—to know. Could they electronically swap the records in the system like that?"

Sydney frowned. "Yeah. I'll look and see if there's evidence of tampering, but—"

"But if they're as good as you say they are, you may be unable to tell," Gray interrupted, frustrated with their lack of leads.

"Right." Sydney nodded. "Let's hope we can get some prints from the gun you pulled. With any luck, that'll lead us somewhere."

Luck. Not on their side right now. But he gave her a terse nod anyway. He looked around the room at the rest of his team, avoiding eye contact with Carter for now. There had to be another way to approach this. Nobody was that good. "We need more help. Maybe bring in Camila. Or what about that friend of yours we worked with before? Former MI6. Zoey-something?" When Gray gave in and faced Carter, he didn't expect the dirty look Carter shot him.

"I'd hardly call Zoey a friend," Carter drawled in a clipped voice. "I don't want either of them coming here. Next idea."

"I know someone who might be able to help us," Sydney announced, her tone hesitant. Not the best sign. "At least, help me find out intel a lot quicker."

"What? Who?" Gray's heart rate jumped.

"Your sister is one of the best at hunting cyber terrorists. But Natasha's on an op with her husband's team right now somewhere north of here, so I doubt we can pull them into the fray. But . . ."

Gray's jaw locked tight when it hit him who she was

about to suggest. "My niece is in grad school, and Wyatt will kill me if I fly her here to hunt a hacker."

Gray's brother-in-law had first found out he had a daughter back in 2021. Gwen was twenty-three now, and Gray's sister was only a little over a decade older than her stepdaughter. But they both happened to be cyber geniuses and badasses.

"Wyatt doesn't know this yet, but Gwen dropped out," Sydney shared. "She slipped and told me while babysitting the kids one night."

Gray blinked in surprise at that revelation, unsure how Wyatt would take the news. And, yeah, that wasn't his problem right now, but Wyatt finding out his daughter left school was a far cry from finding out she'd been pulled to a foreign country into this mess.

"We need her." Sydney crossed her arms. "*I* need her." She wet her lips, and dammit, Gray knew that look. She'd already made contact, hadn't she? "Gwen's confident she can help. We don't need better software, Gray. What we need is a better hacker, and that's Gwen."

"You already asked her to come, didn't you?" he asked, not bothering to mask his concerned tone.

"I gave the go-ahead," Carter spoke up.

"Gwen's visiting friends in New York right now," Sydney informed him. "JFK has a direct flight this evening, so she'll arrive tomorrow around zero six hundred."

Gray turned from the room and clawed at his hair. He had to fight to get his emotions under control.

They had no leads. Not a damn one. It was just a hunch this was somehow connected to Tessa's brother, but he still wasn't quite sure how or why. There were too many bad guys. Too many unknowns.

They needed all the help they could get. Even if it meant his brother-in-law would kill him later.

Gray faced the team. "Fine. In the meantime, expand the list of people you look into and include friends, ex-boyfriends, and her patients."

Carter nodded, finally in agreement on something.

"I want to know about her best friend's boyfriend too. He's with Naomi in Jamaica. The timing of all this is . . . just see what you can find on him," Gray ordered, shooting his attention toward Tessa's bedroom, hoping she was now asleep.

"I'm on it," Griffin said, on the move.

"We should also get a list of every boat, cargo ship, and the like that has come in and out of Istanbul this week," Gray added. "It's possible she was brought here that way."

"I'm working on that myself," Carter noted.

Gray nodded his thanks. "I need to rest my leg for a second. And I'm going to order food. Is everyone hungry?" A few nods and requests followed, then he started for the second bedroom.

"Hold up." Gray turned to see Jack joining him in the room, closing the door once inside.

Gray dropped down onto the bed. He was wiped out, sure, but before his osseointegration surgery, he'd never have been able to go such a distance by foot as he'd done today. The benefits of the surgery, which required learning to walk again, were paying off now.

Another benefit of his implant was the ability to drop the prosthesis off the external fixture easily without removing his pants. Previously, he had to deal with the socket and the thick, socklike silicone liner that rolled on like a condom every time he wanted to remove or reattach his prosthesis. That protective liner may have protected his skin from abrasion, but the liner had turned sweat into his archnemesis. Now, without it, he only had to clean the implant area twice a day.

Gray rubbed his achy thigh muscle as Jack said, "You've had a hell of a morning. I'm worried about you." He set his back to the door, folding his arms across his chest. This was "serious Jack." He got this side of him occasionally, but only when he was concerned about someone or something.

"I'm . . . not sure what I'm thinking or feeling," he confessed, continuing to massage his thigh over his jeans. "I know I need to focus. Think of this like any other operation. But fuck, with Tessa in the mix, I don't know how to do that."

Jack was one of the only people he could open up to. Not sensor or filter his words and thoughts. And right now, he needed his best friend to tell him what to do. To give him the orders because he didn't trust his own judgment.

"I won't use her as bait to draw these fuckers out, Jack, it's not an option," Gray went on. "But I have another idea."

"No." Jack unlocked his arms and pushed away from the door, giving him a stern look. "We're not using you either."

"Just hear me out." Gray held up his hands, knowing it would take a lot to convince his best friend on this.

"I'm not hearing you out on anything. Too many things could go wrong. Not only could we lose the trail if they take you, we could lose you too. Plus, we don't even know how many bad guys we're dealing with," he rushed out his reasoning. "This hacker is better than Sydney, which is saying *a lot*. So no. New fucking plan, Batman. I don't want a new best friend. That's too much work. And God help me, you know Griffin and I would just kill each other. And Oliver? Too young. Jesse? Too busy being obsessed with his wife." He dropped onto the bed next to him. "And Carter?" He laughed. "The only friend that man cares to have is his dog."

"So, what you're saying is—"

"No, brother," Jack cut him off. "I'm saying no to you becoming the taken one."

There was a knock at the door, followed by Sydney saying, "Hey, I managed to find something." She opened up, a tablet in hand.

"What is it?" Gray asked, feeling hopeful she might have good news.

"Tessa's phone is offline. Still no signal. But I decided to hack her best friend's phone. Naomi texted her this week from Jamaica," Sydney shared, looking at Jack before turning her attention back to Gray. "And Tessa texted her back."

CHAPTER TWELVE

"You remembered." Tessa tightened the knot of the robe, ensuring her body was still covered, before going for a slice of pizza from the box.

"Of course I remembered." Gray stood at the edge of her bed. "You always stole the pepperoni from my slice."

"I recall you *pretending* you weren't a pepperoni fan and asking me to eat them for you." She nearly moaned at her first bite. Much better than the hospital food. "And I knew you were faking it. You would practically drool whenever I popped the pepperoni into my mouth."

He quietly observed her, his eyes narrowing on her lips.

"Like you're doing now, I might add," she said with a laugh, peeling another pepperoni from the cheese to eat it. "Unless you just enjoy watching me put meat in my mouth." *Oh. My. God. What is wrong with me?* She set the slice inside the box, closed her eyes, and groaned. "I shouldn't be allowed to talk. Ever." *But somehow, you're managing to distract me yet again. To keep me sane. Diffusing tension really is one of your skills.*

"And yet, you're still talking." Humor cut through his

tone, and if she opened her eyes, she knew she'd see a devilish grin on his face. "But . . . it's possible I did enjoy having you steal my pepperoni back then."

She gave in and looked at him, hoping her cheeks weren't as red as they felt hot. Gray was alongside the bed now and within arm's reach. He'd changed from his long-sleeved shirt into a black tee, more than likely needing a new one thanks to her ducking under the water like she'd been part of a carnival game.

"Raisinets. Pepperoni. What else do you remember about me?" *Why am I asking this? Poking at memories that left me with scars. And no one has ever been able to heal them.*

The way his eyes darted to her mouth made her lick her lips, wishing she'd thought to ask Mya if she happened to have any new ChapStick on hand. Hell, she'd take something off-brand too.

"Blueberries," he finally said, and now she couldn't help but grin.

"So, let me get this straight." She rested her chin on her knuckles as she stared at him. "When you think of me, you remember food?"

"I happen to like eating." He tipped his head, assessing her. But the way his eyes slid over her, as if he could see beneath the robe, sent an explosion of tingling sensations from the tips of her ears down to her toes.

Yeah, you remember more than that. A lot more. I can see it in your eyes. Feel it in that beating organ of mine that you crushed when following through with walking away the next day.

"You still have a thing for scented lip balms?" His arms were at his sides now, and she tracked the curve of muscle with her eyes. Arms like his should have been a sin with all the dips and ridges.

Don't get me started on his forearms. Crap, did it get ten degrees *hotter?*

"Do you still have a disdain for ChapStick?" she challenged back, working her focus to his face. Maybe not a great idea. His eyes were like green glass, and if she looked any closer, she might find her reflection. And maybe he'd even be able to see her thoughts. Know that in thirteen years, no one had ever made her feel like he had in just a few short months.

"I never hated your lip balm."

Sure you didn't. His hate had been stated and obvious, and she used to love to drive him nuts by doubling down on wearing the blueberry-scented ChapStick even more. Applied it three times a day when they were together. "I call your bluff." She gave him her best fake smile, hoping he'd accept it without question. She doubted he wanted to keep walking down memory lane, even if it made her feel better. It helped her forget she'd lost five days of her life.

Gray bent forward, dipping closer as if he might meet her halfway for a kiss. "You know I don't bluff unless we're playing poker."

Yeah, he was right. Back in the day, they not only watched movies, they played heads-up poker. Sadly, not strip poker. But he won every flipping time except once. "Sooo, then, tell me, why'd my ChapStick irritate you so much?"

A dark smirk cut across his lips, and he stood tall, managing to extinguish the intense look from his eyes. "Maybe we should talk about what I learned instead?"

Avoidance, got it. Or maybe he's trying to focus on the issue at hand, and I should too. "Good or bad news?"

"Both." He took a step back, placing what seemed like a mile between them. "The bad news is we're coming up empty on all fronts, which isn't typical for us. But the good news is my niece is a bit of a cyber genius, and she's flying here to help us."

"Your niece?" She lifted a brow in surprise. "How old could she possibly be?"

"Actually, I have two nieces. Emory is a baby. But Gwen is my sister's stepdaughter. She'll be twenty-four in March. My brother-in-law didn't even know about her until a few years ago. Crazily, a cyber case brought my sister and Wyatt together, and that case included Gwen."

"Cyber case? So does your sister work for the government?" She went for her pizza and took another anxious bite at the news Gray's team had no leads.

"She does," was all he gave her, which had her wondering if Natasha worked for a three-letter agency like Curtis did. The way Gray's brows tightened had her worried there was more bad news though.

"What is it?" She set the slice back down and clutched the lapels of her robe.

Gray reached into his pocket and produced a phone. "Sydney found a few text messages between you and Naomi. I can show you the screenshots."

"Wait, I texted her while I was missing?" How was that possible? "Does that mean someone pretended to be me?"

"Or forced you to answer to prevent Naomi from worrying and reporting you missing," he suggested. "I thought maybe you could read the texts and see what you think." He opened the phone and handed it to her.

She let go of the death grip on her robe and accepted it, nervous about the uneasy tightness of his jaw. And the look in his eyes . . . what was that all about?

Naomi: Hey, girl, I know I'm supposed to be offline, but I'm just checking on you. Making sure you haven't broken any of the rules.

Tessa: You're NOT supposed to be online, missy. And no, I'm behaving. How is the view? Are you in heaven?

"That feels like something I'd say," she admitted.

Naomi: Besides the naked couple in the bungalow next door, the view is amazing. Fun fact: a barracuda likes to chill beneath the glass floor of my room. And here my dad was worrying about sharks. Let me send you a photo. One second.

An image of a big-ass fish appeared in the text next.

Naomi: They call him Charlie. And if this naked couple doesn't stop swimming in the nude, I have a feeling Charlie is going to have a snack soon.

Tessa: *laughing emoji* Is it bad I'm secretly hoping for that story next?

Naomi: Same. I'm not in the mood for a schlong in my face while sipping my morning coffee.

Tessa: Schlong? Thank you for the LOL moment.

Naomi: Anytime. ;)

"This is me. Definitely. And I don't know how to feel about it. I don't sound scared for my life."

"There's more." Gray pointed to the phone, and she forced herself to continue reading.

> Tessa: Okay, get offline and try and enjoy yourself despite the schlong view. And only text if Charlie does something interesting. I mean it.

> Naomi: As long as you promise you won't text Mr. You Know Who.

Heat worked up the column of her throat knowing Gray had read that. *And dear God, please tell me I didn't use his name.*

Her hand trembled as she swiped to the next screenshot, and her stomach flipped at what she read.

> Tessa: I won't call Gray. I don't need another broken heart. You're right.

Shit. There was one more message exchange on a different day, so she pressed on and read.

> Naomi: Schlong Guy is gone. Thank goodness. Just popping online to check on you once more. Then I promise I'll stay offline the rest of the trip.

> Tessa: Glad to know he's gone, and you can enjoy your coffee again. And I'm fine. You need to stop worrying about me.

> Naomi: Are you suuuure? I have this weird feeling I can't shake. I'm going to call you.

> Tessa: No, don't call. In fact, if you call or text again, I won't answer. You deserve a blissful break, especially now that the naked couple is gone.

> Naomi: Fine, fine. I'll leave you be. Just promise me you're okay and not mopey over Gray still.

Tessa nearly facepalmed herself at that last message, knowing Gray and his colleagues had read it.

> Tessa: Seeing him again was confusing. But I'm clear-headed now. No mopey-me. Promise. Okay, love you, lady. Not answering another text after this. I'm stubborn, and you know it. *kissing emoji* Have fun for the both of us! Muah!

Tessa swapped the phone for a slice of pizza and stuffed her face, trying to work through what to say and how to feel about what she read.

"Are you okay?" he softly asked.

After swallowing a mouthful of food, she answered, "You'd think by those messages I really was at home just relaxing without a care in the world. But I'm not that great of an actress."

"It's easier to deceive someone with a text." His tone was flat. A little distant. Like he was working hard not to say what was really on his mind.

"I suppose someone could've made me message her, and I didn't want her to worry, so I did my best to sound okay." But why was two plus two starting to feel like five? Nothing made sense.

"Listen, I know I keep saying we'll figure everything out, and I'm sure it doesn't look so hot with our lack of leads after what happened this morning, but I won't let you down." There was that promise she so desperately wanted to cling to again. "And there's something else I need to say."

That I'm crazy? Because she was starting to think, *Yeah, maybe.* "And that is?"

"That I'm sorry." The words came out rough. Not uncut-diamond rough. But the guilty kind of rough that caused sleepless nights and stomach aches. "I don't think I've said that to you. But I'm truly sorry for what I did. I wish I could say it was because I was young and dumb, but—"

"It's fine." She looked toward the covered windows, needing to focus anywhere but on the man who could snatch her thoughts straight from her head.

"Pretty sure nothing good has ever come from a woman telling a man she's 'fine' and him believing her." There was a seriousness in his tone, even though it was possibly his wayward attempt at humor.

"Grayson." She was at a loss for what else to say, unprepared to have that conversation with him right now.

"*Contessa*," rolled from his tongue, and goose bumps peppered her skin beneath the robe. That was the name on her birth certificate she never used and hadn't shared with him. *He's here to help me, so of course, he did his homework.*

"No apology needed," she croaked out with too much emotion. "Please."

He leaned in and dragged the pad of his thumb along her jawline, urging her to look at him. Hesitantly, she surrendered her focus.

"You didn't know I was a virgin," she whispered, hoping to dilute his guilt and wash it away. He was there and helping her now, and that was all that mattered. "I asked you to stay, knowing you had every intention of leaving." *Just secretly hoped you wouldn't.*

He dropped his hand from her face, set it over his heart, and stood tall by the bed. "I should never have stayed since I had already planned to walk away. It was wrong." The genuine sincerity in his tone, and sad look in his eyes, was such a sharp contrast to the asshole he'd so desperately tried to make himself out to be those first few weeks they'd spent together forever ago.

"You don't need to do this." She squared back her shoulders, searching for strength when she felt buried beneath the rubble of forgotten memories from the last five days.

"I won't be able to focus if I'm worried you're still hurting from something I did. Like I started to say, I wish I could blame the fact I was younger and not a hundred percent myself after the accident, but there's no excuse for what I did. I stayed because I was selfish. Because I wanted to be with you. And then I was too much of a coward to stay the next day, and for that, I'm truly sorry."

His honesty was as shocking as it was refreshing. The new norm for all the guys in the last few years was to simply ghost instead of telling the truth or talking about feelings. *Well, you did leave me. But at least you warned me and said goodbye first.*

She thought back to that sad morning. Standing by his car, he'd slid his hands from her cheeks and into her hair. He'd gently pulled her head back as he slanted his mouth over hers. His tongue had stroked hers, and what started as a gentle goodbye kiss became more ravenous.

Her back had wound up against the side of the car while he devoured her mouth. She'd circled her hips, aching for more of him as his hand slid beneath her T-shirt. Long fingers had splayed across her heated skin as she'd moaned into his mouth, resisting the urge to beg him not to go. *Stay with me* had been written into every flick of her tongue, but she'd never said the actual words.

And then he'd pulled away as if some otherworldly power had physically forced him to back up. He'd shot her a depressing look before touching his lips to her forehead. Then he'd whispered his goodbye into her ear and left.

She'd waited until he'd driven away before going back inside to collapse. To cry. To mourn the loss of what could've been if only . . .

"I know I can't fix my mistakes with one apology," Gray said, his words cutting through her memories, and she didn't need him to do this. "But—"

"Gray," she interrupted, because him feeling guilty and remorseful wouldn't help him or the situation. Damn those text messages. "That was thirteen years ago. I'm fine." *Shit. I admitted earlier our shared summer felt like yesterday.* "Would the word okay work better for you?" No shift in expression from him, so she went on, trying to save herself, "How about good? Obviously, I'm not great, because well"— she opened her arms to emphasize her current situation—"but I mean, it could be worse. I could've drowned. Or been *re*taken or killed by one of those men this morning." She let go of a nervous chuckle.

He tipped his head, stealing his eyes toward the window as if disturbed by the thought she'd drawn for him.

"Listen," she began, realizing this stubborn man needed more, "it was going to hurt either way when you left. You were already a lot of firsts for me. My first patient. My first real crush outside of grade school. But then you became the first to make love to me. And hell, to this day, you're still the only man I've never had to fake it with." *Oversharing again.*

He whipped his focus her way, and an uncomfortable

silence stretched between them. "Tessa," he finally spoke, but the heated look in his eyes had her heart racing.

"Seriously. I'm okay. Fine. Good. Grand. At this point, I'll even give you a great. Anything to stop you from feeling guilty." She pointed to the phone sitting by the pizza box, thinking about her texts to Naomi. "Yes, maybe seeing you at the bar that night threw me off. And I possibly unpacked your West Point tee. You know, the one you forgot at my place after I spilled my wine on it while we were watching a movie. You never let me give it back to you. And maybe I even wore it a few times after our bump-in two weeks ago. Of course, if you want it back, it's yours. I mean, it *is* yours."

Gray stared at her, unblinking.

"I'm rambling again. Oversharing. I swear, I'm not this bad around other people. You just make me a little nervous." *Always have.* "Then I share about twenty words too many."

Gray shook his head, a touch of a smile on his lips that time, then he focused on the phone lighting up from a notification.

She was closer, so she reached for it, accidentally reading the first line from the text notification as she handed it over. "Um, here." She shoved it into his hand, disturbed by the flutter of jealousy inside her.

"This is Jesse's phone. That message was from his wife and meant for him."

Unlike Gray, she did bluff. She just sucked at it. So, she knew when she smiled and tried to act cool and not like she was relieved at the news, she was failing. "They sure keep things spicy."

Gray pocketed the phone, then dragged a thumb along his bottom lip. And why was that so sexy? "I guess so. I try not to, uh, know about that stuff when it comes to anyone that works with me." He pointed to the bed. "Just eat. Get your strength. You need it. I'll check in on you soon."

She clutched the lapels of the robe again, nerves taking over. "Is there anything I can do to help?"

He looked at the hardwoods for a moment. "Any, uh, ex-boyfriends that could be involved in this?"

Like the ones who I faked it with? Please, for the love of God, keep that thought in your head. "No."

"Patients?"

"Not any that come to mind." *Wait, that's not true.* "Mr. Whitlock," she rushed out at the memory. "He never misses an appointment, but he didn't show up Saturday or answer my calls. That's not like him. He was in the Army like you."

His eyes narrowed at that last part. "I'll look into it."

"I'm sure it's nothing."

"The day you go missing, your reliable patient doesn't show up. Sounds like something to me."

Right. "My best friend is on vacation. My practice is closed. Brother on a top-secret mission. Dad is backpacking and unreachable with his girlfriend. Tell me the timing of it all doesn't feel weird?"

When he *didn't* tell her that, her stomach dropped, quite possibly all the way down to Hell.

"Maybe your memories, or at least some of them, will come back if you rest?" he suggested, and she knew him well enough to know he was trying to keep her from panicking. "Also, we're looking into the possibility the hacker switched your tox report at the hospital to hide the fact there were drugs in your system. That could also mean when the effects wear off, maybe your memories will come back."

She stood at the news, nearly tripping over his shoe, but she saved herself before he needed to catch her and brushed off the near fall. "Is there a drug on the market that could make someone lose only select memories?"

"Not that I know of, but drugs plus a skilled hypnotist . . . maybe?" He pointed to the pizza box. "Please, eat. You need your strength."

She peeked at the pepperoni pizza, curious if he'd had anything today. He needed his strength and stamina too. *Stamina?* She fidgeted with the knot of the robe and decided, "I'll eat if you do."

"You were always so bossy. I see you haven't changed in that way."

"Well, you were a stubborn patient. I didn't have a choice." She wet her lips, longing for some lip balm, then tipped her chin to find his eyes.

"And you drove me nuts. Looks like you're capable of doing the same to me now."

"Oh, am I?" *How'd I circle back here again? To this feeling of lust I know I shouldn't be experiencing right now?*

"Yeah, you're pretty damn good at it." His nostrils flared, and he mumbled a few curses and stepped around her. She'd take it as a small victory that he grabbed a slice of pizza. He faced her and held the slice on his palm. "And for the record, I really don't like pepperoni. My meat is all yours."

She chuckled and reached for one. "Thank you for making me laugh when all I want to do is cry and panic."

"Anytime, ma'am." He winked, his attention riveted on her lips as she popped the pepperoni in her mouth. "Two more, sweetheart. They're all yours."

Sweetheart? There goes my heart. And with my luck, it'll soon explode into a million pieces I'll have to pick up again.

She stared at his hand, noticing a low ringing in her one ear. *What the hell?* Hesitantly, she reached for the next pepperoni but then slammed her hand to the side of her head at the blinding pain.

"Gray, I'm not feeling so good," she murmured as her knees buckled. He dropped the pizza and snatched hold of her, and she folded right into his arms. She squeezed her eyes closed, trying to focus on the memory pushing to the front of her mind. It was like trying to recall a dream, but it was slipping away, just out of reach.

"I think I remember something," she gritted out as she forced her eyes back on him. "I didn't escape," she whispered. "I think whoever had me let me go."

CHAPTER THIRTEEN

"JUST LET HER SLEEP. SHE'S FATIGUED. STILL RECOVERING from the shock and trauma of everything, but she'll be okay," Oliver suggested.

After Tessa had shared her memory—and practically fallen asleep in Gray's arms—he'd insisted Oliver triple-check Tessa's vitals.

Gray sat at the edge of the bed, which was four times too big for Tessa, and his attention slid from her sound asleep over to Oliver.

"You're sure? What if she needs to be in a hospital? What if there's something wrong? What if they did drug her and she's having a delayed reaction?" And a million other concerns warred in his mind.

He was used to being in control. This damn feeling was downright painful. Torturous even. Throw in the fact his teammates now knew he'd broken Tessa's heart thirteen years ago, coupled with the fact he'd tried to apologize to her, and her pushback only made him feel ten times guiltier . . . it was safe to say he was spiraling. *Right the fuck out.*

Oliver tipped his head, his brow creasing as his boss lost

his cool. "Gray, if we bring her to a hospital, you *know* what will happen. She's safer here."

"I know, I know. Fuck . . ." But what if she needed more care than his team could provide? Back on his feet, he tore his hands through his hair and paced alongside the bed, thinking about what Tessa had said before passing out.

"I woke up on a bench on the dock. An officer yelled for me to go, that I couldn't sleep there. And then, I made it to the street level, and I was confused. I had no clue where I was or what was going on, and that's when I tripped and fell." He'd held her in his arms as she stared up at him. Her big brown eyes full of fear. *"I was just . . . there. All alone. Why does that terrify me even more than if someone was chasing me?"* And then she'd passed out in his arms, and he'd hollered for Oliver, worried something serious had happened to her.

"Why would someone take her, then drop her off at a dock without her memories? It doesn't add up. Maybe she's remembering wrong?" Oliver blocked Gray's path and clapped a hand over his shoulder, waiting for eye contact he wasn't in the mood to make.

Oliver was the youngest on the team, but his life experiences had aged him. From the loss of his brother to his years in the Army, the man had seen a lot. But *Gray* was team leader. He was supposed to keep his emotions in check and make clear decisions.

And what had he done since getting Tessa from that hospital? Had a few hard-ons and nearly admitted to Tessa he used to hate her berry-scented lip balm because it made him think of all the things he wanted to do to her mouth. *God, I'm horrible. No wonder I didn't see a bright, welcoming light those thirty seconds I died.*

He blinked, then finally gave Oliver his attention. "I don't know," he sputtered.

"I've never seen you like this, man. Not even when Sydney was in danger."

Yeah, same, brother. Same.

Gray stole a look at the beautiful woman asleep in the bed, one arm crooked up alongside her face, her fingers nearly brushing her cheek. She had the same angelic features in her thirties that she had at twenty-one. Her cheeks were full, and when she smiled, it was like her entire face came to life in the most incredible way. Her nose would widen a touch while "crinkles," as his sister would say, met Tessa's almond-shaped eyes beneath her perfectly arched brows.

Gray sighed out a heavy breath as Oliver pulled his hand free from his shoulder. "I don't know what to say. But if it was Mya in trouble, and in that bed, what would you do?"

Oliver glanced at the closed door. "You're really asking me that?"

Gray covered his heart, a horrific pain crawling inside his chest. What was that all about? "Yeah," he nearly groaned out his response.

Oliver scratched his cheek, before placing his hands on his hips. "Well, Mya's not mine. You know she drives me nuts."

So did Tessa. And things ended between the sheets with me taking her virginity. If only I had known that information back then.

"But . . . I don't think I'd be able to make any tough calls if anything happened to her." Oliver cleared his throat. "Or anyone on the team, for that matter."

"I can't keep putting the team at risk when I know my head isn't on straight. I mean shit, I didn't even follow protocol when we were being chased earlier, and now my face is on CCTV footage." *And my dick doesn't obey commands. And the woman has me rambling.* But he'd keep those facts to himself. "Carter needs to take point."

"Can you really let Carter make the decisions regarding her life? Can you step back?" He paused to let the idea sink in and take shape. "Carter is a shrewd motherfucker. And he's damn good at what he does. But you two are like yin and yang. And I'm not saying that's a bad thing, but you're just very different. Especially in how you handle situations."

Not as different as you think. I just have a heart. Not so sure Carter does. Not anymore. "We have no leads aside from the gun, so maybe different is exactly what we need." He slowly turned, his gaze falling back on Tessa, and the memory of their kiss that morning sat heavily on his mind. "She's out cold. Are you sure she's okay?"

"Want me to check her vitals a fourth time?" Oliver snatched his medic bag from the foot of the bed, and Gray held up a hand.

"No, I trust you." He angled his head toward the door. "I'll go talk to the team. Let them know I'm stepping back." Before he could change his mind, he left the bedroom.

The team was scattered about the living room, working. As much as he regretted asking his niece to fly to Turkey to help their case, he knew they needed Gwen.

"How is she?" Sydney was the first to ask, but she was looking at Oliver, standing at his nine o'clock, and not him.

"She should be fine," Oliver answered.

Fine? He was pretty sure he hated that word now more than ever. Maybe even more than the generic word *okay.*

"And how are you?" Sydney peered at Gray this time, and you could hear a pin drop in the room as everyone fell silent. "Actually, hold that thought," she said before he could lie his way through an answer. "Levi's dad is calling from his office at the Pentagon."

Gray hated that man. Not because he'd been married to Sydney, but because he'd cheated on her with her former best friend and broke her heart. But why in the hell was he calling now? It wasn't even zero seven hundred in D.C.

"You're at work early," Sydney said straight away. "Is Levi okay?" There was a pause before she looked at Gray while saying, "Oh, hi, Admiral Chandler. Yes, I can put Gray on the phone."

What the hell? Gray's stomach dropped. Alarm flooded his system. The fact his father went to Sydney's ex to get ahold of him was sure as hell a bad sign.

She started his way, and all eyes in the room were on him as she handed him the phone. He quickly brought it to his ear, his heart thrashing wildly in his chest. "My phone is off. I'm on a job. What's wrong?"

"You stepped on a landmine, son. I don't know how you managed to be so unlucky and get yourself involved in this mess, but you need to leave Istanbul and come home, now," his father ordered, using his no-nonsense military voice instead of the easier-going one reserved for game nights and golf with his friends.

"Did the U.S. Embassy reach out to you and let you know I'm here?" Gray asked, remembering the detective mentioned making that call. Clearly, word got back to his father, but he couldn't understand why his father would care. And if CCTV footage had been wiped from the crime scene, no one knew he'd killed a man earlier.

"Of course they did. Because when the son of the Secretary of Defense steals a woman from a hospital, a woman who was being questioned by the police, I get woken up in the middle of the night. Throw in the fact your face is all over the damn hospital cameras, plus they have a video of you pointing your Glock at a detective there—"

"You can't be serious right now?" *THAT is why you're calling?*

"Dead serious. This has become a political nightmare for me."

"Well, you've been misinformed. She's an American citizen. Who's in danger, by the way. There are people after her, and I'm protecting her," Gray quickly shared, hoping to turn this conversation around and fast. "Do you have any idea who she is?"

"She's Colonel Sloane's daughter. And once we get ahold of him, he can help arrange to get his daughter back home. But this can't be our problem."

"It's not 'our' anything because *I'll* handle it. She's in danger, and I'm going to keep her safe," Gray snapped back, still shocked by the call.

"Turn her over to the authorities before you wind up rotting in a Turkish jail. They're an ally, but our relations with the president there aren't so hot right now. He'll use you to negotiate a deal or a prisoner swap for someone we sure as hell shouldn't release."

"What, and he won't use Tessa, the daughter of a colonel, for the same thing if they get their hands on her?"

"The Turkish president will think you're more valuable because of me," his father slapped him with the reminder.

More valuable? Harsh memories from his past clawed their way to the surface. "Same was true back in 2010 when the pilot was ordered to turn around and not save those Rangers, right? I may not have agreed with that decision, but Colonel Sloane was trying to save *your* son. Me," he grunted in anger. "And now, here you are not giving two shits about his daughter."

The other end of the line fell silent.

"Let me make this very clear, I am not leaving Turkey

without Tessa at my side," Gray said, his eye twitching. "You don't need to worry about my capture. It won't happen." He clutched his throat with his free hand. It felt like his father had reached through the phone and was strangling him with his ridiculous order. "Tessa was taken. She fell. She's committed no crime. I'm not sure what bullshit the cops here cooked up and fed to the embassy to push you into making this call, but—"

"Taken?" he cut him off. "They said she illegally entered the country."

"They're lying. Someone, hell, *multiple* someones, are after her." He tossed a frustrated hand in the air. "Maybe the government here realized they're sitting on a goldmine. She's the daughter of a colonel with no record of entering the country. They have the son of the Secretary of Defense on camera pointing a weapon at a detective on the same day a hacker screwed with traffic cams, CCTV footage, and a hospital." He paused to let that sink in. "But that doesn't mean we give them what they want. No prisoner swaps. No deals. You have my word I won't be caught." And if he was going to follow through with that, he needed to get his head back on straight and turn operational authority over to Carter, even if it pained him to do so.

"You've put me in a bad spot, Gray. Your mother is panicking, and you know she isn't one to panic. Your sister is out of the country as well and can't help you. Not to mention, if POTUS finds out about this, he'll have my head for not forcing you to come home."

"I'm not in the military anymore. Your orders are meaningless. Go ahead, remind him of that." Gray slammed a hand to his chest. "It's called free will. Not an easy concept for you to understand, I get it." He squeezed his eyes closed, trying to calm down. "But be my dad for a second and not the admiral. Please." The rough plea broke from his lips.

Silence.

More waiting.

A painful awareness hit him, and his eyes flashed open. "You're tracing this call, aren't you?"

The betrayal came in one simple word: "Yes." What he didn't expect was for his father to tack on, "You have fifteen minutes before I alert the authorities of your whereabouts. I made a deal to hand over your location, and I have to follow through. If she's in danger, let them help her." He paused. "You walked away from this girl once, and if I were you, I'd do it again."

His blood went ice cold, his restraint ready to snap. "Low. Fucking. Blow." But also, how in the hell did he know that? He'd confessed that to his mom over a late-night phone call, when he was drunk and regretting he'd left Tessa, but she'd promised not to tell anyone. "You know I won't leave her."

After a resigned sigh, his father said, "I know, dammit, because I'd do the same if I were you." And then he ended the call.

Gray tossed the phone back to Sydney. "We have less than fifteen minutes to get the hell out of here." He looked over at Mya. "Can you wake up Tessa?"

"Of course," she said, already on the move.

"I know your dad is a rule follower, but damn," Jesse said on approach, tucking his pistol at the back of his jeans.

"Your father's just doing his job," Carter declared, shocking Gray. "He works with POTUS. You know it wasn't an easy decision for him to make. Choosing his country over his son."

"I'm honestly not sure which he just chose," Gray murmured before Carter began directing the others to their next steps. "I want to be outside when the police arrive," Gray decided. "I need to see exactly who plans to come for her. My guess, more of the bad guys from earlier, not just the police."

"Dude, they have your name and face. Maybe let someone else do it?" Jack suggested, circling the table to face him while slinging the strap of a duffel bag over his shoulder.

Gray planted his hands on his hips as he thought back to the hospital. "No. I want to be here." He focused on his best friend. "It's also possible someone is pulling the detective's strings. What if he's working with one of the groups from this morning?"

"And what do you plan to do if he shows up too? Question him?" Jack cocked a brow, clearly worried about Gray and his decision-making skills.

"I warned him this morning exactly what I'd do if I found out he was in any way involved in endangering Tessa's life," Gray remarked in a low, steady voice.

"And that is?" Carter asked.

Gray swallowed the lump down his throat and faced Carter. "I'd do exactly what you'd do."

"You're supposed to be better than me," Carter tossed out the reminder, his dark eyes assessing him amidst the hustle of the team's preparations to leave.

"Yeah, well, sorry to disappoint you. I'm not always a choir boy." Gray snatched a new hat, a white one that time, and rested it on his head, brim facing forward.

"If we're being honest, Gray's not a great singer," Jack joked, attempting to crack through the tension in the room.

"And that's supposed to mean?" Carter focused on Jack while chambering a round in his 9mm.

Jack exchanged a quick look with Gray. "That he'll kill

any fucker who messes with someone he cares about. This morning is a clear example of that."

And yeah, Gray hadn't hesitated to cut down the asshole as he came at him with the knife in the alley.

At the sound of the bedroom door opening, Gray turned to see Mya and Tessa there. Tessa had changed into black sweats and a white hoodie. He snatched the red hijab from the couch and walked over to her.

"Here." Gray's fingers brushed against hers as she took it.

"Running again?" she asked as if getting used to her horrible predicament of danger. Gray nodded, and Mya helped cover her hair with the red silk scarf.

"Carter's taking you this time," he told her. "I'll meet up with you soon, I promise."

Tessa reached for him, and he looked down at her small hand clutching his forearm. "What if something happens to you?"

His frown deepened. "It won't."

"But what if it does?" she whispered, squeezing his arm.

Mya left them alone by the doorway. He knew they needed to get a move on, but he was aware of Tessa's ability to go from zero to sixty in the panic department. And who could blame her after everything that had happened to her?

He angled his head, quietly studying her, and his exhale damn near hurt his lungs. And his heart. *What is happening to me with this woman?* "Tessa," he began, covering her hand on his arm while dipping in closer, ignoring the fact he had an audience behind him, "I promised you I wouldn't walk away this time, which means not even the devil himself can rip me away from you. Got it?"

He just had no clue who the devil was on the mission. But there was always one, and he often had an accomplice. And to protect her and keep his promise, he needed to figure out who he needed to fight.

Gray studied her lips, and with his free hand, he reached out and palmed her cheek. "I'll even bring you some ChapStick later. Deal?"

Her tongue slid along the seam of her lips at his words. "They're that dry, huh?"

"We need to go," Carter barked out from behind him, slicing through the moment he shouldn't have been having.

Gray couldn't help but smile at this beautiful woman. Not only was he calming her down, but she was also dialing down his pulse rate and steadying his breathing. The implications of their reactions to each other definitely didn't go unnoticed.

Still cupping her cheek, he leaned in and brought his mouth to her ear, slipping the scarf to the side in the process. "Oh, I don't know, your lips felt pretty damn good against mine this morning."

CHAPTER FOURTEEN

"Man, I owe you an apology." *Apologies seem to be the theme of my day. Among other things.*

"What are you talking about? Apology for what?" Griffin looked over at Gray from the driver's seat of their rental. They were staked outside the hotel, waiting for the police to arrive.

"Because I'm a hypocrite, that's why," Gray admitted, trying his hand at sharing his thoughts instead of shielding them behind barbed wire and concrete walls like he'd done most of his life.

Gray swept his focus left and right, then twisted to look around to ensure they were still clear. Oliver and Sydney were parked around the corner for an additional set of eyes.

His gut told him there'd be more than just police officers showing up today, and he hoped his luck would finally turn around and he'd get a clue as to what was going on.

"You'll have to elaborate," Griffin said, not letting Gray off so easily with his vague claim. "My mom is an author. My wife is testing her hand out at writing too. So, I'm familiar with big words if you need to use them."

Gray smirked. "I see Jack is rubbing off on you." Better than them constantly fighting.

Griffin laughed. "Don't you dare tell him that." He lifted his shades to meet Gray's eyes, his silent plea obvious, before allowing them to drop back in place. "But really, I have no clue why you're a hypocrite or owe me an apology."

Gray took another look around the property. A woman was walking her dog in a patch of grass. A guy carted luggage toward the hotel from a Mercedes. And a little girl was pulling on her dad's arm and pointing at the red balloon she'd released into the air.

But no police or anyone suspicious. The place wasn't that active, so it'd be easy to spot anyone coming. That also meant he had to stay behind the tinted windows and not get out of the vehicle because he'd also be noticed.

Griffin fidgeted with the brim of his hat, waiting for Gray to share, but his walls were a bit tougher to crack through than he'd anticipated. *Yeah, this isn't easy.* He could talk openly with Jack because the man knew everything about him. But others? He usually needed liquor in his system to open up. Even with his mother.

Then there was Tessa, a sharp curve along the straight line he did his best to follow. She was also the reason for this conversation and apology. "I gave you shit when we were on the op in Greece with Savanna last year. I ordered you to keep your hands to yourself, if I remember correctly." *There. I said it.* Now, looking at Griffin and not feeling weird about it would be a different challenge.

"Ah, I see." An uncomfortable pause later, Griffin added, "And you're struggling with Tessa. So, are you trying to ask me for advice on behaving? Because I failed. Pretty miserably."

"What? No." Gray shook his head, finally looking

Griffin's way. "Just saying sorry that I was a dick. I could've handled things better back then."

Griffin gripped the wheel, eyes on the hotel. "I mean," he began while glancing at him, "sometimes you don't know what you don't know, ya know?" He shook his head. "I swear, that sounded better in my head."

"But you're right, I didn't know it'd be this challenging." *I nearly kissed her back at the hotel. In front of everyone.*

"I'd say things get easier, but they don't. The more time you spend together, the harder it'll be to see more than two feet in front of you. To see more than just her," Griffin said bluntly, hitting him in the head with a necessary reality check.

"Shit, you get that from one of your mom's novels? Or your wife's favorite reads?" Gray chuckled, trying to play off Griffin's heavy comment, but he also knew he was right.

"Speaking of Savanna, she's . . ." Griffin's knuckles whitened as he gripped the wheel tighter.

"Savanna's what?" He shifted on the seat, alarmed by the distressed tone of his voice.

"Pregnant," he laid it on him quickly that time, shocking Gray's shoulders back. "No one knows. She's waiting for Jesse and Ella's baby to be born before sharing the news. Plus, she said something about wanting to be out of the first trimester?" He brought a second hand to the wheel, and Gray looked at the wedding band Griffin never took off, not even on ops. "I'm telling you this because my focus on this op might be as fucked as yours."

"Aren't you happy?"

"Of course. But I promised Savanna we were going on a quick and easy op in Paris, and I haven't told her we're in Turkey yet. Shit might get complicated, and that'll make her worry."

Damn. "Well, if you're asking whether you should lie to

her, I don't know what to say. But I remember my sister telling me that Wyatt felt the same when he found out she was pregnant. He was worried about how to handle operating and remaining focused. But maybe ask Jesse for advice? I'm sure he'd be better at it than me."

Griffin looked at him and smiled. "You know damn well he can't keep a secret from his wife. He'll tell Ella, and then Savanna will kick my ass for opening my mouth before planned."

"Well, I'm no wordsmith like your mother, and you, apparently. But I'm sure you'll force yourself to focus. You don't want to leave your baby fatherless. And Savanna can't lose another . . ." *Husband.* But he left that part off.

"Well, when you put it that way," Griffin grumbled, shaking his head.

"And I can't protect Tessa if my head isn't on straight," Gray said under his breath just as his burner buzzed on his lap. They'd all turned off their phones and had new disposable ones in case his father, or anyone for that matter, tried to track their location again. "It's Carter." He put the call on speakerphone.

"We're at the boat," Carter said. "No tails."

That was a relief. Knowing Tessa was safe, *maybe* he could focus beyond two feet in front of him. *For now.* That relief was short-lived as Carter continued his update.

"I can't get Tessa on the boat. I'll toss her over my shoulder and carry her if you can't convince her. She said boats make her claustrophobic. Though, I'd hardly call a ten-bedroom cruising yacht a small space," Carter said in a clipped, irritated voice.

Shit. "Put her on the phone." He looked over at Griffin and gave him a nod, letting him know to keep an eye on the place in case he found himself distracted by the woman on the other end of the line.

"I'm not trying to be a pain in the ass," Tessa's fragile voice filled the line.

"But you *are* being one," he overheard Carter grumble in the background. Gray had no doubt the man really would snatch her up and carry her on board in a second if he couldn't convince her to go under her own power.

"I just can't get my legs to walk across the plank-looking thing."

"It's not a . . . why do I bother?" Carter cursed, and Gray knew he was seconds away from following through on his threat to haul her aboard like a piece of gear.

"Deep breaths, sweetheart. Just take in a few deep, controlled breaths," Gray said in a steady tone. "You've got this."

"You all must think I'm crazy. But I woke up on a dock yesterday, without my memories, minutes before falling into the water. So, getting back on a boat doesn't do wonders for my anxious state. Especially when I'm claustrophobic," she rattled on in a hurry, sensing her time was nearly up before Carter lost his control.

But wait. Rewind. "You remember being on a boat before the dock?"

"I, um, yeah, I guess I do." She was quiet for a moment as if shocked by her own words.

"What do you remember about the boat?" Carter asked her, realizing that piece of information might be of value.

"I don't know how to explain it, it's more like I just know I was on one," she shared, her voice too soft and quiet for his comfort. "I'm sorry."

"No, hey, this is good. The new memories, I mean," Gray reassured her.

"You have incoming," Oliver's voice popped into his ear over comms. "Three black Suburbans trailing behind a black four-door sedan. I think they're together."

Gray looked over to see four vehicles pulling up the driveway. "I have to go. But, Tessa, you'll be okay."

"Yeah, after she smacks me because I'm about to pick her up," was the last thing he heard from Carter before the call ended.

Griffin tapped his ear, unmuting his comm. "We see them. Three unmarked Suburbans and one sedan."

"Roger that," Oliver answered.

The car and SUVs parked in front of the main entrance, and Gray went still at the sight of the detective exiting the sedan alone. "The detective from the hospital, Onur, is here with ten other men," he said once the men filtered out of the SUVs. "No uniforms. Suits. My guess is they're MİT, Turkish Intelligence."

"And since they know Gray's military background, looks like they brought a lot of someones," Griffin added. "Given your father *and* her father, it makes sense they'd send in intelligence officers instead of the police, especially if their president sees a power-grab play or negotiation deal on the table."

"They're heading into the hotel now," Gray filled the others in over comms. "They don't have a name for our room. And my dad could only track us to the hotel. It'll take some time for them to check the whole place."

"Looks legit so far, right? I mean, the detective is a dick for going along with using a woman in danger, but he's more than likely just taking orders from above," Griffin commented.

"I still have a bad feeling."

"Murphy's Law kind of bad?" Griffin asked.

"Exactly," he grumbled.

At least they were lucky enough Carter had managed to secure a new safe house, even if it was a yacht instead of a freestanding building. And thanks to Carter's money, they also had a compound in Greece if they needed a nearby place to go. It was also the same location where Gray had ordered Griffin to keep his dick in his pants around Savanna. *Hopefully, I used better words than that. But doubtful.*

Five minutes later, Oliver announced, "We have a silver four-door Renault about to pull up as well. Same one you described earlier from the bridge."

"The Americans?" Gray sat taller at the news. As the sedan pulled onto the circular driveway, Gray brought a hand alongside his face to block their view of his profile.

Instead of stopping in front of the hotel, it looped all the way around, parking just shy of the exit.

"They must've hacked the police station and intercepted the address as you predicted would happen," Griffin pointed out.

"Or they have an inside man," Gray said in disappointment at seeing the detective exiting the front door with a phone to his ear, scanning the area as if looking for something. Or someone.

When the man's focus shifted to the Renault, he lowered his phone and started for the vehicle.

"Yeah, he must be working with them." And it had Gray's blood boiling. "The second the car leaves, follow them," he instructed Oliver as the detective neared the vehicle.

"Roger that," Oliver confirmed.

The detective remained on the sidewalk, a few feet away from the passenger side door, and then all hell broke loose.

"That gunfire?" Oliver snapped over the line as Onur crumpled to the ground next to the Renault.

"They shot him," Gray hissed, going for the door handle. "They're driving your way. Don't lose them."

"Roger that," Oliver answered.

"Don't go out there," Griffin ordered, but Gray was already lunging from the car, headed toward Onur. He had to talk to him while he had a chance.

He barely heard Griffin cursing over the screams coming from the front of the hotel as he rushed toward the detective.

Kneeling beside him, he set his hand over Onur's chest as he struggled to breathe; he probably had a collapsed lung.

Onur's eyes met Gray's momentarily as he said, "I was only trying to help."

Gray grabbed the lapels of his jacket, his hands now damp with blood. "Help who? Who the hell are you working with?" When his arms limply fell by his sides, Gray cursed and let go of him to check his neck. A small spark of relief filtered through his mind when he detected a steady pulse.

He lifted his head to see Griffin parked alongside him with the passenger side door open. "Get in," he hollered as more gunfire crackled in the air, striking the taillight of their rental.

Two MİT officers were making their way from the hotel. *And great*—Gray thought as he snatched the detective's phone and jumped into the car—*if he dies, now I'll be pinned for murder. My father is going to love that.*

CHAPTER FIFTEEN

"I'LL STILL NEVER UNDERSTAND HOW THAT MAN DOES THE things he does." Gray eyed the luxury superyacht Carter had secured last minute, then turned his attention to Griffin at his side.

Since they'd been marked by the Turkish officers, they'd ditched their rental a kilometer away from the hotel, and proceeded on foot. It'd taken them an additional two hours to ensure they didn't have a tail before they made their way to the marina.

"I've known him for a long time, and I still don't know how he pulls off this shit, even with his money." Griffin pushed his Ray-Ban sunglasses into his dark hair. "What's the real reason you're hesitant to get on this ostentatious floating safe house? And so help me, if it has a disco room or some bullshit like that, I'll be going man overboard."

Jack really was rubbing off on Griffin. Steely, reserved, and quiet, the man had never been one to crack jokes back when they'd first met. "I think you know."

"She's tough. Look at what she's been through in less

than twenty-four hours. And somehow, she's managed to crack a few smiles. She'll be okay."

He was right about that. Tessa had been through the wringer, but she'd found a way to push through. The lemonade-from-lemons approach.

"Come on." Griffin slapped his back before he boarded.

Gray waited a few seconds to clear his thoughts, then joined him. They found Carter, Mya, and Jack in the living room at the center of the "ostentatious floating safe house." No sign of Jesse, who was probably doing a perimeter sweep.

The interior was modern and sophisticated. Sleek wood. Cream-colored furniture. A wall of books, large flat-screen TV, and a fully stocked bar.

Jack was parked on a barstool, an iPad in one hand, whiskey in the other.

"Where's Tessa?" Gray asked, eyes remaining on his best friend.

"She's asleep somewhere in one of the five thousand rooms on this *ship*," Jack exaggerated. "The yacht even has a nightclub."

"I knew it," Griffin piped up before snatching Jack's glass. "Why are you drinking?"

Jack rolled his eyes. "Who made you captain of this vessel?"

Griffin poured his drink down the drain, and Jack flipped him off only to snatch the bottle of Buffalo Trace from the counter. Since it was Gray's favorite, well, hell, maybe he'd have a finger of whiskey too.

When Griffin went to grab the bottle from him, Jack stood and went to the table where Mya and Carter quietly worked, ignoring the exchange between Jack and Griffin.

"I checked on Tessa a few minutes ago," Mya shared, her fingers moving fast over her keyboard. "She's still sleeping."

"That's surprising." Gray frowned, eyes landing on Carter. "You didn't drug her, did you?"

Carter looked up at him with a blank expression. "What? She had motion sickness. I gave her Dramamine."

"That better be all." Gray cocked a brow, not always on the same page with his partner's methods. "Tell me Oliver and Sydney have a location for the Americans in the Renault." He'd lost connection with his team while on the run with Griffin.

"Oliver and Sydney followed the Renault to the Asian side of the city. Sydney bypassed the gate code and they're parked outside a three-story building. But it has four rental units inside," Mya brought them up to speed as she turned her computer to share her screen. Thanks to Google, she had an overhead view of the property and complex. "The van from the alley you described earlier is parked out front as well. Three of the units have been occupied for over a year. And one was rented out today. No name attached to the rental agreement. I'm guessing this was a rather large, last-minute cash offer for an unknown amount of time."

"We have any idea how many tangos are inside? Did they manage to pull any photos of the Americans?" Gray set a hand to his chest, an aching burn blooming there.

"Windows are closed. Curtains are drawn in that unit. But Sydney snagged a profile shot of the driver and a decent image for the passenger before they entered the building," Mya said. "Running their faces through our software now to see if we get any hits, but something tells me we won't."

"Just like someone is cockblocking us on finding out that Scottish dude's name too," Jack chimed in, sharing news Gray sure as hell didn't want to hear. "If his prints were ever in any system, they're gone now. And the serial number on the gun was filed off."

"Of course," Gray glibly responded.

Jack plopped down on a couch near the built-in bookshelf and asked, "Maybe we should move in now? This is our only lead."

"No, we're in sit-and-wait mode," Carter answered quickly. "Recon and surveillance until we know who we're dealing with." He leaned back in his chair at the table, hooking his ankles around the chair's legs. "Plus, it's not exactly great timing considering Gray is being blamed for shooting a detective in broad daylight." He focused on Gray. "If you weren't a marked man before, you sure as hell are now." He shoved his laptop away from him, folded his arms over his chest and fixed him with a solid "what were you thinking" look.

The fact Gray had risked being captured by running over to the detective outside the hotel was evidence he *hadn't* been thinking. His judgment concerning this case was beyond fucked. "Any word if the detective is still alive?"

"In surgery. We checked the hospital records," Jack beat Carter to the answer. "Bullet went clean through. He should be okay."

"And you really think whoever shot him plans to let him survive?" Gray reached into his pocket, searching for the detective's phone he'd grabbed. He'd powered it off mid-run to ensure the MİT officers didn't track his location with it. "I wouldn't be surprised if they hack the hospital's power grid and their backup generator, so he'll die on the table in surgery."

"That's a fun thought," Jack responded. "You should use that as your opening line when you go check on Tessa."

Griffin sat next to Jack, elbowing him to make more room as he asked, "Why'd they shoot the detective in the first place?"

"Loose end?" Gray proposed. "Or because he broke their deal when he didn't turn over Tessa?"

"What throws me off," Mya began, swiveling on her chair to face Gray, "is why'd they let Tessa go only to come back for her?"

"Assuming it's the Americans who had her, you mean?" Gray asked. "And not the Scots?"

"Shit, I don't know." Mya blinked a few times, clearly as confused as him.

"Well, the Americans didn't rent that unit until today, which tells me they came here after learning Tessa was in the hospital," Jack tossed in his two cents.

"True." Gray offered Mya the detective's phone. "Can you work some magic and break into it? Or do you need me to have Griffin swap with Sydney and come here and help?"

"I'm slightly insulted that you think I can't do the tech stuff without her," Mya said teasingly. "And this lump of joy sitting across from me already sent Jesse to swap places with her before you two arrived."

Carter mumbled something too low to hear. A jab back at Mya, more than likely.

"Grump," Mya said, willing to poke any bear. No holds barred with her, especially when it came to Oliver. The two of them made Jack and Griffin's bickering look like they were singing a love song together.

"Whoever we're up against has better cyber skills than any of us, so I was thinking we need strength in numbers is all," Gray clarified in case she truly was insulted. He'd only worked with Mya on a handful of ops that year, but the woman really was a firecracker.

"Want a sip?" Jack lifted the bottle Gray's way. "I know we're working, but a little whiskey never killed anyone."

Griffin grabbed the bottle from Jack before Gray had the chance to consider it.

"Buzzkill." Jack glowered at Griffin, but Griffin kept quiet and rested the bottle in the crook of his other arm.

Of course, Jack didn't know Griffin was expecting a child, and he had the good sense to want his teammates alert in case shit hit the fan. He had a wife and unborn baby he wanted to return home to, and Gray would do everything in his power to ensure that happened.

He just needed to save Tessa first. "I let the detective use me this morning. I walked right into his trap."

"But you didn't walk into anything. You escaped," Jack reminded him.

"And the fact I'm now going to have my face all over the news? Blamed for shooting him?"

"Yeah, you could've dodged that one by not jumping from the car to go to him." Jack shrugged his apology at the truth.

"Just tell me you all have something else to share. Where are we at on looking into Tessa's friends and patients?" Gray focused back on Mya, assuming she'd been the one to dig into Tessa's relationships.

"Ruled out Naomi's boyfriend, Sam. He's as clean-cut and boring as they come. Naomi and Sam had dinner with his parents the night before they flew to Jamaica. No red flags," Mya told him. "Tessa's father and brother are still unreachable, which feels a little suspect in itself." She paused to let the news sink in. "But one name you provided me is a bit of a question mark."

"Which one?" Gray's muscles locked up with anticipation.

"That patient she was worried about, Mr. Whitlock," Mya began, "he lied about his name."

"What?" He knew where she was going with this, but after the day he'd had, he needed her to spell it out.

"I'm saying Mr. Whitlock doesn't exist. But *Whitney* Howard does, and his face matches that name too. Looks like aside from health care at the VA, Whit has no insurance. He was in the Army as Tessa said, so at least that checks out."

"So, you're thinking insurance fraud?"

"That's what I'm guessing. I'll keep digging, but so far, that's the only anomaly I've come up with. I was waiting to tell Tessa until I learn more, but—"

"Wait," Gray cut her off. "I don't want to tell her anything until we know for certain this Whit guy is only committing insurance fraud." Once Mya nodded, he peered at the staircase. "What room is she in?"

"We chose the innermost room. Thought it'd be safer," Jack spoke up, then told him where to find her on the yacht. "And are you planning to tell Tessa what happened while she's been asleep?"

Tessa didn't need to know he was now a wanted man. She'd blame herself.

And she sure as hell didn't need to know that unlike last time, when it'd been her father telling him to walk away from her, it was now his dad.

Gray let go of a heavy sigh. "No, I'm going to lie."

CHAPTER SIXTEEN

"Hey, you decent?"

"Gray?" Tessa's heart jumped in her throat when she heard his voice on the other side of the door.

"Yeah, it's me. I'm back."

She'd assumed he would've been there hours ago. But between the nausea and Dramamine, she'd lost track of time. There were no windows in her room, but she had to guess it was around seven at night. Tossing back the covers, she hurried to open the door.

She flicked on the light, then swung the door open with so much force it banged into the wall, and she had to catch it before it shot closed again.

His hands were resting on the exterior doorframe, and his head was bowed. He'd changed clothes. Gray sweats and a white tee. His hair was messier than normal as if he'd been running. And had he been?

She let go of the door to wrap her arm across her midsection at the uncomfortable squeeze in her abdomen. He righted himself, catching the door with his palm before it slammed in his face.

"I couldn't get you any ChapStick, I'm afraid. I decided it wouldn't be best to show my face in public."

"Seems you don't want to show me your face either," she whispered, wondering if he'd ever meet her eyes. "Did something bad happen? I mean, aside from all the bad stuff I already know about?"

"The Americans from this morning were outside the hotel," he shared, his voice level, but he still refused to look up. "Oliver and Jesse are watching them. Sydney returned a few minutes ago, and she's helping Mya work on getting names for them."

"That's good, right?" *So, why no eye contact?* "A lead?"

He nodded. "Can I come in?"

"Only if you look at me," she insisted.

He slowly dragged his eyes up her body. When his attention landed on her top, his jaw clenched.

"What?" She looked down at the tank top Mya had given her, which she'd paired with lightweight black sweats with PINK written on the ass. "Oh." *No bra.* Curling her hands into fists, she crossed her arms over her breasts to hide her nipples poking through the thin fabric. "They insisted I sleep after they calmed me down and gave me Dramamine. I can't sleep in a bra."

At her words, he stepped inside and moved away from the door, allowing it to swing closed behind him.

"Do you want me to put on a bra?" Her eyes widened at the flare of his nostrils and how tense his arms appeared at his sides, the ridges of muscle even more evident.

"No," he returned in a clipped voice. "Yes." He sighed as if frustrated with himself, then lifted his chin before saying, "Whatever you want, I mean. Whatever makes you comfortable."

"I think you'd feel better if my nipples weren't showing,

so I'll grab a bra. One second." When she turned to find where she'd tossed it, she bumped into him, her knee landing on the bed, her ass going back, and she was pretty sure that was his crotch she felt against her. He snatched her hips, probably on instinct, and her hands went to the bed in the perfect position for doggy-style sex. "Sorry." Jeez, she wouldn't wish her embarrassing klutziness on her worst enemies.

"It's . . . fine," he ground out, but he still had her hips between his big palms. She couldn't resist arching back, pressing against his groin, and his cock twitched. "Bra," he snapped. "You find it?"

"It'd be easier if you weren't, um, holding me down."

"Fuck." He let go of her, and she looked over her shoulder to see him turning, probably so she could have a moment of privacy to put on her bra.

She righted herself, patted her hot cheeks, then found the bra beneath the covers.

"This room is smaller than I expected. I'm starting to feel claustrophobic myself," he surprised her by saying as she clipped on the uncomfortable underwire bra.

"Just when I was getting used to it," she said with a light laugh. "Now I feel like the walls are closing in, thank you for that. It's safe to look now."

"I thought I was safe this morning during your bath too," he said, not budging. His strong back muscles bunched together, and she resisted the desire to run her hand up his spine and offer him comfort the way he'd been doing all day for her.

"I'm not naked and wet like earlier, so I promise you I'm good."

"Tessa." How'd he manage to pack so much meaning into two syllables?

"Sorry, I didn't mean it like that."

"Sure you didn't," he grumbled, then lowered his hands from the closet door and slowly faced her. But the room really was tight, so when she backed up to give him space, she landed on the bed.

Yup, that was my intention.

Gray set his back to the closet as she planted her palms alongside her. "You worry me."

"I do?"

He nodded. "Yeah, you do." He met her eyes, and a nearly haunted look crossed his face. "I'm afraid I should never let you out of my sight again." He looked around the room. "At least my team was smart enough to give you the only room without windows or a balcony."

She folded her arms. "I'm not that bad. Am I?"

He arched a brow, and a dash of a smile came and went.

"I'll take walking disaster as a flaw over some of the others God could've given me. What I lack in some areas, I more than make up for in others."

"Oh, I remember." The dark rasp of his tone had her squeezing her thighs together. She was sure he hadn't been referring to sex, but now she couldn't help but think about that night thirteen years ago.

Intense. Hot. Passionate. And the pain from him being her first had been short-lived because their bodies had fit so perfectly together.

"So, um, you learn anything else while I was asleep?" she rushed out, hoping to tame her wild thoughts and get back on track.

He pressed his lips into a tight line while studying her. When his eyes landed on her shoulder, she nervously brushed her fingers there. No way he remembered his galaxy comment about her freckles, right?

"They're working on leads. I'm afraid I'm only getting in their way right now," he finally said.

"I take it you're not used to feeling that way?"

His Adam's apple rolled, and he shook his head. "I thought you might need a distraction though." He reached into his pocket and produced a white AirPod case and cell phone.

"Hmm. A phone instead of a kiss for a distraction?"

He squeezed one eye closed for a second as if unsure how to answer.

"Kidding." She slid her lip between her teeth before verbalizing her thoughts, "I really do have two modes, don't I? Perky or panicky."

"Rom-coms or horror flicks," was all he said back, and she smiled at the comparison.

"See." She shrugged.

"I prefer to see you," he said as his eyes quickly landed on her breasts, "perky." His focus journeyed up almost painfully slow. Like he caressed every inch of her skin without touching her. And now she was hot all over. "The only time I want to see you breathless is . . ." He shook his head as if deciding not to continue his thoughts.

But she'd been captivated, ready, and anxious to hear more.

He cleared his throat and peered at the phone. "It's an untraceable phone. Screen is small, but if you want to listen to music or watch a movie, you can. Just no calls or texts to anyone." He closed the foot of space between them and set down the items alongside her before backing up again.

"But I can't log into my accounts to watch anything, right?"

"No, and I'd give you access to my accounts, but—"

"You're afraid I'll judge your watch history? See you

prefer rom-coms to horror films?" It was a dumb joke, but she was mentally and physically fatigued despite the rest. Also, she was nervous about being alone with a man that had her pulse jumping and arousal climbing despite being in danger.

"I hate scary movies," he reminded her with a shake of the head. "It was you who liked them. I see enough scary shit in my life. I don't need to pay to watch it." He offered her a small smile. "And my movie playlists would bore you, I promise. They were much more eclectic when we were together."

When we were together? Her brows lifted.

"I mean, when you forced me to watch movies back in the day," he clarified after clearing his throat yet again, then pointed to the phone. "I created a dummy account for Netflix and YouTube though."

"This is a sweet gesture, I appreciate it. But I'm worried this gift means you think we'll be on this mega yacht longer than planned."

His lips twitched, and where was he going with that? Smile or frown? "We had to leave the Bosphorus. Too crowded. We'll spend the night docked in the Marmara Sea. My teammates can meet us at another marina in the morning. Gwen too."

Gwen, right. Your cyber genius niece. "Oh God, we're moving, aren't we?" Her eyes widened in panic at the realization they were no longer anchored. "Who's the captain? Can we trust him?"

He smirked. "Griffin knows his way around boats. Oliver too. Hell, even Carter."

"Not you?"

He scratched the facial hair on his cheek. "I can manage a boat if need be. Trust me, you're in good hands."

Right. Your father is an admiral. Though, she doubted he'd ever been at the actual helm of a ship. "I know I am," she whispered on a small exhale. "I just don't think music, or a movie will distract me now that I know we're moving."

He tipped his head, eyes narrowing. "What will?"

"Well, you said you're only in your team's way, right? Does that mean you can steal a few more minutes down here with me?"

"I think I can manage a few minutes. Maybe even a whole hour. But then I'm taking you upstairs with me to eat. We're both in need of food."

She smiled and rubbed her stomach. "I thought I'd lose my appetite with all the chaos, but there's a growl happening here for sure."

"Want food now?"

"No, I'd rather wait until we're not moving to test whether I can keep down what I eat."

"Good call." He skated the hand at his cheek down his jaw, then around to the nape of his neck. "So, how can I help take your mind off everything? Which distraction would you prefer?"

Oh God, are you giving me a choice? Asking if you can kiss me? But since he didn't officially ask, she went with, "Talk?"

He gave her an uneasy look. "Do you remember anything else aside from waking up at the dock alone? Or that being-on-a-boat feeling?"

"No, I don't. And sorry, I meant talk as in finally catch me up on the last thirteen years of your life."

"Ah, those thirteen bullet points I never provided earlier. You really do want them, huh?" His smile traveled to his eyes that time, and it warmed her heart.

"Possibly." *Why do I feel like you're not ready to give*

them though? "Or you could just tell me why my ChapStick drove you nuts? Or explain why you stopped emailing me back?"

The blank look he offered in reply had her attention cutting to his sneakers. With the fit of the sweats at his ankles, it was the first time she'd caught sight of even a hint of his prosthesis. He seemed to do his best to keep it hidden.

"Silence isn't always golden," she whispered, pulling her focus back up while waiting for any kind of reaction from him. She could even work with grizzly.

"In my line of work, it saves lives."

Like earlier in the alley when I had to be quiet. When you saved my life?

He let go of his neck and took one step closer. "There's not much to tell you, that's all. I couldn't even fill an index card of notes for you. Work is my life."

Sadly . . . "I can relate to that."

"I don't believe you." His forehead tightened. "You're far more interesting than me."

An awkward laugh tumbled free at his words. "Not true," is all she managed out. When she realized his eyes were on the bed, she wondered if maybe there was another question she should be asking. "Why don't you rest here with me? You've been going hard and nonstop today. And I doubt you did much sleeping by my bed last night."

He smirked, meeting her eyes again. "You want me to climb into that tiny little bed, barely big enough for the two of us, and sleep?"

"We did share a smaller space this morning. I'm sure you can manage this one." She grabbed the AirPod case and phone, then set the items on the end table before getting situated on the bed. "Talk to me. Prove to me your life is as dull as you say it is or get in this bed with me and sleep. Those are your options."

"Bossy again, I see."

"Don't act like you don't like it." *Where'd that come from?*

But the lift of his brows was her answer. He did.

"You should rest your leg. Take off the prosthesis," she suggested.

"Anything else, boss?" He waggled his brows, but at least the dark cloud that'd been hovering over his head lifted a touch.

"No, I think we're good." She winked. "For now."

"Mmmhmm." He sat on the bed and removed his shoes, then pushed up his one pant leg to detach the prosthesis. He let his pant leg drop, then shifted on the bed to look at her.

"I wish you came to me after your last surgery," she shared, keeping her voice as soft as possible but hating how disappointed she sounded.

"So you could hear me grunt and curse while dealing with those frustrating parallel bars all over again? Nah, you had enough of my bad mouth to last you one lifetime."

"I don't think I've had nearly enough of your mouth."

"Well then." He suggestively rolled his tongue along the seam of his lips.

"That's not what I—"

"Yes, you did." He quietly studied her as if curious if she'd take their joking further.

With her back to the headboard, she slid her toe up and down her achy calf muscle, her pant leg pushing up in the process, waiting for Gray's next move. "What else can you do with the new prosthesis?" she asked as he climbed closer. "Walking long distances seems easier. Is, um . . ."

"Are you trying to ask me if sex is easier?"

So, you just went there, huh? Naughty Gray. I like this side of you. "I don't want to know about who you've tested sex out with, to be honest."

"I wasn't planning on giving you a detailed report about my sex life. Or lack thereof lately."

Lack? Her stomach muscles tensed, and a rush of heat settled between her legs.

He adjusted his residual limb, shifting to his side to face her. "But yes, a lot of things are easier. Showering, for one. And more control over my foot position. Less back pain because I have a normal gait again. No pressure points or chafing since I no longer have the socket. And I can sit comfortably on a stool. Hell, I don't even break toilet seats anymore." He lifted a hand. "It happened a few times," he added. "But the thing I love the most that I took for granted before the accident," he continued in a lower voice as his hand fell between them and their pinkies touched, "is now I can feel the ground again. Well, my brain thinks so, at least."

"Proprioception. Feeling the ground underneath you and the awareness and position of your movements." At his nod, she murmured, "You're incredible, you know that, right?"

"Not nearly as incredible as you are. If it weren't for you, I probably would've given up thirteen years ago."

"Not true." She couldn't help but slip her hand inside his, and she relaxed just a little more when he linked their fingers. When he remained quiet, she asked, "Why aren't you under the covers with me?" She slid farther down, bringing her head to the pillow.

He leaned in closer, his mouth mere inches from hers. "Not the best idea. My focus tends to go out the window around you."

She wet her lips. "Good thing there's no windows, then, right?"

"Good thing." His eyes fixed on her lips, and with his free hand, he threaded his fingers through her locks, pushing a few wispy strands behind her ear.

The little touch had her body tingling and alive. And feeling alive was a good thing considering she could've died last night.

Shit, I almost drowned. I'm in Turkey. Lost five days of my life and nearly died today and—

"Tessa?"

She closed her eyes, her chest going tight. "Yeah?"

"What can I do for you? I'm losing you to stress, aren't I? How do I get you back to perky?"

"Am I that obvious?" She could hear the panic creeping back into her voice. But at least her teeth weren't at the chattery stage like back in that spice closet. Oddly, when she'd hidden behind the dumpster, she'd been in some strange numb state of shock, which was probably for the better.

"Walk me through this. Tell me how I can help." His tone was so warm and soft. His words so genuine. She honestly couldn't remember any guy she'd dated who didn't dismiss her feelings with a quick, "Just don't worry" comment.

"Hold me like you did in that closet? Maybe I can turn?" She kept her eyes closed and did her best to shift around without kneeing him in the groin or hurting his leg.

"How's this?" He wrapped an arm around her and eliminated the space between them, and she nestled against him, a relaxed sigh falling from her lips.

She instinctively covered his arm with hers. "Much better." *We're spooning, aren't we?* The comforter served as a barrier between her ass and his crotch, and she guiltily wished nothing separated their bodies. "Sleep for me. An hour, at least."

"Yes, ma'am," he groggily replied as if already on the edge of the dream world.

She was quiet for a minute or two, but her thoughts thundered around in her head, unwilling to cooperate and calm down. "Gray, can I ask you something?"

A husky chuckle moved through her hair, and that sexy rumble slid beneath her skin, heating her body. "You change your mind on sleep?"

"No," she quickly answered. "But I need to quiet my mind first."

"By asking me a question?" He maneuvered his other arm under her body, allowing her to feel fully cocooned in his embrace.

She nodded, and he eased his mouth near her ear, and his warm breath fanned across her skin. Goose bumps scattered everywhere as her nipples went hard. "My concern is any answer I give you will turn up the volume on your thoughts, and I'm supposed to be distracting you. I'm not doing a great job."

She shifted his arm away from her midsection so she could face him. "And I'm supposed to let you sleep, so I'm failing too."

His brows slanted when she shoved down the comforter. "It's hot in here," she lied. "I'm hot, at least."

He snatched her hip, startling her by drawing her tightly against him. But this time there was no barrier, and her breasts smashed against his chest. "Ask me the question." He stared deep into her eyes, and her mouth opened, but nothing came out. "The one you really want to ask, sweetheart."

When that Texas upbringing of his slid into his voice, it had her shivering that much more. She wet her lips, wishing they weren't so freaking dry, as her mind went one way and her heart screamed at her to go another.

His hand shifted a touch, and his thumb moved in small sweeping circles over the small of her back as he quietly waited for her to speak up.

She reached back and moved his hand to her ass, and his jaw tightened. His palm sat unmoving against her now. Conflict warred in his eyes, a mirror of how she felt on the inside.

"Will you touch me?" It was the only thing currently on her mind. Not her original question, but the only one she now wanted an answer to.

"Where?" he growled out.

She brought her lips near his as she begged, "Everywhere."

CHAPTER SEVENTEEN

GRAY CURSED, AND HIS RESTRAINT DISSOLVED BEFORE HER eyes as he did what she asked. He squeezed her ass cheek over the thin fabric and swallowed her moan with his mouth.

She offered him her tongue, and he didn't hesitate, indulging in tasting her. It wasn't a slow dance. Or soft and sensual. It was exactly what she needed. Demanding, possessive, and nearly out of control.

She lost track of how long he kissed her. Touched her. Made love to her with only his mouth while his hands coasted over her clothed body.

Her heart nearly stopped when he pulled away to ask, "About my mouth you said you want more of . . . can I get a yes from you this time?"

"A yes to what, exactly?" she asked, playing dumb as heat pooled in her belly and rushed to her center. She arched into him and rotated her hips, needing to feel the heavy weight of his cock against her.

He peered into her eyes, slipping a hand through her hair to cup the back of her head. "I want my mouth on you. Everywhere." His tone was rough, almost feral. "I've been waiting thirteen years to taste your pussy," he spelled it out for her, and his dirty words had her hot all over. "I'd like to show you I can do much more with my mouth than swear."

Unable to get the words out past the chokehold of her own anxiety, she eagerly nodded, feeling silly. *But I am who I am.*

That boyish smile she'd witnessed earlier, the one that met his eyes, returned, and he shifted his weight on top of her, then traced his mouth along her jawline to the column of her throat.

She buried her fingers in his hair and clawed at the messy locks as he scooted farther down, blazing a trail of heat along her skin. When he reached her stomach, he rolled her tank top up and slid his hands up to unclasp her bra.

She cried out as he circled his tongue around her belly button while palming her breasts. *Is this really happening?*

It felt like yesterday she'd been staring into her office mirror trying to convince herself not to call Gray, and now she was on a yacht, flush with anticipation about him going down on her.

"No faking with me, got it?" he demanded, lifting his head, searching her eyes for confirmation.

"Never with you." And damn, she'd forgotten she'd overshared that detail. When he lifted an uncertain brow, she added, "No faking. Roger that."

He cracked a smile. "Good girl."

Two of the most powerful words in a romance novel, and he just said them to me. Yeah, I'm done.

A few seconds later, Gray had her sweats and panties down to her thighs, and his mouth hovered over her sex as he gripped one of her legs.

"Before I give you my mouth," he said as he skimmed his

finger along the seam of her sex, her head falling back at the simple touch, "tell me I'm not a stranger."

She forced herself up on her forearms to peer down at him, and there was no humor in his eyes or tease to his tone. He was serious, wasn't he? "You're not a stranger," she softly confirmed. It was easy to give him those words because it was the truth.

His brows knitted, and for one quiet moment, he simply stared at her with his hand remaining just over her sex. "Good to see we're on the same page," he acknowledged in his operator voice. She could feel it vibrate and rumble right through.

And then his facial expression softened, his eyes like two light green emeralds holding precious meaning, as he studied her for a few seconds.

"Not a stranger," she shared one more time, worried this man truly needed to knock the words she'd nervously rambled to him that morning from his head.

A terse nod later, he lowered his mouth over her center, and when his tongue followed the same path his finger previously had, she fell back and fisted the bedding at her sides.

She bit down on her back teeth to stop herself from screaming for God. With her luck, the sound would break the spell and Grizzly Gray would reappear and change his mind and retreat.

"Fuck, Tess."

He'd never called her Tess before, but damn, did she like it. Of course, right now, he could call her just about anything short of another woman's name.

Gray pushed two fingers inside her, curled them inward, and held them in that position for the scantest moment before his tongue flicked the sensitive spot just above. "You're so wet. Taste and smell so good," he murmured between licking and sucking her clit.

She let go of the bedding and reached for his head. The sensations were almost too much to handle. The build-up and intensity had her on fire. Burning on the inside.

Her hips lifted off the bed, and he buried his fingertips into her thigh, drawing her closer to his face as she shimmied right along with the movements of his tongue. *Oh my God.* His facial hair tickled her sensitive skin, heightening the sensations.

"You're ruining me for everyone," she cried between yelps and pleas for him not to stop.

But he did stop.

In fact, he went totally still.

He even eased his mouth from her center, forcing her to let go of his hair as he looked up at her.

"What?" She was desperate for him to keep going, on the precipice of coming and hanging by a thread. She was breathing hard. Fast. And then she realized what she'd said. Her "ruin me" comment implied there'd be a "someone else" one day. How could she tell him she didn't want there to be? But that would sound absurd. *Then why does he look upset by that idea too? More than the stranger comment?* "Gray," she begged, unsure what to say or do, but certain that if he didn't place his face back between her legs soon, and finish what he started, she'd have to take matters into her own hands.

Was he about to growl out "mine" to demand she never climax with anyone else? She'd be good with that. Really, really good with that, in fact.

But instead, his warm breath rolled across her skin, and he shocked her by thrusting three fingers inside her while keeping her prisoner with his gaze. Her hips bucked, and her back lifted from the bed. He set his other hand on her abdomen, pinning her down. And he didn't have to use the word, *mine*, because she felt it in his actions and in the way he looked at her.

Yeah, I'm yours, she sang like lyrics in her head just before he sank his mouth over her pussy, flicking that sensitive spot again with his incredible tongue. *Oh holy hell. Wait, holy and hell don't belong together and I'm . . . just shut up.* "I'm—I'm . . . going to . . ."

Frantic breaths. Pants and moans. She cried as she chased her orgasm, riding it as high as it would go.

She collapsed a few seconds later, every thought and breath stolen from her. Snatched straight from the air.

"I should've let you do that thirteen years ago," she admitted as he worked his mouth up her body.

She felt like a limp ragdoll, on the verge of collapsing into a pile of limbs. He scooped her into his arms and hauled her against his body. With her back to his chest, he held her tight. The very definition of *mine* in his embrace.

Her sweats were still at her thighs, and her top was pushed up, so with his arm resting over her hip, she couldn't resist grinding her ass against his hard length as he pinched her nipple.

"I assume you know I didn't fake it?"

"Sweetheart," he began, his mouth near her ear as he lightly rolled her nipple between his thumb and forefinger, "you came on my tongue. It's safe to say I believe you."

"Mmm. True. I—"

"Gray, we need you," a woman rushed out as the door flung open, scaring the hell out of her. "Oh shit. Dammit." The door thudded shut. "I'm sorry. Just come upstairs," she said, her voice filtering through the door.

Gray cursed as Tessa reached for her panties and sweats and pulled them up before flipping to face him. She snapped her bra back in place and rolled her tank top back down.

"Was that Sydney? I didn't look. I'm mortified your teammate saw me like this," she said, her skin hot from embarrassment.

"Teammate, right," he answered in a low voice while shifting to the side of the bed, moving his intact leg around so his foot found the ground. "Yeah, it was Sydney. She clearly forgot to knock."

"I'm so sorry." She hopped off the bed and grabbed his prosthesis and handed it to him.

He attached it and looked up at her. "You have nothing to be sorry about. I, uh, should've locked the door. My focus is not so great lately."

"Do you regret what happened?"

He reached for her wrist, and she slung her arms over his shoulders as he pulled her onto his lap. With his free hand, he brought a fist beneath her chin. "I've racked up a lot of regrets in my life," he began while leaning closer to her, "and getting you off is sure as hell not one of them."

CHAPTER EIGHTEEN

Not even two steps into the living room, Sydney grabbed Gray's wrist and pulled him aside. "I'm so sorry. I never should've barged in like that. I wasn't thinking you'd—"

"That I'd break my own rules?" Gray looked over at Tessa sitting on the couch by Griffin. Her attention was riveted their way, and the flush of embarrassment matched the pink sweatshirt she'd put on over her tank top before they'd made their way up to see what was so urgent that Sydney rushed in without knocking first. "Glad you had that kind of faith in me," he continued, looking back at her. "I guess consider us even since it's not like I didn't nearly walk in on you and Beckett before."

She let go of him, a small smile meeting her lips. "I like her."

He stole another look at Tessa, now chatting with Mya. "I do too," he said with a sigh. When Gray's eyes met Jack's, his best friend shot him a grave look, reminding him something was up. "What's going on?"

"Oliver and Jesse managed to get photos of one more guy

with the Americans. Jack knows him. Says you do too," Sydney shared as they walked farther into the room.

"Who?" Gray stepped away from Sydney, eyes set on his best friend, who looked like he'd been paid a visit by the Grim Reaper.

Jack spun the laptop around to show him the screen, and Gray stumbled at the man in view, bumping smack into Sydney.

"Sorry," Gray absentmindedly apologized to her, then covered his mouth with his hand, shock stealing the rest of his thoughts.

"What's going on?" Tessa asked.

Gray wanted to look her way, but his pulse was going too fast. Chaotic beats of his heart made it to his ears.

At the feel of Tessa reaching for his arm, realizing she was now at his nine o'clock, he focused on her while sharing, "The man on that screen is Dale Franklin."

Tessa's eyes widened with recognition. "Wait, your friend, the one I met at Walter Reed?"

He slid his hands to his hips, but she didn't let go of his arm in the process. "Yeah, the one you met."

"The three of us were best friends growing up in Dallas." Jack tugged at the brim of his hat, probably trying to shield his eyes. To hide the anger and pain Gray was feeling as well. "Dale joined the Marines instead of the Army. He also worked at Gray's security company in California, the one he ran before Falcon, until—"

"Until I fired him," Gray cut him off, lifting his chin to find Jack's concerned eyes. "I have to go there. Talk to him." He pulled away from Tessa's grasp and turned, but Sydney snatched his other arm to try and stop him.

"Think this through," Sydney advised as Carter stalked his way, stopping in front of him as a barrier to block Gray from rushing off to throttle information from his former friend.

"This doesn't change things. We're still in sit-and-wait mode," Carter said, his tone dead even, letting Gray know he wasn't interested in arguing.

"It sure as hell changes things. He sent men after Tessa. After me. He had his guys kill those Scottish men in the street in broad daylight. Has a hacker on his team to cover his tracks and—" He abandoned his words, knowing he was wasting his breath on Carter.

"Why would Dale be after Tessa, that's what we need to figure out," Sydney said, remaining focused on the mission. "And we need to make sure it was him and his men who had Tessa in the first place."

"Gray." Tessa's soft voice roped him her way, grounding him a touch, especially when their eyes met. "How can I help you?"

She was offering him the same words he'd provided her not too long ago. But he wasn't so sure this situation could be fixed with anything other than Gray going after Dale and demanding answers.

"Why'd you fire him?" Carter asked, beginning to roll down the sleeves of his dress shirt before cuffing each at his wrists.

Gray looked toward Jack, hoping he'd answer for him.

"Dale got hurt on a job," Jack took the lead. "Became addicted to Oxy. Drank too much. He was becoming reckless. Putting our team at risk on missions. We told him he had to go to rehab and get help if he wanted to keep working with us."

"He chose not to. So, I fired him," Gray surrendered in a low voice of defeat, thinking back to that dark day with Dale, wishing there'd only been one bad memory.

But no, the memory of a much shittier confrontation after that had the hairs on the back of Gray's neck standing.

"I should've killed him when I had the chance," Gray rasped, goose bumps covering every square inch of skin beneath his clothes. At the feel of everyone's eyes on him, he dragged his palm down his face, searching for the will to continue when all he wanted to do was head straight for Dale's place.

"Can you be more specific?" Carter asked. "When and why did you nearly kill him?"

Gray stepped back, needing some space from everyone. His memories were already crowding him, making it hard to breathe.

"Dale's not just a former friend. He was once engaged to my sister, Natasha." He thought back to the day Dale had become a runaway groom, leaving his sister there to send away the guests on her own. He'd chased after him, roughed him up a little. But in reality, he'd been relieved the marriage never happened. They weren't the right fit, and his sister barely shed a tear over it because she'd known that too. "Dale left her at the altar. He actually wound up marrying Wyatt's ex-wife." He peered at Tessa since she wasn't clued in on the next detail. "My sister's married to Wyatt, a Navy SEAL."

Tessa blinked in surprise. "Wow, small world."

Crazy small. "But what I'm about to share next remains in this room. Never leaves here, are we clear?" He looked around at everyone before continuing, "Last year, I went to my cousin's wedding in Dallas. Wyatt couldn't go with Natasha because he was working. Gwen offered to go with her since Natasha was pregnant, not that she was showing yet." His stomach roiled at the memories from that night.

"I was also invited to the wedding, but so was Dale," Jack

spoke up. "Dale's wife, Clara, didn't come. It was our first time seeing him since he left the company."

Gray thought back to that night, not at all in the mood to relive what happened. "Natasha walked in on Dale being aggressive with Gwen. He was shitfaced. Handsy. Trying to kiss Gwen when my sister said Gwen clearly didn't want him to. So, Natasha went after him, and he hit back." He dropped his eyes to the floor. "My mother and I happened to be walking by the room, so we rushed in, and I intervened."

"Wow," Mya said under her breath. "So, you almost killed him then?"

"No, not then. He was so drunk, one punch knocked him out." Gray lifted his eyes, looking for Tessa. Needing to see her to stay grounded so he didn't lose control over the memories. "Once Gwen and Natasha left the room, my mother and I waited for him to wake up and spoke to him. My mother told him she'd bury him alive under endangered plants and promised she'd make the evidence of his death disappear."

"But you didn't just let him walk away, I'm guessing?" Carter asked, knowing Gray wouldn't let shit go after that. None of his teammates would.

"Natasha and Gwen made my mother and me promise not to tell Wyatt about what happened," Gray shared, avoiding Carter's question.

"Why?" Tessa whispered, her brown eyes glistening with unshed tears.

"They blamed Dale's addiction. And they knew what Wyatt would do if he found out," Gray replied. "Wyatt wouldn't show mercy. Touching his daughter. Striking his pregnant wife. Not to mention the fact Wyatt was still friends with his ex, and Dale was married to her, so . . ." He shook his head in disgust. "But I couldn't let it go.

The next day, Jack and I tracked him down and brought him as close to death as possible. Made him promise to get clean and change his life, or we'd be back to finish the job."

"And now he's here," Carter remarked in a low tone.

"Did he get clean?" Sydney asked. "Does he work for another company? Mercenary?"

"I never followed up to find out. I didn't think I could stomach checking in on him. I felt guilty for keeping what went down from both Wyatt and my father. But Natasha and Gwen didn't want Dad to know either. He's not so forgiving either." His hands tightened into fists at his sides. "I need air." He stole a look at Jack. "Find out where he works now and why in the hell he'd be here." He took off from the room before anyone could stop him.

When he made it to the deck on the starboard side, he snatched hold of the railing, setting his eyes on the city, a lit-up and beautiful backdrop to their gloomy evening. They were anchored at sea for now, a safe distance from shore. Gwen would be there early in the morning. And having her there after learning Dale was in the mix nearly had him leaning over the railing and emptying the contents of his stomach. Not that there was much in there.

His body went still at the awareness that he wasn't alone. "You didn't need to come out here."

"How'd you know it was me?"

"Wild guess." He turned to the side, setting his forearm on the railing to put eyes on Tessa. "You should get back inside."

A light breeze blew a few strands of hair across her face as she approached, her steps surprisingly stable given her fear of boats. "I'm not claustrophobic up here." She ran her hands up and down the sleeves of her sweater before folding her arms over her chest. "But if you're worried I might fall overboard, then I can see your point."

He frowned. "Well, I hadn't been thinking that, but now I am." He lifted his chin. "You're cold, that's why."

"I'm okay." She closed the space between them but kept her distance from the railing.

Good idea. He wasn't in the mood to go night swimming.

Her eyes landed on his T-shirt. "But aren't *you* chilly?"

"My anger is heating my blood just fine."

Her lip caught between her teeth as she quietly studied him, clearly unsure how to navigate the metaphorical waters. They were rough and choppy right now. "You're thinking about Gwen, right?"

How'd you know? He looked up at the sky, finding an open patch between thick clouds that offered a narrow view of a few stars. "I'm just wondering if this is my fault."

"What do you mean?"

He set his gaze back on her beautiful eyes, searching his messy mind for how to explain his thoughts and have them make sense. "What if I hadn't fired him? Just forced him into rehab even when he refused. What if I didn't almost kill him? Or, at least, checked in on him afterward. Maybe I would've discovered he switched sides to work for an enemy?" *If only I knew which enemy.*

"You can't blame yourself." She reached for his bicep and squeezed. "You can't be responsible for someone else's actions. You must know that."

"But I'm responsible for mine. The choices I made." He swallowed. "Those choices may have brought him to the breaking point." With his free hand, he tore his fingers through his hair. "He was one of my best friends. I've known him since I was five. How'd we end up here?"

"Sometimes the people closest to us are the ones who hurt

us the most." She rolled her tongue over her teeth. "Sounds like another movie line. But it's true. And I can't handle seeing you feeling guilty about this."

"I'm more mad than anything else at the moment," he replied as she smoothed her hand up and down his arm. "I should have told Wyatt though."

"I can imagine keeping what happened a secret wasn't an easy decision for Gwen or your sister to make." Her expressive eyes cut straight through him, and his stomach squeezed.

"They didn't want Wyatt going to prison for murder."

"You really think Wyatt would've killed him?"

"Absolutely." He closed his eyes and let go of a gruff breath. "Hell, you and I didn't even officially date, and I wanted to murder your boyfriend when I saw him kissing you."

She stopped stroking his arm, and it took him a second to recognize what he'd shared. Damn his anger for opening his mouth and sticking his foot in it.

"What are you talking about?"

When he opened his eyes, her hand was gone from his arm, and she was too close to the railing. "Come here, you." He snatched her wrist, hauling her closer, and her hands landed on his pecs.

He gently gripped her arms as she tipped her chin and looked up at him, waiting for more. "What boyfriend?" she whispered, brows slanting with curiosity.

He considered how much to divulge, then settled on the only option. The truth. "Three months after you left for grad school, I came up with the idea to open my own tactical security firm." He thought back to that day. To the decision. To the hope in his heart. "I knew it'd take time and resources, plus I had to get stronger, but I figured if I could operate, I'd be me again. And then maybe I'd deserve you. I wouldn't ruin your life if I was in it."

Her eyes narrowed, and he looked down to see her fingertips curling into her palms, but she kept her little fists on his chest. "My dad made you feel that way, didn't he?"

He didn't need her feeling bad about her old man, so he pushed forward with the story, sharing, "I came to see you in Boston. I wanted to surprise you. Since I couldn't get you out of my head, I thought maybe you felt the same."

"When?"

"A week or so before your Christmas break. It was snowing out when I made my way down the street to your brownstone in the city. And that was when I saw you outside, kissing your doctor boyfriend." How was that memory so vivid in his mind even after so many years? Same with the feelings it'd once evoked? "I realized I was too late, and I didn't want to ruin your happiness."

"Oh, wow." She shot him a funny look. "How'd you know he was a doctor?"

Now I'll sound crazy. "I needed to make sure he was safe for you. A good guy. So, I, uh, did some recon." His mouth twisted with worry as he waited for her to look at him with disgust.

She rolled her tongue along the line of her gorgeous mouth and surprised him by saying, "That's kind of sweet."

"Not the reaction I was expecting."

"But it's the truth." She unfurled her fingers, laying her palms flat on his chest again. "I wish you'd surprised me anyway."

"How could I? I really did want to choke the life from that man just for kissing you. I knew then I had to move on. Let you be happy. I told myself you'd be better off if you never heard from me again. That's why I didn't answer those last few emails you sent. I decided to forget you ever existed."

"Ouch." She winced.

"Now, looking at you, I know I did that because messaging you back, remembering you, would hurt *me* too much," he confessed.

At the sight of tears filling her eyes, he was met with regret once again. He'd said too much. Hurt her again. That hadn't been his intention.

"The thing is, if you'd shown up, I would've left him for you." A single tear chased down her cheek and hit her wobbly lip. "In a heartbeat."

Fuck.

"But we can't change the past."

"I know." He pushed the lump of regret down his throat, feeling it magnify the pain as it settled in his chest.

"Which is why you can't blame yourself for anything, including what happened with Dale." This sweet woman was always trying to let him off the hook. He didn't deserve it. But he knew she'd never change. It was who she was. Kind and caring. Unrelenting in her mission to help bring light to others on their darkest days.

He cupped the sides of her face and bowed his head to hers. "It hasn't even been twenty-four hours and here you are . . . bringing me back to life the way you did thirteen years ago," he admitted, his tone harsh and husky. "Crazy thing is, I didn't know I'd been so dead on the inside until now."

Her hands slipped from his chest and rested on his arms. "Is this our second chance?"

"I don't deserve a second anything," he hoarsely said. "But you deserve the world. You deserve whatever you want."

She met his eyes. "And what I want is *you*."

CHAPTER NINETEEN

BACK INSIDE THE YACHT, JACK WAS SAYING SOMETHING, AND he was pretty sure it was to him, but Gray barely heard a word. All Gray could focus on was Tessa from the corner of his eye as she talked to Mya and Sydney while he replayed Tessa's "second chance" offer in his head, the one she'd made less than ten minutes ago.

Was she ready to give him another chance so fast? Did he deserve it? The stranglehold of guilt tight around his throat told him he didn't. How was she able to forgive him for hurting her? And was she concerned he'd do it again? It had to be in the back of her mind, right? *Maybe that's because it's still in the back of mine.*

"Gray?"

He blinked, shaking free his thoughts and eyed Jack. "I'm sorry, what were you saying?"

Jack's brows pinched with worry. "You okay?"

"I'm . . . the same as you, I suspect." He grabbed the back of his neck and squeezed. He was tight. Tense everywhere. And it certainly didn't help he'd gone down on Tessa not that long ago and hadn't found relief between his legs afterward.

Interrupted by my ex. He owed that bit of information to Tessa at some point, but he doubted now was the ideal time.

"I can't believe Dale is part of this." Jack steepled his fingers and tapped them against his chin twice. "We grew up together. Built forts. Hunted. Threw parties that got us grounded. Did a bunch of other stupid shit together. How is he our enemy now?"

"Didn't we ask ourselves that question after we nearly killed him last year?" Gray reminded him as he glanced over at Tessa again. He sure as hell hoped Sydney and Mya weren't sharing anything with her he wasn't ready for her to hear. They had enough on their plate without worrying Tessa even more. "Anything new from Oliver or Jesse?"

"No, Carter still has them in sit-and-wait mode." Jack lowered his arms to his sides as they both faced the room.

Carter had a phone to his ear. And Griffin was nowhere to be seen, most likely missing his wife and calling her in one of the bedrooms.

Tessa looked his way, still talking to Mya and Sydney, not that he could hear their conversation.

"We're trying to track down who Dale works for, but—"

"Dammit," Gray cut Jack off when a sick thought hit him, and everyone in the room peered his way. "Dale knows my moves." He looked back at Jack. "He worked with me long before you joined. Hell, he helped design the company's playbook."

"What are you saying?" Mya's dark brows arched while waiting for him to go on.

"I'm saying Dale knows what to expect from me. And he'd know I'd never allow myself to get captured at the hotel. He'd also assume I'd have eyes on the place to see who came for Tessa." He mumbled a choked string of curses at how truly bad having Dale in the mix was. "If someone on Dale's team hacked the hospital's system, they would've seen me pull a gun on that detective this morning." He hadn't walked into the detective's trap today. It'd been Dale's. "The detective is probably innocent. They called him. Baited him over to the car and shot him."

"To put the blame on you. Make it tough for you to move around the city as a wanted man." Jack huffed out a breath.

"Wait . . . what? He was shot?" Tessa shot up from the couch. Her balance was decent, which meant the effects from her fall last night had more than likely worn off. But now he'd have to share news with her he hadn't planned to reveal yet. "And you're being blamed?"

Here I am the one to open my mouth when I was worried about others doing it.

"Gray's dad gave away our location after Gray refused to turn you over at his order," Carter shared, and Gray shot him a hesitant look. "She should know."

Tessa lifted a hand to her chest, her breathing appearing to become more shallow. Panic setting in. He went over to her and threaded their fingers together, bringing their united hands to his chest so she could feel the steady beats of his heart. Show her he was still calm. Some-fucking-how.

"I got you," Gray promised. "Breathe."

The room fell silent as their eyes locked and he waited for her breathing to even out. After a stuttery exhalation, she murmured, "I'm okay."

"I'm sorry for not telling you. I didn't think it would help you to know any of that."

"I had a feeling you were keeping something from me."

Tessa's brightness, that gorgeous light that she carried around inside her, blinding to people so dark on the inside—people like Gray—felt like it'd gone out. Extinguished. He had no idea how to make things right for her, but he'd work his ass off to do it.

"Are you ready to hear more?" Carter asked. "I was just on the phone with a contact of mine, and I have information about Dale Franklin."

Gray hesitantly let go of her hand and faced Carter. "And what'd you learn?"

"Dale got back his government clearance late last year. He mostly handles private military contracts. His last post was in Qatar for four weeks."

"So, he works for the good guys?" Tessa asked in surprise. "Is that why he took down the bad guys? What if he was trying to save me from them? And he and his friends weren't out there to hurt me?"

"Dale clearly knew Gray was with you in the hospital," Carter stated. "If he was trying to help you, he should've reached out. Gave Gray a heads-up."

"He'd never reach out to me." Gray stroked his jaw, thinking. "And it was clearly his guys who set me up with the shooting of the detective today."

Tessa's shoulders fell. "Right, I forgot about that."

"He wants you away from me." Gray turned to face Tessa. "That's what I *do* know."

Carter scratched his trimmed beard as he added, "The company who signs his check is reputable, that's the best I can give you right now."

"Then why would Dale have his guys shoot a police officer to set you up if he works in private security for a reputable company?" Tessa asked.

"It was a clean shot. Maybe it was never meant to kill him," Jack spoke up before Gray could. He knew Jack wasn't defending Dale, but if someone on Dale's team wanted the detective dead, at that range, they could've easily made it happen before fleeing the scene. "Dale plays by his own rules. I just never expected he'd go that far outside the lines and shoot an innocent person. Well, assuming the detective is innocent. He could've still helped them."

Gray thought back to the hotel and when the detective had walked out with the phone to his ear. Thinking about it now . . . "No, he didn't know. He looked confused when he had the phone to his ear. I think the detective helped us get out of the hospital today because he believed we were in danger." *And I was a dick to him.*

"And now he might die because of me," Tessa whispered with regret.

"He's going to be okay," Gray did his best to reassure her while giving her a terse nod.

"If he was shot just to throw some heat on Gray and cause him more problems, then there's no reason for Dale to finish off the detective," Sydney shared her thoughts on the matter.

"Dale's not a murderer. He just lost his way," Jack said in a low voice. He had to be feeling the same as Gray. A weird mix of guilt and anger about everything.

"We need to find out who Dale's working for and what his team wants with Tessa. Any chance your father knows what's really going on? Or hired Dale and his team?" Sydney asked Gray. "You said your father doesn't know what Dale did last year, so perhaps Dale hasn't burned all of his bridges with your family."

"My father hire Dale?" The thought made him sick. "No. Besides, Dale was here before my dad found out I helped Tessa leave the hospital. If something else is going on, and my dad knew about it, he would've given me more than just a fifteen-minute head start, he'd have given me a clue. So no, it's safe to say he's in the dark on Dale's involvement here."

"The fact we can't find Tessa's brother or father, and now this Whitlock guy is not who we thought and—"

"What about Mr. Whitlock?" Tessa stepped away from Gray to look at Mya, and Mya closed one eye, more than likely regretting the fact she'd spoken her thoughts aloud.

She already knows almost everything anyway. "Just tell her."

As Mya filled Tessa in on the fact her patient gave her a fake name, Griffin walked into the room and scanned the worried faces. "What'd I miss?"

"You missed a lot." Jack went to the bar and grabbed the whiskey. "And screw this, I need a drink. Don't give me shit," he warned, and Griffin lifted a hand in surrender.

Gray went over to Carter and pulled him off to the side of the room away from everyone else. "I need to talk to Dale. He's our best hope at finding out what's going on once and for all."

"Don't you think he's expecting you to do exactly that? He probably also knows we had his guys tailed from the hotel and that they have eyes on them right now. He showed his face to bait you," Carter snapped out what Gray knew in his gut to be true, but he didn't want to believe it. "Until we can make sense of his motives, I'm saying no."

"And you're taking charge, is that what you're telling me?" Hell, it'd been Gray's original plan, but he hadn't told Carter that yet. And he wasn't so sure he wanted to sit in the backseat now that his father and former best friend managed to wind up in the mix. It was a clusterfuck of a situation.

"Yeah, that's what I'm telling you. Dale is in a hurry. He's making bold, quick moves because he must be on a short timeline. Let's make him wait. See how that forces his hand," Carter said decisively.

Dale was never a patient person in general. But Gray

didn't want to see any more innocent people get hurt because of that impatience.

"It's our only play right now. We need to learn more before we do anything else. Gwen might be our best hope at figuring out where Tessa was those five days." Carter looked over at her. "The best thing you can do right now is to do nothing and let us handle things. Take her out of here and keep her calm. Keeping her safe is *your* mission. Finding out who wants her back and why is *mine*."

CHAPTER TWENTY

"You do realize I'm getting into this room one way or another, right?"

Tessa set her back to the door while clutching the towel above her breasts. "I just . . ." She peered around the small guestroom. Now that she was thinking about it, the room was probably meant for a yacht employee rather than a guest since it wasn't all that cozy. "I needed a second to breathe like you did earlier."

"In a room that makes you claustrophobic? Don't lie to me." She knew he'd just winced at his last words, even if she couldn't hear or see it happening. "I lied . . . I'm sorry. Tessa, please."

"The room is growing on me, by the way." Not a total lie. But not quite the truth. The walls just didn't happen to be closing in on her right now.

"I gave you ten minutes of space, and that's ten too many considering I heard the shower running when I first knocked. You could've hit your head."

"I'm not dizzy. My head feels much better. I think the

effects of the fall have worn off." *Which means my memory issues are most likely not related to my tumble.*

"Let me in," he pleaded. "I can't handle you being alone."

I don't want to be alone either. "Rationally, I know why you lied to me. I get why you kept the stuff about your dad and the detective from me. Even the insanity about my favorite patient lying about his name. I get it." She freed a harsh breath from her lungs.

"But irrationally?"

"Irrationally, I need someone to be mad at because I'm scared and confused."

He was quiet for a few seconds before saying, "You can be mad at me. If that helps you, I'll take your anger. I'll happily be your target."

"Why would you do that?"

"Because I'd do anything for you," he said in such a sobering tone she couldn't help but face the door and unlock it.

She slowly opened it to find one of his hands braced against the frame, his body leaning forward a touch. His eyes lifted, speeding over the fact she was only in a towel to find her face.

"Gray." She kept a tight hold on the towel, worried it'd fall. With her luck, one of his teammates would happen to walk by if it did. "I'm not really—"

"It's okay. I deserve it." His forehead creased as he studied her.

"No, you don't." She tipped her head, motioning for him to join her, then turned and listened as the door clicked behind her. She went still at the feel of his big arm wrapping around her waist. He drew her against his hard body, and she squeezed her eyes closed as she relished in the comfort of being so close to him. "I'm sorry. I'm just overwhelmed."

"Can I admit something?" He paused for a heartbeat, then went ahead and shared, "I'm overwhelmed too. We're in the same boat."

"Quite literally," she whispered before turning into him, uncertain of what to think, feel, or do next. "Naomi will be home tomorrow from Jamaica. And the practice reopens on Monday. What am I going to do?"

"Do you want to talk to her when she gets home? I can arrange that if you—"

"Yes, please. I was holding off while she was on vacation, but I need her," she cried and slipped her hands up his chest. He snatched hold of her wrists but kept her palms in place. "You seem to know what I need before I do. You're very good at your job."

"I'm pretty bad at my job right now."

"Not true."

"Maybe a little true." Just the side of his lip lifted. Not quite a full smile. "I'm useless to them tonight."

"Well, you can't argue with me on this point. I'm safe because of you."

"Your safety won't ever be in question. I won't let anything happen to you."

"You proved that this morning." *Kept me safe from a lot of people.*

He lifted her hands from his chest, but in doing so, her towel fell to her feet. His gaze plunged between them, and she followed his eyes to her peaked nipples. "Sorry." He let go of her, as if prepared to grab the towel, then stopped himself. "Yeah, if I go down there," he rasped, meeting her eyes again, "I'm not coming back up."

A flare of heat shot through her belly and down between her legs, his words igniting the memory of his tongue between her thighs earlier.

Another orgasm was off the table. *Well, it should be, right?* She parted her lips, about to defend her dirty thoughts with all the reasons why sex *should* be on the table, but the pad of his thumb sliding over her mouth stopped her.

He closed his eyes and said, "I can't." The words came out with force. Like it'd taken all his willpower to say them. "I want you so fucking much. You have no idea. But the mood I'm in . . . I wouldn't be gentle, and you deserve that." His Adam's apple rolled as he opened his eyes. "You deserve so much more than I can give you right now. Maybe I have two modes too. And I'm at the very dark end of the spectrum right now."

"I don't believe that." She stepped onto the towel, which gave her a little boost to get closer to his face. His arms remained locked at his sides, and she held on to him and brought her body closer.

He groaned as if in protest of their proximity but didn't budge.

"Listen, you have every right to be angry. Way more than me. You're hurting." She couldn't even begin to imagine that kind of betrayal from someone she cared about. "The pressure from your father too." That part hurt her to say. "In the last twenty-four hours, you've given me everything I need. You've been there for me. Let me give you what you need now."

"No." The word cut through her. Left a mark, it was so harsh. His chest puffed out on a deep exhalation before he added, "I would never use you like that."

She stroked his arms up and down, attempting to calm him, knowing how it felt to be on edge. Riled up. Breathing hard. Heart thundering. "You have me," she repeated what he'd said to her back in that spice store.

He set his hands on her hips, and she went up on her tippy-toes to arch into him, wanting to feel his hard length press against her. Looking up, she found his mouth parted, eyes focused on her face. "I don't have a condom," he announced as if his resolve was slipping. He dipped his face, drawing his lips closer to hers, and a hint of whiskey she hadn't expected wafted between them. In those ten minutes apart, he must've had a drink, and she didn't blame him. "But I just can't," he said while turning his cheek.

"I have an IUD." She doubted that would convince him, but she wasn't ready to give up, even if it was insane to have sex while they were being hunted in a foreign country.

"Tess." He faced her, his brows slanting with determination. "I want to pin you to every surface of this room and fuck you so hard that nothing can possibly muffle your cries," he gritted out. "Which is why I can't."

"Gray." *Not my best rebuttal.*

"That's why I hated your ChapStick back then. It drove me nuts." His nostrils flared as he focused on her mouth. "It made me want not only to kiss you, but to fuck you there too. Then move on to every one of your holes after that while you wore only blue high heels."

Every. One. Of. My. Holes? Each word from that statement punched through her mind, making her wetter than she'd known was possible. If he touched her right now, he'd discover she was on the edge of an orgasm already. *Word porn.* Yeah, that was what that was from him. Words turned her on more than any visual or video ever could.

But also . . . *blue* high heels? That was oddly specific.

"I'm forty-one, not a twentysomething anymore. I should have better control than I do right now, and it's throwing me off." His hand shifted to her ass cheek, and he buried his fingertips into her flesh, drawing a gasp from her at his tight grip.

His eyes dropped to her breasts, and she wished he was shirtless too. Did he still have hair on his chest? *Probably.* He didn't look like a man who shaved his chest. And what about those deep V lines he'd once had? Were those still visible? *More than likely.*

Based on the muscle she felt when touching him, he was even more ripped now than at twenty-eight. She wanted to run her fingers over the ridges as he made her cry out in ecstasy.

"Not here," he bit out. "I can't."

Then why wasn't he letting go of her ass cheek? Why'd he just lick his lips while staring at her mouth as if imagining his cock there?

"I could hurt you." The way he spoke, it was like he was working to convince himself to back off. "I'd sooner kill myself before I'd ever hurt you," he added in a nearly broken tone.

He slowly let go of her and his back hit the door before he dragged his palm down his face as he hung his head.

Shivers wrapped around her limbs, and she snatched the towel from the floor, but the last thing she wanted to do was add a barrier between them.

"I'm just, um . . ." *Turned on. Painfully so.*

"Let go of the towel and touch yourself." He shoved his hands into his pockets. "Find relief."

She stared at him, a blazing trail of heat in her stomach. "You want to watch me?"

He arched a brow and angled his head as he lifted his chin in a silent command for her to obey.

The towel fell, and she slipped her fingers between her legs. Damn, she was wet, and when Gray pulled his bottom lip between his teeth, she couldn't help but moan. His eyes were focused between her thighs, and her knees buckled at the sight.

"I don't trust myself to touch you, but I want to watch you fuck yourself with your fingers. I want to watch you fall apart," he murmured as she kept moving her fingers along her sex. But then his tone softened a touch as he added, "And I'll be here to catch you."

Her hand went still for a moment as she replayed his promise.

"Show me how you like to be touched." The heat in his tone and how his words delivered tingling sensations throughout her body had her fingers moving again.

His sweats were tented from his arousal, and he moved one hand inside his pants, fisting his cock. Stroking lazily. A low groan escaped his parted lips as he continued to clock her movements.

Licking her lips, she wished he'd come closer so she could be the one touching him.

"Cup your breast with your other hand, then pinch your nipple for me." His order was rough as he added, "Harder, sweetheart. A little pain can feel good."

"Then come closer and touch me yourself," she challenged. "I can handle the pain." She pinched her erect nipple and continued to work her fingers over her sensitive clit.

His eyes raked over her body. "No, sweetheart, I'm enjoying every second of this, trust me."

Damn this man and his self-control. What she wouldn't give to see that control snap right now?

"I'm close." Her breathing picked up as she touched her swollen center.

"Come for me." He paused, removing his hand from his

pants. "Right now." The order shot through her, and she came harder than she'd ever come before by her own hand.

She collapsed, falling forward, and as promised, he was there to catch her. Breathless and panting, he helped her stand.

He cupped her chin and gave her a soft but quick kiss on the lips before scooping her into his arms to carry her to the bed.

"Orgasming while standing is a first. As well as having someone watch me."

An unexpectedly harsh look slid across his face as he set her down. "I lose my mind when I think about the fact you've ever been with anyone else."

"Maybe I feel the same about you." And it was more than a maybe. She couldn't stomach the idea of wondering where Gray had learned to become such an expert with his tongue, let alone wonder about his ex-girlfriends.

"I think we're both—"

"Crazy?" She let her head fall back onto the pillow as he rounded the bed and joined her, but he remained sitting rather than lying next to her as she'd hoped. "I feel like I'm inside that TV show *24*. Every hour since you've arrived has been an episode."

"It's been a long day for sure." His eyes landed between her legs, and when he brushed his knuckles over her knee, she parted her legs for him. He focused on her wet, slightly pulsing sex. "The things I want to do to you."

"So do them," she whispered, her body too spent to talk much louder than that.

He hooked his arm around her leg and trailed his fingers along her inner thigh, bringing his palm close to her sex.

"It can be our next episode."

"Hour twenty-five?" he surprised her by teasing back.

"Anything but a cliffhanger." She lifted her hips, desperate to feel him even though her body was worn out from climaxing twice in one night—not to mention the rest of the day's events.

A small smile played across his lips, but he withdrew his hand and gave her the disappointment of the century by covering her with the comforter.

"You're trying to behave, and I'm begging you not to." She swallowed. "When, then?"

Standing by the bed now, his fists were back in his pockets. "When I can trust myself not to be a savage in bed with you, that's when."

What if I want savage? "You'd never hurt me. Not physically, at least."

His brows slanted, and he opened his mouth to say something but then slammed his lips shut.

"But that's not it, is it?" she asked with a sad shake of the head. "You're not afraid of hurting me during sex. You're afraid if we make love, you'll break my heart afterward." *That's your problem, isn't it?*

He pulled his hands from his pockets, and for a second, she thought he would return to bed. But no such luck. "I'm pretty sure that kind of pain hurts even more than the physical," he shared. "But no, Tessa, that's not it."

She swallowed. "Then what?"

"The last time we had sex, I took your virginity without knowing it." He kept his eyes focused on hers as he continued in a low voice, "So the next time we're together . . . I'm doing things the right way."

CHAPTER TWENTY-ONE

"Tessa?" Gray felt around the bed, searching for her. Groggy, he rolled over, finding the bed and room empty. *What time is it?* He checked the Apple watch on his wrist, shocked he'd slept so late, then hurriedly attached his prosthesis to go find her.

It'd taken all his restraint not to take Tessa into his arms and have sex with her while he'd watched her touch herself last night. But his head had been off, and his heart out of order in a way that had him not trusting himself. He didn't want to use sex to combat the pain working its way into every crevice of his body. Hell, even into his prosthesis.

After she'd fallen asleep, he'd slipped away from the room to take a cold shower and jack off.

But an orgasm didn't help any more than the shower had. His anger over Dale's involvement only intensified, and sometime around zero dark thirty—thirty minutes after midnight—he went to the deck of the yacht and collapsed onto a lounge chair, fighting back the urge to scream into the night air.

At some point, Jack had found him and forced him to go

to bed. Once back in the room with Tessa, he'd wrapped her up in his arms and most of his anger melted away moments before he'd crashed.

"Tessa?" he called out once upstairs.

"In the living room," she hollered back.

He'd known she'd be safe on board, but that didn't stop the swell of relief from filling him at the sight of her. He set both palms to the interior doorframe and simply stared at her.

Her smile was like a bright beam of sunshine shooting back at him. She'd always be the sun. He hated he'd always be the cloud, and God help him, he didn't want to be what smothered her light.

"Why didn't you wake me?"

She was alone in the room, sitting at the center of the leather sofa. Her legs were folded beneath her, a cup of coffee nestled between her palms. The mug hovered just in front of her mouth as she focused on him, her long lashes fluttering a few times.

"Because you didn't come to bed until sometime after three. I know, thanks to the phone you gave me. I rolled over and checked the time."

His hands dropped from the doorway at the sad look in her eyes as she sipped her coffee.

He finally made his way farther into the room, testing his self-control. He'd woken with a "boner," as she probably would have called it, and his dick had yet to go limp. Seeing her look so stunningly beautiful, all sweet and innocent before him, wasn't doing wonders for the de-boning effort. *De-boning? She has me making up words now too.*

Tessa scrutinized him with her signature "don't give up" look, the one she used to kill him with back in the day. Downturned lips with a hint of a pout coupled with sad brown eyes beneath slanted brows. All that was missing was her playing, "No Easy Way Out," from the *Rocky 4* soundtrack to motivate him to get his head back on straight. "How are you feeling?"

"I'm fine." Her answer was far too manufactured. A lie. "How are you?"

"I'm fine." If they were going to play that game, he'd give her the lie right back. But for whatever reason, the concerned look in her eyes and the way she continued to stare at him had his pulse climbing. He might actually need her to play the song from his favorite movie to snap him back to being solid. To actually being "fine."

"Aw, there you are," Mya said, walking in just as bright-eyed as Tessa. She maneuvered around Gray and went to the bar, popping a coffee pod into the Nespresso machine.

"Where is everyone?" Gray asked her, noting the table lacked laptops and some of Sydney's other techy gadgets that had been there last night. "Shouldn't Gwen be here by now?"

"I'm right here," Gwen chirped, and he pivoted to see his niece entering the room from the back hallway, walking alongside Sydney.

Gwen set down her laptop, which had stickers plastered over every square inch of the back, and he ate up the space between them. He pulled her in for a hug like he hadn't seen her only two weeks ago.

Wyatt's going to kill me. "Thank you for coming all the way here. Who picked you up?"

"Carter. He's in the dining room yelling at someone in another language, so Sydney and I decided to come to this room." She smiled. "And of course, I'm here, I bloody live for this stuff," she added, her British accent sharp in her tone. Gwen glanced at Tessa and tossed out, "Sorry for the reason though."

"Just glad you're here to help," Tessa spoke up, lowering the mug from her lips, and . . .

"Your lips." Gray blinked a few times. Was he still in a foggy haze of sleep? Or was he losing his mind?

"What about her lips?" Gwen elbowed Gray in the side before dropping down in a chair as Oliver walked into the room.

And when did you get back? I can't believe I slept in so late.

"Oliver gave me his ChapStick." Tessa set her focus on Oliver as Gray mindlessly accepted a coffee mug from Mya, cocked a brow, and waited for Tessa to elaborate.

Oliver held up his palms and a smirk spread across his lips as he dropped onto the couch next to her. Gray was feeling all kinds of stupid and jealous, and Oliver must've recognized that because he left a respectable amount of space between them. "While you were getting your beauty sleep, she asked Sydney for some ChapStick. I happened to have a new pack."

"What, not a fan of dry lips?" Mya shot Oliver a funny look.

"We work a lot of cold-weather ops. And no, I'm not a fan of chapped lips." Oliver rolled his eyes at Mya. "Hell, I even carry some tubes in my medic bag." He glanced at Tessa and winked. "It was her lucky day, and I was able to satisfy her obsession with lip balm."

"Coconut flavored," Tessa said, her eyes glinting. "Not blueberry." A knowing smile teased her lips, and he remembered what he'd said to her last night—including the truth about how he felt about her lip balm and the things it made him want to do.

"You have coconut lip gloss?" Mya chuckled and joined Sydney and Gwen at the table, flipping open her laptop.

"It's *balm*." Oliver shrugged. "And yeah, I like to feel like I'm at the beach when my nut sack is freezing off in whatever Arctic-cold areas y'all drag my ass to."

"I can punch him for you if you'd like," Mya piped up, and maybe that wasn't such a terrible idea? "It'd make my day. Really."

Gwen smiled as she kept typing without joining in on the conversation. Now, sitting next to Gwen, Sydney appeared just as engrossed in whatever she was doing. *God help us, hopefully getting leads.*

He set his back to the bar and sipped the coffee, stealing another look at Tessa. Her hair had dried in her sleep, so it was wavy and messy over her shoulders. Mya must've provided Tessa an entire wardrobe. She had on jeans today paired with a white hoodie with **Wait . . . What?** written on it in bold blue.

"When'd you get back?" Gray finally asked Oliver, needing a distraction from thinking about sucking the balm free from Tessa's lips.

"Jack and Griffin swapped places with Jesse and me," Oliver answered around a yawn while he stretched, nearly whacking Tessa with his elbow in the process. "Jesse's getting some rack time now."

"Maybe you should get some sleep too?" Tessa suggested, eyes on Oliver.

"Nah, Jesse let me sleep in the car last night while we were there. I'm solid."

"Jack shouldn't be there." *He might go after Dale.* And damn, now he'd have to let Gwen know Dale was involved, and he wasn't sure how she'd take the news. "Also, not the best idea to put him in a car all day with Griffin. They'll kill each other."

"They'll be fine." Oliver patted his stomach. "I don't need

sleep, but I am famished. I'll go see what's in the kitchen." He stood and flipped his ball cap backward, starting for the hallway.

"Make something for me too. I'm starving," Mya called out, halting Oliver mid-step.

He looked back at her. "Not on your life, buttercup."

"Call me buttercup one more time. I dare you." Mya leaned back in the seat, peering at Oliver with narrowed eyes.

Oliver fully faced the room, then proceeded to stalk her way with determined strides. He gripped the back of the empty chair next to her and leaned in close. "Buttercup. Honey. Sugar. Doll face. I can keep going if you'd like." He kissed the air, and Mya covered his lips with her palm.

A second later, Mya winced and pulled her hand back. "You nipped me."

"Don't put your hand in places it doesn't belong, then, *buttercup*." Oliver righted himself, sending her a cocky smile.

It was too early for Gray to deal with their usual back-and-forth.

"Do yourself a favor, stay away from him if you value your sanity," Mya said, eyes on Gwen, and Gwen shot Oliver an amused look.

That smile on Gwen's face had Gray's heart thundering. *Oh, hell no.* He lowered his cup to his side, remembering Gwen had a thing for guys over thirty-five. He'd recently helped Wyatt scare off Gwen's thirty-seven-year-old boyfriend.

"Anyone other than Mya hungry?" Oliver focused on Gwen, surely just to piss off Mya. "Can I make you some flapjacks?"

"Sure." Gwen tucked her blonde hair behind her ears, her cheeks tinted with a hint of pink, before returning her fingers to the keyboard.

"No, she doesn't need your pancakes. Or flap-whatever." Gray peered out the window and noticed they were docked. Of course it made sense given they had to pick up Gwen. And Oliver and Jesse were now on board. "Bagels. See if there are bagels or donuts or something. For *everyone*. If not, go buy some."

"Roger that." Oliver mock-saluted him, then left, leaving Gray alone with the four women.

"So," Mya jumped right into it, "I thought you'd want to know we identified those other Americans from yesterday. They served with Dale in the Marines."

Our enemy is a bunch of Marines. What the hell? "And where are we on the detective's phone?" He also needed to follow up on the detective's surgery, find out whether he was still alive.

"His last incoming call was from an unknown and untraceable number," Mya answered. "And all of his previous messages and calls lead me to believe the man is innocent."

He'd more than likely been a pawn in Dale's game, and that had Gray's blood heating.

"Also," Mya continued, "he received some encrypted messages from Turkish Intelligence. Seems the detective was opposed to using you or Tessa in any political games, but his superiors ordered him to escort the officers to the hotel anyway."

"So, he was a stand-up guy." Gray didn't regret being cautious, but he couldn't help but feel like a dick because of it.

"Looks that way," Mya said. "Carter's planning to make some calls and check on his status."

"Okay, good. Keep me posted." Gray turned his attention back on his niece, ready to rip the Band-Aid off and get the uncomfortable conversation over with. "Gwen, can I talk to you outside?"

She stopped typing and looked up. "Yeah, of course." Pointing to her screen, she said something to Sydney about layers of encryption and firewalls before standing to follow him.

"I think we're getting close to finding the source of all the hacks," Sydney said. "Thanks to your niece."

Gwen shook her head. "You were pretty much knocking at the hacker's door before I arrived. Don't sell your cyber skills short."

"I appreciate the ego boost. It may have been needed." Sydney smirked, and then Gray motioned toward the exit.

"We'll be right back," he told Tessa before leaving the room through the side exit to head for the deck.

Once up top, Gwen grabbed hold of the railing, focusing on the bustling city. "Warmer than I expected here for November." Yeah, she was about as good at small talk as he was.

"Sure you're not cold?" He frowned at her ripped jeans and the T-shirt barely covering her abdomen. Arching a questioning brow, he asked, "You realize there are holes in your jeans?"

"What? Really?" She hip-checked him. "You sound like my dad." When she faced him and crossed her arms, he noticed goose bumps there. Probably not from the weather, but because she knew he was about to drop shit news on her. "But we're not here to talk about my jeans."

He squinted against the sun in his face as he cut straight to it. "Last night we discovered that Dale Franklin is here. And he's after Tessa. I'm not sure how he fits into this, or why he's here, but I wouldn't have asked you to come had I known he was involved."

She opened her mouth, but nothing came out. He caught sight of the tongue piercing her father hated as she said, "You don't need to worry about me."

"Of course I'm going to worry."

Silence gripped the morning air and Gray wondered if Tessa was right. Silence wasn't so golden, especially when on the receiving end of it.

"It's *you* I'm worried about," Gwen finally spoke up. "Jack too."

He reached for her arm and lightly squeezed. "We're fine." Damn that word. The lie that weaved through it almost every time it was used.

"Natasha and I asked you to keep the truth from Wyatt and your father." Her regretful tone made his chest tighten. "That's a heavy weight you've had to carry."

He let go of her. "I understand why you asked."

"Because Dad would've killed him. You know how obsessed he is about my safety. Natasha's, too, of course." She ran her fingers through her blonde hair and released a heavy breath. "And my guess is now you wish you had."

"I, um." He cleared his throat. "I nearly did last year."

"Wait . . . what?" Now Tessa's sweatshirt felt that much more on point today. Hell, this whole trip could be summed up into those two words.

Why am I thinking about that? My focus is so F'ed. He blinked in surprise. Being around Tessa had him wanting to curb his sailor's mouth, even in his head.

"Anyways." He did his best to abandon his wayward thoughts. "I'm thinking Dale's going to be gunning for me now that he knows I'm in his way, and I have no intention of letting him have her."

"You like her, don't you?" A small smile played across her lips. Gwen may have been twenty-three, but she had the wisdom and maturity of someone his age. Maybe, in part, he understood why she dated older guys. Not that he'd ever tell Wyatt that. He didn't have a death wish. "Do you have a history together?"

A history? Yeah, I'd say so. "We do, and it's complicated."

"Well, nothing good in life is ever easy. You know that." She sighed and set her eyes back on the postcard view of the city.

He didn't want Gwen feeling the need to hide her feelings about Dale's presence, but he wasn't quite sure how to navigate the waters with what to say.

"On my flight here, I worked on a few things," she shared, her tone a bit distant as if working hard to ignore her true feelings on the fact Dale was in Turkey too. "The hospital records were altered."

"The tox report you mean?"

"Yeah. I can't see her original results, but I can tell the records were messed with."

What in the hell is going on? Before he could say more, he realized they had company. He turned to see Carter there.

"I have an update on the detective," Carter revealed. "He pulled through surgery. Still alive. And according to the police reports, he told his team the shooter was masked and in a Renault. The hotel security footage was screwed with, so the police never saw what happened on camera. But since you were seen getting into a different car after the shooting—adds enough reasonable doubt for the department here to believe you may not be the suspect."

"Tessa will be relieved to hear that," Gray said as he caught sight of Sydney joining them on deck.

"Your program worked," Sydney rushed out. "We know who's responsible for the hack at the hospital yesterday, and it's not a hacker." She looked back and forth between everyone. "And now it makes sense how they could pull all of this off."

"Who?" Gray snapped out, not in the mood for suspense. He'd had enough for a lifetime.

"Not so much a who as a what." Sydney came closer before revealing, "The National Security Agency." She focused on Gray and freed a deep breath. "I'm pretty sure they're responsible for taking her. And it looks like someone at the NSA wants her back."

CHAPTER TWENTY-TWO

PACING? *CHECK.* FINGERS CLAWING THROUGH HER HAIR? *OF course.* Wild, thumping slaps against her rib cage from her heart? *Without a doubt.*

Nope, I'm not good. Not even close to okay. And screw fine.

Tessa's eyes were so blurred from unshed tears she barely saw Gray rejoining them.

Without hesitation, he wordlessly pulled her into his arms and held her tight. When he cupped the back of her head, she turned her cheek to his chest and slipped her arms around his body, the movement jostling free a few tears.

She was on the verge of full-blown panic because a United States government agency wanted her. *But why?*

"I've got you," he whispered, taking his time with her as he always did, despite the gravity of the moment.

"I know," she mouthed, catching a teardrop on her lip.

Gray didn't seem to be in a hurry to let go of her, and she'd swear, the way he was staring at her mouth, he was moments away from kissing her. Not to silence her panic amidst the fear and chaos this time. To possibly silence the storm going on inside himself. She could see it brewing. A mix of anger and worry in those light green eyes. A need to punish someone for putting her through this.

"Does this mean someone at the NSA hired Dale and his team?" she overheard Gwen ask, and at her words, Tessa untangled herself from Gray's comforting arms.

She had to focus. Get calm and quiet her mind. *Who am I kidding? Normal for me is a million thoughts running every which way.*

"Government agencies often outsource to private contractors who have military clearance, yes," Carter explained, and his words had her shivering. "The fact the NSA is willing to use such extreme methods must mean they're dealing with an issue related to national security."

Gray kept a hand at her back while turning his attention toward the others, most of whom sat with a laptop or device in hand in the crowded room. "I think it's safe to say Tessa was taken, only to be let go because someone needs her as—"

"Bait?" The word popped from Tessa's mouth, and she released a shaky breath.

The room fell silent, leaving her alone with her chaotic thoughts, which weren't nearly loud enough to drown out every little sound around her.

Mya's chair creakily tipping back. The vibration from a text pinging in Carter's hand where he leaned against the wall. Gwen's swift fingers flying over a keyboard. The whistling from the Nespresso machine as a fresh brewing cycle ended.

Sydney faced the room with the mug in hand and took a sip, her nose wrinkling as if unsure how to navigate the "bait" topic and not because her coffee was bitter. She exchanged a look with Gray, and Tessa wasn't sure what Sydney saw in his eyes, but it was enough for her to break the deafening silence and say, "Tessa was most likely dropped off in a crowded area to draw someone out. Dale and his teammates were probably following her to see if whoever they're after would intercept her, but then—"

"I fell," Tessa cut her off. "Those other men, the Scottish guys . . . what if they're who the NSA is after?"

Gray and Sydney exchanged another look she couldn't read before Gray answered, "Possibly. But the NSA clearly still wants you back, so my guess is they've yet to get their hands on their actual target, whoever that may be."

Not what she wanted to hear. "So, we're not out of the woods."

"I'm afraid not," Sydney confirmed, her brows pinching in apology. "Since we're dealing with a clandestine government agency, they'd have access to pharmaceuticals not yet approved for the market. They more than likely used something to erase specific memories."

"Did they, um, do that because I'm horrible at keeping my mouth shut?" *Who'd they think I'd tell? The media? My father?*

"No," Gray spoke up, his frown deepening. "If you were supposed to be bait, they were more than likely worried that if you were caught before they could save you, the enemy would get you to talk. Share their plan."

Torture? She spun away from him, and his hand fell from her back, but he circled her and set a fist beneath her chin, guiding her eyes up to meet his. "If they still need you for that reason, it doesn't matter. I won't let it happen. Dale was probably brought in to get you away from me." Gray moved his hand to palm her cheek, smoothing his thumb over her skin in small circles. "You can't be bait if you're under my protection."

"I just . . . can't, um, believe the government would do

this." Fluid speech was becoming increasingly impossible, but she had to push through. Be strong. *Soldier on,* she reminded herself. "If they still don't have who they're after, well, it's hard for me to believe the NSA would order Dale and his teammates to shoot a detective to blame you just to get to me." *There's line crossing. And then there's THAT.*

"That might be Dale's doing." Gray's shoulders fell, disappointment in his former friend grabbing hold of him again. "But he probably has whatever-it-takes orders, and the government went private-hire because they can't be tied to his extreme methods."

"What about your dad?" Tessa asked him, and his hand fell from her cheek.

"Gray's father *should* know about national security threats, but that doesn't mean he knows every detail on how different agencies may go about handling the ops," Sydney spoke before Gray could.

"The NSA director reports to Under Secretary of Defense Jacobs, not my dad," Gray shared.

"And that means your father may not know?" Tessa looked at Gray for clarification.

"It's more than likely General Jacobs didn't alert my father to what's going on. At least, not the operational details involving you." Gray paused as if considering an idea. "My father would never approve of an op involving kidnapping an American, using her as bait for any reason. And he sure as hell wouldn't approve of what they're doing regarding me to get to you," he added in a low voice. "No, he only called me yesterday because Turkish Intelligence reached out, and he's trying to prevent a political issue. He has no clue what's really going on."

"At a very fundamental level, I know the NSA spies on people, but aside from that, my dad never really spoke about that agency. And not much about the NSA is ever in the news. What am I missing? Why would they want me?"

Sydney discarded her coffee and folded her arms over her black dress shirt. "They design cryptographic systems to protect U.S. communication systems. Collect and process intel on foreign adversaries. Have mathematicians isolate weaknesses in foreign adversaries' intelligence agencies."

Say what? "You're basically speaking Greek to me."

"Well, like you said, they're spies. They also spy on other governments, and they do their best to intercept and stop anyone from spying on the U.S. They gather and decrypt intelligence from all over the world. From a phone to a secure data network, to your favorite social media network," Sydney shared.

I get they're like big brother, but still . . . why do they want me? Tessa lifted a brow, and Gray frowned, appearing uneasy with the entire conversation. He seemed content to let the woman do the talking on this one. And Broody Dude remained as stoic as ever, his phone still in his hand, his ankle now casually crossed over his foot, quietly studying everyone in the room.

"Their budget and a lot of what they do is classified. They're one of the most secretive agencies out there. They weren't created by Congress, so they can act outside of congressional review," Sydney went on with her googled-sounding answer, still not sharing her guess as to why the NSA may want Tessa.

Annnd that's because you probably don't know.

"Not to mention in 2008, FISA basically allowed the NSA to monitor *domestic* communications without a warrant too," Mya tacked on what felt like bad news.

Tessa smoothed the Turkish evil eye on the bracelet between her thumb and forefinger, searching for some protection. And a way to calm her nerves. She was on the verge of panic mode again, and she knew that wouldn't help anyone.

"So, what Sydney is trying to say is that a top-secret spy group that is every conspiracy theorist's wet dream wants you, and we don't have a clue why," Gwen said, the only one willing to be blunt. "But we'll find out why."

"I'm a physical therapist. There should be zero reasons why." She made an O with her hand. "But clearly," she added as she gave in to the reality of her situation, and her shoulders dropped, "there must be, or I wouldn't be five days memoryless in Istanbul."

"I think there's only one thing left for us to do right now," Gray said, finally breaking his silence. "I have to talk to Dale. He won't be happy or likely forthcoming with info, but he won't kill me."

"He may not let you walk away either." Carter joined the conversation and pocketed his phone. He began adjusting his sleeves at the wrists, as if ensuring they were properly cuffed, as he added, "If he's desperate, he'll—"

"Maybe you should stop protecting me," Tessa took a bold chance to cut off the intimidating man. Carter's lips tightened, but he didn't look upset. "If I'm that important to national security, or somehow a threat to it, then you should let me go. If lives are on the line and I can somehow help people, I can't choose myself over others. It's not right."

Gray snatched Tessa's shoulders, forcing her to face him, a dark look in his eyes. "Absolutely not. We'll find another way. But over my dead body will I let you sacrifice yourself for anyone or anything."

She searched for the will to argue with him, knowing the man was stubborn, especially regarding her. *You left me thirteen years ago because you thought you were protecting me.*

"This is nonnegotiable," Gray added. "Don't argue with me on this."

She wasn't anxious to become bait, but she refused to let anyone get hurt if she could stop it from happening. And something in her gut told her that whoever had her those five days, convinced her of that very point.

"Dale knows you'll refuse to give her up," Sydney pointed out. "Which is probably why he didn't just call you at the hospital and ask for help. He and his men had to keep a low profile if they're working with the NSA. Hence the fire alarm hacking to draw you outside instead of an infil."

"That might have also been to prevent the other bad guys from going in and causing a mess as well," Carter noted.

The fact those unknown other men were still a question mark in everything had her head spinning. And she'd thought she was done being dizzy.

"If you go talk to Dale," Tessa began, trying to focus, to keep her sanity, "what if you're the one he tries to use as bait? Won't he try and force your teammates to choose? You or me?"

Gray's jaw tightened. "Then my team will swoop in and save my ass if it comes down to that. They'll know where I am."

"Hold up, Jack's calling," Mya announced, and Gray let go of Tessa.

Mya placed the call on speakerphone. "Hey, we have news."

"You do, do you?" an unknown voice answered. From the way Gray's face drained of color and how Gwen's shoulders fell, Tessa knew it was—

"Dale," Gray bit out, starting for the phone. He snatched

it from Mya's palm, his back muscles bunching together. "Why do you have Jack's phone?"

"Blame your teammate Griffin for that. Must've lost his edge joining your team," Dale said. The deep rasp to his tone slid under Tessa's skin, and from the looks of it, gave Gwen chills as well since she pushed away from the table and began rubbing her arms. "I knew you'd have my guys followed after they left the hotel yesterday. It just took me longer than I would've liked to find the fuckers watching me." A deep breath on the other end of the line crackled through. "Jack gave himself up in exchange for me removing the red dot laser sight pointed at Griffin's chest. I declined the offer. Got my hands on both. But you know who I need."

Need. Not want. That distinction mattered, didn't it?

"And you can't have her," Gray hissed. "So, next idea. I'm sure you've already relocated before calling, so—"

"We really do need her, Gray," Dale said, his tone grave. "Don't make this harder than it already is."

"Harder for who?" Gray turned to the side, offering Tessa his profile. "Just talk to me. Tell me what's going on. I know you're working for the NSA, and using Tessa like this isn't the way. The end never justifies the means when you take advantage of innocent people."

"If you knew what was going on, you might think differently." Dale paused as if reluctant to share more. Maybe he had orders not to? "My guys saved your ass this morning, by the way, and what'd you do? Run? But you're good at that, right?"

Gray bowed his head, his entire body visibly going tense.

"And we wouldn't have been in that situation had the NSA not kidnapped Tessa and dropped her off in Istanbul in the first place," Gray said a few deep breaths later. "What in the hell is going on?"

"I never thought I'd see the day when you're on the wrong side of things." Dale's voice was even-tempered. No hint of assholery. More like he truly believed what he was saying. "I'm the good guy here. And you're the one standing in the way of what needs to be done."

"What's your mission? Aside from getting Tessa away from me?" Gray pressed as if he truly believed Dale would answer, but her gut told her he'd never give up the truth. "You wouldn't still be after her if those men this morning were your marks."

"Unfortunately, those men were useless piles of limbs," Dale grumbled. "They knew nothing. We need to try something else."

"Nothing about what exactly?" Gray continued to fish for information. "What does the NSA want her for?"

"I'd have to say, Tessa falling and calling you was quite the curveball. We had no contingency plans in place for such a thing. Although, considering her rambly-klutziness type behavior when she was with us those few days, I should've had concerns," Dale said instead, ignoring Gray's questions.

"You son of a bitch." Gray's face went red, and his bicep muscle flexed as the vein shooting down his forearm became even more visible.

Dale was quiet before sharing, "We're on a tight timeline here, so I have orders to do whatever is necessary to get her away from you and your team. You have until twelve hundred hours to bring Tessa to the American Embassy. The brass would prefer you don't wind up in a Turkish prison for a prisoner swap, so they want you at the embassy with her. We also don't want you running rogue trying to pull some cowboy shit and derailing what needs to be done. You'll be detained until this is over."

"First of all, fuck you," Gray barked out. "Not happening.

And secondly, I'm not a lone wolf. I have a team. You get rid of me, fine. You still have them to deal with." He paused for a breath. "And if you so much as touch Jack or—"

"You'll what? Beat me to a pulp again?" Dale cut off Gray's warning, his voice flat. Not smug or pissed off like she half expected.

Gray grimaced before asking, "And you plan to let them go if we show up at the embassy?"

"My men will drop them off at a central location in the city if you play ball, yes."

"This isn't you." Gray faced Tessa, but then his eyes fell to the floor as if it were too hard to look at her. "You won't hurt people like this. Jack used to be one of your best friends." His tone unexpectedly softened. "We need to work this out. There has to be another way."

"She's our only hope right now. There is no other way," Dale was quick to respond.

Only hope? "What happens if you don't get me?" *Please, just give me that.*

Gray whipped his focus back to her, visibly swallowing as Dale dropped the hammer on them all. "Thousands of people will die, Miss Sloane, that's what will happen."

CHAPTER TWENTY-THREE

As Oliver rejoined the room carrying a box of donuts, it reminded Tessa of Whit and the donut he brought her every Tuesday. He'd assumed she was a sprinkle-type girl, and she never had the heart to tell him she really only liked glazed donuts.

"I need alternatives to the embassy," Gray remarked in a deep, commanding voice. Throwing his arms open in frustration, he knocked the box free from Oliver's hand, sending the donuts flying. "Shit, sorry."

Oliver took a knee to clean up. "Sounds like I missed something when I went on my donut run." He looked around the room. "What's going on?"

I can prevent people from dying, that's what.

"You missed a lot." Gwen rounded the table and blew past Gray, crouching to help Oliver clean up.

"Fill me in, then?" Oliver lifted a brow, eyes on Gwen. He set a chocolate donut back into the box, getting icing all over his fingers.

"Sure," Gwen offered, and Oliver gave her a lopsided but cute smile.

Tessa sat on the couch, drawing one knee to her chest, and she couldn't help but stare at the two of them doing something so innocent. Exchanging a few looks and smiles during the cleanup process. It was much better than facing the reality of their stark situation.

"It's my fault Jack and Griffin were captured," Gray ground out. "Griffin warned me his focus was as jacked up as mine."

Tessa's stomach squeezed at Gray's words. *I'm screwing with your focus.* Guilt sliced through her. He was starting to unravel, which she doubted was the norm for him.

Gray peered at Tessa with slanted brows and a determined look in his eyes. "Not your fault," he mouthed to her as if reading her thoughts. "Mine."

"No," she whispered, the word barely audible.

"Why is Griffin's focus off?" Oliver asked.

"Don't worry about that right now." Gray lowered his head into his palms. "Dale knows my playbook. He knows my moves. It's like fighting myself, except he's backed by a clandestine agency with a multibillion-dollar budget."

"But that means you know Dale's moves too," Sydney reminded him.

Tessa prepared herself to stand and go to him, but Sydney beat her to it.

Sydney grabbed hold of Gray's arm and smoothed her palm up and down his bicep while murmuring something too low for Tessa to hear.

I'm jealous. This is nuts. Sydney had an engagement ring on her hand. *She's not interested in Gray. Right? But why does my stomach hurt looking at the two of them?*

When Gray lifted his head and peered at Tessa, her cheeks flushed, feeling as though she'd been caught witnessing a private moment. Gray frowned, and Sydney let go of him before returning to her laptop. There was something in his eyes that . . .

You're keeping something else from me, but what? she thought as Carter rejoined the room, pocketing his phone.

"What if the hostage swap at the embassy is just a ruse?" Mya suggested. "And then he 'reluctantly'"—she used air quotes—"agrees to let Jack and Griffin go but his plan was to track them back to us all along?"

"No," Gray was quick to shut her down. "He knows Jack well enough to know he and Griffin wouldn't run the risk of being tracked back to the yacht. They won't come here."

"Then what's his play?" Sydney leaned back in her seat, eyes on Gray. "He's failing, and he knows it."

"And there's one thing Dale can't stand more than anything. Not accomplishing a mission," Gray said in a firm tone. "I need to think outside the box. Do something he'd never expect me to do."

"The only thing out of character would be to turn Tessa over," Carter pointed out, which had Gray glowering at him.

"He won't hurt Jack and Griffin, right?" Tessa couldn't help but ask.

Gray cupped his mouth before dragging his hand down the column of his tan throat. "I don't think so."

Tessa peered over at Gwen and Oliver quietly talking by the bar. Gwen must've filled Oliver in on everything because he turned to the room and said, "I should go wake up Jesse."

"I'll do it," Mya offered.

"I'll come with you," Oliver replied as she stood.

Mya gave him the once-over. "Thanks, but I know my way around this yacht." She waved him away, and Oliver mumbled something while crossing his arms.

"She okay?" Gwen asked while heading back to her laptop.

"That woman is a mystery to us all," Oliver said with a shrug.

"Well, I definitely don't think you should go to the embassy," Gwen said once seated, "but I've been working on a tracking prototype, and I brought it with me." She dug into a bag by the chair legs and brought out what looked like a sheet of clear, nearly transparent stickers.

"Those are tracking devices?" Gray asked in surprise as he took the sheet from her.

"Yup. Embedded in each sticker is a code. It's not like anything on the market. Not even off-market," Gwen answered. "So far, I've only tested them at short-range distances. Three kilometers. Like I said, they're prototypes. But if we need to track anyone, the sticker will blend in with your skin. No one will see it. No devices, not even ones the NSA has, can detect it."

"Damn." Sydney took the sheet from Gray. "If these work—"

"Then use one on me." Tessa stood before she lost her nerve. She was in a room full of brave people, and she needed to be one as well. "The NSA needs me for some reason." She opened her palm. "Let me wear one. I'll go to the embassy, but without you."

Gray shot Tessa a dark look, then ignored her before facing Gwen. "This may come in handy at some point. But it won't be used on Tessa because she will never be bait." He looked over at Carter. "We clear?"

Instead of responding, Carter went for his phone and took the stairs, probably to make another call to scare someone.

Forget Broody Dude as a nickname. He was more than that. Jack was right. Frightening, for sure. She was just glad they were on the same side.

"Thousands of people might die," Tessa reminded Gray.

"Dale could be lying about what he said to you. You can't trust him," he shot back, fire in his eyes.

"Gray, I—"

"I need a word alone with you," Gray cut Tessa off, snatching her hand as he spoke, and she knew a lecture was coming.

"Keep thinking. I need a plan. One that keeps Tessa as far away from everything as possible. And one that gets Jack and Griffin away from Dale."

Oliver nodded and took a seat opposite Gwen and Sydney. "Tell me how I can help you two," Tessa overheard him ask the women as she and Gray started for the exit.

Before they'd even reached the door, Gray halted at the sound of someone calling out to them from just outside the room.

"Don't shoot," a guy yelled, and Gray stepped around Tessa like a shield. "It's me. Wyatt."

Tessa looked back to see Gwen popping upright, knocking her chair over as she shrieked, "Dad?!"

CHAPTER TWENTY-FOUR

Tessa stretched her neck and pushed up on her toes to peek over Gray's shoulder, trying to match the voice to a face.

"How'd you find me?" Gwen flew past Tessa and Gray to get to her father, now hovering near the living room entrance, a snarl on his lips as if unsure who to yell at first.

And yeah, he was pissed. An angry bull ready to charge. The brim of Wyatt's black hat didn't conceal the heated look in his eyes. And his long-sleeved black shirt didn't hide the broad barrel chest and huge muscles appearing locked and loaded, ready to throw down.

But the moment he snatched Gwen's wrist and pulled her in for a hug, the harsh look fell away. He'd only been worried about his daughter.

"I shouldn't be hugging you. I'm pissed," Gwen said, but she didn't pull away from her dad. "You clearly violated my privacy somehow if you're here."

Tessa stepped around Gray to stand alongside him instead of craning her neck like an uninvolved bystander driving by an accident.

"Gray," Wyatt ground out while letting go of his daughter.

Gwen stood off to her dad's side as she waited for him to explain why he was there.

Yeah, how? Why? She was on the same page as Gwen.

Gray held up a palm, patting the air. "I can explain."

"I received half of an explanation from your father when my op finished in Moldova." Wyatt stole another look at his daughter, shaking his head. "He said you were in some trouble here."

"But how'd you know I was involved?" Gwen stabbed at her chest, then her eyes darted to the charms jangling on her bracelet. "Oh no, you didn't?" Her mouth popped open, and she quickly released the clasp, removing the bracelet. "The SEAL trident you gave me for my birthday has a tracker in it, doesn't it?" She chucked the bracelet at him, and Wyatt snatched it from the air before it hit him.

"Of course it does," Wyatt casually answered. "You have a tendency to get yourself in trouble."

Gwen's arms landed across her chest as Mya and Jesse returned. Carter was there a moment later.

"What's going on?" Jesse asked, stealing the words Tessa was sure would've fallen from Carter's lips at any moment.

Mya tipped her head hello to Wyatt, shot an apologetic look at Gwen, then went over to the table and sat.

"Meddling fathers is what's going on." Gwen's clipped response had Wyatt scowling. "Gray's dad called Wyatt, and my dad tracked our location."

Jesse hung back near the door, looking back and forth between Gwen, Gray, and Wyatt, waiting for more information. His eyes were red. Clearly, he hadn't rested enough.

"I forgot you two haven't officially met." Gwen tipped

her head toward her father as she peered at Tessa. "Meet my overbearing father, Wyatt Pierson."

Tessa swallowed her nerves and nodded. Best she could do.

Gray closed in on Wyatt while asking, "Where's my sister?"

"I sent her home to be with Emory instead of coming here," Wyatt said, a grit to his tone. "I didn't give her a choice. She doesn't know your father contacted me. She doesn't know Echo Team was being redirected to Turkey because of her brother."

Gray opened his mouth as if about to reprimand him for lying, but then he slammed his lips shut, clearly remembering the lie about Dale.

"How'd you know to track me?" Gwen asked as Wyatt offered her the bracelet, and Gwen frowned but took it.

"Your phone was off when I tried calling to check on you. Your phone is never off unless you're up to something and don't want me to find you," Wyatt admitted. "Imagine my surprise when I turned on the tracker and discovered we're in the same city."

"Did you tell my father you found us?" Gray asked.

Wyatt redirected his attention to Gray. "Not yet."

"Where's the rest of Echo Team?" Gray followed up.

Wyatt peered at Carter, then focused on Gray again. "I told them to hang back in the city for now. Your dad thinks they're running leads trying to locate you." He folded his arms. "What in the hell is going on, and why'd you drag my daughter halfway around the world?"

"So, my dad still doesn't know the truth?" Gray turned to the side, catching Tessa's eyes.

"What truth would that be?" Wyatt's brows dipped together. "He called my team to come here to prevent you from winding up in a Turkish prison. Not my normal gig, but you're family, so . . ." He let go of a heavy breath. "Where are Jack and Griffin?"

Gray motioned to the couch. "You may want to sit."

"I think I'll stand, even though I've been going nonstop for days." Wyatt shot his daughter another angry look.

"Fathers," Gwen bit out. "Overbearing. Frustrating." She looked at Tessa. "Your dad this bad?"

Tessa nodded, unsure if speaking up about her dad right now was the best idea. The colonel was still MIA, but hopefully, he really was backpacking in the Philippines.

"Fathers," Gray said under his breath, his eyes narrowing as if an idea hit him. "There's something else Dale would never expect me to do."

"Wait . . . what?" Wyatt asked, and Tessa dropped her focus to her sweatshirt, reading the same phrase there. "Dale, as in my ex-wife's husband, Dale? Just tell me we're not talking about him."

Gray faced Wyatt. "Unfortunately, yes, that Dale."

Wyatt dragged a palm down his face at the news.

"What's your idea?" Carter asked Gray while Wyatt processed how small of a world it seemed to be.

"Ask my dad for help," Gray announced.

After a few seconds, Carter responded, "I'm listening."

"If the NSA has a mission they need handling, one that involves national security," Gray mused, his eyes meeting Tessa's, "then we make him aware of the fact they're keeping shit from him. Then get my father to turn the op over to someone else. Someone we trust. Someone we can work with."

Wyatt's attention snapped to Gray. "Please tell me that someone is me." His forehead creased. "And while you're at it, tell me what in the bloody hell is going on."

CHAPTER TWENTY-FIVE

"Dad, you still there?" Gray set the heel of his hand to his chest, the throbbing pain growing by the second.

"I'm . . . processing." A deep breath cut through the line from his father. "I knew Dale had been having a rough time the last few years, which is why I'd called in a favor to a friend of mine to get him that job with the security company, but to repay me by using you like this is—"

"You helped get him that job?" Gray's stomach dropped, and an unrelenting pain twisted into one of the advanced sailor knots his father taught him as a kid.

"He asked me for help last Christmas. He said he was trying to get his life back on track, and he hoped I'd make some calls."

I should've told you the truth. But he'd leave the conversation about what happened at the wedding to his mother or Natasha.

"But I guess I understand why General Jacobs opted to keep me in the dark," he continued. "Not that I agree with that decision, but he knew my judgment would be clouded because of your involvement."

I understand that more than you know. His own cloudy judgment kept leading to mistake after mistake.

Gray looked out at the city from where he stood on deck, unsure what to say next. He wasn't used to having such talks with his father.

"I doubt the NSA director anticipated Turkish Intelligence would try and use me for some kind of political trade deal," Gray divulged his thoughts, unsure why he was defending the NSA. But deep down, he assumed decisions were being made to protect the "greater good." He just didn't agree with their tactics to get the job done.

"More than likely." An unusual dramatic pause from his father had Gray's temperature climbing a few degrees with every beat of silence. "Also." Damn that pause again. Not good when it came to the admiral. "There may be another reason they didn't pull me into the fold. And that's more than likely because of Tessa Sloane's involvement. More specifically, because of her father."

Where are you going with this? When his father didn't elaborate, Gray rasped in frustration, "I'm waiting for you to talk, but all I hear is that weird gurgly sound you make when you're bluffing at poker."

"Let me have this meeting first before I share classified intel."

"Classified intel about the colonel?" Gray pressed.

"Yeah," was all he'd give him.

Just perfect.

"Be in touch soon," his father announced, letting him know the conversation was finished. But then he surprised him by tossing out, "And, son?"

"Yeah?"

"I'm sorry for the call yesterday." A reluctant-sounding

throat clear followed. "For what I said." And then he hung up.

Gray pocketed the untraceable burner he'd used to call him, tabled his emotions the best he could, then headed for the living room to share what he'd learned with the team. He wasn't so sure he'd share his father's cryptic words about Tessa's father. The last thing he wanted to do was add more to Tessa's already heavy and confusing plate.

When Gray returned to the living room, he found Tessa on the couch with a pillow clutched to her chest.

Gwen and Sydney were at work on their laptops, and Wyatt hovered over Gwen's shoulder, watching her screen. Jesse, Carter, and the others weren't there, and Gray assumed they were off somewhere making calls. Chasing leads as the clock wound down.

"What'd he say?" Wyatt asked as Gray sat alongside Tessa and lightly squeezed her leg.

Gray zipped up his emotions for the second time in the last sixty seconds, then gave Wyatt his attention. "Apparently, the NSA director and Under Secretary Jacobs called my dad already and requested an emergency meeting at the Pentagon. He was en route when I called him."

"That must mean Dale called his point man at the NSA to let them know we discovered their involvement," Sydney said. "Something they most likely never expected, so they didn't have a contingency plan for it." She smiled her thanks to Gwen. "And now they're scrambling."

"I have no idea how they plan to do damage control after everything they did under Dad's nose." Gray grunted, irritated at the entire mess and at the NSA who'd helped create it.

If Dale had given the NSA the heads-up, that meant Dale *had* expected Gray to call his father. *He really does know me.*

"What are you thinking?" Sydney asked Gray, her fingers going still on the keyboard.

"Just that this is more than likely Dale's last-ditch effort to get us to play ball. He never expected me to go to the embassy. And he knew I'd put my pride aside and ask my father for help." *That's what happens when you grow up with someone, I guess.*

Wyatt cocked a curious brow. "And what? Dale wants to work with you?"

"Not going to happen," Gray bit back, the idea ludicrous. But terrifyingly possible, considering his father didn't know what happened the night of the wedding last year. "This job is a paycheck for Dale. If he doesn't get his hands on Tessa, he doesn't get paid. And he's proven he'll do anything to try and make it happen."

"You told your dad he's why Turkish Intelligence is after you, right?" Tessa asked, her voice small. "That he set you up. Shot a detective. Surely, your dad can't forgive those things, and let him keep working the case. Dale has to know that."

"Well, my dad will force the NSA to turn operational authority of their mission over to him." Gray tipped his chin toward Wyatt. "Then to your team." *And hopefully, ours too.* Not that he had plans to bail regardless of whether his father officially allowed Falcon to work the case.

"How'd the NSA not expect blowback on this one?" Wyatt stood tall, crossing his arms.

"Because the powers that be at the NSA think they're untouchable. That they can do whatever they want in the name of protecting America," Gwen shot back, a bitter edge to her voice. As a hacker, she wasn't the biggest fan of the government. "And are you surprised? The CIA gets its hands pretty dirty too. Not as bad as overthrowing regimes like they used to," she continued, "but still." She twisted in her chair to peek back at her dad. "End never justifies the means," she repeated what Gray had told Dale earlier.

"Don't tell me you're also a conspiracy theorist," Wyatt begged while wrinkling his nose. "And also, why does your comment feel directed toward me as well?"

"I'm not sure what I am," Gwen said casually. "And yes, it was intended for you too."

Wyatt arched a brow. "I don't regret the tracker. I wouldn't have found any of you if not for that gift."

"I'd hardly call my invasion of privacy a gift." She rolled her eyes and returned her focus to her computer screen.

"Are you okay?" Tessa whispered to him, pulling Gray's focus away from the tennis match between Gwen and Wyatt.

He wasn't remotely okay. The list went on and on as to why he was far from it. But he smiled and said, "If you're okay, I'm okay." When her sleeve slipped down, baring her shoulder, a memory from their past catapulted to his mind at the sight of her freckles. "Still have a galaxy there." And there it was, what he needed—a genuine smile from her, one that met her eyes.

"I really could fall in love with you again," she shocked him by blurting before squeezing closed her eyes as her cheeks tinted pink.

Again? You loved me before? His heart thumped harder. Beats of regret for hurting her when he'd walked away.

Sydney stood, sending him a funny smile like she was happy for him, then she angled her head toward the door. "I should find the others and tell them what your dad said."

"Right." Gray tore his hand through his hair. "That should've been one of my first thoughts."

"It's fine. You have a lot going on," Sydney said, already heading for the door.

Gray looked back at Tessa to see if she'd peeled open her eyes and shed the embarrassment she didn't need to have.

"Sorry," she whispered, eyes on him.

He leaned in and set his mouth to her ear, unable to stop himself, "Your rambling bluntness happens to be something I love about you." *Love.* Her word. Now his. And he was shocked at how comfortable it felt rolling from his tongue.

"When's the rest of your team getting here?" Gwen asked her dad, and her question had Gray returning his focus back to Wyatt.

"I'm hesitant to fill this yacht up to capacity until we know what Admiral Chandler says," Wyatt said. "And we don't have our version of Sydney with us."

Tessa chuckled. "Your version of Sydney?"

"Echo Four's wife normally works with us, but she's home with their daughter. My wife filled in for her on the job in Moldova."

"So, what you're saying is you need a woman to do the heavy lifting and without one . . ." Gwen let her words trail off before winking at her dad.

"Sounds about right." Wyatt discarded his uneasy smile before saying, "I still can't believe the NSA approved of Dale using Tessa like this."

Gray spotted Gwen's shoulders flinching when her father used Dale's name. She peeked over at Gray, a plea in her eyes not to share the truth about Dale, and although his shoulders fell a bit more under the weight of so many secrets, he discreetly nodded.

"I knew you and Dale had a falling out, but damn," Wyatt went on, reaching for the brim of his hat and spinning the cap backward.

"When was the last time you talked to your ex, Clara?" Gray couldn't help but ask, curious if Dale's wife wound up forgiving Dale for putting her through all the rough times that led up to Gray firing him from his company.

"Honestly, we lost touch. I'm assuming she pulled away when things became hard with Dale. But they're still married. No kids," Wyatt answered.

Gray was focused on Wyatt, but he didn't miss Gwen's startled reaction to whatever was on her screen just before she peered at Tessa with a dismayed look.

"What is it?" Gray stood, prepared to react quickly to whatever intel they were about to hear.

"Sydney and I have been trying to track down where Tessa was before her fall," Gwen began, her gaze shifting from Tessa to Gray's as he approached. "And well, I just found her in Cyprus . . ." She hesitated, and the hairs on his arm stood in anticipation of what was to come. "But she's not alone on the surveillance footage."

"What am I doing?" Tessa asked, standing alongside Gray now. "Who am I with?"

Gwen's eyes were sympathetic as she swiveled the screen around and unpaused the footage, allowing it to play.

Gray checked the time and date stamp. Wednesday night. A day before Tessa woke up in Istanbul. It was a parking lot outside a nightclub. There was a black Suburban with the door open and two men motioning for her to get inside, and then—

"My *dad* is with me?" Tessa covered her mouth at the sight of her father stepping into view of the camera. Gray looped his arm protectively around Tessa's back as she leaned into him for support.

There was no sound in the video, but it was obvious the two men wanted Tessa and her father to get into the SUV. Her dad was holding her back, refusing to allow her to get inside.

Gwen paused the footage and looked up at them. "You may not want to see what happens next."

Tessa's hand fell from her face as she stared at Gwen. "Why not?"

"Because your dad is um . . ." Gwen started, "about to kill those men." She cleared her throat. "*All* of them."

CHAPTER TWENTY-SIX

GRAY FOCUSED ON TESSA AS SHE SAT NEXT TO GWEN AND stared at the screen. It was her third time watching the footage of her father pulling a gun from the back of his pants and shooting the two armed men who'd been trying to force Tessa into the SUV. Once they'd been neutralized, he'd taken out the driver with a single headshot, then one in the chest for good measure.

He'd never witnessed such moves from high-ranking officers back in his Army days. Colonels and the like usually sat safely behind computer screens while barking out orders. Sometimes Gray forgot men like her father had once gone outside the wire, and they'd been successful and survived to make it to such a rank.

Now more than ever, Gray couldn't help but wonder what "classified intel" about the colonel his father was holding back.

"So, from the looks of it, we refuse to get into the SUV, they draw their weapons on us, and my dad kills them. Then the camera footage goes black." Tessa stared at the screen, her hand at the column of her throat. She wasn't in perky or panic mode. From Gray's vantage point, she was in a state of shock.

Gray would have been more shocked had his father not planted the Easter egg in his head about the colonel on their call. "Whoever is heading the mission at the NSA must've wanted someone to see that clip, but they didn't want them to see how you left or with *who*."

"I guess your father is off the grid, just not backpacking in the Philippines. He's been with you. I knew we all called him Bryan Mills for a reason," Oliver said, and Mya slapped him on the back of the head. "He certainly proves age is just a number."

Mya glowered at him. "Not the time for jokes."

"I wasn't joking." But then Oliver winced, eyes landing on Tessa in apology.

"If I'm here, where's my dad now?" Tessa whispered, ignoring Oliver's comment.

Gray wanted to stamp out her worry. To provide her reassurance. But he could only give her false hope and lies if he spoke up. So instead, he chose avoidance, lifted his eyes to the ceiling, and kept his mouth shut.

"I'm sure he's fine," Oliver said, doing what Gray couldn't. "Probably at a safe house."

"Thanks." Tessa's small voice had Gray looking her way, but her attention was back on the screen as Gwen replayed the footage.

"Wait." Gray stepped forward. "Pause there, will you?" He leaned in between where Tessa and Gwen sat, setting a hand on the table, which earned him a whiff of whatever sweet-smelling soap Tessa had used in the shower last night. "Zoom in." He pointed to one of the men's hands. "I think these guys are with the Scots from yesterday. They have the same tattoo on the back of their hand as he did."

"That tattoo's called the Lion Rampant. Definitely Scottish," Mya shared, then snagged the image of the tattoo and dragged it over to upload into their symbols identification database. "Let me see if this tattoo is connected to any organizations or gangs. Give me a few minutes."

Gray turned his head, his eyes meeting Tessa's face. Her gaze dropped to his mouth before slowly rising back to peer at him. He could smell her coconut-scented lip balm. As if sensing the direction of his thoughts, her tongue peeked out between her lips to moisten them. He pushed away from the table and straightened his posture. Yeah, he didn't need to be thinking about kissing her right now.

When he shifted his focus toward Carter, nearly forgetting he was even in the room, he found him quietly studying him with concern. *Broody Dude. Yeah, that's how I'll be thinking about you now, thanks to Tessa.* Not that broody was strong enough of a word for him.

"Not sure why the NSA would have Tessa and her father at a nightclub in Cyprus. This isn't exactly what they do," Mya spoke up. "The CIA, sure. But I guess it now makes sense why those Scottish guys came after Tessa yesterday."

"No other footage found from Cyprus, right?" Gray peered at Gwen. "Just this clip?"

"Nothing else yet," Gwen answered without looking away from her screen. "I'm assuming the NSA is after whoever hired those men, and they haven't caught him. Otherwise—"

"We wouldn't be in Istanbul right now," Gray finished for her.

"And since Dale must be a private contractor for this NSA-backed mission, and he's still after Tessa, my guess is those Scots yesterday are only hired guns. And they're still looking for the head of their operation, group, gang . . . whatever they are."

Gray nodded in agreement, then focused on the screen. It was paused on Tessa as she stood near the open SUV door, one man directing her inside. She wore a skintight black dress with black heels, and it was a look he wasn't used to seeing her wear. "Anything yet on the tattoo?"

"From what I can tell, it's a symbol these guys all have. Kind of like a biker gang of contract killers, but I don't think there's a ringleader for their organization. A *Knights of the Round Table* kind of thing, maybe?" Mya suggested.

"I never want to hear the word knight again, thanks," Wyatt said after a grunt, then dropped onto the couch. He was more than likely remembering the infamous hacker, The Knight, that Natasha had dedicated her life to hunting once upon a time ago.

"Sorry." Mya focused back on the screen and opened a map. "They appear to be based in Dundee, Scotland."

"Any group member names?" Gray asked, but he wasn't hopeful, given they'd hit a dead end yesterday with the man's 9mm.

"No, but I'll keep digging," Mya said, her tone almost hopeful. "They were chosen for a reason."

"Right, rarely is anything coincidental," Gray agreed.

Tessa twisted in her chair and rested her forearm on the top of the seat. "Are these guys why Dale's men didn't just grab me from the hospital after my fall? Were they waiting for them to show up?"

Gray tipped his head, narrowing his eyes on her. "I think so."

"Colonel Sloane was under General Jacob's command. And Lieutenant General Torres, the NSA director, worked with Sloane as well. They all served together," Wyatt spoke up a few seconds later.

And my dad knows something classified about the colonel.

"Do you think that—"

"No way would my father agree to kidnapping me and erasing my memories," Tessa interrupted Mya. "My dad would never put me at risk. Not even to save thousands of lives."

"He's like me," Gray said under his breath, agreeing with Tessa. "He'd never let anything happen to her, no matter what. And if they were supposed to get into that SUV, her father calculated the risks and opted not to. Potentially blowing whatever the NSA had planned since they were obviously out by that club for a reason."

"This Scottish group was probably hired to deliver her and the colonel to someone else, and my gut tells me that 'someone else' is unaffiliated with their group. Hired help to add a layer of protection," Carter spoke the thoughts Gray had been pulling together in his own mind.

"So, Dale's team was forced to go with a contingency plan," Gwen suggested. "Using Tessa to try and draw out whoever they're after in Istanbul."

"And to prevent Colonel Sloane from mucking up the plan," Mya theorized, "they didn't include him in their new one."

Tessa's eyes fell to her lap where she wrung her hands together. "What could I possibly have that anyone would want?"

No clue. When his phone vibrated in his pocket, he announced, "Hopefully, we're about to find out. My father's calling."

"Put him on speakerphone," Carter requested, and Gray went to the center of the living room and answered the call.

"I'm here with NSA Director Torres and Under Secretary

Jacobs," his father stated, and the two men quickly introduced themselves.

"They've advised me of the situation, and after what I've learned," his father went on, "it's been decided it'll be best to keep Dale as part of the operation moving forward. You'll be included in the mission, but you'll work with him."

The blood drained from Gray's face. "What? No." Every part of him locked up. "Hell no," he added in case there was any doubt. "New plan."

The line went quiet and there were mumbles in the background. "Give us a second," his father said before muting the call.

But a moment later, Gray received a text from his father's "off-the-books phone," one he reserved for emergencies.

> Dad: Echo Team will run point alongside your men. But Jacobs and Torres are unaware Echo Team exists. I'm not permitted to tell them. Just go with this. Keeping Dale on the mission working with you is what they'll THINK is happening.

> Gray: And when Dale sees Wyatt here, and he runs his mouth to the NSA?

> Dad: Wyatt's men will use their alias, Scott & Scott Securities. Tell Dale when you meet up that you called him in for help. I can't publicly tie myself to them.

> Gray: You can't ask me to work with Dale.

Gray stopped typing when Wyatt came alongside him, and he showed him and Carter the message thread.

Wyatt muted the call on their side as well and said, "We're off the books. Only your dad, the CIA director, and the President know we exist." He looked around the room. "And you all, I suppose."

Gray's shoulders slumped, but he wasn't ready to accept defeat. He unmuted the call and declared, "My team can handle whatever the hell is happening. We don't need Dale."

The line clicked over, and Gray doubted the other men knew his father had been texting him.

"Dale's been running point internationally from the start," his dad said, "and it's been decided he should continue until the mission's complete."

"So, he wasn't the one who kidnapped her from the U.S. and brought her here. Is that what you're saying?" Gray caught Tessa's eyes for a moment, and she visibly trembled.

"A team of agents here intercepted Miss Sloane and explained the situation to her before she made the trip overseas," General Jacobs said.

"Intercept? Trip?" Gray faked a laugh. "Is that how you'll describe kidnapping an American citizen and taking her to multiple foreign countries against her will in your intelligence briefing? Or will those words be redacted?" Gray snapped out. "Oh wait, you don't report to Congress, so no one will ever know your unethical methods, will they?"

"Son," his father remarked, his voice dripping with a cautious warning to stand down.

"You don't have to like us, but you *do* have to work with us," the general fired back.

Maybe Gwen was right, and these bigshots—hell, even his father—believed they were above the law. All in the name of national security. *Now I'm starting to sound like a conspiracy theorist. But fucking A, if the shoe fits.*

"Dale knows all of the details," the general went on. "We've agreed with Admiral Chandler we can bring your men into this, but *only* if you play ball. Dale can send the rest of his crew home. Too many cooks in the kitchen."

"Remind me of which game we're playing exactly. Football? Basketball? Baseball?" Gray glared at the phone. "Nah, you're probably golfers." He nodded, not that they could see him. "Is that the kind of ball we're playing? You looking for a hole in one, *sir?*" He spat out that last word as if it were dirty.

"Are you done spewing bullshit?" the general asked, seemingly unaffected by Gray's words.

You're too comfortable. "Dale can't be trusted. He shot a Turkish detective and framed me for it. He took two of my men as hostages."

"And we apologize you were pulled into this," Director Torres spoke up, taking a softer approach than the general. "That shouldn't have happened. We never expected her to call you."

"And what did you expect?" Gray bit out. "For someone else to get ahold of her? Who? What in the hell is really going on?"

"And where's my father?" Tessa called out, and Gray shot her a sympathetic look. "Is he okay?"

"How'd you . . .?" Director Torres left his words hanging.

"We know more than you think." *Just not enough.* Story of the damn mission. Kept falling short by about five damn days.

"Colonel Sloane is alive and safe," the director finally answered, and Tessa put a hand to her chest. "We need to get you all out of Turkey. We'll get Gray's name cleared with the authorities, but it's still too hot there. The original plan was shot to hell in a handbasket the second Miss Sloane fell and called Gray."

"It looks like your plans went south before that. When

Colonel Sloane and Tessa didn't get into that SUV in Cyprus," Gray pointed out. He was met with a long pause he didn't like, so he continued, hoping to bait them into giving in to his demands. "You drugged her. Used an innocent woman. There aren't enough apologies or excuses in the world that will ever cover what you've done," he hissed, seeing red at the memories.

"Miss Sloane agreed to help us in Cyprus," the general attempted to once again sell him on the idea.

"Yeah, and we have no choice but to believe you since you stole her fucking memories," Gray challenged back, his free hand bunching at his side.

Tessa nearly knocked the chair over when she stood to get to him. To calm him down? Ha. No one could lower his blood pressure right now. He was lit up with rage.

"Gray." Tessa squeezed his bicep, urging him to look at her.

Forget two modes. I only have one right now. Anger. Because he couldn't even give this beautiful, sweet woman his attention right now.

"It'll make sense when we explain. But we did what needed to be done," was all Director Torres said, and that wasn't remotely close to good enough.

"We'll work on your next location and fill you in on the details of the mission over a secure video call once Dale is with you." It was his father this time. How in the hell could his dad agree to allow Dale to continue to work the op?

Frustrated, Gray unfurled his fingers and sent another message to his father.

> Gray: You outrank them both. Tell them to go fuck themselves.

277

Dad: Doesn't work like that. Director Torres doesn't report to me.

"Please confirm you understand," General Jacobs spoke up.

Gray turned to shoot Carter a quick look to gauge his thoughts.

"We understand," Carter answered in a nearly cutting tone.

"Dale's methods are not just questionable, they're unethical. He crossed lines," Gray reminded the room in case anyone forgot. Because he never would.

"And you wouldn't cross lines to protect the country?" General Jacobs retorted.

"What if we won't work with Dale?" Gray asked, ignoring the fact Carter had agreed.

There was silence for a few seconds before the general warned, "Trust me on this one, son, you don't want to find out."

"Not your son. Let me speak to my actual father. *Off* speaker," Gray hissed, unable to calm his mind or body.

"It's just me," his father said a moment later. "I wouldn't ask you to do this if I didn't believe it was in the best interest of the nation. And I trust you'll protect Colonel Sloane's daughter."

Now she's Colonel Sloane's daughter, not Tessa? That change meant something, something important, didn't it? "Dale's not a good guy," Gray tried again, unsure how this was happening. He stole a look at Gwen, an uneasy expression crossing her face when their eyes met. "I don't trust him. I can't work with someone I don't trust."

His father sighed before saying, "I'm not a fan of his methods, trust me. But he did what I couldn't do."

Gray scoffed. "And what's that?"

"Choose the country over family," his dad shared. Gray was shocked he'd admitted that given he wasn't alone in the room at the Pentagon.

"Dale's not my family," Gray said flatly. "If you make me work with him, I can't promise a stray bullet won't find a way to his chest."

"That's a risk I guess we'll have to take." His father paused. "But I know you, you'd never take an innocent life."

"Well, that 'innocent man' punched your daughter when she was pregnant, so—" Gray stopped himself and hung his head. He'd let the rage do the talking, and he'd slipped up.

"What?" The word had snapped hard and fast from Wyatt.

Gray looked down at his phone, realizing the signal had dropped. His father more than likely hadn't heard his last words. But Wyatt sure as hell had. And now Gray would have to do damage control.

Before he could say anything to Wyatt, another text popped up from his father.

> Dad: Dale will be calling soon. Give him your location. When he joins you, call us back. We'll be waiting.

Gray swallowed and handed the phone over to Carter, then gave Wyatt his attention. The room fell eerily quiet as Gwen slowly stood.

"Why do you look like you know something too?" Wyatt focused on his daughter, his palm in the air as if he wanted to push away the words he'd heard Gray accidentally share.

"We can explain," Gwen struggled to say, her words catching in her throat.

"Someone better. And fast." Wyatt looked back and forth between Gray and his daughter.

Before Gray could say anything, his teammates decided it'd be best to clear out. Mya hooked her arm with Tessa's, urging her to leave as well. Tessa hesitantly let go of Gray, a nervous look in her eyes, before she left.

Once Gray was alone with Wyatt and Gwen, Wyatt snapped his arms across his chest, his jaw locked just as tight as his muscles appeared to be. But then Wyatt's gaze seemed to soften as the realization hit. "The wedding last year. When I Facetimed Natasha from my op that night, she said she ran into a waiter's serving tray, and that's how she got a black eye." His nostrils flared. "Why in the hell did Dale hit my wife? And why'd she lie to me about it?"

"It's, um, my fault. Natasha and I begged Gray and Mrs. Chandler not to tell you." Gwen closed her eyes as she pressed her hand to her stomach.

Wyatt's arms plummeted to his sides, and the color drained from his face as he stared at his daughter. "What happened?"

Gwen slowly parted her lids and peered at her father. "Dale was drunk, and he cornered me in one of the rooms at the wedding reception. He was getting handsy. I told him to leave me alone, but he wouldn't. Natasha found me struggling to stop him from trying to kiss me, and she slugged him."

Wyatt faltered back a step, his eyes landing on the floor. Gray knew that look. Knew the anger. He'd felt it last year himself.

"Dale hit her back, almost as if on autopilot before realizing it was her," Gwen added when Wyatt silently processed the news. "And that's when Gray and his mom came in, and Gray knocked him unconscious. He was so drunk that he went down fast," she rushed out, her lip trembling as she smoothed her hands up and down her arms. "And Gray's mom threatened to kill him for it."

"I don't understand. Why wouldn't you tell me?" Wyatt asked, his shoulders falling. He stared at his daughter as if he'd just suffered a broken heart.

"Because you'd kill him, Dad," Gwen said.

"You're right, because what he did was inexcusable." Wyatt snatched her arm, drawing her in for a hug. "And today will be the day that son of a bitch finally atones for his transgressions."

CHAPTER TWENTY-SEVEN

"Maybe him killing Dale isn't such a bad idea," Jesse said to Gray as they observed Wyatt and Gwen's animated conversation near the bar.

Gray faced his teammate, some of his anger finally dialing down a couple of degrees. Jesse's dark humor seemed to be taking a bit of the edge off them. "He'll be convicted of murder."

"We can always help make sure the body is never found." No hint of humor to Jesse's tone that time. But Gray still doubted he was serious, even if the man had once been an assassin for the CIA.

Dale was drunk. Had an addiction and was struggling. And Natasha and Gwen asked me not to kill him, Gray reminded himself of the reasons he hadn't ended Dale's life himself, and why he couldn't do it now. He'd have to remind Wyatt of the same.

"Unfortunately, we can't let him. We have to talk him down." *That still doesn't mean I want to work with Dale.* At the feel of his phone vibrating in his pocket, Gray snatched it and frowned. The last thing he wanted to do was interrupt

Wyatt to tell him Dale was calling. "I'm going to take this in the dining room," he told Jesse. "Keep an eye on them, okay?"

"Yeah, sure." Jesse gave him a tight nod, and Gray quickly left.

He made his way down the hall and to the dining room where Tessa and the rest of his team had gathered. "Dale's calling," he announced as he entered, and Tessa's worried gaze volleyed back and forth between his face and the phone. Feeling every bit under the spotlight, he simply answered, "Gray."

"You called your father," were Dale's first words, and Gray opted not to place him on speakerphone. "I wasn't sure if you'd tuck your tail between your legs and do the unthinkable, but you did it."

"You didn't give me much choice. Clearly, you anticipated that move. You gave your bosses the heads-up, so they knew a call from the admiral was coming. But I'm guessing you didn't run the plan by them first. They never wanted my father involved."

"Desperate times call for desperate measures," Dale said, far too matter-of-factly for his liking. "You and me working together again. Wild, right?" There was a touch of nostalgia in his tone, not the coy or smug satisfaction of "winning" Gray had expected.

"Lead the way, brother. You know I trust you. I'll follow you into any dark hole," Dale's words from one of their last ops together echoed in Gray's mind, and his posture sagged a touch at the memory. "Just put Jack on the phone," was all he could stomach for a response. He set his back to the wall near the doorway for support.

"Whether you believe me or not, my goal has always been to protect national security. Everything I've done has been for that reason," Dale shared, straightforward yet again, then the line went silent before Jack came on.

"Hey, it's me." Jack's voice was a welcome change.

"You okay? Griffin?" At Gray's question, Tessa and the others focused on him, waiting for an answer.

"Yeah, we're fine. I'm sorry we put you in this situation," Jack apologized. "But is it true the NSA is involved?"

Gray gestured to the room that Jack and Griffin were okay while answering, "Yeah. Shocked Dale told you."

"Yeah, not much else though. Just tried to convince me he's not a bad guy. But are we really going to work with him?"

"Looks like it. It may be the only way to end this thing once and for all. You can bring Dale to the boat, but only him." He paused to give Jack a moment to absorb that unwelcome information. "But just a heads-up, Wyatt's here. And he knows what happened last year." His eyes met Tessa's as he tried to keep calm. "Don't let Dale know that."

"Damn. Yeah, okay." Jack's tone was more reserved than Gray was used to. "This is a bit much, even for me." He was quiet for a few seconds before adding, "We're about twenty minutes from your location."

Gray needed more time to get comfortable with the idea of Dale coming on board. But he hesitantly offered a quick, "See you then." He ended the call before Dale could come back on the line.

"Jack, Griffin, and . . . *Dale* will be here in about twenty minutes." He pocketed the phone, and his gaze fell to the floor, his thoughts all over the place. "I need a second alone before I see him. Excuse me."

He cut out without making eye contact with anyone, quickly bolting to the deck like his life depended on it. Once up top, he snatched a deep breath of air while lowering his head into his hands.

"Does alone mean without me too?"

He slowly lifted his head to find Tessa standing at a distance, fidgeting with the sleeve of her sweatshirt. "Never." He extended his arm and offered his hand. "Come here."

She stepped forward and took his palm, and they sat on one of the benches with a view of the sea. The water softly lapped against the anchored boat, and birds sang while soaring somewhere overhead.

It felt . . . peaceful. A sharp contrast to the chaos of his mind.

"I'm so sorry," she whispered, and he balked in confusion at her words.

"For what?" He peeked at her profile, finding her eyes on the blue sky.

"For getting you caught up in my mess. I mean, I don't even know what the mess is, but it seems pretty messy." That innocence from her was exactly what he needed. Just like thirteen years ago, she could lead him away from the road of despair and back to the right path.

"This is not your fault." Turning on the bench, he set a hand to her thigh and lightly squeezed. "And thank God I'm involved. I can't imagine what would've happened had you not called me."

She sat in silence for a few moments before asking, "So, what do we do now?"

"What I need to do is talk to my sister. Warn her that Wyatt knows and ask her to convince him not to kill Dale."

"Isn't she on a flight back home? And I thought Wyatt didn't want her knowing he was in Turkey because of you?"

"I think that ship has sailed." He laughed at his own stupid joke. The irony of being stuck on a boat with several people who wanted to kill Dale wasn't lost on him. "I have to tell her now, even mid-air. She's the only one who can stop him." He frowned. "And shit, sorry, I didn't even ask you. Can you handle seeing Dale right now?"

"He has the answers I'm desperate for, so yeah, I'll be okay." She shot him a semi-crooked smile, one that didn't show her teeth or cause "crinkles" around her eyes, so he knew it was fake. "I'm just not so sure we should trust whatever the NSA and Dale tell us."

Yeah, that's an understatement. He looked back out at the water, struggling to process it all. All the things he could have done differently in life. The choices he'd made. The *what-ifs* that nagged at him. "I keep thinking back to that night at the wedding last year when my mom morphed into some kind of badass and threatened to bury him beneath endangered plants, so he'd never be dug up. I just wish that whole night never happened."

"I can imagine." She rested her hand on top of his.

"Believe it or not, Jack, Dale, and I were once nicknamed the *Three Stooges*. The three humorous hellions." His eyes dropped between them at the mention of his former best friend. "I feel like I've lost that side of me over the years though . . . after the accident, after everything with Dale . . ."

"Well, I can still see that side of you. It's still there, and then some. After all, you're the reason I'm smiling amid all this chaos." She smiled, gently squeezing his hand. "Plus, you're the reason why I'm safe. I'm not sure what will happen between you and Dale after all this, but life has a funny way of working itself out."

He stared into her eyes, her internal light once again shining bright even in the darkness of their shitty situation. It was something he'd always loved about her. *I just wish she didn't have to be near the darkness.*

"Can I ask you something totally unrelated?"

"Yeah, I could use a little unrelated right about now." He chuckled, happy to have a distraction from his thoughts.

"Well, I was just wondering how you managed to live in Dallas your whole life with your dad in the Navy." She popped one shoulder. "Told you, totally random."

"It's a good question." He smiled. "Mom was a well-known prosecutor in Dallas, and my parents made the decision once they had kids that she'd stay there with us instead of her moving every time he had to. They made it work. He was always spinning up anyways." He flipped his palm on top of her thigh, turning it facing up in a request to hold her hand, and she accepted, linking their fingers. "What about you?"

Her slender neck went taut as she lifted her chin, allowing the sunlight to wash over her. "Even after my parents' divorce, Mom kind of moved whenever he did so he could stay in my life until I was eighteen."

"And what about your brother?"

She scooched a little closer. "He stayed with his mom and stepdad in New York. Spent his summers and every other holiday with us."

He lightly nodded. "So, where's your mom now?"

"Once I was in college, she followed her dreams and joined Doctors Without Borders. Last I heard, she's in Peru."

Last you heard? "You two don't talk much?"

"We schedule a call once or twice a month. But work is her life right now, and I'm happy for her. Living her dream. She gave up a lot for me. For my dad."

"I bet you learned to be patient from her?"

"What?" Her smile stretched. "You never saw the soft, cuddly side of the colonel?"

"I rarely saw him at all, to be honest. Our paths didn't

cross much because of his rank." *And now I'm wondering what else I don't know about him. My guess is you're missing a few pages on your dad's life as well.* "But no, never took your dad as much of a cuddler." Reality settled back in hard and fast at the mention of her father. "But take a bullet for his daughter? Yeah, for sure. I mean, I saw what he did to those guys on camera."

She frowned. *Shit.* He popped their bubble, didn't he?

"Can we go back to talking about normal stuff?" She made a dramatic *oomph* sound. "Pretend the world doesn't suck so I feel normal again?"

"Not sure if you've ever been normal-normal," he taunted and pinched her cheek with his free hand, trying to comfort her. "Don't worry, I dig *not* normal."

"Oh, you do, do you?" She angled her head, one expressive brow lifting. "And what would you call me exactly?"

That's easy. "Unique. Special. Kind." He stared into those big brown eyes as he leaned in closer, his focus dropping to her lips. "Beautiful."

"Mm. You forgot quirky. Rambly. A klutz." She smiled. "Really, I could go on and on."

"Well, I love quirky. And we established your ramblings are damn cute." *But . . .* "I'd feel better about you not tripping so much. That makes me nervous. We can work on that."

A genuine smile cut across her full lips that time. "We can, can we?"

"Yeah, if you're not too stubborn to listen to me. You're similar to me in that department."

"And do you have any evidence to back up the stubborn accusation?" she asked, her tone inching into husky territory, unexpectedly making his balls tighten.

He closed one eye, taking a quick tour of his memories.

He extracted one and said, "Remember how hard it was for me to convince you to trade in your flip phone for an iPhone back then?"

She chuckled. "Okay, me getting that phone was for your benefit. You couldn't stand listening to the sounds my flip phone made while I was sending a text."

"Yeah, the tap-ding-tap sounds could be used to torture someone into submission." He winked, and she rolled her eyes.

"The texting sounds were not *that* bad."

The fact some of the color returned to her cheeks as they slipped back into "normal" conversation had him realizing just how much she needed the distraction. *Me, too.* It was better to be up there on that deck with her than for him to stew in his thoughts alone, that was for sure. "I'm proving how stubborn you are right now, by the way. You can't even admit how much you loved the iPhone after I pushed you into buying one."

"Shiny new gadgets never impressed me. Still don't. But I do recall one benefit from that purchase—that selfie you sent me the day after I bought it was pure fire."

"Selfie?" He scoffed. "I do not take selfies."

"Then what do you call the photo you texted me? You were in front of a mirror, shirtless, in the picture you sent me."

"I'm sure my text was related to something medical. I had concerns about . . ." He snapped his fingers, trying to produce something. Anything. *Well, damn, something important, surely.*

"So, showing me your abs and the V lines disappearing into your sweatpants, an image that lived in my head forever, was for medical purposes?"

"I mean," he said with a fake pout, "there had to be a

good and valid reason." He skipped back through his memories, trying to recall the selfie, and then it clicked. Only because he remembered her text to him that resulted in his shirtless response. "Wait a minute, missy. *You* sent me a selfie first, so don't start with me. You're leaving out that important detail from the story."

"It was to drive you nuts as retaliation for forcing me to upgrade my phone." There was that beautiful laugh again. A slightly nervous, awkward chuckle that he wished he could capture and bottle up. Listen to every day of his life. Then again, a sound like that deserved to be free.

"Sending me a photo of you puckering your lips was retribution?" He grinned. "Sign me up for that kind of revenge any day of the week."

Leaning into him, she playfully swatted his chest. "It was to show you my new ChapStick. So, I sent you my lips to rub in—"

"I'm fairly certain I rubbed something that night after your text." He playfully waggled his brows, officially feeling younger again. Lighter. Free of any burdens.

"You know, some days I really did think you hated me," she said without any real sadness in her voice. Just giving him a hard time like she used to in the past.

"Some days I really did." He pinched his index finger and thumb together. "A little."

"Probably on the days I refused to let you quit."

"Pretty sure you not giving up on me is another example of *your* stubbornness, sweetheart."

"And I'll take that as a compliment." She sent him a cheeky, satisfied grin.

"But since we're making confessions," he began, pretending to feign seriousness, "I have one to make as well."

"And what's that?"

"I may have cheated one night while we played poker and *let* you win. There was a lot on the line." He thought back to that night, erasing the smile from his lips with the back of his hand.

"Like what? If I won, I got to pick the movie that night. I remember it crystal clear."

I remember everything about you so damn clearly. How was that possible when he could barely keep track of what countries he'd been to in the past twelve busy months? "Well," he began his confession, "you wanted to watch the movie *The Proposal*. And to save my manhood, I couldn't admit I wanted to watch it too. So, I let you win instead of watching my pick, the fourth *Rocky* movie."

"I think your manhood," she said, miming air quotes around the last word with one hand, "wouldn't be tested even if you asked me to watch a classic like *Pretty Woman* or *Dirty Dancing*."

"Okay, *Rocky* is a classic." He adamantly shook his head. "I'll even give you *Die Hard*. But let's not ruin this perfectly good normal-but-not moment now."

"Your signature bad-boy panty-melting devilish smirk is going to be kissed away in a second if you argue with me on the definition of a classic movie," she warned, her gaze thinning. He fought to smother a grin. The woman struggled to pull off "bad girl" when everything about her was bright and sunny.

"That's a lot of descriptors." He winked. "And kissing me is not a deterrent, by the way. Plus, I think you just provided me with another example of your stubbornness by threatening to kiss me as punishment. And let's not forget, you told Naomi over text you're stubborn. So, there's that too." He lifted his brows. Wet his lips. Then waited for this incredible woman to make her move.

"Youuu," was all she blasted him with, a little flustered, then fisted his shirt and tipped her chin as if offering her mouth.

And he took it. Slanting his lips over hers, allowing the insanity of their situation to continue to fade away. For the warm November day to wrap them up in a moment he never wanted to escape.

It lasted only a few quiet seconds before Tessa freed a small moan, and he realized it was because she was about to pull away.

When their lips parted, her shoulders fell. The weight of reality settled in, pushing down on her. Her eyes fell to the bracelet on her wrist that the young woman at the spice market had given her. "I've never much believed in luck or something protecting me. You think this thing will work and keep us safe?" She lifted her eyes, and he cupped her cheek at her innocent tone.

"Believe in me," he offered, his words rough, raw in his honesty. "Believe in me to protect you," he clarified before kissing her again. Close-mouthed, chaste this time, meant to do nothing more than reassure her.

"I do," she whispered once he eased back. "And now you know what you need to do."

He hated that their moment of normalcy had been ripped at the seams and was falling apart as the reality of what had to be done next closed in on them. "Yeah, I know. I have a call to make, and a sister to piss off."

CHAPTER TWENTY-EIGHT

"WYATT'S ONE OF THE WORLD'S BEST SNIPERS. LIKE THE best-best. His only competition for the number one spot works alongside him," Oliver said to Tessa as they hung back in the living room. She figured Gray had asked Oliver to keep her away from the possible line of fire when Dale arrived.

"So you're saying he can kill Dale from far away and no one will be the wiser?" She fiddled with the bracelet on her wrist, trying to collect her thoughts. She'd give anything to slip back into Gray's arms and the comfortable conversation they'd shared before he'd phoned his sister and told her the truth of their situation.

From what she'd overheard, Natasha didn't panic. But Gray had confided to Tessa before the call to his sister that she was CIA. So, she supposed Natasha would react differently than Tessa given the same circumstances. But still, the conversation understandably hadn't gone well.

"I'm saying if Wyatt doesn't kill Dale on this mission, there's nothing stopping him from doing it behind a long gun at some point." Oliver rounded the bar and handed her a cup of coffee.

"You're not very good at making people feel better." She lifted her brow and took a sip, grimacing as the brew hit her tongue. She liked her coffee to taste more like dessert and wasn't a fan of the plain black stuff Oliver had offered. "Oh, unless the idea of Dale dying makes you feel better?" She faced him and abandoned the bitter coffee on the bar top. "Also, Wyatt won't commit murder. I just don't believe that."

Mya joined the room before Oliver could reply. She barely glanced at Oliver before asking Tessa, "Is he bothering you?"

"Not everyone gets so annoyed at the slightest of things," Oliver returned, keeping his tone casual. "I can't breathe around this woman without her losing her mind," he tossed out as if accidentally verbalizing his inner monologue. "I swear, she'll suffocate me in my sleep one day."

Mya rolled her eyes. "Get over it. We shared a room. Once. And that was for an op. We had no choice and it'll never happen again." She looked at Tessa as if worried she'd get the wrong idea about her and Oliver.

Oliver's coffee mug hovered near his lips as he said, "Believe me, buttercup, I never want to share a room with you again either."

"Ugh, you drive me nuts." Mya clenched her hand between them and mimed an explosion. "I wish it was you Wyatt was pissed at instead."

Tessa backed up a few steps, trying to decide whether to bail.

"Oh, I know, maybe date his daughter," Mya hissed while folding her arms. "Then I can watch Wyatt wipe the floor with you."

Oliver set his coffee mug on the bar and leaned closer to Mya, his mouth nearly touching hers. "Maybe. I. Will," he remarked, enunciating each word for dramatic effect.

And yup, now seems like the perfect time to leave. She doubted they'd notice her hasty exit. They were too busy locked in some kind of staring contest. It was a shock they were able to work together at all.

She made her way from the room but went still at the sound of a loud crash coming from one of the other rooms. Or maybe that was furniture flying against the wall?

As she got closer, she overheard Gwen begging, "Natasha said not to kill him. She'll never forgive you if you do this."

Oh shit. Dale must be here.

She rounded the corner to see the dining room crowded, chairs scattered and knocked over. Wyatt had Dale up against the wall, his hand around Dale's throat. He had a lot more muscle on him than Dale, but oddly, Dale didn't seem to be fighting back.

Gray was at Wyatt's side, trying to pull Wyatt away from Dale, and Gwen was at his back, her arms circling his waist in what was clearly a wasted effort. She'd have more luck pulling the yacht out of the water alone.

Wyatt seemed unstoppable. But Dale was still breathing and not totally red in the face, so Wyatt was obviously withholding from choking the life from him.

"You can't kill every man who touches me," Gwen hissed, tug-tugging away with no change in Wyatt's position.

Without missing a beat, Wyatt rasped, "Oh yeah? Give me a list of anyone who has ever set their bloody hands on you without permission, and you'll find out exactly what I *can* and *will* do."

"Dammit, Wyatt," Gray bit out. "We need him. You're—"

"Don't you dare tell me I'm overreacting," Wyatt snapped back at Gray, tossing him an intimidating look from over his shoulder. His snarl punctuated exactly how serious he was.

Beast mode unlocked. Well, was bull mode a thing? Shut

up, Tessa. Do something to help. But what? She looked around, noticing everyone else quietly observing the scene, same as her.

"How'd you not kill him?" Wyatt's back muscles snapped together as he grilled Gray. From her vantage point, she spied the veins popping at the side of his neck. The situation was continuing to escalate quickly. "He hit your pregnant sister and—"

"We almost did," Jack said, almost too low to hear, but based on Wyatt's slight startling of his shoulders, he'd heard him.

"You knew too?" Wyatt spat out. "Did everyone but me know?"

Shockingly, just as rapidly as things had spiraled, everything stopped. Wyatt released his hold of Dale and took two steps back, and Gwen and Gray let go.

Dale slumped to the ground and wrapped a hand around his throat, but he wasn't gasping for air.

Because Wyatt's not a murderer. Angry, yes. But, like Gray, Wyatt wouldn't kill someone unless he had no choice. Like in the alley yesterday.

Wyatt spun around to face the room, his nostrils flaring. A new target acquired. And he'd set his crosshairs right on Jack. "Clarify."

"Gray and I beat him up so bad we nearly killed him." Jack's shoulders dipped with disappointment. But she wasn't sure if it was regret he hadn't finished the job or him recognizing he'd "almost killed" someone that wasn't an enemy of the state.

Tessa leaned into the interior doorframe, unsure whether she should leave, but she also couldn't get her feet to move.

"I'm sorry." Hearing Dale's apology, Wyatt spun back around to face him. Dale lifted his hands in surrender, remaining on the floor. "I know that's meaningless at this point, but I am. What I did was wrong. Drunk or not." His attention shifted to Gray. "You made me promise to get my shit together or you'd finish me off, and that's what I've been doing. Believe it or not. I even told Clara what I did, and we separated because of it. And she only recently took me back."

"You never bothered to apologize to Gwen. To Natasha," Gray snapped out.

"Would you have really let me go near them?" Dale's hand dropped to his lap.

Gray silently stared Dale down, breathing nearly as hard and fast as Wyatt. "You went to my father for help. After what you did, how could you?"

Dale bowed his head and tore his hands through his messy hair, his hat upside down on the floor by his side. "I was desperate. If I didn't get another job, I knew I'd spiral, and Clara would never take me back. I asked everyone else I knew first. I figured since your father and Wyatt never came for me, they didn't know what happened."

"It's unforgivable." Gray's hands went to his hips. "All of it. Including you shooting a detective yesterday to set me up. What kind of right-path BS is that?"

Wyatt moved back a few more steps from Dale, and he leered at his daughter as if uncertain what to do.

"Violence is never the answer," Tessa's mom always said.

Her dad? *"If you ask them to stop, and they don't, it's their problem if they wind up with a bloody nose."*

Yeah, her parents were two sides of a totally different coin. No wonder it didn't work.

Tessa watched Gwen cautiously approach her father as if worried she'd scare away a buck, and she hooked her arm with his.

"I wasn't lying when I said thousands of people could die.

At least, that's what NSA Director Torres told me," Dale said, his tone broken. Not heartless and cold as she'd expected. "My team was hired because we can go outside the lines when his officers can't."

"You shot an innocent man. That's more than outside the lines." Gray stole a look at Tessa, his gaze softening a touch when their eyes met.

"My guy was only supposed to clip him in the arm. The detective shifted at the wrong time. But he'll be okay, and the company will compensate his family. Trust me." She doubted Dale's explanation would be enough for Gray, let alone Wyatt.

"I forgive him," Gwen spoke up, and Dale's eyes snapped her way. "You were grabby. Tried to kiss me when I said no. Nothing a dozen other men haven't tried before. But nothing happened." She ignored the growl from her father and went on, "But I can't forgive you for hitting Natasha, even if she does."

"I really am sorry," Dale replied hoarsely. "I'll have to live with what I did for the rest of my life." His eyes fell closed. "And not being able to get drunk to handle that pain is torture. I learned. I'm sober."

"There will never be an excuse for touching a woman. For setting your hands on my daughter or wife. Alcohol or not." Wyatt stabbed the air. "So, you live with that guilt. You let it eat you until there's nothing fucking left." He pulled away from his daughter and crouched before Dale. Dale's eyes flicked open, wary but focused. "But if you so much as look at my daughter again on this op, I'll forget they asked me not to kill you." He angled his head. "We clear?"

"Crystal," Dale said in a low voice, then fixed his eyes on Gray as if searching for an assist Tessa knew he wouldn't get.

"We really are short on time, though, so if you want to save lives . . . we need to get you up to speed."

CHAPTER TWENTY-NINE

"I NEED TO SEE MY FATHER. SHOW ME HE'S OKAY," TESSA inserted herself into the conversation with the Penta-freaking-gon . . . *How is this my life?*

But the three high-ranking men on the web call, including Gray's dad, were stalling. She could feel it. And nope, no patience right now. All maxed out. She needed to know where her father was and what in God's name she'd been doing with him in Cyprus.

When no one bothered to answer Tessa's demand, Gray repeated it, nearly word for word, and she tipped her head in thanks. He stepped alongside her and threaded their fingers together, a visible show of support to the men on the web call.

"Well?" Carter prompted, growing impatient with their lack of an answer.

"One second," Director Torres remarked, and the call was muted as the men talked with one another, only their profiles on screen.

It was hard to believe Gray's father was on the other end of the call, and her own dad was the subject of the conversation. Before today, of the three men, she'd only seen Gray's father. A few times too many, in fact, since he was always on TV at the White House press conferences.

But after this call, all three men's faces would be forever cemented in her mind. The director and general both looked to be in their early sixties, with stubbled square jawlines and tired green eyes that lacked empathy.

"This is bullshit," Tessa overheard Jack say somewhere in the room, and she turned to see him sitting at the bar. His eyes were laser-focused on Dale, a glowering look instead of the amused expression that she'd grown accustomed to seeing from him.

And Jack wasn't the only one staring at Dale. If looks could kill, well, Wyatt was on another level. With his hands visibly straining in his pockets, his jaw tense as if he were grinding his back teeth, she assumed he was busy playing out different ways to kill a man and make it look like an accident in his head.

"We can't patch your father through right now," the director said, showing his face again. "But we can assure you he is secure at a CIA safe house near you." He held up a palm. "Before you ask, it's a classified location."

"The CIA is mixed up in this now?" Carter asked, stepping closer to the screen, his tone dropping low as if that was news he hadn't been itching to hear.

"They've been involved from the start." The words came out a bit rough, like Director Torres hadn't been eager to admit that.

"Start from the beginning," Gray demanded, squeezing her hand a touch. "I want to know everything."

"There's a lot to go through," Director Torres started, "so we're going to be as succinct as possible."

"Time is of the essence, yada yada yada." She spied Jack rotating his wrist, twirling a finger, his other hand gripping the bottle of whiskey.

"Just get to it," Carter urged.

"Three weeks ago," General Jacobs began as Tessa prepared herself for a long-winded monologue, "the CIA reached out and informed us they'd intercepted chatter that one of the NSA's highly encrypted programs had been breached. Three batches of classified documents were set to be sold to a singular overseas buyer. One sale had already happened. Two more sales were planned."

"Protocol dictates we do a thorough investigation to check for evidence of a breach," Director Torres added. "We have some of the best minds in the country working for us, but we came up empty. And there were no signs of outside interference or any bugs in the intelligence software the CIA told us was at risk. Either CIA intel was wrong, and there was no breach, or—"

"You have a traitor," Gray cut him off. Tessa peeked at him, witnessing his jaw tensing as he stared at the screen.

The director reached for his neck as if planning to loosen the knot of a tie that wasn't there. "We had to do our due diligence and determine whether we were dealing with someone at the NSA selling our secrets or if the CIA had bad intel."

Gray once again tightened his hold of Tessa's hand, and that little touch helped keep her steady on her feet. Rooted to the ground and to reality. Even a reality that sucked was better than not knowing what had happened.

"What'd you find out?" Gray asked.

"It took two weeks to pore through everything and every employee. During that time, the CIA reported the second batch of classified documents had been sold," the director said. "And yet, our search came up empty. No red flags within the NSA. We were about to close the case and consider it a nonissue when one of our own intelligence analysts intercepted an encrypted transmission over the dark net. We were able to decrypt and read the communication, then trace the message's origin. And well, that took us to Miss Sloane."

Shocked, Tessa stumbled back. "I don't understand." Her hand slipped free from Gray's, and he turned to face her.

"Neither did we," the director stated. "But the email came from a server at your office, telling the buyer they were ready to make the third and final sale."

"That wasn't me. No way. And Naomi and my colleagues would never—"

"We know." The director patted the air.

Gray stepped alongside her again and wordlessly hooked his arm around her, pulling her tight to his side, and he stroked her back up and down, trying to keep her calm. "Explain," was all Gray said.

"Tessa *and* her father were framed. It was a trap meant for my agency to uncover," the director shared.

"Framed?" *I'm going to be sick.* Her stomach roiled, and she pinned her arm across her abdomen.

"Why would anyone frame a retired colonel and his daughter when neither have a connection to the NSA?" Gray asked, managing to keep his tone even-tempered.

"Because Colonel Sloane worked for the NSA for eleven months before his actual retirement a little over a year ago. He was the manager of the very project the CIA claimed was targeted, leading to the supposedly stolen classified intel. Only those in the room with me now and those who were on that project were aware of your father's role."

Tessa waved her hand in the air. "I'm sorry, no, that can't be true. My dad's not a spy." She blinked, her gaze falling to the floor as she processed the impossible.

"Your dad was hardly a spy." She wasn't expecting humor in the director's tone, and she wasn't thrilled to hear it. "When he retired from the Army, we asked him to sign a consulting contract to work specifically on one project. We needed someone with real-life experience dealing with signals and human intelligence to help guide a team in creating a new and improved security communications system."

"Security communications system is a mouthful when you could just call it by its name," Gwen blurted. "*Spying.*"

General Jacobs frowned. "Who is she?"

"She's my granddaughter," the admiral said, the warning to drop it clear in his tone.

"What'd the program do?" Gray asked.

"Something you'd appreciate," Gray's father answered that time. "It was designed to try and mitigate risks for operators in the field. Prevent bad intel from sending our men into dangerous situations that didn't warrant our involvement. Reduce ambush-type scenarios like what happened to you and those Rangers thirteen years ago."

"Using A.I., the program filters through intel better than any person out in the field can," the director added. "Colonel Sloane dealt with those bad-intel ops multiple times, and we believed he could offer more personal insight on the matter."

Oh, wow. Now this is personal for Gray. Well, personal for all of us. Tessa peered at Gray, worried about him. He simply blinked at the screen as if uncertain what to say.

"But the colonel's involvement is another reason I was left in the dark on this," Admiral Chandler began. "Colonel

Sloane and I are friends. This situation would be personal for me."

"Some friend you are. You were willing to turn Tessa over to Turkish Intelligence to save me," Gray remarked, nearly whispering as if still trying to work his mind through the news.

But really . . . our dads are friends? Like what, golfing buddies? Why does that feel so weird? Maybe because it is. Because my dad told Gray to stay away from me. And yesterday, his dad told Gray the same. I'm in the land of make-believe, aren't I?

"You know I'm innocent though," Tessa began, pulling herself free from her thoughts, "so . . . when do you get to the part where you figured that out? I'd like to hear it."

"We didn't know who was innocent or guilty until last Saturday, to be honest," Director Torres admitted. "But yes, the traitor wanted it to *look* like your father was a traitor and you were his accomplice to cover their tracks with the NSA."

"And who was the traitor?" Gray asked before Tessa had a chance to get the words out. "I'm assuming not one of you in that room, so it had to be someone from the project, right?"

Director Torres nodded. "Last Saturday, we discovered the traitor was a former employee on that project. Your father fired him a few days after the completion of the project, just before he retired."

"That's kind of an asshole thing to do," Gwen said, and Tessa caught Wyatt nudging her in the side. A request, more than likely, to abstain from interjecting again.

"The man the colonel fired may have been an asset to the NSA, but he'd disagreed on how to use the program. He had ideas we weren't on board with, and he kept butting heads with the colonel. It was decided it'd be best to let him go," Director Torres answered, fidgeting with the buttons of his shirt while looking toward the ceiling as if . . . Was that his "poker" tell? Was he bluffing?

"You want us to believe that?" Carter asked, a mirror to her thoughts.

"Surprised you guys let someone like that walk away alive. Don't you spooks make people who know too much disappear for good?" Jack asked around a hiccup, and Tessa looked back to see the bottle of whiskey hovering near his lips.

"Jack, watch it," Gray's father said as if scolding a child. Then again, he'd known Jack most of his life, so he was probably like a father to him.

"We have protocols after employees quit or are fired," the director announced. "He was monitored for a year, and it was deemed he wasn't a threat to national security."

"And he knew your protocols," Gray remarked. "That's why he waited until recently to make his moves. But he'd probably had the plan in the works for a long time."

"So, let me get this straight," Tessa began, somehow keeping her tone steady. Not a single nervous tremor shot through her body. *I'm soldiering on, I guess.* "A pissed-off former employee with a beef with my father set us up? And although he no longer works at the NSA, since he had knowledge of the project, that's how he broke through your systems unnoticed to steal the intelligence? I assume for both money and revenge," she rambled on but with a decent amount of confidence. "Am I understanding this correctly?"

"There was no hack," Gwen spoke up. "There didn't need to be since he was one of the project's architects. That's why the NSA couldn't detect a breach. There wasn't one. I bet that while he was still working there, he was somehow siphoning out information as a backup plan for a just-in-case rainy day."

"Yes," Director Torres said, his frown lines becoming

deeper as if pained by the admission. "We think he was worried we'd catch on to him around the time of his third sale, so he decided to try and throw us off with that transmission we intercepted originating from Miss Sloane's medical practice."

"And you weren't the only one who traced the communication back to Tessa's office, right?" Sydney spoke up for the first time. "The buyer did."

"And the bad guys did their homework and learned who Tessa's dad was, and they decided they wanted to meet in person," Jack piped up, now standing, the bottle still in hand.

The director nodded. "But that in-person-meeting request meant the traitor would need Tessa or her dad for the final sale to happen."

"What was to stop the buyer from just coming after Tessa or her father themselves if they wanted their hands on them and now knew their location?" Sydney asked.

"Tessa was bait before she even knew it." Gray's arm fell from her back. "That's how you found out the traitor's identity. He came for her first, didn't he?"

There was a touch of painful silence before Director Torres answered, "We had a joint task force staked outside her office and home. When the power went out, we realized someone was coming for her. Agents rescued Tessa, but the traitor put up a fight and was killed. We sent agents to get Colonel Sloane from the Philippines, and we kept Tessa in protective custody until we determined the best course of action." He squeezed the bridge of his nose, then huffed out a gruff breath before looking toward the screen. "We couldn't find any intelligence at his house or on his servers. Whatever intel he had was hidden elsewhere. But we found seven million dollars in an account in the Caymans we believe was his. Another seven million in a bank in Europe."

"There was one other thing their men discovered," Admiral Chandler informed them. "This man had been watching Tessa for months." He pinned Tessa with a sympathetic look. "He'd been coming to your office bi-weekly as your patient."

CHAPTER THIRTY

"Please don't say it was . . ." *Mr. Whitlock. Well, Whitney Howard.* Hell, she couldn't even finish that thought.

Gray grabbed hold of her sides and crushed her to his chest, clearly sensing she was about to break down over the potential betrayal of her favorite patient.

"He used the name Matt Vizor with you." At the director's words, Tessa wilted in relief. "Last name was fake."

She collected her thoughts, then eased away from Gray and mouthed, "I'm okay." *Because Whit isn't a bad guy.* "Sorry, I was just worried it was someone I actually liked. And I didn't like Matt."

"Did he bother you?" Gray's brows snapped together in alarm as if he wanted to go kill an already-dead guy.

"Not like that." She shook her head. "He was just a jerk face."

Gray gave her a hesitant look, then reached for her hand before facing the screen again.

"I need you to skip back a few steps and walk me through everything that went down, starting with what happened after you saved Tessa, only to use her as bait *again*." Gray twirled the finger of his free hand in the air. "You're not off the hook. Not even close."

Right. There was still the unknown-buyer bad guy out there.

"Since we couldn't determine the buyer's name or whereabouts based on anything found at Matt's home, we realized Tessa and her father might be our best shot at finding out who the hell purchased the intel," the director explained. "On Sunday, using the dark net, we sent an encrypted message back to the buyer agreeing to their requested in-person meeting. But we insisted on choosing the location. We chose Cyprus."

"Just hand her right over to the bad guys so they don't even have to come find her, huh? Save yourself some time," Gwen popped back into the conversation.

She loved Gwen for speaking her mind. She gave zero F's about the rank of the men on that call.

"We decided it'd be better for Tessa, as well as her family and friends, if we didn't have her sit around and wait for the buyer to come to her. In fact, that was a requirement for her to agree to help us. We had to keep her friends and patients from danger," the director calmly explained.

"Sounds like something I'd say." *But I guess I have to take your word for it.*

"With her practice closed, best friend out of town . . . the timing wound up working in our favor. The only thing lucky about any of this," the director noted.

Luck? Sure.

"We did put in a request to her brother's boss at the CIA to ensure he was kept in the dark and didn't wind up complicating things." The director's focus cut straight to Tessa. "That wasn't coincidental."

"So, you convinced Tessa to help you catch this bad guy, and then you flew her to Cyprus for the meeting. Brought her father there too," Gray said as if still trying to wrap his head around it all.

"We picked up Colonel Sloane and his girlfriend from their backpacking trip. We couldn't have his girlfriend talking, so she's under our protection right now as well. And yes, then we brought Tessa and the colonel to Cyprus so Dale could take over from there," the director answered.

"Now, tell me how you convinced the colonel to agree to a plan endangering his daughter. Knowing him, he'd lock Tessa up somewhere safe for all eternity before letting her in on a mission." Yeah, Gray was right about that. Her dad was overprotective, almost to a fault.

"That was all Miss Sloane," General Jacobs tossed out, his tone stern. "She told her father she'd help us whether he went along with the plan or not. Said she refused to be put in some box for safekeeping forever."

"And you also made her believe thousands would die if she didn't help," Gray said.

Jeez, I nearly forgot Dale's words.

"She needed some motivation, yes," Director Torres confessed. "We also had Sunday through that Wednesday night to coach her through everything. And we promised her before we flew to Cyprus, we could mold her into being who we needed her to be."

"Me, a spy? I'm struggling to believe you could mold me into that." Tessa frowned, then looked around the room. *But I am facing my fears. Not a total disaster lately.* "I guess with the proper motivation, I can do anything."

"Was that 'motivation' you fed her an outright lie?" Gray pressed. "If not, how do stolen classified documents from that project equate to thousands dying?" He jerked a thumb toward Dale. "Even that idiot is sold on that idea. So what's the real story?"

"There is a national security threat, that much is true," was all General Jacobs offered.

"I'm assuming the first two sales still jeopardized your program and national security, regardless of the third sale, or you wouldn't be going to this trouble to put Tessa at risk just to save her life. Sounds counterintuitive," Carter tossed in his two cents.

"Of course her life would matter either way," the director answered. "But yes, our program is still at risk."

"What exactly happened in Cyprus?" Carter asked, his voice poking through her distressed thoughts. "We only saw part of the footage."

"The buyer didn't show up. He sent hired guns in his place. They explained to your father they had orders to take you both to an undisclosed location where you'd be stripped and checked for trackers, then wait for further instructions. *Not* what was agreed upon in the email. The risks of you getting into that SUV now outweighed the benefits of finding the buyer. And the men wouldn't let you walk away when you refused," the director said, eyes on Tessa now. "So, your father killed them. We were forced to move to a new plan."

"One neither Colonel Sloane nor Tessa agreed to. Am I correct in that assumption?" Gray let go of her and stepped forward, his back muscles drawing together.

The slump of the general's shoulders was all the answer he needed. "We had her safely monitored by Dale's team the entire time she was in Turkey. We hoped we'd have better luck the second time around."

A fake laugh fell from Gray's mouth as he turned toward the room and tapped his fist against his mouth. "Better luck, huh? That's how you run the NSA? Do you make decisions by flipping a coin? A little *rock paper scissors* to decide whose life you put on the line next?" Tessa reached for his arm, realizing he was on the verge of snapping. He shot her a pointed look, then his gaze softened into one of sadness. "You used her as bait, not her father. Why? At least he could've protected himself." When no response came, he spun back to face the screen. "What if the buyer realized Cyprus was a trap? Same with Istanbul. Maybe they gave up on getting that third batch of—" Gray abandoned his words and dropped his head.

"What is it?" Tessa asked, urging him to look at her by gently tugging at his arm.

"The buyer doesn't need that third batch of information," Jack semi-slurred. Tessa turned to face him without letting go of Gray. "When that traitorous bastard from the NSA offered the intel for sale on the dark net in the first place, he had to prove he had credible information up for grabs."

"What Jack's saying," Sydney began, looking toward Tessa while sliding her hands in her pockets, "is Matt must've shared on the dark net that he helped create the security program. And he somehow proved his intel was solid, and he was a credible source. But he kept his identity hidden to protect himself."

"But then he led them to believe my dad was the project manager. So, they think my dad can give them everything they need with or without the sale taking place," Tessa said, putting it together. "That's why we're in danger no matter what. Even if we were to prove to the bad guys we aren't the ones who ever had the intel for sale, they're still convinced my dad can give them what they want anyway." *Holy shit.* "You told me all of this before hitting control-alt-delete on my memories, right?" She dropped her hand from Gray's arm and spun to the side, her focus cutting to Dale, to the man who'd had her in his "care" for some of those lost days she no longer wanted to remember.

"If the buyer gets their hands on your father, they'll torture him until he gives them what they need to fill in the gaps. Until they know everything about the program that can then be used against the United States," the general said, harsh lines of worry deepening his frown.

"The risk-benefit scenario. The enemy getting their hands on the colonel is too dangerous. It'd be even worse than them getting the third batch of intelligence," Sydney said, her tone soft. Surprised.

Tessa shook her head. "My dad would never talk."

"Oh, I don't know about that." Jack lifted his bottle in the air, meeting Tessa's eyes. "What better way to get a Bryan Mills–type hero out of hiding *and* get him to talk . . . than to take his daughter."

* * *

"You okay?"

Tessa looked over her shoulder to see Gwen walking her way on the deck. The low fifty-degree temperature, coupled with the horrifying news, sent chills down Tessa's spine.

"Stupid question." Gwen held up a hand, and the sun seemed to bounce off the silver rings adorning nearly every finger.

"I just need a second to breathe. That was a lot."

"Gray was going to follow you when you took off, but I begged him to let me come up instead. Figured he could yell at the general and director a bit more that way." Gwen came up alongside her, pushing her blonde hair blowing from the breeze away from her face.

"The NSA is using me to catch a bad guy. And the buyer

THE TAKEN ONE

is after me to catch my dad." She blinked, still unable to wrap her head around it. "And all of this is really because some jerk was fired?" She fully faced Gwen, thankful she was steady on her feet and didn't feel there was a chance of going overboard. "You think what the general said is true?" She replayed the last exchange before she'd run from the room, desperate for air.

"That there's a target on your head?" Gwen squinted, then shielded her eyes from the sunlight with her hand. "That part, yes. But I don't think this buyer will tell anyone about the goldmine he thinks he has on his hands. Well, is trying to get. So, if we take him out, you should be safe."

"What makes you say that?"

Gwen smirked. "Bad guys aren't so great at sharing, and they don't play well with others. Nah, he'll hog this intel for sure. So, yeah, time is of the essence if we want to prevent anyone else from hunting you to get to your old man."

Hunted? Last week I was giving myself a pep talk and checking my teeth for food. And now this. Tessa thought back to the general's words following Jack's drunken declaration. "Protective custody, allowing the NSA and our country to be at risk, and letting the bad guys go free, or . . . used as bait. Are those really the two options they presented?"

Gwen tipped one shoulder. "I would've run from the room too."

"No, you wouldn't have." A surprising smile met Tessa's lips. "You would have told them where to shove it."

Gwen laughed. "You barely know me, and yet you know me so well."

"I'd love to have your courage. Also, your computer skills. I can barely operate Excel without a meltdown."

"First of all, you're a courageous badass. You risked your neck while also facing your fears—I may have heard you're

315

afraid of flying, boats, and small spaces. Now they're asking you to save yourself and your dad while also protecting the U.S. and take down an enemy *again*." She held up three fingers. "They say the third time's a charm, right?"

"Maybe for lucky people."

"You know what I think?" Gwen smiled. "You're actually very lucky. If bad stuff keeps happening to you, but you live to tell the tale, well, you survived. Not everyone does."

"Shit, I never looked at it that way. Maybe you're right."

"Also, you may have run from the living room, but you didn't make a beeline off the boat and abandon ship, so to speak." She slapped a hand to her shoulder. "Oh, and fun fact, Excel makes me cry too. Don't worry."

"You're pretty wise for your age."

"Which is why I tend to go out with men in their thirties. Not because I have daddy issues." She held up her palms. "I mean, yes, I only just met my real father a few years ago, but most of my life, the guy who raised me, well, I thought he was my old man. Never knew any different."

"And where is he?"

Gwen looked up at the sky. "Dead," she said under her breath, her eyes falling back on Tessa.

"I'm so sorry."

"But I don't want to make this about me. Just tell me what I can do to help."

"Now you sound like your uncle."

"And speak of the devil." Gwen tipped her head, and Tessa followed her gaze to see Gray hanging back by the entrance to the deck.

There was a stoic, reserved look on his face. Tight jawline. Eyes steady on them. "You want to swap places with me?" Gwen asked him.

"Please." Gray nodded.

"I'll happily go give those men a piece of my mind," Gwen offered.

"Sure your dad will love that." Gray sent her a crooked smile and Gwen waved over her shoulder to Tessa as she made her way back down to the meeting room.

"Hi," Tessa uttered what was more like a passing breath between them.

"Hi." His brows arched over his beautiful light green eyes as he gently returned her greeting. "I don't know how to ask you to help them again, but I also don't know how to ask you to live in hiding for the rest of your life. It's not who you are. You're bright and cheerful. And you need sunlight and joy. And to help people."

"I am. And I do." And she knew now more than ever she had to say yes to helping. Of course, she was still pissed the NSA had Dale's men drug her, detain her father, and move on with plan B without her consent. Dropping her off in Istanbul without her memories, hoping the bad guys would follow her, was insane. But since the NSA's plan was foiled when she fell into the water and called Gray, maybe everything happened for a reason. "We should help regardless. And remember, it was decided on this very deck, I'm stubborn. So don't try and talk me out of it."

"*So* stubborn."

"And you love that about me." She ran her tongue over her lips, not expecting the salty taste she found there. Was she crying? *Shit, maybe I am?*

"I do." He reached out and dragged the pad of his thumb across the contour of her cheek, catching more of her liquid emotion. "But I'll hate that about you if something happens to you because of it. I'll hate it. Hate myself. Hate the whole fucking world if you're taken from me, and I—"

Tessa pressed up on her toes and kissed him, cutting off

317

his fears. It was her turn to shush the chaos battling inside him.

He groaned as if momentarily forgetting his concerns, and she did the same. She gave herself over to him. His hands wrapped snugly around her body like she belonged in his embrace forever. Like she always had.

"Make it go away," she pleaded between kisses. "Make this all go away."

Her tears fell more steadily between their close-mouthed kisses as he rasped, "I'll do anything for you." He slid his tongue between her lips, kissing her passionately. One last time before they'd have to face reality.

At the sound of a nearby boat horn and birds scattering overhead, startled from their perch, she untangled herself from his arms. "We should go back in. I need to let everyone know I'm helping."

"I'm not letting you get taken, just so we're clear." He gently snatched her chin, commanding her attention. "Even coming up to this deck without me made me nervous."

"Pretty sure Gwen could take a bad guy down with a click of a mouse. I was safe. Your niece is a badass."

She was hoping for a laugh, but the concerned look in his eyes didn't dissipate with her joke. She didn't want him worrying every second until this was over just because she was dangling herself out in the open for the bad guys. Well, assuming that was the plan.

"You're a badass too," he said without washing away that stern look in his eyes.

"Hardly. But my dad apparently still is, even in his sixties."

"You're his daughter. Apple. Tree." He shot her a cocky wink.

And there you are. Her grizzly guy, but with a killer smile and a touch of humor. "Oh, really?" She snatched his shirt with both hands and hauled herself closer to him, lifting her chin to find those stunning green eyes. "And do you forgive that tree?" *Forgive my dad for the accident? For pushing you to walk away from me?*

"Hmm. It did bear some pretty delicious fruit." He slid his tongue along his lips, then leaned in and kissed her. "Mmmm, a coconut-flavored apple." He reached around and squeezed her ass cheek. "I just might need another bite."

CHAPTER THIRTY-ONE

"Give us seventy-two hours," Gray told his father over the phone from the top deck. "Between my guys and Echo Team, we'll deliver the results you're looking for."

"I'll talk to Director Torres. In the meantime, the NSA will continue to work leads on their end. And they'll handle preventing the Scottish group from becoming a future problem for you all," his father said. "The Scottish guy Dale's team interrogated yesterday couldn't answer who hired him. But the NSA managed to track the money transfer to their account in the Caribbean. The Scots must've closed it." He paused to let the dead-end news sink in. "Also, I'll work on clearing your name with Turkish Intelligence, but it'll take time. You're going to need to get out of Turkey another way."

"Nothing we can't handle," Gray reassured him. "I'll be in touch when we're on the move."

"Stay safe."

Gray swallowed. "Roger that." He ended the call and shoved his phone into his pocket. "Ready to figure out the next steps?"

Tessa nodded. "But first, I need a favor."

"Anything," he said without hesitation.

"If I'm going to be bait again," she began, and his stomach sank at the mere mention of that word, "what if they go after someone I love to try and draw me out?"

"Naomi," he said in understanding. "Your mom."

"Right." Her beautiful eyes narrowed in concern. "Naomi arrives home later today, and I'll be sick with worry if I don't know someone's protecting her. And my mom may be off the grid, but that doesn't mean if someone is desperate . . ."

"Consider it done."

"Done?" She snapped her fingers. "Like that?"

He smirked. "Like that." He reached for her hips and held her, then nuzzled her neck before bringing his mouth to her ear. "I told you, sweetheart, for you, anything."

"Thank you," she whispered, and he could physically feel some of her worries wane with her favor granted.

He pulled back to find her eyes again. "Naomi's phone may be tapped because of all of this. I can arrange a secure call once her protection picks her up from the airport, but I think it'd be best to let them explain what's happening if that's okay with you?"

She frowned. "She won't trust just anyone."

"We'll send Natasha with the security team. She can relay the message. As for your mother, we can have her watched from a distance if you prefer?"

"Yeah, that'd be better."

"Come on, let's go figure out a way to keep you safe while also catching this bastard." He leaned in and kissed her before guiding her back inside the yacht.

As soon as they rejoined the team in the living room, Carter shared, "I have an idea." Standing by the bar, eyes focused on his phone while his fingers flew over the screen, he added, "It's a bit unorthodox, but I think it'll work."

Oliver chuckled. "Have any of your ideas ever been orthodox?"

"Oliver has a point," Jesse said, standing off to the side of the table by Sydney as they shared a tablet.

While waiting for Carter to continue, Gray motioned for Tessa to sit. She tipped her head in agreement and crossed the room to settle between a grumpy-looking Wyatt and a growly-looking Griffin. *And wow, this woman has me describing my teammates with her adjectives.*

"So, boss man *numero uno,* you going to leave us hanging? Or clue us in on your unorthodox plan?" Jack shot Gray a lopsided smile. "He's got the money, bro. Writes my checks. He's *numero uno* there." He covered his heart with his free hand and smiled. "But you're my best friend, so *numero uno* in that department."

"Someone get him a banana bag," Gray begged, looking over at Oliver. "Sober him up."

"On it." Oliver stood and left the room to grab what he needed.

"Just finalizing a few details to ensure everything will work. Give me one more second," Carter said, continuing to work on his phone, ignoring Jack and his drunken rambling.

Gray swiveled his focus toward Dale, the reason why Jack was more than likely a few drinks beyond okay. A glass of whiskey wasn't uncommon for them. But drunk? Hell no.

Nope. This is Dale's doing.

Gray kept his eyes on Dale as the man stood about as far away from everyone else as possible, nearly in the doorway.

For a fraction of a second, the pained look in Dale's eyes almost made Gray feel sympathetic for him. Because damn, they'd been best friends. Risked their necks for each other.

Dale even got his pilot's license after the Marines, just so he could be their pilot on ops when they'd worked together at his old company. Dale had saved his ass more times than Gray could count by swooping in for an extract.

But Gray doubted he could ever forgive Dale. He was with Wyatt on that. There was no excuse for what he did. "Anything helpful you can share with us that your boss forgot to reveal on that call?"

Dale peered at Gray but immediately looked away as if he couldn't stomach the eye contact. "Nothing that will help, no."

"And do you trust all the intel the NSA provided you?" Gray asked, earning him another brief look from Dale.

"They lied to me about people dying if I didn't help. So no, I don't necessarily trust them." He shook his head. "Then again, I don't make it a habit to trust anyone anymore."

"Fact-check the fuck out of them is what I say," Jack suggested, twirling a finger in the air as Oliver returned with the IV.

"I agree." Gray nodded his thanks to Oliver as he hooked Jack to the IV. "We need to do our homework and check out their story."

"I started digging the second the call ended," Sydney informed him, slipping back into a seat at the table, swapping her iPad for a computer.

"Okay. It's done," Carter abruptly announced while shoving his phone into his pocket.

"What's done?" Gray moved off to the side of the table so he could have eyes on Tessa while also giving Carter his attention.

Carter uncuffed his sleeve and began working it to his elbow. "I think I can draw out our buyer while also keeping Tessa safe."

"How?" Tessa planted her hands on each side of her, nearly bumping the two operators she was wedged between.

"Just outside Zurich, there's a stretch of land right on the line near Germany that was designated a neutral territory during the Cold War. Neither Switzerland nor Germany can claim it. A billionaire snatched up the acres and built a resort with a reputation as a haven for criminals. It's a no-man's-land sitting outside the law of either country," Carter explained. "The only weapons permitted inside the hotel are the ones carried by security. You're thoroughly checked upon arrival. Reinforced hotel room doors require your thumbprint and a personal code to enter your suite as well. They may cater to criminals, but they take their safety very seriously."

"Are you talking about The Sapphire?" Wyatt stood, sliding his hands into his pockets. "I thought that place was a myth."

"Guess you weren't kidding about all of this being unorthodox," Oliver said, sitting across from Mya again now that Jack had his IV going.

"I've heard of The Sapphire," Sydney said. "And I won't be able to hack their guest log to see the guest names."

"Maybe I can?" Gwen suggested.

"No, it's not that." Sydney shook her head. "The guest log can't be hacked because it's a ledger. Pen and paper. Guests pay in cash too."

"I'm just . . ." Gray held his hand up, needing to pump the brakes for a second and slow down. "You want me to take her to a hotel full of criminals?"

"I've already reached out to my contact there to let them know I have friends in need, which is code for seeking a safe place from arrest. I secured us four suites. It's a service they provide for their . . . regulars," Carter shared.

Jack grinned. "I forgot you were a shady motherfucker

before joining us. Of course you'd belong to a hotel straight out of a *John Wick* film."

"I had to create a certain reputation for myself to get some jobs done," Carter shot back, obviously not a fan of that jab. "And a haven for bad guys comes in handy. Especially when people think you're one of them, but you're really just—"

"Looking to catch one," Gray finished in understanding. "And if we want the buyer to come himself, we need him to feel safe from the NSA. With Turkish Intelligence after Tessa, her seeking asylum at a place like that adds credibility to the idea of her and the colonel being traitors."

Tessa blinked in surprise. "So, our cover story is to go as criminals?"

"Not a stretch for Carter," Jack said around a hiccup.

"Looks like you don't want those checks signed after all." Carter joking? That was new. Or hell, maybe he was being serious?

"Well, I'm in." Oliver popped up to his feet. "Love playing the role of a bad guy. They have so much more fun."

Mya rolled her eyes. "Of course, you'd say that."

"I just need to process this all for a second." Gray looked at Tessa, trying to gauge her reaction, but shock was all he was getting from her statue-like state.

"No one but hotel security will be armed at the hotel," Carter reminded him. "And technically, you're not supposed to attack other guests."

"And by 'technically,' you mean you broke that rule before and just didn't get caught since you're still a member?" Oliver asked.

"There's a loophole, yes," was all Carter gave them, which wasn't exactly reassuring.

Shit, this might be our best option. "Are you sure you can leak the fact that Tessa and I will be at The Sapphire without it blatantly looking like bait?"

"With Gwen's help, yes," Carter said, and Gwen nodded that she was in. "Many deals are often done at this hotel between criminals worried about a double cross. If the buyer finds out Tessa's there, he might be worried Tessa's also there to sell the intel to a new buyer."

"And he won't want that to happen, so that'll motivate him to come himself and not send someone else in his place to grab her again," Gray said, slowly getting on the same page as Carter.

"And no one knows you all work together at Falcon, right? So, if you show up at the hotel, the other criminals there won't have questions?" Tessa asked, breaking through her frozen-like state. It was a valid concern, but thankfully, not one she had to worry about.

"No, we're safe. Falcon doesn't have a digital footprint," Oliver answered. "No webpage to keep up with or emails to answer."

"Maybe I'm missing something though," Tessa said, "but how do we get the buyer out of the hotel alive if it's so secure? And, for that matter, how would he plan to get us out?"

"I have an idea. And it'll require us narrowing down our suspect list to ensure we beat him to the punch and make our moves first," Carter was quick to answer.

"Let me guess, with Gwen's help?" Wyatt piped up, removing his hands from his pockets to set them on his hips as he trained his attention on his daughter.

"I need an extremely skilled hacker to break into the hotel's security network unnoticed. We can't access their guest log, but we can see any new guests checking into the hotel over security cameras," Carter explained.

"And I think we can narrow down that list to anyone from the U.K.," Sydney announced, looking up from her screen.

"You find something new?" Gray asked her. "Or is this just because those guys were Scottish?"

"When I started fact-checking the NSA twenty minutes ago," Sydney began, "I wound up down a rabbit hole on the dark net, and I think the NSA missed what I found. I would've too if I didn't practically trip over the intel."

"Tripping is something I normally do," Tessa said, then blushed as if she'd meant to only think that, and Gray couldn't help but smile. Even now.

But also . . . he needed good news, and it sounded as though Sydney was about to offer a much-needed lead. "What'd you find?"

"With Gwen's help," Sydney said, "we tracked down the encrypted message the buyer sent to the Scottish men hiring them to go to Istanbul. And she traced the signal to somewhere in the U.K."

"Not to a specific location there?" Gray asked.

"I'm afraid not," Gwen replied. "The signal keeps bouncing around in a looped pattern, making it impossible to know its origin point."

Talking with her hands, Sydney explained, "Think of surveillance footage that's been put on a looped feed to hide what was originally there. That's what this signal is doing."

This isn't my specialty, but thank God it's yours. "Tell me you can remove that layer and see what's under it and isolate where the email originated."

"While we're traveling, I'll modify an existing program I created to basically unknot the loop and find our starting point," Gwen said with a smile. "He wouldn't have sent a transmission like this from his house or office unless he's an idiot, and based on the sophisticated code, he's not. He also likely has a skilled hacker on his team. So, the best I can get you is a city."

"And once we have a city, we can narrow down our list to any known criminals or suspects with the funds and motive to pull this off," Gray said, and damn was he grateful for his team. "And whoever from our suspect list takes the bait and walks through the hotel doors is our mark." *This is starting to feel like a plan I can get behind.* "If I agree to this, we're back to Tessa's question. How are we removing our mark from such a secure site?"

"We can discuss the extraction plan on the plane. We should get a move on now if we're doing this." Carter looked toward Wyatt. "I have a place outside Zurich. Your men will stay there, which will also be part of our plan to take down the HVT."

"I didn't know you had a safe house in Switzerland." *Not a shock I'm in the dark.*

"The house belonged to my late wife's family. We inherited it, and I haven't had a chance to sell it since she . . ." Carter cleared his throat. "So, it's not really a safe house, but it'll work for what we need on this op. It's isolated and near the hotel."

"So, are you on board?" Wyatt asked Gray, clearly waiting for his go-ahead to get a move on.

Am I? He looked at Jack, who gave him a quiet nod, but when his gaze skated over to Tessa, finding her lip caught between her teeth, her nervousness gave him pause.

"This place is basically a spa. A getaway for criminals. Most are looking for peace, not problems." More cryptic talk from Carter.

What if something goes wrong? "I don't know what to say."

"We'll handle it," Carter said with a nod. "I can have my

pilot fly to the closest Greek island that has a landing strip. We'll meet the plane there and fly to Zurich and meet up with Echo Team." Carter turned to Wyatt as if everything was a done deal. "But I'll need your daughter to fly with us *and* stay at the hotel."

"And you're sure Sydney or Mya can't handle hacking the hotel cameras?" Wyatt asked him, tossing a hand in the air. "You already have Gwen unknotting the loop thing or whatever you said. And I know you're working on other leads, but—"

"As I said, to hack one of the most secure sites on this side of the globe, I need one of the best hackers," Carter cut him off.

"Dad, I got this." Gwen stood and gave him a firm look.

Wyatt only scowled back. "Who else is going to the hotel? You said you got four rooms."

"Gray and Tessa will be in one." Carter set a hand over his heart. "I sleep alone." He looked over at Jack. "Assuming you sober up in time, you can go with Gwen as a couple."

"Ohh. No, no, no." Gwen winced. "Jack's like an uncle. I just don't think I can pretend to be his girlfriend." She waved a hand in the air and tossed out a quick, "Sorry," Jack's way.

"Then nobody will believe you're at the hotel together. If we're going to pull this off, you need to be with someone you have chemistry with," Mya said, her eyes moving around the room in search of the perfect fit.

"And who do I have chemistry with?" Gwen asked, but Gray saw the answer in his niece's eyes because her attention was fixed on Oliver.

"Well, Griffin and I are out," Jesse spoke up. "Our wives prefer us not to play pretend with other women. And I'm not a fan either."

Griffin quietly nodded in agreement, then peered at Oliver

as if he were the only viable option left and lifted his chin in his direction.

"Wait, uh." Oliver frowned at Griffin's gesture, then quickly focused on Wyatt, scrubbing a hand over his jawline, clearly uneasy with that option.

Wyatt cocked a brow and crossed his arms, staring at a man seconds away from becoming his new enemy. In Wyatt's mind, Dale was probably like wallpaper in the room now that Oliver would share a suite with his daughter.

"Why can't Gwen just be Jack's niece instead of going as his girlfriend?" Oliver proposed.

"The hotel only has king-sized beds left. No double rooms available either," Carter shared. "Guests and hotel management will have issues with an uncle and his niece sharing a bed. They won't believe Jack will choose the couch instead. And these types of criminals shockingly have morals about certain things."

"Is Mya going?" Oliver asked. "How about Mya and Gwen bunk together?"

"I'd prefer someone with a kill count longer than my arm to share a room with Gwen. The same goes for Mya," Gray spoke his thoughts aloud. "No offense."

"Trying not to take any," Mya mused. "Sydney's the only one of us women who meets your kill count requirement." She looked over at Carter next. "I do think I should be at the hotel to help Gwen with some of the backend stuff. I'm not as tech illiterate as you all make me out to be."

"Can you pull off appearing to have chemistry with Jack?" Carter asked Mya, and she peered at Jack, and Gray noticed him staring right back at her.

They quietly studied each other for a moment before Mya shook her head as if freeing herself from a dazed state and said, "Much more than I can with Oliver."

"Fine, it's settled," Carter decided. "Mya and Jack. Oliver and Gwen."

Oliver glanced at Gwen, and she quickly looked away from him and down at her keyboard, a blush working up her throat.

"I don't think I need to spell out what happens if I hear you share a bed with my daughter instead of sleeping on the floor or couch." Wyatt's bark was just as big as his bite that time. Because he nearly showed his teeth when talking.

"And *you* realize I'm not a child, right?" Gwen fidgeted with her charm bracelet as if remembering Wyatt's overreach. "Not a virgin, either."

Wyatt turned his cheek as if she'd slapped him.

"I get that you missed out on my life, but that's Mum's fault. You don't need to try and make up for that time by snarling at every guy who looks my way," she went on, her tone softer that time to try and get Wyatt on board. "And Oliver's not my prom date you have to scare off."

"But if you wind up in danger while in that hotel, then—"

"You'll storm the gates and save me, I have no doubts," she cut off her dad. "Now go. You have your own team to bark orders at and scare into compliance, right?" She playfully shooed him away.

Wyatt grunted, then leaned in and kissed the top of her hair. "You drive me nuts, you know that? Just stay safe." He faced the room, glowered at Oliver, then stole a look at Dale. "Before I go meet up with my team to fly to Zurich, what are we doing with him?"

"Shiiiit. Forgot you were even there," Jack said dismissively. Gray doubted that was true, considering Dale was probably the reason Jack had been walking down memory lane with a bottle in hand. And memory lane was littered with landmines and broken glass. It sucked. The whole damn thing.

"We don't have enough room for everyone on the jet," Carter remarked. "Griffin and Jesse fly with Echo Team. We'll keep Dale so Wyatt doesn't—"

"Throw him from the plane?" Wyatt finished for him.

"There is one problem with this plan," Tessa interrupted them at the mention of the jet, and Gray already knew where her thoughts were going. "The flying part." Tessa gave him a cute but nervous smile. "I'm not so sure I can get on a plane without fainting." She looked at Dale. "How'd the NSA get me to you in Cyprus?"

Gray turned toward Dale, and his heartbeat ramped up. He was pretty sure he wasn't going to like his answer.

"The agents, um, said you panicked the second they had you on the plane, so . . ." Dale tugged at the brim of his hat. "They drugged you."

"Excuse us for a moment." Gray reached for her wrist and guided her from the room and into the hall, leaving his teammates to work on the next steps while he ensured she was truly okay and understood the ramifications of what his team was suggesting.

Once out there, he pinned Tessa's back to the wall and leaned into her, angling his head as he held her eyes, silently imploring her to confide in him what she was truly feeling.

"Not sure if I can fly without being drugged." She frowned.

"You didn't have me then. But you have me now. And I've got you, I promise."

"Says the guy who probably jumps from perfectly good planes." Her lips twitched into a beautiful smile, and she slipped her hand over his heart.

"True. But I promise you, we won't be doing that." He

cupped the back of her head and brought his mouth to her ear. "But I know something we can do once we're alone, and it's *safe* for us to be distracted."

"What?" she asked, arching into him, and he knew her mind was far from thinking about their afternoon flight. For now, at least.

"Showing is so much better than telling, don't you think?" He rotated his hips a touch, unable to stop his cock from getting hard at the mere idea of being with her. He was done fighting how this woman made him feel, even in the face of danger. Hell, he might actually become the "bad guy" he was about to pretend to be and take her the second they walked into that hotel.

"Gray, if you don't fuck me sometime soon, I'll—"

"Not sure if I've ever heard that word come from this sweet mouth before," he cut her off, easing back to find her eyes. He brushed the pad of his thumb along her lips and implored, "Say it again, and maybe I'll give you exactly what we both want sooner than I planned."

She wet her lips, taunting him. "Fuuuck," she purred.

Gray growled out a curse before slanting his mouth over hers to swallow the word when she dared to say it a third time. Their tongues met. Dueled and danced.

She moaned before pulling away to declare, "You just love to use your tongue to distract me from my fears, don't you?"

"Is it working?" He teased his brows up and down.

Tessa snatched hold of his shirt and pressed up on her toes. Her lips hovered near his as she peered at his mouth briefly before meeting his eyes. "I'll take your kisses to relax me any day of the week. And if I play my cards right, and I'm good at being bad later, maybe you'll even distract me with something else . . ."

He loved that idea, but . . . "Are we really agreeing to this plan?" He needed complete confidence in her decision to be on board with any of it, including her being naughty at that hotel later. "Tell me you don't want to do this, and we don't. You get a say. Always."

She pursed her lips together, then said with a tight nod, "Let's do this."

CHAPTER THIRTY-TWO

UNDISCLOSED LOCATION - JUST OUTSIDE
ZURICH, SWITZERLAND

GRAY SQUEEZED HIS HANDS INTO FISTS, COUNTED BACK FROM five, then unfurled his fingers. He repeated the move he'd been doing for thirteen years, hoping his tension-stress relief method would work. But chills racked his spine, sweat dotted his back, and every part of him was strung tight. *It's not working. That's because Tessa is about to enter a hotel full of criminals. As bait.*

Of course he trusted himself and his team to protect Tessa, but the woman had already been through so much. And after a boat ride to a Greek island, she'd faced her fear of flying with only one glass of wine and her death-grip squeeze of his hand to get to their new location. He was so damn proud of her.

Inside the foyer of the "safe house," which was nothing like he'd expected—a charming cottage in the middle of nowhere, surrounded by snow-capped mountains—Gray anxiously stood alone at the base of the staircase. He felt like a prince in one of those Disney movies, adjusting the cuffs of his suit jacket as he waited for his true love to descend the stairs and greet him.

Tessa appeared at the top of the stairs a few heartbeats later, holding the rail, and began his way. Knowing her, she was probably concentrating on not tripping in the brown high-heeled boots she'd paired with a sexy, light cream-colored sweater dress. And now he couldn't help but envision her wearing only those boots while they made love.

Shit. Do I have a thing for shoes? The ridiculous idea popped into his head, and he nearly laughed. Of course, it was always thoughts of Tessa naked, wearing only heels, that infil'ed his brain in the past. *But hell, I lost my foot. Maybe it's some—*

"Gray, you okay?" Tessa interrupted his Freudian self-analysis as her gaze coasted over the tailored suit Carter had provided. As promised, he'd had their wardrobes and vehicles there waiting for their arrival. The man had to be a wizard. How'd he do it?

"You've rendered me speechless," Gray finally answered, taking her hand. He had her do a little twirl. And he officially hated the dress once he remembered a bunch of criminals would get an eyeful of how it clung to every curve of her body—from her full tits, hips made for holding, to an ass that was downright sinful.

"You look dapper. Handsome. All the adjectives," she said with a smile. When he let go of her hand, she reached for the collar of his shirt and adjusted it. "No tie?"

"Not really my thing. Neither is the jacket, so that'll be off soon."

"Surprised Carter managed to rope you into dressing up like him," she teased. "But I'm not going to lie. You make one sexy bad guy." She rolled her tongue along her glossy lips. Her smoky-brown shadow and liner made her brown eyes pop that much more. And her cheeks had a touch of pink on them.

"And you look . . ." *Still sweet and innocent.*

"I feel pretty," she mused as if reading his thoughts. "But still like a good girl."

"That's because you are." He reached for her shoulders.

Her dark brows rose with uncertainty. "I guess you and I are kind of going as ourselves, though, so I'm just me. A traitorous version of me."

"Hard to remove the angel-esq quality from how you look, I'm afraid. Even if you did use lip gloss instead of lip balm today," he admitted with a wink.

"Well, trust me when I say Gwen and Mya certainly have the bad-girl look covered. Wait until you see them." Her gaze cut over Gray's shoulder, and he turned to see Oliver on approach, in an entirely different outfit from Gray.

"Got holes in your jeans, buddy," Jack said, striding into the foyer in an all-black suit, not his normal fit, from the opposite direction as Oliver.

"Gwen chose my clothes." Oliver fidgeted with the collar of his long-sleeved black shirt that was untucked over his jeans. He cleared his throat, eyes dead set on the stairs, which meant someone was coming. Gwen or Mya?

Jack stood alongside Oliver and set his finger beneath Oliver's chin to close his mouth. "Down, boy." Thankfully, Jack was now sober and just his typical humorous self.

"How do I look? Fierce?" Gwen asked, and Gray finally turned back toward the stairs. He'd hoped it'd been Mya stealing Oliver's breath, not his niece.

Gwen wore skintight leather pants with black combat boots and a tank top beneath a black leather jacket with the collar popped. Her shoulder-length blonde hair was wavy instead of straight, and her eyes were done up in a smoky black. "I'm a notorious jewel thief, and Oliver's my getaway driver, so I thought this was fitting."

"Never thought I'd enjoy being a sidekick so much," Oliver said with a laugh that was borderline flirty.

Gray slipped his hand to Tessa's back as Mya came to the top of the steps next. She slowly descended, and once she reached the bottom, she shifted her long mass of brown hair to her back.

Mya had gone with a different look from Gwen. She wore a fitted red dress with strappy heels, and Gray was a bit thrown to notice it was *Jack* staring at her legs.

"You're going to be cold," Oliver said, eyes on Mya. "You realize we're in Switzerland in November, right?" He reached into his pocket and produced ChapStick. "See. Cold-weather ops. Lip balm needed." He applied it while Mya simply stared at him as if contemplating whether she wanted to swat him or steal the balm and use it too.

"You look . . ." Jack coughed into a closed fist, clearing his throat. ". . . Nice."

"Thanks, Jack." Mya smiled, her eyes sweeping around the foyer at the six of them crowded there. "Where's Carter?"

"Down the hall with the others," Gray told her as Oliver tossed Gwen a set of car keys.

"I know I'm your getaway man," Oliver said, "but since you're the true baddie, you want to drive?"

Gwen closed her hand around the keys. "That sick Bugatti out there Carter got us?" Her eyes widened in excitement. "Hell yes."

"You know how to drive stick, right?" Oliver asked as Gray reached into his pocket and fidgeted with the keys of the luxury ride Carter had given them for their cover story.

"Oh, you could say that." Gwen teased her brows up and

down. She shot Gray an apologetic look as if embarrassed by making the obvious "dicks" as "sticks" joke in front of her uncle.

"Your father is down the hall with his team," Gray grumbled the reminder. "They're finalizing the plans." *The ones I hesitantly agreed to on the plane ride here.*

"And this whole thing might even happen tonight?" Tessa asked. "I'll get my life back."

"Yeah, you can get your life back." Gray's forehead tightened. *Hopefully with me in it,* but he kept that thought to himself. "I need a second alone with Jack. We'll meet up with y'all in the war room in a minute." He squeezed Tessa's hand, and she smiled, letting him know she was okay.

Once everyone else left the foyer, Gray eyed Jack and cut straight to it, "Are you okay? You've never been drunk on an op before." He'd wanted to talk to him sooner, but Jack had slept off the alcohol on the boat ride to the Greek island. Then Gray hadn't left Tessa's side as she gripped his hand the entire flight to Switzerland.

"Yeah, shit. I'm sorry about that." Jack fidgeted with the knot of his skinny black tie, focusing on the hallway where the women and Oliver had gone down.

"Did Dale do or say something to you this morning that set you off?"

"No, not really. Him being here is throwing me off, sure." Jack let go of his tie. "But I guess when I saw that red dot on Griffin's chest this morning, it messed with my head. For a second, I thought Savanna was going to lose another husband."

Gray would've felt the same. Damn. "And you offered the trade."

"Don't tell him I actually give a fuck, okay?"

"I think he officially knows," Gray pointed out. "But what else is it? What's the real story behind your drinking?"

He shrugged, trying to be casual, but Gray called bullshit. "This morning put things in perspective. It made me realize I have no one back home to worry about me. Never will. And it's . . . depressing. I don't know." That slump in his best friend's shoulders was a brutal sight. "Between seeing Dale again, and then . . . it was all just a lot."

Depressing wasn't a word Jack ever used. He was the one always bailing his friends out from the darkness to bring them into the light. "Why didn't you tell me you're—"

"I'm fine. Really." Jack waved a dismissive hand. "I had a moment. Got stupid drunk. It won't happen again. Sorry." He started to walk past him, but Gray grabbed his arm, stopping him.

"You've always been there for me," Gray told him when Jack stole a look back over his shoulder. "I have your back too. If something is bothering you, don't hide it. Tell me, okay? I don't want a new best friend, either. Got it?"

"Don't get any stupid ideas about me . . . you know me. I'll be fine. So, you can derail your shitty train of thoughts, please." Jack rolled his eyes. "You can't get rid of me that easily. Well, not unless I need to swap my life for someone who's worth more."

Gray let go of Jack's arm. "Just so we're clear, Griffin's life isn't worth more just because he's married. You're both—"

"I get it, I get it. But don't tell me you wouldn't trade yourself for someone else too," he poked back. "Enough sappy talk. Let's go." He faced forward and started down the hall before Gray could say more.

Gray blew out a gruff breath, trying to calm his nerves, which felt damn near impossible considering what they were about to do—then followed him. He found the team gathered in their temporary "war room." There was no furniture, but it was jam-packed with gadgets and weapons, along with operators talking and going over plans.

When they'd arrived an hour ago, introductions had been hastily made. With Dale in the room, Wyatt left out the part where Echo Team ran off-the-books ops for the President.

Gray smirked at the sight of Tessa kneeling alongside Bear, Echo Team's canine. She scratched his belly as his tail flopped from side to side, hitting the wood floors. His tongue hung to the side as he enjoyed Tessa's company. When Bear set his eyes on Gray, he'd swear the dog frowned at him and gave him a territorial look, claiming Tessa.

Tessa kept rubbing Bear's stomach while searching the room until her gaze landed on Gray as he hung back in the doorway. He collapsed his arms over his chest and leaned into the doorframe, unable to look beyond the vision before him. There was a glint in her eyes and a glow to her skin as she smiled that warmed his chest.

"My wife, Rory, called while you were getting ready," Gray overheard Chris, Echo Three, saying to Tessa, drawing her attention away from him. "She went with Gray's sister to visit with Naomi and explain what was going on. Introduced Naomi's new security detail as well."

Tessa's hand went still on Bear as Chris squatted on the other side of the dog and scratched behind Bear's ear. Although Bear worked for the team, he was Chris's dog. He'd married Jesse's sister, Rory, after a case involving Carter brought the two of them together. Amusingly, they'd believed Carter was a bad guy, and look at them all now. Appearances could certainly be deceiving.

Gray quietly observed them, waiting for Chris to continue.

"Rory and Natasha were sparse on the details they gave Naomi, but they promised her you'd be okay. And we intend to keep that promise." Chris swiveled his head, stealing a look at Gray, and Gray nodded his thanks for the update.

Tessa lifted her hand from Bear, who groaned out his displeasure at being interrupted, and she reached for Chris's wrist while saying, "Thank you. And also, I met your wife two weeks ago when she was with Jesse."

"You did, did you?" Chris smiled.

"Small world, huh?" she asked, and Chris nodded.

It really, really is.

"So, we ready to do this?" Jack snapped Gray from the spell of staring at Tessa. And Bear rolled to his side and popped to all fours as if being called into alert mode. Chris and Tessa pushed upright as well. "Good with the plan? Contingencies and all?"

There were several "if this happens, then we do this" scenarios they'd run through on the plane ride there. And once they'd met up with Wyatt's team at the cottage, Echo Team had offered a few tweaks to the plan that Gray and Carter had agreed to make.

"Yeah." Carter shrugged on his black suit jacket as he casually remarked, "There is one thing I should probably mention before we roll out. One other hotel rule."

Ah shit, here it is. Gray straightened in the doorway at his words.

"The hotel may be a haven from authorities, but you put a bunch of criminals together, and someone is bound to break the rules and go after a guest," Carter began. "It rarely happens, but when it does, there's a protocol they follow."

"Explain," Gray demanded, thinking about that loophole Carter referred to earlier.

"If someone attacks another guest, the fight doesn't stop

until someone loses. And the only way to lose, is to die. If you don't finish the person off, *you'll* be finished by management," Carter explained, his tone too casual for Gray's liking.

"Even if you're just chilling? There for a facial?" Jack joked. "Doesn't seem fair."

"Management assumes if someone is willing to risk hotel rules and their life to make a move, it's for a good reason," Carter said, adjusting his jacket sleeve to hide his watch. "If you start the fight and win, you still lose your membership permanently. But if you're the one attacked and you win, you just cover the damages, and you're not kicked out."

"So, you motivated someone in the past to make the first move, so you could take them out and keep your membership intact?" Jack probed, smiling.

Carter nodded his answer. "We'll be fine."

"Sure," Jack said, echoing Gray's concerned thoughts. "What can go wrong always does. Murphy's Law . . ."

Gray did his best not to let the *Fight Club* rule put him even more on edge as Carter spun a finger in the air and declared, "Let's do this. It's near dinnertime already."

Gray looked over at Tessa as she patted Bear on the head and said, "See you soon, buddy."

And she would. Because Bear was part of the takedown plan. He'd be one of the teammates who'd keep Tessa safe since Gray would be the one dangling himself as bait at the cottage.

CHAPTER THIRTY-THREE

TESSA STARED OUT THE WINDOW AS GRAY SAT BEHIND THE wheel of their white Aston Martin, flying gracefully around a sharp corner. It was after eight at night, so it was too dark to take in the scenery, but she was sure there'd be an incredible view of the Swiss Alps with the sun splashing over them in the morning.

Following Carter in his Audi R8, they were sandwiched in the middle with Gwen and the others behind them.

"Ten more minutes until we're there." Gray reached for the radio and turned on some tunes, keeping the volume low to serve as background noise. "You okay? Want to go over the plan once more?"

"I don't know, do I?" Her nerves were catching up with her with every stretch of road they sped down.

"Are you nervous?" He stole a look at her expression before his eyes slipped to her exposed thighs. In her seated position, the sweater dress had hiked up a bit, and if she parted her thighs, it wouldn't take much effort for him to get an eyeful of the scrap of silk between her legs.

"This is me we're talking about," she said with a *nervous*

344

laugh as he whipped the car around another bend in the windy road, managing to do it with ease.

He snatched her hand, urging her to hold his, but she pulled back.

"Don't you need two hands on the wheel?" *Where is the oh-shit handle?* She looked up and grabbed it.

"I'm good, sweetheart. You have nothing to worry about. The roads aren't icy. I can drive this bad boy with one eye closed while my fingers strum your clit and never miss a beat."

Her nipples pebbled at his surprising words, and she eased up on the handle and peered at him, catching a smoldering look in his eyes. When her gaze wandered to his crotch . . . a different idea popped to mind, one that might ease her nerves so she wouldn't feel like they were in a *Fast & Furious* flick on their way to a hotel full of criminals.

"Tessa, I know what you're thinking, and no," he drawled, but that hand he claimed he didn't need on the wheel went to his dick, and he adjusted the pronounced bulge there.

"You know what they say?" She cocked a brow. "When in Zurich . . . road head?"

A husky laugh rumbled from him and hit her between the thighs, the sound relaxing her muscles, easing her legs open.

"Give me another first, Gray. I've never . . . and I want to." She licked her lips, catching some gloss on her tongue. "Go over your operational plan again while I distract myself between *your* legs. It'll calm me down. Plus, these bendy roads in this fast car have me—"

"You want to put my dick in your mouth while I share operational details with you, so you're not scared of my driving?" he asked with a laugh.

"Precisely." She shifted the front strap of her seat belt to her back. "I'm supposed to be bad, right? This feels like a thing a bad girl would do."

"Tessa," he gritted out, his eyes falling to her lap. She hadn't even realized she'd moved her hand between her thighs, and her nude-colored panties were now visible, tinged with the evidence of her arousal.

He adjusted himself again and elongated his neck to be upright against the leather seat, eyes back on the road as he freed a harsh-sounding breath of what she hoped would be concession. His knuckles whitened as he held the wheel, and she decided to go ahead and make her move. Take distracting herself into her own hands.

She reached over the console and moved his hand away from his crotch. He dropped his focus to her fingers, and she searched for the zipper and tugged it down.

"Tell me about the plan, Grayson." She reached into his dress pants, through the hole of his boxers, then fisted his cock. He snarled. Cursed. And she didn't stop.

With his girthy length visible, she stroked him up and down, then swiped her tongue along her lips, wanting to lick the precum from his tip.

"The plan," she urged, leaning in. "Tell it to me while you *fuck* one of my holes."

More curses rolled from his tongue like wax melting from a flame. They came out fluid and easy from this man. Somehow, he managed to make the F word sound erotic and sexy every time he said it, especially when it came to his reactions to her.

She sank her mouth over his cock and swallowed every inch of him, nearly gagging herself as she tried to slide down as far as possible.

"The plan," he said after a low growl-gasp escaped his

lips. Then another curse while he slid his hand into her hair, moving her locks away from her face. "Tessa, fuuuuck."

She eased all the way back up, searching for her breath for a second. She flicked her tongue, circling the head of his cock, then moved her hand up and down in time with her mouth.

"The plan is . . . that first we figure out the city where the buyer's from, and Gwen's close, so that's gooooood." The last word stretched out with a hot moan. "Then we narrow down the list of sus-suspects." He snatched her hair, urging her to slow down as if he'd come too soon. "And when someone from that list makes an appearance, shortly after you and I fake a . . ." A string of curses left his lips when she swallowed his whole length again, choking on him. "We fight. We're going to fight in the lobby." He guided her head up and down, faster. His tone pitching lower. Deeper. Rougher. As the pressure more than likely built up inside him.

"Then I grab your car keys and take off," she said as her lips brushed his crown. "And you chase after me in one of the other cars."

"Riiight," he confirmed as she sucked him again, hard. "Then . . . four of our guys pose as the American authorities who are waiting, um . . . to catch us outside the hotel." He cursed again, and his body tensed. He was close.

She lifted her mouth and craned her neck to look up at him. "They'll be waiting at a safe distance outside the hotel to grab me for being a bad girl."

His eyes snapped down to meet hers. "Tessa, so help me. Get your mouth back on my cock. Now," he hissed, his chest lifting and falling from quick breaths.

"Yes, sir," she taunted, then slipped her mouth back over his hard length, and his hips bucked up from the seat. She swirled her tongue around his crown before dropping over him. Gagging again. The man was big. Thick. And just . . . damn. "The plan," she reminded him after easing up, tears in her eyes from taking as much of him as she could.

"They do a vehicle . . . inter . . . diction." Their car jerked to the side a touch as if veering off the road, but she felt him quickly course-correct back onto the road. "The buyer will hopefully have us followed, see us getting detained by authorities and taken to what they think is a safe house to be questioned and—" His words died when she took as much of him as she could again. He grunted and held her head down on him while coming hard. She swallowed every drop before sliding up, desperate for air. "Holy shit," he added a beat later while letting go of her hair.

She carefully tucked him back into his pants and zipped him up. Satisfied with herself for getting him off, and grateful she hadn't caused an accident, she righted herself in her seat and fixed her seat belt.

It was the first time she'd seen the man look truly relaxed. "You good?"

He swiveled his head, a drunk look in his eyes. "You just fucked the life right out of me. I'm having an out-of-body experience." That edge of exhaustion in his tone gave her no reason to doubt him.

She smirked. "Well, I feel better. So, thank you."

"You're thanking me?" He laughed and reached out to pat her knee.

"I am. I like seeing you look sated."

"Sated? Well, that's one way to put it." He glanced at her. "Can I 'sate' you with my hand?"

"Mmmm. I think we're almost there. Let's be good bad guys and wait." She chuckled at her own words. "That makes no sense, but you know what I mean."

He grunted in protest, then murmured without looking at

her, "I wish I didn't understand. Because I want to finger-fuck that tight little cunt of yours so much right now, I might just pull over."

Holy . . . She squeezed her legs closed.

"But later, right?" He shot her a quick devilish look. Oh, he was playing dirty.

Now she was the one pouting. "Later." She squirmed on the leather. *I need a distraction now.* She reached for the purse she'd been given at the cottage and searched for her lip gloss, then busied herself with fixing her swollen just-gave-road-head lips. "So, the plan."

His hand was still on her knee, so she grabbed his palm and locked their fingers together.

"You realize you've ruined all future operations for me, right? How will I ever go over plans without you servicing my cock simultaneously?"

"Mmm. I serve. You protect. We'd make a great team." *We did thirteen years ago, and we still do, don't we? Even in danger.*

"I like the sound of that." He lifted their united palms over the console and leaned over to kiss her knuckles, never losing sight of the road in the process.

"But um," she said once he rested their hands on her leg again, "do you really think this plan will work? Will the bad guys follow us from the hotel and truly think American agents grabbed us? And will the bad guy have his team show up at that cottage to try and take us from them?"

"It's our best play. We can't just leave the hotel and head to the cottage. The buyer will sense a trap. But if we make it look like agents were staking out the hotel, waiting for us to leave, then he'll try and seize that opportunity to get ahold of us."

"And your men will be there waiting for him," she said

349

with a nod. "But you guys don't think he'll show up himself though, right? He'll stay behind at the hotel?"

"We still don't know who we're dealing with. But he's already spent fourteen million on those first two transactions, so he's rich and more than likely powerful enough to have others get their hands dirty for him."

"And why do we have to split up again? Why can't you go with me through that secret exit into the woods to that little shelter place where I'll hide with Wyatt and Bear?"

"I need you away from danger, but we need the buyer's men to see at least one of us inside the cottage when they first arrive. Otherwise, we risk them pulling back and calling their boss to let him know it's a trap. And then Carter may not be able to snatch the buyer from the hotel as planned," he explained as if it all made perfect sense. But Gray placing himself directly in the line of fire would never sit well with her.

She looked out the window, noticing a set of gates coming into view. Since Carter was ahead of them and slowing his speed, she assumed they were nearing The Sapphire. "Okay," she hesitantly agreed, still hating the idea of Gray winding up in the middle of a gunfight. "The NSA wants the buyer alive for questioning, so Carter won't kill him, right?"

"Carter will do whatever he must to neutralize the threat. And if killing him is the only way we can get him out of the hotel and keep you safe"—Gray squeezed her hand and shot her a look as they slowed down near the gated entrance— "then so be it."

CHAPTER THIRTY-FOUR

"You can't keep her in the room. I know you want to lock her up behind closed doors and protect her from a hotel full of assholes," Carter rasped on the other side of the bedroom door, "but that defeats the purpose."

"Are you eavesdropping?" Oliver's tone was light and full of humor.

Tessa pulled away from the bedroom door to face him. "Listening and eavesdropping are two entirely different things." Her sorry excuse sounded ridiculous even to her ears, and Oliver returned her words with silence and a shit-eating grin.

"I can hear them from all the way over here, by the way," Gwen said before biting into a chocolate-covered strawberry while continuing to type with her other hand. Oliver had ordered room service for the two of them while Gwen settled in to hack the hotel's security cameras.

They'd only been at the hotel for an hour and a half, and Tessa had spent most of that time at dinner in the hotel restaurant, where Gray had about lost his mind with every passing minute.

"I can't do this. I thought I could, but I can't. Everywhere I look, I see problems," Gray had hissed under his breath, snatching Tessa's hand while standing from the table.

"That's because criminals are everywhere you look. But we're fine," Carter had returned in a low voice so no one overheard.

"No one from the U.K. has checked in today. Until they do, she doesn't need to be so exposed," Gray had said back in a calm but biting tone.

"I'm with Gray on this," Jack had agreed, tossing his napkin on his plate while standing. *"Let's go check on Gwen and Oliver. See if they have any leads."*

"She's been texting me updates on every new guest entering the lobby to check in," Mya had reminded Jack. *"I think Carter's right, and we should hang out in the open as much as possible."*

Jack had grumbled a protest and remained standing while Gray ignored everyone and practically hauled Tessa to her feet, rushing her to the elevators.

The second everyone reconvened in Oliver's suite, Carter had dragged Gray into the bedroom. Although, dragged wasn't quite descriptive enough for what Tessa had witnessed. Carter had stalked to the bedroom, opened the door, and then did some Jedi mind thing that had Gray cursing and following him in before the door slammed shut.

"Earth to Tessa?" Oliver waved a hand before her face, pulling her back to the moment.

"Sorry, I was reliving the insanity of the last hour." *Talking about being in a hotel full of dangerous criminals is much easier than being in one.* "Why do you think it's better for me to parade out in the open, even if we don't think the buyer is here yet?" she asked Mya since she'd said as much at the dinner table.

Mya was on her tablet, pacing the length of the couch while she worked. At Tessa's question, she stopped walking and swung her attention to Jack in the armchair. He held up his hands, palms out as if saying, *Don't look at me for an answer.* Then she pivoted her focus on an unlikely source of help.

Oliver's lips curled at the edges, relishing in her request for help before he faced Tessa. "If the buyer is smart, he'll send someone else in first to assess the situation. Get eyes on us and confirm you're here."

"That person could walk in the door any minute, and it'd be better for you to be visible," Mya added, then gave a hesitant nod of thanks to Oliver for being on the same page. "And that lead man may not be from the U.K."

"But not one of the Scottish guys, right? I overheard you all planning on the plane. And didn't someone say Admiral Chandler dispatched a SEAL Team to keep tabs on every member of that Scottish group to ensure they don't come here?" Tessa sank down onto one of the chairs by Jack, then tugged down her sweater dress.

"Right. For now, the SEAL Team needs to keep their distance from the Scots, so it doesn't look like they're working with you. But they'll discreetly intercept them if they try to come after you here for revenge," Jack reassured her. "They won't be a problem for us. And once we wrap this op up, we'll ensure they're never a problem for you again."

She supposed that was a little comforting to know. One thing checked off.

"I know it's not easy asking you to put yourself out in the open when you've got a bunch of basic bad guys all the way up to high-level criminals all over the place," Mya began, and there went that tiny sliver of comfort, "but we have your back. You don't need to worry about it."

"I'm not the one protesting the idea." *I'm not a fan, but still.* "Gray's the stubborn one you have to convince." She pointed to the closed bedroom door where their heated conversation continued, but they'd dialed down the volume, so she couldn't hear word for word what they were saying anymore.

"I got it!" Gwen abruptly announced, nearly jumping up from the couch. "London. The buyer sent that email to the Scots from London."

Carter and Gray must've overheard her because the door opened a second later, and they joined everyone in the living room.

"What do you know?" Carter asked, striding across the room.

Gray tossed his suit jacket on a chair as he closed in on where Tessa sat, and he began working his sleeves to the elbows as he fixed her with a distressed look.

"The buyer was mobile when the signal was transmitted," Gwen told them. "I can pinpoint it to the London Bridge."

"Big city. Big pool of suspects," Carter said. "And it doesn't mean he's local to London. He could've been passing through, but let's focus there as our prime location for now."

"I'll let Sydney know," Jack said, phone to his ear and already on the move, heading to the bedroom Tessa doubted Oliver would share with Gwen later that night.

Carter checked his watch. "There's a bar. Or a poker room. Where do you want to go? We need to be out in the open so it can be confirmed you're truly here."

"I hate this," Gray grumbled.

"I'll be okay." Tessa stood and reached for Gray's hand before facing Carter. "I'd rather be in a room full of bad guys who prefer drinking to a high-stakes poker game."

"I told you this place is where people come to relax and

escape the law. Get off the grid. It's not meant to be dangerous." Carter frowned as if not exactly loving his own words. "I mean, it can be dangerous because the guests are criminals, but it's supposed to be mostly safe."

Mostly. Loopholes and all.

"Well, I think I'm going to hang back here," Mya said, joining Gwen on the couch. "I'd like to work on compiling a list of existing guests we've flagged from the surveillance feeds and check their backgrounds. Do a threat-level analysis."

"In case the loophole clause arises?" Oliver asked, his eyes cutting to Carter as if assuming he'd be the cause of any problems.

"Yeah, in case anyone has a beef with our regular here," Mya said with a chuckle, and Carter glowered at her.

"Don't act like you don't piss people off in every city you go to," Oliver said, wiping away his smile with the back of his hand before taking two steps back from Carter as though the man might bite.

"Fine. Just the three of us, then," Carter decided, motioning toward the door. "Tell Jack we're heading out." He peered at Oliver. "Keep an eye on Gwen and Mya."

"Oh, I'll be sure to keep an eye on them." Oliver playfully lifted his brows while snatching a strawberry from the room service tray nearby.

Mya dropped her attention to her red dress. "Maybe we should change if we're going to be hanging back?"

"You both look fine to me." Oliver winked when Gwen looked up from her screen briefly, a quick touch of blush meeting her cheeks. Her reaction didn't go unnoticed by Gray, who didn't seem to be a fan of his niece developing an obvious crush on Oliver.

"Behave," Gray snapped out. "And when anyone learns something, let—"

"Wait," Gwen cut him off. "I just identified a British national who entered the hotel ten minutes ago."

Oliver rounded the couch to see Gwen's screen, and his forehead tightened as if in recognition. "Well, she's not a threat. Not for most of us, at least." He shot Carter a funny look. "It is someone who doesn't have much love for *you* though."

"Who?" Carter's hands went to his hips as he stared at Oliver.

"Just a rogue MI6 officer." Oliver grinned. "Between Dale and now her, this trip is turning into a real frenemies reunion."

* * *

"YOU OKAY?" *AM I REALLY ASKING BROODY DUDE THAT?* Tessa fidgeted with the hem of her dress, pulling it down, not in the mood to have any eyes on her that weren't Gray's. They were at the far end of the bar that stretched the length of a mirrored wall. And she'd spied too many guys checking her out in that mirror as they walked behind her.

Carter met her gaze in the reflective glass and asked, "Why wouldn't I be?" He took a sip of his whiskey neat.

Gray slipped his hand to Tessa's back, pulling her protectively to his side before his hand wandered down to the slope of her ass. It took her only a second to realize he was shielding her derrière, not trying to cop a feel. In the mirror, she spotted Gray's piercing gaze fixed on a guy in a suit at a high-top table, and his eyes remained on her ass.

"If Zoey's here, she's here for me. It's no coincidence," Carter said, drawing Tessa's attention back his way. Not that he'd yet to make eye contact with her in the twenty minutes since they'd been there. He was too busy searching for this mysterious woman Oliver had described as the equivalent of Bond before going rogue from MI6.

"You think Zoey knows why we're here?" Gray asked him.

"I barely know why we're here," Tessa mused. "How could she?"

"She has a point," Carter drawled.

When Gray grunted his frustration at being there for the umpteenth time since they'd arrived, she turned to face him. Instead of letting go of her ass, he only tightened his hold of her, and she planted her hands on his chest. She worked her gaze up the starched material to the top two buttons he'd left undone. The lights had been dimmed, but she could make out the movement of his throat as he swallowed down his discomfort.

"You okay, sweetheart?" That wasn't Gray's normal, reassuring tone. No, that was his *I-want-to-F-you* one. He brought his mouth to her ear and his warm breath there set off butterflies in her stomach and created a flash of heat between her legs. "Say the word, and I get you out of here."

She wet her lips and whispered back in a teasing voice, "Word."

He pulled away to find her eyes, a smile sliding across his lips at her joke.

"Well, hell," Carter said, stealing her focus a moment later, "you were right about Murphy's Law."

Tessa twisted around to see who or what had Carter's attention. She didn't even make it full circle before Gray spun her around, placing her behind him. He threw his forearm up, using it to block a barstool that must've been launched their general direction. The stool went off to the side and knocked into a table.

With Gray guarding her, she had to peek around him to figure out what was happening.

"Carter Dominick," someone said, and his voice boomed and echoed all around her, competing with the music still playing.

Definitely not Zoey. Did the guy escape a Viking movie? The sides of his head were shaved, but he had a knot at the top that transitioned into a braid that wrapped around his shoulder. Brown leather pants stretched across mammoth thighs, and his flowy white shirt looked like it belonged in another century.

Reaching back over his shoulder, he pulled the shirt over his head and tossed it, then cracked his neck while staring at Carter. *This doesn't bode well.* Gray continued to pin Tessa to the bar top behind him, one arm stretched to the side as if to stop her from going around him.

"You plan to break the rules?" A man in a three-piece suit stepped between the Viking and Carter. Management?

The Viking snarled and pointed at Carter. "Yes."

"And you know the consequences?" the manager asked the guy. "If you lose, you die."

Tessa held on to Gray's sides, trying to wrap her head around Carter's "it rarely happens" situation that was, in fact, happening. *My luck, seriously.* And yet, somehow, she hadn't slipped straight into panic mode.

The Viking guy made a come-hither motion toward Carter as his response. So yeah, he must've understood the rules. But he also had at least four or five inches and a lot more muscle on him than Carter.

The music kept playing as if a fight wasn't about to go

down. Even the guests didn't startle or panic. *And why would they, Tessa? They're a bunch of criminals.*

The manager turned toward Carter, hands casually sliding into his pockets as he waited for some type of response from him. "No help," is all he said as if it were a reminder. "But you remember the drill, don't you, Dominick? Not your first rodeo."

The man's accent was . . . *Southern?* Not Switzerland Southern, but American Southern. So, management's from the Deep South? *Okay, was not expecting that one.* Not that it mattered, she supposed, but what the hell was going on? They were there for the buyer, not for some WWE matchup between Carter and some guy who stepped out of the 11th century.

"You're not allowed to help," Carter casually remarked to Gray. "Just keep her back. Okay?"

"You sure about this?" Gray asked him.

Carter tossed his suit jacket, then uncuffed one sleeve and began working it to his elbow as he replied in a low voice, "No choice. This may work in our favor anyway. Ensure our mark knows we're here." He then focused back on the manager. "I understand the rules," he said. "The only way to lose is to die."

She buried her nails into Gray's sides as panic settled in. From the corner of her eye, she spotted some of the guests at the bar going for their wallets. Pulling out money. *You're making bets?*

"Stay behind me," Gray gritted out, standing like an impenetrable statue of protection. "He won't touch you. I won't let him."

"What does he want?" Tessa whispered as Carter worked at his second sleeve.

She wasn't certain he even heard her until he answered, "I

killed his twin brother. He must've heard I checked into the hotel. His brother was an assassin. And so is this guy."

"Don't die," Gray bit out, reaching around as if to confirm Tessa was still there despite the fact her nails probably dug into his skin with how hard she was holding him.

"I'll be fine." Carter stepped forward, and Tessa kept her head to the side of Gray to keep an eye on what was happening.

The manager casually flicked his wrist. "The rules are understood. Whoever wins pays for the damage times ten." He stepped back and motioned for his two armed guards to remain nearby.

A few guests finally decided it'd be in their best interest to move. They didn't leave, just backed up and gave the two space to square off.

The Viking guy came at Carter without delay, but Carter shocked her by sliding straight under his tree trunk of an arm before spinning around, grabbing that same arm, and from the looks of it, dislocated it from the shoulder.

Tessa buried her face into Gray's back and hid her gasp in his shirt. Deciding she couldn't watch, she kept her face hidden, listening to the grunts, blows, and sounds of flesh and bone smashing against each other.

She counted back from ten, hoping it'd soon end. When it didn't, she lifted her head and chanced another look, immediately regretting it. Carter, who had a bloody nose and streaks of red all over his white dress shirt, had just thrust his fingers into the man's eye socket.

And I'm going to be sick.

She hid her face again as Gray murmured promises under his breath that everything would be okay. Based on Carter's insane fighting skills, she was truly beginning to think so.

A minute later, she checked the scene again, finding Carter on top of the guy, appearing to crush his Adam's apple with the knuckles of both index fingers.

"Don't look," Gray begged, sensing she'd been peeking.

"Okay." She let go of his sides and folded her arms between his back and her chest, burying her face in her palms to prevent the stupid curiosity in her from checking again.

"It's over," Gray announced not even a minute later.

"As in someone's dead?" she asked, cringing.

When she peeled herself away and scooched to the side of Gray's tall frame, she spotted Carter standing tall while patting the blood beneath his nose with a napkin. Then he swapped it for another and wiped his hands clean before tossing the linen.

The Viking assassin was motionless on the floor with a fork in his throat. *A fork?* Where'd he even get that? *Stick a fork in him, and he's done? Really?!*

Carter tossed a look toward the manager and said, "Add the damage to my tab."

The manager nodded as the two guards grabbed the Viking's ankles. The rest of the guests returned to their drinks as if nothing earth-shattering had just happened.

"I'm just . . ." Tessa covered her mouth, and Gray pulled her into his arms and cradled her head, shielding her from the view of the dead man being dragged out.

"Sorry for that," Carter said before snatching his whiskey and throwing it back.

"You had no choice," Gray told him, freeing Tessa from his embrace. But Gray's attention was elsewhere now. Tessa turned to see a stunning woman in a red pantsuit peering at them from across the bar.

"Zoey," Carter said, discarding his empty glass. "Give me thirty minutes alone with her." He grabbed his suit jacket from where he'd tossed it and casually strode from the bar. Zoey nodded what appeared to be a hello to Gray, then quietly followed Carter.

Tessa blinked, shock still knocking around in her body, making her feel a little lightheaded. "Can we go?"

There was already a cleaning crew on scene. Mopping up the blood. Hiding the evidence of death.

Gray wordlessly snatched her hand, maneuvered her around the cleaning crew, and rushed them to the set of elevators. No sight of Carter or Zoey along their way.

She looked up at him, the queasy feeling now gone. And in its place, something unexpected. Arousal? "Should we meet up with the others, or . . .?" *Or what? What am I asking? To be forked? I mean, fucked?*

Once the doors opened, Gray quietly pulled Tessa into the empty elevator. As the doors slid shut, he pushed her up against the wall, and his palms skimmed her silhouette.

"What do you want to do?" Gray brought his mouth close to hers, barely a whisper of space separating them, then he pinned her with a dark, heated look.

"Is it bad that what I want is—"

"Exactly what I want," he rasped and sealed his mouth over hers.

CHAPTER THIRTY-FIVE

THE SECOND THE DOOR TO THEIR SUITE WAS SECURELY locked, Gray pounced, pinning Tessa against the wall. Sliding up her dress, he kissed the column of her throat, working his mouth over her soft skin.

Tessa arched into him, moaning when he slowly trailed a finger along the slit of her panties.

"Fuck, sweetheart, you're so wet." No, wet was an understatement. Her panties were damn near soaked. And he suddenly found himself stupidly jealous of the silk barrier. "Does fighting turn you on?" he murmured into her ear before hooking the silk to the side.

"I hope not," she mused, her voice husky with desire as he touched her pussy. His balls tightened the second his hand made contact with her clit. "But that kiss in the elevator . . . oh my gosh, it definitely got me hot," she labored out.

He stroked her sex, painting his fingers in her arousal, then dipped a finger inside her while simultaneously caressing her sensitive spot with his thumb. "I know I said the next time we're together I'd do it right," he began, his mouth near her ear as he continued to stroke her, relishing in her little whimpering sounds, "and yeah, we're in a hotel full of criminals, Carter just forked a guy to death, and we're short on time, but—"

"Gray?"

He leaned back to find her eyes, his hand going still. He cocked a brow in surprise at the wicked glint in her eyes and the smile on her lips.

"You're starting to ramble like me."

He bent in and nipped her bottom lip. "Am I, now?" he teased as she parted her lips for him. The second his tongue met hers, he resumed his featherlight ministrations over her sensitive flesh. "We do have a slight problem though," he said between kisses and intensifying brushes of his fingers over her clit.

"What's that?" She grabbed hold of his biceps, shimmying against his hand wedged between her thighs.

"I don't have a condom. Do you?"

"And if I say no, but I'm on birth control, will you make love to me anyway?"

His body tensed at her words. He remembered her saying the same on the boat. But hell, take this woman bare and not be a sixty-second man?

"I've never done it without one," he confessed before kissing her again, sweeping his tongue with hers in a dance he felt no one else had ever known the steps to before her. Like they really were made for each other.

What could have been if I hadn't walked away?

"I've never either," Tessa cut off his thoughts before they had a chance to really steal him from the moment. "Gone bare, I mean."

He stopped kissing her. Stopped touching her. He stepped back, and her dress slowly slid back into place. "I have no right losing my mind at the idea that anyone else has ever touched you, watched movies with you, kissed you, loved you." He took two more steps back, and an uncomfortable band of pressure built in the walls of his chest. "But here I am, losing my mind anyway."

She stared at him, drawing her fingers along her thigh. Bunching her dress to her waist, he watched as she worked her panties down until they snagged at the top of her boots. He slowly lowered his eyes to her swollen cunt, beautifully on display for him. "We can be each other's *onlys*," she murmured seductively. "I probably just butchered the English language, but I think you get what I mean?"

"Yeah, I think I do," he rasped, and a second later he had her pinned against the wall again, her dress sliding back down to her thighs.

Their fingers interlocked and their hands landed on the wall off to her sides. He stared deep into her eyes, the words, *I love you*, burning and racing through his mind. Weaving right around his heart. *Mending* that once barely beating organ of his. But for whatever reason, fear maybe, he couldn't get himself to share what was on his mind.

"So, what do you say, you want to be my only?" She traced the seam of her lips with her tongue, that sexy glint returning to her eyes as he leaned in.

"Yes, I want to be *each other's onlys*." He kissed her hard. His control snapping. Maybe his sanity too since they were about to make love at such an infamous location. In the middle of an op. And he couldn't bring himself to care about any of it.

He released her hands and stepped back to lift her dress back up. He cupped her pussy, resisting the urge to growl out some sort of caveman grunt of ownership. But fucking fuck, he wanted her. All of her. Every piece of her. Forever. He'd never in his life felt such a wild sense of need to possess another. To touch, fill, and just be with someone so much in his life.

"I'm yours," she said like a promise, like she'd read his mind. "Take what's yours," she added, her lower lip wobbling.

He let go of her dress and began working at the buttons of his shirt, struggling to make sense of the emotions pushing through. "Take everything off," he finally managed to grit out.

"Boots too?"

"Everything-everything," he demanded gruffly.

Eyes glassy with need, lips swollen and slightly parted, she nodded and freed her panties from where they'd caught on her boots, tossing them aside. While he removed his clothes, she peeled the dress over her head and removed her bra, giving him an eyeful of her luscious tits. Her pink nipples were erect and puckered.

He shoved down his boxers and gripped his shaft, anxious to fill her. He kept on his prosthesis, knowing she'd never judge him, to see him as "less than" because of it. And damn, he felt whole again under her heated gaze, and his heart jumped a little at the thought.

She turned and wiggled her gorgeous ass as she took her sweet time removing her boots, and he stroked his cock, knowing exactly what to do with that ass when they had time.

"Tessa, so help me, you're going to get spanked or have that third hole filled if you shake your ass anymore while you take your time removing your boots," he remarked, dead serious. He tightened his hold on his dick, pulling slowly, almost painfully, in controlled movements up and down, doing his best not to totally lose it.

She shot him a saucy look over her shoulder and played with fire, moving her hips from side to side. That was it . . .

He lifted her up to toss her onto the bed. She landed on all fours, ass in the air, just like he wanted.

Following her onto the bed, he shifted his residual limb in the right position to settle on his knees behind her. He bent forward and swatted her pussy with his palm, then followed the same path with his tongue.

"Oh my God," she cried as he flicked her swollen clit with the tip of his tongue.

"Tell me what you want," he demanded, digging his fingers into her sides as he devoured her beautiful cunt, tasting the promise of a million *what-could've-beens* on his tongue with every sweeping motion. Hating himself for losing thirteen years because he'd been an idiot and scared.

"I want you inside me," she begged.

"You sure? You don't want me to get you off with my mouth first?" She whimpered, then called for God. "Just me, sweetheart. Sorry to disappoint."

"Oh, trust me, I'm . . ." She began bucking against his tongue, and he eased back before she came. He knew what she really wanted—for him to fill that tight pussy and bring them to the perfect release. Together. "Please. Make love to me, Grayson."

He flipped her to her back and climbed on top of her, taking care to shift his residual leg to a position that would ensure the metal from his prosthesis didn't rub up against her while they made love.

She stared up at him, placing her hands on his chest as she wet her lips. *Such a tease.* He leaned in, prepared to kiss her, but she shook her head.

"Don't even think about it. I have no desire to know how I taste," she said with a light laugh, pushing on his chest as her eyes fell to his muscles beneath her soft palms.

"Oh, but you taste so good." He lifted his brows a few times. "I promise."

"I'll take your word for it." She swiped her hand over the bit of chest hair and whispered, "I knew you didn't shave your chest."

He smirked and dipped in again, but she turned her cheek, forcing him to brush his lips along her jawline. "You ready for me, Tess?"

"Mmm. Yes, please." She lifted her hips off the bed, and he dropped from his palms to his forearms, drawing himself closer. She reached between their bodies and positioned his head at her soaked center.

With their eyes locked and his heart pumping harder than maybe ever in his life, he pushed inside her. He was fairly certain everything went black for a moment as their bodies connected without any barriers between them.

"Gray, are you with me still?" At Tessa's words, and the feel of her hands on his cheeks, he pulled himself free from his blissed-out haze and focused on the most beautiful woman he'd ever seen in his life.

"I'm here," he promised. "I'm with you." He blinked, surprised to find his eyes glossy with unshed emotion. He resumed moving, in and nearly all the way out, feeling her warm, tight walls squeezing every inch of him. *Perfection.*

He knew whatever was happening between them right now was so much more than just sex. It would never be *just* sex with Tessa. And then he remembered her *I could fall back in love with you* comment from the yacht and—

"I loved you too. Thirteen years ago," he confessed what he hadn't truly understood until now, acknowledging it all as emotion swelled in his chest. "I loved you too," he repeated, his voice strained. "And I should have told that doctor in

Boston to piss off, you were mine. I'm so sorry it took me so long."

Her lips skimmed along his jawline, and she lifted her chin and brought her mouth to his ear, and he felt the quiver of her lips and the promise of her words when she said, "I forgive you." Then she slid her hands down to his arms and held on to him as he moved. Took his time. Wanting it to last forever.

Face to face again, her expressive, beautiful eyes remained fixed on his with every thrust.

At the feel of her body tensing as she shifted her hips from side to side, rubbing her sensitive spot against the short hairs at his groin . . . he knew she was close.

"Come for me, sweetheart," he begged. "Take us both to Heaven," he pleaded, his voice a hoarse whisper of emotion and intensity. He felt the tremor shoot through her body, her back arching off the bed as her breasts smashed against his chest. She cried and cursed. Screamed for God again. Then screamed for him.

With one final thrust, his vision went black just before he saw the light, pretty sure the only woman he could ever truly love really had just sent him to Heaven.

CHAPTER THIRTY-SIX

"Third pair tonight."

Gray peered at Tessa as she slipped into her panties, shooting her a cocky grin. "If I have my way, those will be just as ruined as the others before they come off later." He tipped his chin toward the wall of glass. "I have ideas, and all of them involve you naked against the window, pussy fisting my cock while your tits are crushed against my chest, and—"

"Am I only wearing high heels in this fantasy?"

"Fantasy implies it may not come true." His fingers went still on his belt buckle. Instead of clasping it, he let it go and ate up the space between them. "Wait," he directed as he grabbed her bra dangling in her hand. "I need to feel these tits before you hide them." He captured one heavy breast in his palm, then dipped his head and lowered his mouth there. He rolled the nipple of her other breast between his thumb and forefinger, and a little whimper escaped her as he pinched her nipple between his teeth. Then he eased back just enough to look up into her eyes and murmured, "And yes to the heels."

She reached between them for his belt buckle. "I wish you were naked and not in those jeans right now."

He'd opted for a long-sleeved black shirt and his favorite pair of well-worn jeans instead of the wardrobe he'd been provided for the trip.

"Later," he promised, squeezing her breast again before leaning in to circle her nipple with the flat part of his tongue, soothing the sting his teeth had delivered moments before. His cock was already straining against his jeans, begging for freedom. To slide back inside her.

"Mmm. That patience you think I have is going to be tested." She sighed as he let her go so she could finish getting dressed.

He kept his eyes on her as she clipped on her bra, then covered up with a cream-colored cashmere sweater.

"I have to admit, this raw and dirty sex you're promising does sound appealing," she mused while pulling on a pair of skintight jeans. "But don't knock what we just had. It was one of the best moments of my life."

He finished buckling his belt, the only thing hanging limp on him. "And what are some of these other moments? How can I earn my way to the best, not just 'one of the best'?"

She laughed while putting on her ballet-looking flats. "Who says you aren't already there?"

He closed the distance between them and snatched her hip, drawing her against him. "Am I?"

"Is a moment between us at the top of yours?"

Before he could answer, a hard knock at the door had him reaching for his back, instinct priming him to draw his weapon. *I'm unarmed, dammit.* "Who is it?" he barked out, letting her go.

"It's Jack. We've been calling. No answer. You two okay?"

Gray's shoulders relaxed. "Sorry. I thought we had thirty minutes." He checked the time. *Shit.* Thirty-*seven* minutes had passed since Carter gave them what felt like "recess" while he dealt with Zoey.

When he opened the door for Jack, his best friend smirked and lifted his wrist to peek at his Apple watch. "I can give you two more minutes. Any more, and Carter will fetch you himself. And he's particularly grumpy, even for him. Between Zoey showing up and the guy he forked to death—that was quite the show on the security cams, by the way—he's in a shit mood."

"Why's Zoey here?" Gray asked, grabbing his phone, motioning for Tessa to enter the hall. The rest of the team's suites were only a few doors down. Gray moved slowly, using the short walk to get as much information from Jack as he could.

"She was in Germany. Heard through the grapevine that Carter had checked into The Sapphire and that goliath of a man was on his way for him," Jack explained.

"So, she came to warn Carter about that guy?" Tessa asked.

"Yeah," Jack began, "and she figured if Carter checked in here, it couldn't be for a good reason. She put two and two together that he'd be looking for someone. Or someone was looking for him. Lucky for us, she's British, former MI6, and has a catalog of baddies in her head from her time in the U.K."

"Oh." Tessa stopped in front of Gwen and Oliver's suite and fidgeted with the bracelet on her wrist. "That really is lucky for us."

"I'd say so," Jack went on. "Because our genius team narrowed down a list of suspects while Carter was finding creative uses for cutlery, and Zoey is fairly certain she knows who our mark is based on the information we provided her."

"That was fast." Gray shook his head in surprise.

"Fast talkers and thinkers." Jack knocked twice. "Oh, and maybe don't make any jokes about how Carter and Zoey used the first twenty minutes while alone before joining us." He smirked. "It might poke the bear."

"I'm guessing that means you already poked the man who just killed a Viking?" Tessa chuckled as Gray banded his arm behind her back and pulled her to his side.

Jack shrugged. "It's how I roll," he teased.

Oliver opened the suite door a moment later, and his smile said it all. Gray wasn't sure how Carter spent his time alone with Zoey, but Oliver was damn confident in how Gray and Tessa shared those thirty-seven minutes.

Gray spied a blush creep up Tessa's cheeks, and she tucked her hair behind her ears, and he let go of her, motioning for her to enter the room ahead of him.

Once they were all inside, Carter looked up from where he'd been standing behind Gwen's laptop. He'd changed into new clothes, and his hair was slicked back as if he'd taken a quick shower to clean the blood from his body. He tipped his chin toward Zoey, directing her to talk.

Zoey's green eyes landed on Gray. "Hey." He nodded back his hello, and she relaxed her arms from their folded position as she walked around the couch to approach the newcomers in the room. "Ever heard of Maxwell Sherlock?"

Gray flipped through the internal file of bad guys he kept buried in the back of his mind for days like this, finally securing the name. "Of course. Wealthy English businessman who was accused of . . ." *Oh, shit.* "Buying intel on the dark net. Intel stolen from someone who hacked MI6. But Maxwell wasn't charged, right? That was what, two years ago? And you think he's our guy?"

"I do," Zoey confirmed. "MI6 knew Maxwell was their buyer. They had all the evidence they needed. Their so-called ducks were in a row for an iron-clad case. But there was one fatal flaw in their plan to put him on trial for treason. If it were to ever surface that the intel existed, the agency would be in just as much trouble as he was. And to make it worse, Maxwell only got his hands on the data, hoping to sell it to a much bigger fish. Well, a shark. And the government didn't want anyone to know that North Korea had been close to accessing a highly classified program that wasn't supposed to exist in the first place."

"Hold up there." Gray lifted his hand. "Rewind. Start again." He shook his head in surprise. "I know I'm tired and on edge, but are you telling me Maxwell Sherlock didn't just buy intelligence documents, he purchased an entire spy program on the dark net, one that's off the books, and then he planned to sell it to North Korea?"

"Yeah, for five hundred and sixty million pounds. Thankfully, he was stopped just in time," Zoey responded. "But yeah, a much bigger price tag than the twenty-five million pounds he paid the hacker on the dark net for it."

"So, to keep this from going public, most of the evidence they'd need to share for a conviction had to be redacted? Suppressed?" Gray followed up, and she nodded. "And MI6 didn't just throw him in some black site to rot and forgo the trial?"

"When the police let him go," Zoey started, "MI6 officers discreetly tried to catch him, but he went dark."

Gray looked over at Tessa, checking for her reaction. Her eyes were on her lap, her skin pale. *Shock? Yeah, me too.*

"The only thing that'd drag that arsehole out of hiding is a second chance to make half a billion," Zoey said. "And I can guarantee whatever Maxwell purchased from that NSA traitor is something similar to what was stolen from MI6. He probably has a very motivated buyer. Russia. China. Iran.

North Korea again. Pick any dictator who'd love to get their hands on a top-secret American program."

"But the project my dad was managing was supposed to help operators. Prevent bad intel from leading to unnecessary risks for soldiers, right?" Tessa spoke up, her eyes going to Gray.

Like the day of my accident. The day those Rangers died. "So, you think the NSA lied to us? Maxwell Sherlock wouldn't care about an NSA program like that, right?"

"I've been doing some digging," Sydney said, taking point over the secure connection on Gwen's laptop, "and I think Zoey's right. They're keeping secrets."

"Shocker," Gwen said, catching Gray's eyes before she focused back on her laptop. "They were probably using that program to spy on Americans instead. That MI6 program was spying domestically, right?"

Zoey peered at Gwen and remained quiet, which was an answer in itself.

"We need to get NSA Director Torres back on the phone. See what in the hell they're keeping from us," Carter said. "But regardless, the second Maxwell shows his face here, we enact the plan and take him down before he can go off the grid again."

"Um." Gwen pointed toward her screen, brows lifted. "Looks like the NSA will have to fess up to their lies later. Maxwell just walked into the hotel lobby. And he's not alone."

"We figured the buyer would have security detail with him," Carter said.

Gwen shook her head. "Not just that. He's got one of Britain's best hackers at his side, which means we'll have company watching that surveillance footage soon." Her shoulders fell. "And he's not just any hacker, he's one of my ex-boyfriends."

"I swear," Wyatt said, popping onto the secure line, "your choice of men is going to give me a bloody heart attack one day."

* * *

"THIS IS ALPHA TWO. STATUS?" SITTING INSIDE THE LOBBY by the fireplace, Gray tapped his ear to check in with his team. Zero dark thirty. What a fucking time for the op.

"Alpha One. I have eyes on the HVT's room. Third floor," Carter shared over comms. "His team is in the suite with him."

And his team consisted of four big-ass men and one surprisingly muscular hacker.

"Alpha Three, status?" Gray asked Jack next.

"This is Alpha Three. In position. I've got the others on the line, waiting for next steps."

"Roger that." Gray peered at Tessa sitting nervously at his side, her hands bunched into fists on her lap, eyes focused on the flickering flames of the fireplace. "Alpha Four, you good?" he followed up with Oliver.

"Little Bird and Buttercup tapped into the drones the hotel uses to ensure there are no aerial threats and everything looks clear," Oliver shared.

I'm sure Mya and Gwen love the code names you gave them. Based on the grumbles in the background, they were definitely not fans.

"Be sure to keep them safe in that room when this is over. They don't engage with any tangos," Gray reminded him, refusing to use those nicknames. He wasn't looking to get slapped later.

"This will work, right?" Tessa whispered.

Gray muted his comm. "Assuming Maxwell has a second team on the outside . . . yeah, it'll work. He'll more than likely remain back at the hotel to keep at a safe distance from the action." *Then we draw that second team away and Carter and the others here handle Maxwell and his security.*

"Okay." She wet her dry lips, and he was surprised she'd forgotten to grab ChapStick from the room.

Then again, they'd been in a hurry. But he'd made time to place several of Gwen's little clear tracker stickers all over her body for a "just in case" situation. And then he'd had her swap her ballet flats for warm and comfortable boots.

When they'd checked in earlier that evening, he'd left her winter coat in the front seat of the Aston Martin in preparation for this moment. She'd be trekking out into the cold to a little hut once they were back at the cottage, and he didn't need her freezing to death.

"Are we sure it was a good idea to keep your dad in the dark on this?" she asked a few quiet minutes later.

"They might have told us to wait. Change course with the new information. And we don't want to take the risk this thing lasts any longer than necessary," he quickly explained, confirming what he and the rest of the team had decided minutes earlier before they'd advanced into their current positions. Gray tapped his ear again. "Alpha Four, anything yet? Has the ex hotwired the feed yet?" I.e., had Gwen's hacker ex-boyfriend hacked the surveillance footage to put eyes on them?

"Not yet," Oliver answered. "Hopefully soon."

"Roger that." Gray muted his comm so his teammates couldn't hear him chatting with Tessa. He peered around the mostly empty lobby, an uncomfortable thought invading his mind to accompany the uncomfortable feeling settling in his gut. They would need to begin acting shortly. They looked too cozy together for a couple about to fight. "We should probably—"

"Not look like we love each other?" Tessa closed her eyes and wrinkled her nose. "Sorry, I mean . . ." A beautiful blush traveled up into her cheeks, reaching the tips of her ears, making him forget where they were for a moment.

He'd admitted he'd been in love with her thirteen years ago, even if his young-ass self hadn't realized it then . . . but they'd yet to share those words in the "here and now."

Once she parted her lids, Gray smirked and pointed to her ear, reminding her she was on comms.

"I remembered to mute us," she said with a smile.

Yeah, pretending to be mad at her was going to be hard. How'd he do it thirteen years ago?

He tipped his head, silently requesting her to scooch back on the bench to put some space between them for their impending fight. Then he did his best to scowl, trying to play his part.

Tessa had to stifle another smile with the back of her hand, probably in response to his ridiculous fake scowl, before she cleared her throat and shook her head as if trying to focus and get into character.

Gray was about to say something when static cut over his comm. Did Oliver unmute his comm or did someone else? Did someone have news?

Gray's heartbeat jumped into his throat when he realized he was *overhearing* Gwen talking in the background over Oliver's comm.

"Sydney was the love of Gray's life. And I know it was hard on him when she chose Beckett, but—"

"You're. On. Comms," Jack hissed, beating Gray to the punch. Gray's head was too busy spinning at listening to his niece talk about Sydney, knowing Tessa had just heard everything she'd said.

"Shit, sorry," Gwen said, then the line fell quiet.

Gray slowly worked up the courage to peer at Tessa. His stomach dropped at the sight of her slack-jawed, her complexion lacking its normal color. That gorgeous blush was gone. And her eyes were coated in a watery sheen.

"I can explain." Unable to stop himself, he reached for her hand, but she pulled back and stood.

She covered her mouth, her eyes narrowing on the marble floors. "We're supposed to look unhappy. I'm just, um."

Fuck. He stood and went for her hand again, but she lifted her palms between them. *No, you're definitely not acting.* "I . . ." *Shit.* "Sydney was my girlfriend at West Point. I proposed to her, and she said no," he rushed through the messy truth of what he'd withheld from her. "I was going to tell you, but I didn't know how to bring it up."

"West Point," Tessa said, her tone somber. Heartbreaking. "I was wearing your college shirt, and that was . . ." She closed her eyes and a tear dropped down her cheek.

All he wanted to do was wrap her in his arms and tell her it was okay. To ignore what Gwen had said. Forget whatever horrible picture Tessa was now painting in her mind.

But before he could say more, Oliver was on comms, and this time, on purpose, "You've got the green light. It's time."

Tessa lowered her palms, a few more tears spilling. "I thought this was our second chance," she cried, her lip wobbling, "but I didn't realize I was your second choice."

CHAPTER THIRTY-SEVEN

Speeding down the dark, tree-lined road, Tessa swiped away as many tears as possible with one hand as she clutched the steering wheel with the other. She'd broken into an embarrassing sob back in the lobby, then snatched the keys to their Aston Martin from Gray's pocket and took off as planned. Her tears being real? *Not* part of the plan.

In her rearview mirror, she spotted Gray trailing behind her in Oliver and Gwen's Bugatti.

The love of your life? Sydney . . . that genius, gorgeous woman? And you kept it from me because—

"Slow down," Gray popped into her ear, interrupting her thoughts. "Please. It's late. Dark. And the roads could be icy," he begged.

She wasn't sure if the rest of his team could still hear them on the earpiece or not. Maybe they were now out of range? Was it worth taking the chance? She brought her second hand to the wheel, refusing to unmute the comm either way. Because what would she say? She was a mess. Not thinking clearly enough to respond to him.

Maybe it wasn't fair to be mad at Gray over a past

relationship when they'd only had a handful of days, and one summer thirteen years ago together. It was unrealistic to think he'd never been in love before.

Love. Of. Your. Life. Those are big words though. HUGE.

How would she compete with that kind of love? She'd always believed her dating life sucked because the love of her life walked away from her thirteen years ago. Dammit, *Gray* was that person for her.

You proposed. You didn't walk away from her. She walked away from you by saying no. Don't men always want the ones they can't have?

Her stomach was queasy, and she choked out another sob, unleashing too many tears that'd obstruct her vision if she didn't get control of herself fast.

"Tessa, please. I'm so sorry. Just slow down," Gray pleaded, his voice breaking. Catching in the cracks now forming in her heart, breaking in real time.

She slowly eased her foot off the gas pedal just a hair, listening to him without responding. She didn't want to die in a car accident while trying to save herself from Maxwell Sherlock.

"Thank you," Gray said when her speed dropped to below sixty kilometers per hour. "In thirty seconds, part B begins," he added, keeping his tone steady as she heard him slip back into operator mode.

Vehicle interdiction is part B, she reminded herself.

Wyatt and Jesse's SUV would pull out in front of her car, forcing her to stop. And two guys from Echo Team would roll up behind Gray's car, pinning them in with nowhere to go. They'd have on military uniforms with the U.S. flag visible on their vests to help sell the idea the NSA sent operators to grab Tessa and Gray the second they left the hotel.

"Slow to thirty," Gray told her. "They're about to pull out, and we don't want a collision."

Tessa did her best to fight back additional tears, then she did as Gray instructed. A few seconds later, on the windy and empty back roads, a dark SUV pulled out up ahead, blocking her path.

She slammed on her brakes and watched as Gray's car slowed behind her.

Wyatt and Jesse exited their vehicle, armed with rifles while moving as if in battle. Heads low. Weapons pointed her way.

Wyatt barked out a series of orders as he strode toward the driver's side door: *Exit the car! Get on the ground! Hands behind your head!*

With a trembling hand, she opened the door and put her hands behind her head while dropping to her knees. Shit, she'd forgotten her coat.

On the cold hard road, Wyatt urged her flat onto her stomach and then gripped her wrists at her back. "Sorry," he whispered in her ear while zip-tying her wrists, and her comm fell to the ground. Wyatt snatched the earpiece and pocketed it. "Maxwell has a drone overhead watching."

Ohh. "Oh-okay." Once he had her standing again, she looked back to find Gray. The headlights of the Bugatti illuminated the scene, and she saw Gray on his feet, too, hands behind his back. He was maybe fifty feet away, but she knew if he was closer, she'd see the apology in his eyes.

"Come on," Wyatt said. "Gray will be in the second vehicle. We're leaving these cars here."

She tossed one last look back at Gray. He was still on the road just staring at her as one of Wyatt's teammates tried to urge him to walk. She couldn't read his lips, but he was mouthing something to her.

She shook her head, giving in to tears she couldn't keep at bay.

"You're one hell of an actress," Wyatt remarked once she was safely tucked into the back of the SUV. With Jesse behind the wheel, they were on the move in seconds.

Jesse peeked back at her in the rearview mirror, and she knew he'd heard what happened in the hotel lobby when he murmured, "I don't think she's acting."

* * *

"WE'LL TALK SOON, I PROMISE. BUT YOU NEED TO GET OUT of here," Gray pleaded with Tessa inside the cottage that might soon be riddled with bullet holes. "Wyatt won't let anything happen to you."

Tessa stared at Gray as he strapped on a chest plate beneath a vest full of magazines. His movements were methodical and focused as he geared up and slipped back into operator mode. She'd yet to talk to him since running from the hotel lobby. Not a single word had fallen from her lips. But she didn't want to walk away from him before he went to war and not . . . say *something*.

"Tessa?" It was Wyatt this time, trying to free her from her numb state.

Gray frowned and grabbed a heavy jacket from a nearby duffel bag. It was two sizes too big for her, but he quietly helped her into the coat. He began to zip her up as if she weren't up for the task herself, his eyes slowly following the zipper before landing on her face.

"We need to go out the hidden exit, so the drone doesn't see us leaving," Wyatt said. "The exit drops us off in the woods."

"And you need to do it now," Chris said from

somewhere in the room. She knew he was talking to her, but she couldn't take her eyes off Gray. "Sydney's in my ear saying there are four SUVs flying down the road, only one klick out."

Gray clutched hold of Tessa's arms, leaned in to bring his mouth to her ear and murmured, "You're not my second anything. You're my meant-to-be." Chills erupted over her skin at his words. And then he let go of her, backed up and turned, tossing a hand in the air as if begging Wyatt to take her away, unable to watch the sight of her leaving.

Wyatt reached for her arm as Chris gave a few commands to Bear, but she couldn't budge. Tears filled her eyes as she stared at Gray's bowed head, his back muscles pinching together. The last thing she needed was for him to be worrying about where her head was at while fighting off bad guys to keep her safe.

"Gray," she cried, but he didn't turn. And she wondered if he physically couldn't look at her right now. Like it was all too much. "We'll be okay," she whispered, doing her best to let him know she meant that in every way possible, even if she'd yet to wrap her head around the news about Sydney. "Stay safe. Please," was the last thing she managed out before Wyatt began hauling her from the room.

Her body went still when Gray rasped from behind, "For you . . . anything."

She stifled the weeping sound that nearly broke free from her lips, then allowed Wyatt to take the lead. To get her to safety so Gray and his teammates could focus on the mission.

She remained in a foggy daze as she followed Wyatt through a short tunnel that dropped them off in the woods at the back of the cottage.

"You need to wear these so you can see where you're going." Wyatt handed her a pair of what she assumed were night-vision goggles like the ones on his helmet. He helped her put them on, and a green hue filled her line of sight.

"Steer clear of any open patches above," Wyatt reminded her once they were on the move in the forest.

Right. The drone. The bad guys would focus on pursuing her if they knew she wasn't in the cottage, and their plan would go to hell.

"Almost there," Wyatt said a minute later, which meant the shelter area wasn't more than a few acres away from the cottage. He remained at her side, keeping his pace matched with hers. He had a pistol drawn in one hand, a rucksack of gear on his back, and there was a rifle slung across his body.

Tessa looked back to see Bear trotting behind them with his ears pointed up. His dark eyes moved left and right, assessing. Nose to the ground for a moment, then to the air, sniffing out potential threats on their dirt path.

Bear abruptly halted, going stiff like a statue. Wyatt stopped walking when she did, and he turned toward Bear as if alarmed by something as well. He knocked his goggles away from his face and focused on the screen on his wrist, which was half the size of her iPhone. Not a standard watch.

"What is it?" she whispered.

"They sent men to cover every side of the property," he said, his tone low, but she still heard the disappointment. Clearly, not what he wanted to happen. "I have a heat signature on approach." He swapped his pistol for a knife, then knocked his goggles back in place. "We can't give away our position." He made some hand signal she didn't recognize to Bear, who understood the command even in the dark, and went into a nearby brush and crouched in hiding.

"Behind the tree," Wyatt told Tessa, and she quietly did as he said, careful not to whack herself in the face with one of the low-hanging branches.

Her heart thundered in her ears as she waited for what would happen next. And she didn't have to wait long.

Unlike Carter's fight with the guy earlier, she had no intention of watching this time. She listened to the sounds of death. Bear's low growls were accompanied by something deeper, as if gnawing at flesh. Moans and muffled cries assaulted her senses before all she could hear was the thudding of her own heart. *Just breathe.*

"Okay," Wyatt said a moment later, and she hesitantly peeked around the tree to see Wyatt wiping the blade of his knife along his cargo pants, standing by an unmoving lump on the ground.

Dead? Her stomach turned, and she slowly left her position to join her two heroes.

Wyatt tucked away his knife, then quickly tossed a few dead branches over the body. "You okay?" he asked while grabbing his pistol from where it was strapped to his outer thigh.

She nodded, the words stuck in her throat as she stepped around the now partially hidden body.

Wyatt checked his screen again. "They're converging on the cabin now."

"How do you know?" she asked while moving her goggles up to see his screen.

"Because Sydney has eyes in the sky for us too. Thermal signatures." He pointed to some purple-looking blobs inside the cottage. "Our guys are tagged with a dye so we know who is who," he explained. "The other figures about to engage are the enemies."

"That's a lot of people," she whispered, returning her goggles back in place.

"It's what we do. No worries." He patted her shoulder, then tipped his head. "Let's go. More are coming. I need to set up. We're almost there now," he added as they began walking again, and she spied the little hut up ahead.

"More will come to the woods? The hut?" she asked for clarification as he unlocked the door to the shelter a few seconds later.

"Unfortunately. This guy has an army. We weren't expecting this many, but like I said—"

"It's what you do," she finished for him as he stepped aside so she and Bear could enter.

"Stay in that corner by Bear." He pointed to the back of the tiny empty space. The shelter was the size of a small bathroom. The sheltered area in the woods had seemed like a good idea in planning, but if bad guys were going to come anyway, maybe she should've stayed with Gray?

Shivering from the cold, even with the big coat on, she sank down onto the wood floor and pinned her knees to her chest. Bear dropped next to her and began licking his paw. She opted not to consider whether it was blood on his fur.

"This is Echo One," Wyatt said to presumably someone over his earpiece. "Confirming I have the package in position. One tango down en route."

"Am I the package?" she asked him as he removed his rucksack and took a knee before pulling something out and perching his rifle on it in front of the open window.

"Yeah, letting Gray know you're safe."

"Did he respond?" she asked.

Wyatt stopped what he was doing and looked her way, their goggles still their only way of "seeing" each other in the dark. "The cottage was breached. He can't talk."

Ohh. She recoiled at his words but tried to calm herself down at the fact Wyatt seemed unaffected by the "breach" happening.

"I thought we didn't want them to know our—" She let

her thought end unfinished when heavy gunfire erupted in the distance.

Wyatt shifted flat on his belly, removed his goggles, then set his eye behind the scope of his rifle. "Yeah, let's hope the men still think they're only fighting off a military team sent by the NSA that intercepted you two outside the hotel. We need to buy as much time as possible for Carter to make his move on Maxwell."

Bear stopped licking his paw and army-crawled away from her, sliding himself on his stomach to get next to Wyatt.

"You hear something I'm not seeing?" Wyatt asked him.

"Other than bullets flying?" Tessa whispered under her breath what she'd meant to only think.

"Shit," Wyatt cursed. "They have a helo, and someone just took down our drone. Who the fuck is this Maxwell guy?"

Okay, Wyatt being worried was not what she wanted to hear.

Tessa clutched her legs even tighter to her chest, hating the fact she had no clue if Gray was even still safe.

"They're landing in the field behind the cottage. Not fast-roping in. I can handle them. Long distance, but I'm solid," Wyatt said. She assumed he was no longer talking to her, but to whoever was in his ear. Maybe Sydney, since Tessa knew she was safely hidden in an SUV down the road from the cottage.

Sydney. Shit. Don't think about her right now. Not the time, Tessa.

Wyatt fired off a round from his rifle a second later. "Well, if they were planning to exfil and take you out via helo, they'll be needing a new pilot."

"You shot the pilot?"

"Yeah, and I'm about to take these two other guys exiting

the bird down as well. Hold on." Wyatt dialed something on his gun and shifted around a little. And then sent a round. A few seconds later, he sent another shot. "All three tangos from the bird down."

World's best sniper, for sure.

"Yeah, I can hear you, go ahead," Wyatt said, talking to his earpiece again, and chills scattered down her arms beneath the bulky weight of the coat. After listening for a bit, he murmured, "Roger that."

"What is it? Good news?" Based on the fact there was still an exchange of heavy gunfire coming from outside, the fight wasn't over yet.

"Maxwell's men out here realized this was a setup, but they're still pushing forward, which means they're coming after you regardless," he quickly explained. "Maxwell and one of his guards took off from the hotel at the news, but he sent a diversion to buy himself some time. His other three guards attacked Jack, Oliver, and Carter before Carter could make his move. Clearly, he decided they were part of our trap and a threat."

"What does that mean?"

"It means the armed hotel guards will force the three of them to engage in a fight if they don't want to be gunned down. Winner wins. Loser dies," he reminded her of what she'd witnessed earlier.

"But I thought Jack and Oliver were in the room with—"

"Gwen and Mya are okay," he cut her off. "Hotel rules dictate a fair fight. One-on-one. Mya called Sydney and let her know what was going on."

"So, Maxwell will get away if they can't hurry up with the fight and chase after him?" *This won't be over after all?*

"Zoey went after him. She won't let him out of her sight," Wyatt said, his tone confident.

Zoey? Maybe it really was lucky she had shown up.

"Tessa, the phone in my back pocket is ringing. The only one who'd be calling that line is my daughter. I can't look away from the scope, so I need you to answer it," Wyatt said, his confidence now replaced with worry.

She crawled over to where he was stretched out and awkwardly patted down his ass in search of his phone.

"Got it. Want her on speakerphone, or will someone hear us?" She went to Wyatt's other side, keeping herself away from the window.

"Speaker but near my ear," he directed, and she did as he requested.

"Dad?" Gwen said straight away. "We have a problem."

"Yeah, I know. Mya told Sydney, and Sydney told—"

"No, another problem," Gwen rushed out. "My hacker ex-boyfriend is how we were all found, including tracking us down to our suite. He hacked my signal. He figured out I'm here at the hotel, and he . . . it's my fault. He was better than me."

"Are you okay? What's happening?" Wyatt asked while shockingly remaining focused on his rifle. When he took another shot, Tessa nearly dropped the phone.

"I had to go after him. I couldn't let him get away. Even if you catch Maxwell, he'll be just as much of a threat to the NSA. To Tessa."

"No. Stand down. Wait for Jack and the others. They can go after him." Wyatt shifted away from his scope that time, and Bear groaned as if worried. Tessa looked back and forth between Wyatt and Bear, unsure what to do.

"I have to catch up to him before he gets more than three kilometers away and I lose him," Gwen quickly shared, her tone breathless as if she were on the move. And was that Mya yelling in the background for her to stop?

"Tracking him how?" Tessa couldn't stop herself from asking. "Oh," she said as the realization hit her. "The stickers. You managed to get one of those on him? How in the world did you get close enough to do that unnoticed?"

"I caught him by surprise in the lobby before he made his way out," was all Gwen said. "But then he took off, deciding not to start a fight requiring one of us to die."

"Just let him go. Wait until Carter or the others are free to follow him," Wyatt demanded, sitting back on his heels now.

Assuming they all won their fights. *Oh God, they better.*

"No. We may lose him after three kilometers, remember?" Gwen shot out the reminder, then began talking to Mya. "You drive. I'll hack his car to try and stop him that way."

"No!" Wyatt shouted. "The both of you, stop."

"Sorry, Dad. But I won't let you down." And then the call went dead.

Wyatt pivoted to look at Tessa, breathing hard. Although the sounds of gunfire outside began to slow, it hadn't ceased. Cursing, he tapped his ear and said, "Alpha Two, this is Echo One. Change of plans. Get back here now. You need to protect the package."

And you need to save your brave daughter.

CHAPTER THIRTY-EIGHT

GRAY PUSHED HIS PROSTHESIS TO ITS LIMITS AS HE TORE through the woods to get to Tessa. Enemy fire had died down, but they weren't in the clear yet, so Jesse and Griffin had covered him in his hurried exit to get to her.

His lungs burned, and as he ran down the same path Tessa had previously gone, he resisted the urge to give in to fear. To worrying something would happen to anyone he cared about.

The small army Maxwell had sent to the cottage made the Scottish men look like angels. But he supposed with a half a billion on the line, Maxwell decided to leave nothing to chance. Gone no holds barred in his last-ditch effort to get his hands on Tessa.

"This is Alpha Two," he said over comms, catching sight of the shelter up ahead through his NVGs. "Twenty seconds out."

"Roger that," Wyatt answered.

Sydney had filled Gray in on what was going on just after Wyatt had asked to swap places with him.

Zoey was currently chasing Maxwell. And Gwen and

Mya were hunting a dangerous hacker. None of that had been planned for. No contingencies mapped out for such an event. But he needed to save the blame game for later and focus on his current objective.

Gray hissed, "It's me," the moment he set his hands to the door and pushed it open.

He spotted Tessa in the corner, crouched alongside Bear, and did his best to focus on the issue at hand instead of running to her like he wanted to.

Wyatt snatched his rifle from the ground and slung it across his chest. "I need to get to Gwen. She's still following him, and she couldn't hack his car. He's driving a Mustang, and it's old school. No A.I."

Gray blocked the door, needing to talk to Wyatt before he attempted to chase after Gwen with no chance of ever catching up to her without help. "You need a lift. You can't drive to her. You'll never catch up in time." He pointed out the window in the general direction of the helo. "We've nearly got this location secure. And then you'll be clear to fly to her."

"My team doesn't have a pilot. Neither does yours. I sure as hell can't fly that bird out of here." Wyatt tapped his wrist. "But she's still wearing her charm bracelet, so I can find her. Now move out of the way."

Gray didn't budge. "Dale's a pilot. And I've already spoken with him and the rest of your team, and they've agreed to the plan. Dale's been instructed to meet you at the bird once it's clear."

Wyatt stumbled back and Bear winced as if his tail had been stepped on. "Are you insane?"

"Do you want to get to your daughter before she gets to the hacker, and he has the chance to hurt her and Mya?"

Wyatt was quiet for a moment before thankfully relenting, "Fine. Make it happen. I'm heading out now though. I'm not waiting here." He grabbed hold of Gray's arm, urging him to move, and Gray slowly stepped aside.

"This is Alpha Two," he said once Wyatt was gone, focusing on Tessa while speaking. "Echo One is en route. Are we clear yet?" He hadn't heard any more gunfire in the last minute, so he sure as hell hoped so.

"This is Echo Three," Chris said. "All clear from our vantage point. Not sure about where you're at. Working to get new eyes up in the sky."

"Roger that." Gray knocked his NVGs away from his eyes. "Are you okay?" he asked Tessa, offering his hand. He couldn't make out her facial expression in the dark, and it'd take him a second to adjust to the setting without his goggles, but he needed to look at her with his own damn eyes.

Tessa abruptly flung herself into his arms, knocking him back onto his ass. Relief swelled in his chest at being able to hold her. He buried his nose in her hair and cupped the back of her head, wrapping her up in his arms.

"I'm so glad you're okay," she cried.

"You too," he choked out. But before he could say more, Sydney's voice popped into his ear.

"Carter, Jack, and Oliver are okay. Carter took off after Zoey to catch Maxwell. He snuck one of Gwen's trackers on Zoey, probably without her knowing."

Thank God for that. Gray reached for his ear and unmuted his comm. "Wyatt's about to take the bird to get to Gwen."

"I'm almost to the hotel now to pick up Jack and Oliver since Carter took off without them," Sydney shared. Right, all four of their vehicles were now off hotel grounds, so Jack and Oliver would need a lift. "We'll pursue Gwen, but Wyatt may beat us to the punch. He's transmitting her signal from her bracelet to me now."

"It sounds quiet out there, so we should be fine now," he told her. "Stay safe," he added before muting his comm.

"Sydney?" Tessa asked, easing back from his embrace. Her pained tone broke him in fucking half.

"Yeah." He snatched her cheeks between his palms, prepared to say more, when Bear snarled, attention on the window, and the hairs on the back of Gray's neck stood. In one swift movement, he pushed Tessa away from the window, grabbed his rifle, quickly dipped his chin so the goggles fell in place, and got off a shot before he had a chance to warn Tessa they weren't alone.

At the sound of something thudding to the ground just outside the shelter, Bear peeked out the open window and shifted back to a seated position alongside him, letting Gray know the threat had been neutralized.

Gray let the sling catch his rifle, and he pivoted to find Tessa on the floor, her back against the wall, arms wrapped tightly around her legs. He reached out and set his hand on her knee. "We're okay."

"Any more people out there?" she whispered. At her worried voice, Bear stood and trotted around to plop down and curl up next to her.

Gray kept his NVGs in place and returned to the window to check for movement. The familiar sound of blades slicing through the air broke the silence, but he didn't release his pent-up breath until the whooping sounds moved farther away, letting him know Wyatt had safely exfil'ed.

"Echo One is in the air. All good," Chris told him over comms, and Gray relayed the message to Tessa.

He tapped his ear. "This is Alpha Two. How are we looking?"

"This is Echo Three. I've got eyes back up in the sky, and it's just us purple blobs on the screen. Plus, the package and Bear with you. You're clear."

"Roger that." Gray muted his comm and took a second to catch his breath, then he shifted over to get to the other side of Tessa, hoping Bear would share her. He reached for her other hand and laced their fingers together. "You ready to go home?"

"Home?" she whispered. "What about Maxwell and the hacker?"

He tightened his hold of her hand, utterly exhausted. "My people will stop them both." He wasted a smile in the dark. "It's what we do."

* * *

SUNDAY MORNING - ZERO SIX HUNDRED HOURS

After the hell that had been unleashed into the early morning hours, Gray couldn't believe he was standing outside a private hangar in Zurich with the sun trying to slice through the sky in the distance.

The hangar was bustling with people, including Tessa's father, and he'd felt a bit claustrophobic, so he'd stepped out for some air.

Colonel Sloane had been brought straight to Zurich and was picked up by the same SEAL Team that'd been keeping tabs on the Scottish group. Their C17 had arrived only thirty minutes ago, and Tessa's father had run straight from the plane and wrapped her in his arms.

And then the colonel did something unexpected and hugged Gray. Thanked him profusely. And Tessa had stared at the two of them during that moment, slack-jawed in surprise.

"Nothing went as planned," Gray said with a sigh at the sight of Jack casually strolling his way.

Jack had on a bulky coat with his suit pants and a black ball cap turned backward—a funny look that seemed to work for his best friend. But he hated to see his busted lip, bruises around his eyes, and the marks on his neck from getting strangled nearly to death.

"That's usually how it goes," Jack remarked, lifting one shoulder, then winced and held it as if in pain.

"Yeah, not normally this bad." He was grateful that even if half of them were a little banged up, they'd all survived. Of course, Mya and Gwen had barely survived the verbal lashing from not only Wyatt, but Jack and Oliver as well. They'd caught up with them just in time to watch Wyatt beat the shit out of the hacker ex-boyfriend.

Gray's attention shifted to the little BMW sports car Carter was tucking Zoey into, saying his goodbye. By the time Carter had caught up with Zoey, she'd already crashed her car into Maxwell's and engaged him in a firefight on her own. After taking out his bodyguard, Carter and Zoey had successfully detained Maxwell alive. Something both the NSA and MI6 were thankful for.

Zoey was more than likely hitting the road now before the alphabet soup of agencies arrived to claim their prize; she had to be eager to avoid any confrontation with her former agency given she'd gone rogue.

A groan from Jack pulled Gray's focus back to his best friend. "You got the worst of it, huh?"

"Well, Oliver's guy was more of a wrestler. Carter's was just an overconfident but underprepared asshole. And mine was basically straight out of a Jean-Claude Van Damme movie, so . . ." He let his hand fall to his side, then shoved both palms into his puffy coat pockets.

"Shit really went more than just Murphy's Law wrong."

"But at least none of us wound up with any holes in our bodies." Jack faked a laugh that turned into a cough, most likely because his lungs hurt from the movement. "But are you as shocked as I am that Wyatt didn't kill Gwen's ex-boyfriend? I thought for sure he'd take his anger out on him. I mean, he kicked his ass all the way to Germany." He shot him a coy smile. "Almost literally. But hey, he's still alive."

Gray frowned, hating he still had a bad feeling despite the outcome of the mission. Was it because Tessa had barely spoken a word to him since they left that little shelter, spending every hour since practically lost in her own thoughts with Bear as her shadow?

"Stop with the glum look. I can't handle it. The NSA and MI6 have their guys. From the sound of it, the program they lied to us about will remain safe. And the rest of the Scots are toast since they decided to instigate a face-off against the SEALs." Jack paused to let that all marinate. "Your name is cleared with the Turks. That detective is fine, and he'll be getting a nice gift basket of money from the NSA for everything."

"I got it. I hear it. But I still just don't . . ." Gray shook his head. "Why don't I feel good about it all? Why do I feel like we're still missing something." He shifted the brim of his black hat, turning it backward before locking his arms across his chest.

"Because the NSA fucked us over with their lies." Jack's tone softened when he read Gray's thoughts and added, "And maybe because your op started with your niece calling Sydney the love of your life over an open comm and Tessa heard it."

Gray bowed his head and answered without a doubt in his mind, "Sydney's not the love of my life."

"Does Tessa know that?"

"Not yet." When Gray looked up, he focused on the hangar to find Tessa staring out at them. Sydney was talking to Tessa and the colonel, and he wasn't sure if Sydney knew about the "hot mic" moment from earlier. "We should go in there. I have a feeling the colonel has plans to fly Tessa back to the States on that C17 with him."

"Maybe that's for the best?" Jack slapped his back, then moaned and shook his hand as if even that minimal contact had hurt. "Give her space. Time to process the shitshow of what happened. I mean, the NSA stole her memories and used her as bait for a psychopath who planned to sell a secret program to Iran."

Iran. Yeah, what a kick to the nuts that was. Maxwell had confessed an hour ago that the Iranian government had offered up six hundred and fifty million pounds for the stolen program.

But it was on the NSA and MI6 to handle that mess. Gray was done. As long as Tessa and her father were forever safe, he'd consider his mission complete.

They are safe, right? Damn that bad feeling in his gut.

"I still can't believe the BS the NSA fed to us," Jack said, referring to the call they'd had with NSA Director Torres and Gray's father twenty minutes ago—a call that had included Colonel Sloane, which meant the director couldn't feed them any lies.

Carter and Gray had demanded the truth and details, but Director Torres hadn't been all that forthcoming.

"It's wild, that's for sure," Gray agreed, thinking back to what Director Torres had eventually revealed when they'd pressed him.

"We realized the software had the potential for other more valuable uses. We had to make a choice between the original purposes and the newly discovered one," Director Torres had stated on the call, remaining vague. *"Matt was upset about that decision. Making too much noise. We had to let him go."*

"Colonel Sloane, you didn't retire after you learned they were using the program differently than originally intended, right? You quit. You were pissed too," Gray had spoken up, and the colonel quietly nodded. *"And did you know, Dad? The President? Were you in on the lies?"*

"I never told your father the truth about what happened when I left. I was forbidden from speaking about my work there with anyone," the colonel had answered before Gray's father could. *"I wish I had told him or POTUS though."*

It was shocking the NSA could keep so much hidden from the White House. But crazier things had happened.

"I wasn't aware of the change in plans for the software. Nor President Bennett," his dad had added to reassure him. *"And they lied to us during the meeting yesterday as well. We'll make sure this kind of thing never happens again,"* he'd promised.

After the call had ended, the colonel revealed more of the story, sharing that Matt had lost his brother in Afghanistan three years earlier, and he'd spent years researching similar incidents that had resulted from bad intel.

Matt had familiarized himself with every case going all the way back to Gray's failed op. He'd spent time with families, and it'd become even more personal for him. Promises were made, and they weren't kept. He'd felt betrayed.

"So, Matt clearly bided his time, then tried to get his revenge," the colonel had shared. He went on to add, *"I*

doubt Matt did any of this for the money. He wanted vengeance. He dragged Tessa and me into this to force the truth out into the open about the NSA. And he was willing to die in hopes the chain reaction he set off would do exactly that."

"Well, looks like Matt won," Jack said as they returned to the hangar. "With everything Torres and Jacobs did, plus keeping it all from your father and POTUS, they're getting canned. So, that's something. And your father and the President promised to shut down their spy program."

"And Dad said they'll restart the original program to protect our operators from going on ops because of bad intel," Gray affirmed as they entered the hangar. He peered over at Tessa, and the sad look in her eyes when she looked his way, crushed him.

"I'll, uh, go help Wyatt and Oliver lecture Gwen and Mya again." Jack tossed a thumb over his shoulder, indicating he'd give him and Tessa some alone time. Well, as alone as they could be in a hangar maxed out with people.

Gray tipped his head, silently requesting Tessa to join him. She met him halfway, still wearing the jacket he'd zipped her into, and she looked so small and fragile standing before him.

"Hi." He removed his hands from his pockets, unsure what to say next. There was so much to be said between them, but did he want to do it there?

Bear dropped down between them, sitting on their feet. A chaperone or a protector? Maybe a little of both.

"Hey, boy." Tessa knelt next to him, and he rolled over to his side so she could scratch his belly.

Yeah, I'm jealous of a dog right now.

Tessa lifted her gorgeous eyes up to his face while continuing to pet Bear. "Gwen's heading back with her dad's team. You're going back with your people. And I guess I'm going back with my dad."

"I thought that'd be what you decide." He did his best to hide the devastation her words brought him. He'd been with her almost every hour of every day since Thursday night, and he never wanted to be without her again.

"Thank you for saving me. For everything. I'll never forget what you did for me. And really, for my dad too."

Gray set his hand over his heart, hating the agonizing pain there. Because why'd this sound like a goodbye? Was she about to tell him she had to walk away as he'd done thirteen years ago? "Tessa, can we, um . . . talk?"

She patted Bear on the head and then stood tall. "We will." She closed her eyes. "I just need to go home first. Talk to my mom. Brother. Naomi." A single teardrop rolled down her cheek. He reached out, hoping Bear wouldn't jump up and stop him, and slid his thumb along her jawline, catching it from falling. "I just need to get my head back on straight before we talk." She parted her lids. "I believe you care about me, and it's not fair I'm upset that you've ever loved anyone else just because you're the only man I've ever loved."

Fuuuck. He faltered, stepping back as if she'd physically struck him, his heart splitting in half at her confession.

What could he say to make it right? How could he prove to her Sydney wasn't the love of his life, that he'd been wrong about his past feelings for Sydney? And it'd taken Tessa falling, quite literally, back into his life for him to see the truth so clearly.

Gray opened his mouth, preparing to respond, but she lifted her palm, a plea not to say more, and he slammed his lips shut out of respect for her request.

"I'll reach out, I promise," she said with a nod, more tears falling now. Each one crushing him more than the last.

"When?" he rasped, sweat dotting his spine despite the cold air, his body in knots of despair at the idea of losing her again. First time, his mistake. Second time? *Still mine.*

She closed her eyes and murmured, "I don't know. Hour twenty-five?"

CHAPTER THIRTY-NINE

WASHINGTON, D.C

Tessa plopped down on her living room couch and snatched Gray's West Point tee and held it to her chest. It was hard to believe it'd been one week since she woke up in that hospital in Turkey, and this was her fourth night back home.

Her dad had crashed in the guest room for the first three nights, but she'd finally kicked him out that morning, demanding he fly out to see his girlfriend. This would be her first night alone, and Naomi would more than likely remain glued to her side with worry if she didn't kick her out too.

"I FBI'ed too hard and broke my own heart," Tessa admitted, unsure how her friend would take the news she'd done what Naomi told her not to do—looked into Gray's ex-girlfriend.

Naomi snatched Gray's shirt from her, balled it up, and hid it under a pillow before joining her on the couch. "Stop with the mopey-sad brown eyes." She circled a finger in the air. "You should not have looked into Gray's ex-girlfriend."

She reached for their wineglasses from the coffee table and handed Tessa hers. "But what'd you find out?"

She took a healthy swallow of the red wine before saying, "Archer's not just Sydney's last name, she's an actual archer. How can I compete with a badass with a bow? A gorgeous badass, I might add." An exasperated sigh fell from her lips as her gaze landed on her new iPhone inside a light pink case on the coffee table.

On Tessa's first night back, a package had been delivered to her doorstep. Inside it was the new iPhone and a message from Gray: **So you can reach me when you're ready. X, Gray**

She'd had to hide her tears from her father, who'd been hovering over her shoulder, as she'd held Gray's gift. She'd yet to work up the nerve to call or text him with it.

"Okay, let's get one thing straight. You're a gorgeous badass too. Do you think I'd have a best friend that's not a baddie like me?" She winked and lifted her wineglass to clink it with Tessa's. "And seriously, look what you went through last week. The NSA asked you to go undercover to take down an international criminal and you said yes. Then you did all the things I said not to do. Even though now I'm kind of glad you did them."

"You mean like fall into the water and call Gray?" *At least I'm smiling right now.* "Sorry about the fake texts I sent you, by the way. And for you needing protection."

Naomi popped up one shoulder as if to say, *No worries.* "But back to this ex-girlfriend as the 'love of his life' nonsense . . . did Gray ever admit that to you? Or did you only overhear his niece say that?"

"You know the answer to that." Tessa frowned.

"Exactly." She set down her wineglass, then pulled one leg up on the couch as she shifted to better face Tessa. "As much as I want to be mad at Gray for making you all mopey again, I don't know if I can be. He saved your life and—"

"I know. He's kind of perfect." She eyed her phone, wanting to give in and call him. "I guess I just want to make sure last week wasn't a fairy tale, you know?"

Naomi laughed. "Only you would describe what you went through as a fairy tale."

Tessa jokingly rolled her eyes. "You know what I mean. Everything between us happened so fast. But we did spend like every second together, so we squeezed a lot into that time."

"Based on what you said, Gray would trade his life for yours in a blip of a second. Sam would use my body as a shield." She grabbed her glass again. "I'm breaking up with him Saturday. Your adventure has inspired me to find a rugged hero of my own."

"Good. I hate that guy," Tessa finally revealed with relief.

Naomi smiled. "Mmmhmm. I figured." She waved her free hand in the air. "But we're not talking about me now. Tell me what you're going to do about Gray."

The wine was starting to go to her head, and she blinked a few times. "He works with Sydney. I saw their connection. How do I handle them going off on ops together to beautiful countries and having intense moments . . . knowing they've slept together?"

"They were together twenty years ago."

"And I didn't get over Gray after thirteen years," she challenged back.

"But wait, isn't she engaged to some detective here in D.C.? Surely he knows about Gray and Sydney's past, and he's fine with them working together. If you really think he's 'the one,' then you just need to trust him."

"I know, and I do. It's my own intrusive thoughts and

overthinking that's messing with me." She swallowed. "What I need to do is give him a chance to talk to me, but I've been too scared to do it." She checked the time when Naomi tried to hide a yawn behind her wineglass. "Go. It's late. You have a patient at seven in the morning."

"I don't want to leave you alone with your dad gone."

"I'll be fine. Really. I need to get on with my life. Move forward." Tessa stood and placed the glass on the coffee table. "And maybe I'll use this liquid courage and reach out to Gray when you go."

"Fine. You win." Naomi rose and pulled her in for a tight hug. "Love you. Stay strong. Keep your chin up. And just remember, I'll always have your back."

Tessa hugged her again, then Naomi left. And it was Tessa's first time alone in what felt like forever. She snatched her phone and went over to the window, drew open the curtains and peeked outside, confirming Naomi made it to her car. But there was also a mysterious SUV parked in front of the house for sale that grabbed her attention. The engine was running, and the windows were tinted, but she was pretty sure someone was behind the wheel.

She let go of the curtains to scroll to Gray's number in her contacts and hesitantly messaged him.

> Tessa: Hey . . . tell me you're stubborn and overprotective and that's why there's a black SUV parked near my house with the engine running.

The man didn't make her wait, thank God.

> Gray: Hey, you.

407

> Gray: Your dad and I decided it'd be best to hire a bodyguard once he left until I can kill my worry that I missed something. He's stubborn like someone I know, and he had to pick a guy he trusted.

She turned from the window, grateful she didn't need to panic about the SUV. *But wait, you and my dad have been talking?*

> Tessa: You two working behind my back to keep me safe is . . . strange.

"And also adorable," she whispered as if someone might overhear her.

> Gray: We have something in common. We're fiercely protective of you.

There goes my heart again. His words wrapped a hand around it, squeezing.

She flicked off the lights and went into her bedroom and changed into pajamas, glad she'd taken the leap and finally reached out to him. Even if it was to soothe her own suspicious anxiety. But whatever the reason, she hoped it wouldn't stop with his confirmation that she was physically safe.

When she opened her phone again, there was another text from him.

> Gray: I miss you.

> Gray: More than just a little.

> Gray: Is that okay to admit?

She kind of loved he'd sent multiple texts instead of just one long rambly one.

She stared at his words, contemplating what to say.

> Tessa: I miss you too.

Bubbles from his typing came and went. When he didn't say anything, she decided to ask him a few "icebreaker" questions.

> Tessa: How's your team? Are you home? Working?

> Gray: I'm in D.C. at a hotel. Team is good. Jesse and Griffin are back home in Alabama. I'm not working right now. Well, aside from double-checking we didn't miss anything.

She turned on the light on her nightstand, peeled back the covers, then slipped into bed. She could hear Gray's husky voice in her head as if he were talking instead of typing. God, she really did miss him. How'd she go thirteen years without him?

> Tessa: And are you double-checking things with Sydney?

She regretted her text immediately. Watching those nerve-wracking bubbles coming and going as if he was unsure how to respond was torture.

> Gray: Yes.

Well, that was a whole lot of nothing for such a long wait on his response.

Tessa: I'm jealous.

"And did I really just admit that?"

Gray: That's the last thing in the world you need to be, I promise.

His answer was immediate that time, and she wanted to feel better, but the irrational side of her brain kept getting in the way.

Gray: Jack said to me yesterday that it's the women on a man's "blocked list" you have to worry about, not the ones who stay in his life.

"Blocked list?" *Huh?*

Gray: I don't do social media, but if I had a blocked list, you would've been the only one on it. I blocked you from my mind and my life years ago because it made me crazy I couldn't be with you.

Gray: Tessa, I never had to block anyone else.

Oh.

Ohhhh.

"You can work with Sydney because you don't . . ." She released a heavy breath. And tears welled in her eyes.

Tessa: Gray?

Gray: Yeah?

Tessa: I kind of love Jack for that.

> Gray: Not allowed to love anyone else. Especially not my friends. *winking emoji*

"Love anyone else?" *Just say it. Tell him you fell hard.* "No, dammit. Not over text." *And jeez, I'm having a conversation with my inner thoughts.*

> Tessa: Can you help me with something?

She slid a hand down her pink silk pajama shorts.

> Gray: Anything.

This man. He really was amazing. One of the truly good ones.

> Tessa: I haven't been touched since last Saturday, and I'm touching myself now.

> Gray: You trying to kill me? *emoji cocking a brow*

> Gray: But how can I help you, sweetheart? I'd come over, but I'm thinking you're not ready yet.

She considered his words. Heard the "sweetheart" roll through her mind in his voice. She coated two fingers with her arousal, remembering when it'd been his hand touching her instead.

> Tessa: When was the last time you sent a selfie?

> Gray: 13 yrs ago

She smiled at that.

> Tessa: Send another?

> Gray: Do I get one back?

> Tessa: Mmm. Maybe.

> Gray: Hold please. *sly-smile emoji*

She kept working her fingers over her clit, picturing all the delicious things he could do with his tongue, and when the picture from him popped up, she snatched her lip between her teeth at the sight.

Gray was in bed without a shirt, but his face was cut off from the angle he'd been holding the phone up. His hard abominable muscles were flexed. The V-line veins evident, dipping down below his waist. And he gave her a hint of his hand circling his shaft without showing the crown.

Oh. My. Damn. She pushed her pink cami up to show her tits, then shoved her shorts down to her thighs so he'd get a view similar to the one he'd provided her. "Am I doing this?" *Be bold, Tessa. Be bad.* She covered her pussy with her palm, not quite ready to go full-blown naughty. *Baby steps.* Then she snapped the photo and hit send before she could change her mind. But she had to admit, her breasts looked damn good.

> Gray: Time for us both to get new phones. I can't run the risk of anyone ever getting their hands on that photo.

She laughed, her fingers going still on her wet center.

> Tessa: Ever heard of the delete button? You can even delete your deleted.

> Gray: Not good enough. Can't take any chances.

Knowing this man, he was serious, and she loved him for that.

> Tessa: Okay, mister, I'm going to get myself off and go to bed. Early morning tomorrow. But thank you for helping. And for the unneeded protection outside.

> Gray: I wish I was there to help you finish and be the one to protect you.

"Me too."

> Gray: But I'll wait for you to be ready. I told you before, and I'm "saying" it again. I'm never walking away. Not ever, Tessa. You're stuck with me.

A shiver darted down her spine at his promise. "No one in the world I'd rather be stuck with," she whispered, hoping she'd soon be able to tell him that in person.

* * *

"OKAY, THIS MAN IS SETTING THE BAR TOO HIGH FOR ANY future guys I'll ever date." Naomi set down the card accompanied by the thirteen roses Gray had sent to her office. One rose for every year he'd missed since he walked away.

"Also, a pack of blueberry-scented ChapStick and a box of dark chocolate Raisinets. For real?"

Tessa opened the box of candy as Naomi slung her purse strap across her body, preparing herself to go meet Sam to break up with him. "Yeah, I think I'm going to ask to see him tonight if he's free."

Naomi smiled. "He'll be free for you. He'd cancel plans with the President if you asked to see him."

Tessa poured a handful of Raisinets into Naomi's hand before tossing some in her mouth just as a text popped up.

"Him?" Naomi asked, arching a brow.

Tessa grabbed her phone and smiled. "He sent me a song on YouTube without any message."

"Now the man is texting you songs?" Naomi slapped a hand over her heart. "Okay, I'm done. I'll have to stick to book boyfriends forever now since your man is ruining everyone."

"Noooo, you'll find someone," Tessa said while opening the song "Wannabe" by an artist she'd never heard of before, Dylan Schneider.

They stood together silently as the song played, and tears filled Tessa's eyes as she listened to the heartful lyrics.

"Holy shit." Naomi pointed at her arm when the song finished. "I have chills. That man is hopelessly in love with you. You better call him." She patted her hand holding the phone, another urge to call him. "Okay," she said with a sigh a few seconds later, "I'll be late if I don't go." She hugged her, then started for the door before pausing and whirling around. "I have some serious—"

"Déjà vu?" *Yeah, me too.* "That's because three weeks ago to the day you left just before seven at night, and I apparently was . . ." *Taken. Abducted. Not that I can remember it.*

"That hot bodyguard friend of your dad's is still parked outside the office, right?" Naomi smirked.

"Oh, is he hot?"

"He almost gives your smoking-hot brother a run for his money," Naomi teased, then took off as if she didn't just drop that on her.

"Wait, you like my brother?" Tessa called out in shock. *How'd I miss that?*

Naomi only waved a hand in the air and kept on going. Tessa blinked in surprise as she watched her walk away. *Okay, Curtis and Naomi together? Now that's something I can get behind.* Smiling, she snatched her phone, preparing to respond to Gray with an *I want to see you and now* message, but then the front office door buzzed.

Was her bodyguard checking on her? Gray making a surprise visit, reading her thoughts?

She opened the security app on her phone to check the view of the hallway. Her practice was inside a building with three other doctors' offices, so anyone could get into the building, but she knew Naomi had locked up on her way out.

"Whit?" she whispered in shock seeing him on the security camera.

She'd been trying to get ahold of him all week since he'd missed his appointments. She wasn't sure why he'd stopped coming—it wasn't like he'd known she'd discovered his fake name—but she was relieved to see he was okay.

She hurriedly left her office and went down the hall to the empty waiting room, then unlocked the door and opened it. "Whit," she exclaimed. "I've been worried. Are you okay?"

He slowly lifted his dark, sad eyes to her face while also sliding down his jacket zipper. She stumbled back in shock at the sight of what was under his jacket, lost her balance and fell.

"No," she cried, lifting her hand up to push away the betrayal. "Don't do this," she choked out, on the verge of hyperventilating.

Because Gray's bad gut feeling was right. *We did miss something.*

CHAPTER FORTY

"WHAT'S WRONG?"

Gray looked up at Sydney's question and frowned. What could he tell her? That he'd sent roses to Tessa and texted her a love song. That it had been radio silence from her ever since. No, he'd sound pathetic.

Hearing from her Thursday had sent his pulse through the roof and had him grinning like a schoolboy with a crush. But it was now Saturday night, a full week since the night of the takedown in Zurich, and too many days had passed since he'd held Tessa in his arms.

"Nothing," he lied.

"Suuure," Sydney countered dramatically without looking up from her screen where she sat at the kitchen island inside Natasha and Wyatt's home. "If it were nothing, we wouldn't be working tonight."

Gray rolled his eyes, glad she couldn't read his mind, then scrubbed a hand over his stubbled jawline. He hadn't shaved, but he'd dressed up in hopes of maybe seeing Tessa later. Well, dressed up as in he put on his favorite well-worn jeans, boots, and a plain gray cotton button-down.

"If you build it, she'll come," Mya had teased him yesterday while she and Jack helped him drown his sorrows at his favorite whiskey bar in Brightwood. *"Get dressed daily as if expecting to see her, and maybe you will."*

"And stop worrying that something is wrong, man. We didn't miss anything. Just relax. Tessa will come around soon enough," Jack had tacked on to Mya's words, nudging him in the ribs.

But Gray was still worrying. Obsessing. Feeling as though the case wasn't closed. He wanted nothing more than to convince himself that feeling was due to being away from Tessa, but he couldn't shake it. So, he was having Sydney and Natasha check one more time. Pore over everything they could get their hands on. Including every single thing the NSA traitor, Matt, had touched from his first day with the NSA to his last dying breath.

"Nothing is *always* something," Natasha said a moment later as if she'd only just heard the exchange. And knowing his sister, that'd been the case. She always became hyper-focused when using her cyber skills, which she was currently doing to help Sydney comb through everything.

"Exactly," Gray snapped out, referring to the case and not his overall state of misery. "Which is why I think we missed something."

"This is our third time checking the files," Sydney remarked as if he didn't already have a running tally of "failures to find something" in his head. And not finding something would be great if he didn't know in his gut they were supposed to find something. Something had to have been missed. He wouldn't have this feeling otherwise, right?

"Tessa's dad still has that bodyguard outside her office and home twenty-four seven, right?" Natasha asked him.

"Yeah. I'd have preferred it was someone I vouched for,

but I'm just relieved Tessa didn't push back on the bodyguard idea." *She can be stubborn.* He checked his watch. It was getting late, and he knew Emory would need to go to bed when Wyatt returned home with her. "When will they be here?"

"They should be back from running errands any minute." Natasha snatched the stem of her wineglass while her other hand continued to fly over the keyboard.

"And how are things with Wyatt?" He needed a distraction before he grabbed his truck keys and said, *Screw manifesting a call or a visit, I'll go to her myself.*

"He's . . . Wyatt, you know him. Scowly and overprotective. But he forgave me for lying. And while he won't ever forgive Dale, he won't kill him since he helped save Gwen's life with that helo ride last weekend." Natasha set down her glass of red and stole a quick look his way. "But we've decided, well, *Mom* decided, not to tell Dad about what happened last year with Dale. She's worried it'll give him a heart attack, and he's been through enough lately." She wet her lips and shrugged. "Maybe I was the problem? I was hormonal, and I went all 'mamma bear' mode seeing Dale try to kiss Gwen when she didn't want him to, and if I'd just used my words instead of my fist, I—"

"Your right hook was justified," Gray cut her off. "Never blame yourself. Ever."

"You sound like Wyatt."

"Good. Because neither Wyatt nor I will ever excuse a man for setting his hand on a woman like that, even if you and Gwen claim it was an 'autopilot' return of fire." He folded his arms, standing his ground. "I'll always have a zero-tolerance policy when it comes to assholes. And I refuse to let any woman, my sister included, feel at fault for the poor choices of a man. I don't care if a woman walks naked across a room while shaking her ass, if she tells the guy no, it fucking means no." And he'd die by that stance, dammit. "And then to raise a hand to a woman and—"

"Easy there," Natasha said, her tone calm. "It's okay." She stopped typing, eyes set on him. "We're on the same page about that, I promise." Her brows knitted with concern. "But you're obviously tense and on edge right now, and for valid reasons." Her gaze softened as she studied him, trying to do that CIA mind trick of hers to read his thoughts.

He did his best to dial down his heart rate and get a handle on his anger. Dale wasn't his current target, and he knew after last week, he'd never have to worry about Dale again. For the sake of his sanity, it was time to move forward.

But right now, he just needed Tessa safely in his arms and for all the bad shit in the world to just go away. *For once, could it just go the hell away?*

"Oh shit."

Gray's arms fell to his sides at Sydney's two small words that had a big impact on his pulse rate. "What is it?"

Sydney spun her screen to the side to show both Natasha and Gray what was there. "An hour ago, someone tried to access the second bank account Matt had set up in the Caymans."

"What do you mean? Spell this out for me." Gray set his hand on the counter and leaned in, his palms growing sweatier by the second.

"What if Matt had help?" Sydney suggested. "What if the second account wasn't just because there'd been two sales to Maxwell Sherlock but because the money was being split?"

"And someone waited for the heat to die down to collect? They had to know they were burnt, why take the chance?" Natasha asked, then pointed to the screen. "And clearly, their electronic-wire-transfer request was declined."

Gray did his best to rally his thoughts. "Because they don't want the money, they want the NSA to know they missed something."

"But who would Matt work with?" Sydney turned the screen back around and began working fast.

Chills scattered over every square inch of his body as his skin grew clammy in shock. He pushed away from the counter and tore his hands through his hair. "Matt spoke with a lot of families who lost someone in the military because of bad intel. He personally got to know them during the project." He grabbed his phone when it began vibrating from an incoming call. It was a number he didn't want to see. "Her bodyguard." He placed the call on speakerphone. "What's wrong?"

"Tessa didn't leave her office when she normally does, so I went into the building to check on her. She's not answering the door. Her SUV is still outside. And I had eyes on the only exit," he rushed out. "Her mobile is off. No answer on her work line."

It took Gray a stunned second to accept the truth of what he was suggesting before demanding, "Break down the door. I'm on my way."

"I tried. I can't get in, not without a breaching charge. It's not a typical door," the man shared, his tone breathy as if he'd been banging at it already.

Gray's stomach revolted, and he clamped down on his back teeth as he gritted out, "I'm sending help. Do not leave."

He ended the call, not ready to accept reality. To accept he'd been right about his bad feeling. "What if he has her? This second guy? Can you get Beckett to help? Her place is technically outside D.C., but it's right on the line."

"Of course." Sydney had her phone to her ear a second later.

"I have to go there." He grabbed his truck keys and Natasha popped up to her feet as if prepared to come as well. "No, stay here. Get me a name. If he has Tessa, it's for a reason. It's because . . ." His stomach dropped at the realization as he shared, "It's someone who blamed her father for someone dying in the war."

Natasha quietly nodded and sat back down as Sydney shifted the phone from her ear.

Sydney's face was pale as she shared, "Metro PD were already en route before I called Beckett. The local PD station by her office doesn't have a SWAT team. Or a hostage negotiator."

"Hostage," he whispered, his stomach flipping, and the keys in his hand dug into his skin as he clenched his fist around them.

"Demands were made," Sydney went on, his body and mind going numb. "He says he's going to kill her unless the NSA director confesses what he did on national TV."

* * *

"GRAY, IT'S NOT GOOD."

He swung his focus to Sydney in the passenger seat as he tore down the road, ignoring every traffic law to get to Tessa's office.

Sydney lowered the phone from her ear and continued, "They made visual contact. He didn't show himself, but he showed Tessa in front of the window so the police could confirm she was with him, and . . ."

"What?" He white-knuckled the wheel, his heart pounding wildly.

His thoughts were chaotic and messy. A blur of memories from his time with Tessa last week, along with moments from their summer together thirteen years ago, competed with the intrusive dark thoughts he didn't want to have as he flew down the road.

Thankfully, Beckett had warned all local patrol cars not to stop his truck en route to the scene. Not that he'd pull over for anyone right now anyway.

"What is it?" he asked again, realizing the fearless woman at his right was terrified to share something.

"He's wearing a vest with enough explosives to level the entire office building," she finally shared. Gray lifted his foot from the pedal, his world grinding to a halt as disbelief tore through him. "And he had a pistol pointed at her head and the remote detonator in his other hand."

"This is my fault." He blinked and pushed down on the gas pedal again when he realized the truck was slowing to a stop. "I missed this."

"I have to go. We'll be there soon," Sydney said to Beckett and ended the call. "This is not your fault. The NSA kept Matt's true motives from us, so we never knew to dig deeper. There was no evidence until an hour ago he had help. There was nothing more we could've done with what we knew."

Nothing she said mattered right now, not with Tessa's life on the line. He had to get to her. Save her. Find a way inside the ticking time bomb of a building.

"We thought it was over," she went on as if worried she needed to talk sense into him. Not happening. "We would've—"

"Should've, could've, fucking would've doesn't matter," he growled out, control gone. "If something happens to her, I'll . . ." He swallowed, realizing his hand on the wheel was trembling and liquid filled his eyes.

"He has demands, Gray. That means we have time. If he

wanted her dead, she'd already be gone." She punched him with her grave words as he ran a red light, narrowly dodging a collision with another car.

"Call my dad. He must know about this already. And the NSA might've already tracked down a name," he barked out, his brain finally working.

"Well, your sister is calling me, so maybe she knows something." She placed the call on speaker.

"I have a name," Natasha cut to it. "It's her patient. It's that Whit guy."

For the second time, Gray lifted his foot from the pedal, unable to process what he'd heard. Her favorite patient had a bomb strapped to his chest and a gun pointed at Tessa's head? No. He refused to believe that. "We checked him out," he said under his breath in disbelief. "He faked his name for insurance, but—"

"And you all didn't have a reason to keep poking into his background," Natasha interrupted him. "But if you had, you would've discovered his *son* was one of the Rangers who died the day of your accident. And I'm fairly certain Matt convinced him it was the government and the colonel's fault his son never made it home that day. That's how he got Whit to help him."

"No, no, no. This . . . no." He lifted one hand from the wheel, tremors moving from his hand up his arm. As memories from that accident clawed through his mind, pain in his residual limb—pain that shouldn't have been there—blazed to life. "James Whitney Howard," he choked out. "I didn't attend his funeral because I was hospitalized." He remembered reading about him in the report. "He was only twenty-three. Just got his Ranger tab."

"I have to tell Beckett who we're dealing with. I remember Mya sharing on the yacht that Whit has military experience. He's a veteran. Clearly knows his way around explosives," Sydney rushed out.

"The police already know," Natasha interjected as Gray continued to process the fact he was somehow tied to all of this. His accident. His failed op was now why Tessa was in danger. "Dad called and provided the name. He'd already heard about what's happening. The NSA learned Whit's identity from the attempted money withdrawal, but they couldn't get to him in time."

Gray swerved abruptly before crashing into another car as he ran a stop sign. But they were almost there. Tessa's office building was just up ahead. He could hear the sirens. See the flash of blue and red lights in the distance.

"What does your father plan to do?" Sydney asked Natasha. "Will he have Director Torres address the media?"

"The President says it'd set a dangerous precedent," Natasha said what Gray already knew would be the White House's position. "Plus, if the news were to get out about the spy program, the President has concerns it'd create . . . well, problems."

"If Whit doesn't get what he wants, he'll kill her," Gray rasped. "A life for a life. His son's for the colonel's daughter." Chills flew down his spine at his own words, and liquid disbelief escaped his eyes, screwing with his vision.

"They'll try and talk him down. Offer something else. Now that we know who he is, they can make their conversation more personal. But he has no living family. His wife died last year," Natasha shared. "He has no money. He lost his home a few months ago."

"He has nothing left to lose," Gray said hoarsely. "And there's no one to talk him off this ledge." *No one but me.* He had to find a way.

"We're here," he told his sister, skidding to a stop in the

middle of the road and throwing his truck in park. He jumped from the truck without a second thought, knowing Sydney would follow. He hadn't even removed the keys from the ignition. What was the point? Nothing mattered if Tessa was taken, not just from him, but from the world.

Gray rushed toward the barricades, but the police swarming the area began shouting for him to get back. He was about to trample right over them, but Beckett pushed through and cleared the way for him. Gray spied Sydney from the corner of his eye, and Beckett snatched her hand.

"They're with me. They're coming in," Beckett informed the officers.

"I need to talk to Whit," Gray roared, following Beckett toward where SWAT was assembling. "My father can talk to whoever is in charge here and make it happen, but I'm telling you, I'm her only hope."

"What do you plan to say? Do?" Beckett asked him, a worried look in his eyes.

Gray hung his head, his hands slamming to his hips. "I'm going to do exactly what you'd do for the woman you love."

Beckett stole a look at Sydney and murmured in understanding, "You're going to make a trade. Your life for hers."

CHAPTER FORTY-ONE

"WE HAVE ORDERS NOT TO LET YOU GO IN," THE HOSTAGE negotiator said to Gray. "Just so we're clear, if you plan to do anything stupid, my men—"

"Who gave you those orders?" Gray barked out as an officer attempted to put a plated vest on him. He jerked his arm free, waving him off. Tessa wasn't safe, why in God's name should he be? "Don't even spew some bullshit about my life being more valuable because of my father." He'd heard that line enough to last him five fucking lifetimes, and he was done with it.

"If you want on the phone with this man, I need assurances you won't offer yourself in exchange for her," the negotiator said.

Gray shot Beckett a quick look, realizing he might need help distracting an army of officers if they thought they'd deter him from getting into that building.

"Give me a second." Gray grabbed his phone from his pocket and walked a safe distance away from the man who thought he stood a chance in hell of stopping him from helping Tessa.

"What are you going to do?" Beckett caught up with him, and Gray peered at the curtains fluttering behind one of the office windows. His stomach clenched, knowing Tessa was there. So damn close and alone with a man with nothing left to lose.

The building had been cleared out. At least Whit had allowed that. He'd said he only wanted one hostage—one specific person. What Whit didn't yet know was he'd never have his demands met no matter who he took. The White House wouldn't play ball, and Gray refused to let Whit sacrifice Tessa because of it.

"I'm calling my father." *There's no other choice.* "I need his help."

Beckett looked back toward Sydney hanging by the SWAT truck, then focused on Gray. "He won't want you in there."

"He won't need to worry about meeting Whit's demands or setting a precedent," Gray shared, waiting for the call to connect with his father. "Because I'm going to give Whit an alternative," he went on, his voice breaking, knowing Tessa would hate him for what he was going to do, but at least she'd be alive. "Whit wants justice for his son by taking the life of someone else. So . . . he can take mine."

"Gray?" his dad answered two rings later, and Beckett stepped back to give him privacy. "I know what you're thinking and—"

"I have to, Dad. I love her." Goose bumps popped on his forearms with what he was about to say next. "She belongs in the world far more than I do. She's the fucking light, Dad," he rasped. "She's the light, and the world needs the light." He almost fell to his knees when reality settled in hard and fast. "So, tell them to let me in when I convince Whit to make the swap. I'm begging you. If you really love me, Dad, you'll let me do this. Please." His emotions had a stranglehold on his voice, and he barely managed to get the words out. He hoped his father heard him. Would listen to him.

A gruff sound rumbled over the line. "Go," his dad said, sounding like he was holding back tears. "I've got your back."

"Tell Mom I love her. Natasha too. And that I'm sorry. Take care of everyone for me. Tessa too." He swiped the back of his hand across his cheek, brushing away his tears. "And I love you too." He ended the call before his father could respond. "It's done." He pocketed his phone as Beckett turned to face him, then hurriedly rid the remaining tears from his face. He needed to get a grip so he could talk to Whit and not totally lose it.

"You sure about this?" The hostage negotiator met Gray and Beckett halfway. *Damn, Dad works fast.* Thank God for that.

"A hundred percent," Gray answered gruffly, then opened his palm, waiting for the phone.

The negotiator shot Beckett a hesitant look before offering Gray the phone. "We bought some time, and he says Tessa is still unharmed and untouched. But we lied and told him the NSA director will be on TV in an hour."

"We don't have that much time." Gray accepted the phone, his hand trembling. "Because he won't believe you."

"The only number in that phone is his. I hope you know what you're doing." The man twirled a finger in the air, motioning for some of the men to fall back and give Gray space.

Gray clutched the phone and faced Sydney, allowing her to pull him in for a hug.

"When you get in there . . . find a way out of this," she cried into his shoulder. "I'm not saying goodbye. Not promising you I'll look after her or your family." She pulled back, crying. "So, you find a way to save you both."

He swallowed and pushed away from her. "I'll try," was the only acknowledgment he could give her. She turned away from him, and Beckett hauled Sydney into his arms, holding her as she fell apart.

Beckett gave Gray a quiet nod of support, maybe it was his goodbye. Gray nodded back, then faced the building and called the only number in the phone.

The line connected on the third ring, and Gray said without delay, "This is Grayson Chandler. Secretary of Defense Chandler's son. And also, the real reason your son died that day."

"I'm listening," was all that came back.

Gray curled his fingers into a fist at his side, trying to keep calm. To push through so the fear of losing her didn't control him. "If Matt shared the report about your son's death with you, that means you already know my name. And you know the colonel ordered my men to turn around and not go in and save the Rangers on the ground that day." His stomach squeezed and he bowed his head as he added, "The government chose to save my life that day because they thought it was more valuable than your son's. Because of my training. Because of my father." Tears of guilt fell unfettered down his face. "They chose me over your son. It's my life that's owed to you. *Mine,* not hers. I should have died, not your son," he added, his tone trembling. "Take me instead and let her go."

The line was quiet for a moment before he heard Tessa cry in the background, "No, no, no. Please, Gray. Don't!" At the sound of her cries and pleas, Gray's knees buckled, and he fought to keep the bile in his stomach down. "He won't hurt me. I—I know you won't, Whit. He can't . . . but you . . . he might," she begged.

Her sobs encouraged more tears from his eyes to fall. "Please, let her go. It's me you want."

"Because you're worth more than her, is that what you mean?" Whit asked, his tone deepening with disgust. "Because you're of more value to the government, they might give me what I want to save you?"

Shit, he had to feed into his hate of him to get him to play ball, but . . . "Her life is worth more than mine to *me*," is all he could say because that was the only truth he knew.

"No, Gray. Please," Tessa sobbed.

After the longest minute of Gray's life, Whit declared, "Fine. Your life for hers. Come in."

Gray never thought four words could hit him so hard. *"Your life for hers."* He slammed his fist over his heart. "Thank you," he whispered, his voice broken.

He tossed the phone to the negotiator, shot one last look at Sydney, finding her covering her mouth as tears poured down her cheeks, and then he started for the main entrance.

The officers peeled back at someone's command, moving farther away from the possible blast radius, expecting that'd be the way Gray died. That Whit was going to take himself out right along with Gray.

Without hesitation, Gray opened the main door, then turned down the hall to get to Tessa's office. Once outside her door, his hand trembled as he reached for the handle. Finding it unlocked, he opened the door and slipped inside. The second he was in the small waiting area, he lifted his hands in surrender. "I'm here."

As the door clicked shut behind him, Whit slowly walked his way, jacket open to reveal the explosives vest, 9mm trained on Tessa. Gray dropped to the floor, landing on the knee of his good leg, his palms falling flat at his sides, breath catching in his throat as the true reality of the situation hit him.

Tessa had her hands up, and black streaks from her mascara marred her cheeks. Her eyes were swollen from her sobs, and her skin was pale. But she was still alive. Untouched. And he'd do everything in his power to keep it that way. "Gray," she cried. "He wouldn't have hurt me. I—I know that. Go—go while you—you still can."

He shifted back on his heels, not giving a damn how awkward it felt with his prosthesis.

Whit stopped her from coming any closer, and Gray didn't dare move another muscle. He still had the detonator in his one hand and the pistol pointed her way. He wouldn't chance anything happening to her if Whit panicked at a perceived threatening motion from Gray.

"I'm sorry," Gray told her, his shoulders falling. Every part of him sagged as his hands went to his thighs. "I can't risk your life." He shook his head, letting the tears fall as he trained his attention on Whit. "Let her go, please." Chills racked his body as he waited for him to let her leave.

Whit stared at him, a haunted look in his eyes. He may have been in his early sixties, but he didn't look his age. He looked capable of fighting. Of killing too. How'd he fool Tessa? How'd he do it when Matt couldn't?

When Whit remained quietly observing him, Gray turned his attention back on Tessa. She was barely keeping it together, and she'd more than likely collapse from the stress and fear if she didn't leave soon.

"Before you go," he told her, fighting to get the words out, knowing they might be the last ones she'd ever hear from him, "I need you to know and believe that *you're* the love of my life. It's always been you. I'm so damn sorry it took me so long to realize that." Tears met his lips as he went on, "I love you so fucking much, Tess. We didn't have much time together, but it doesn't matter. It doesn't change how I feel about you." He set his hand over his heart, barely able to see straight at this point. "I love you." He swallowed. "But please don't be stubborn after this and blame yourself. Please live your life. Don't—"

"No," she cried, then rushed his way, disregarding the gun Whit had trained on her. She flung herself into his arms, and Gray fought to stay upright as he caught her. Straddling him, she hooked her ankles behind his back, refusing to unlock herself from him. "I'm not leaving you. And you're not leaving me." She buried her face in his neck, and he wrapped his arms around her back, holding her tight, wondering why they both didn't have bullets in their bodies by now.

Gray looked up at Whit, the 9mm hanging by his side now, but the detonator was still firmly clenched in his hand. If he could disarm him, then maybe . . .

"He tried to save your son," Tessa cried, turning her head toward Whit. "He tried so hard. He refused orders. He begged the pilot to turn around. To save your son." Tears flooded her cheeks. "I bet that wasn't in the report, but it's true. And then his helicopter was shot down before he could get to him. But Gray's a good man. He's a hero. He was willing to risk his life to get to your son because that's the kind of man he is." She pulled farther back from him, and all Gray could do to keep it together was cup her cheeks and stare into her eyes. "Look at him now," she whispered while sniffling, "offering to trade his life for mine." Her eyes fell closed, her lower lip trembling hard, then she bowed her forehead against Gray's. "Your son would hate you for taking his life. He'd never forgive you."

A few seconds later, in a somber tone, Whit asked, "Is it true?"

Gray shifted his focus, unsure what to say. He didn't want him to change his mind about the trade. Choosing to end Tessa's life instead of his.

"I'm not going to kill her," Whit added, reading Gray's thoughts. "I was just trying to get the NSA to confess the truth. She's . . . she's Tessa." His eyes surprisingly became glossy. "But I have nothing to live for." He stared at them both with a dejected look etched on his face. Before Gray could answer the question he'd asked, Whit announced, "Just go. The both of you."

Gray jerked his shoulders back when what he was saying sunk in. Tessa worked to untangle herself from him, not taking her eyes off Gray as she stood. Once on her feet, she shot a timid look toward Whit as if unsure what to do.

"The program was supposed to honor men like my son. Make his death mean something. But they turned it into something disgusting. Spying on our own people. How many more men like my son have to die?" Whit stumbled back a step and Gray cringed. One wrong move, and he might accidentally set off the explosives.

Gray shifted his residual leg, then did his best to get upright. "They didn't tell you what happened?" he asked, trying to wrap his head around that.

"Tell me what?" Whit tipped his head forward, tears falling now.

Gray pulled Tessa behind him, shielding her with his body. Not that he could save her from a blast that way, but it made him feel better. He shook free the haze of emotions still slipping down his cheeks to tell him, "The program as originally developed will be restarting in January. My father is seeing to it. And Director Torres and Under Secretary

Jacobs have been fired. Clearly, this was never about money for you. You wanted your son's life to mean something, and it will. You have my word." He gave him a terse nod. "I promise."

Whit stared at him, an uneasy look crossing his face.

"I have no reason to lie," Gray reminded him. "You're letting us go."

"But you don't need to die." Tessa tried stepping around Gray, but he shot his arm out to stop her, worried any sudden steps would . . . well, he didn't want to contemplate that possibility. "Please. Your wife and son would never want you to do this."

Gray's shoulders fell at Tessa being Tessa—trying to bring someone from the dark into the light—but he had no idea if she'd be able to convince someone who felt they had no reason to live to save themself.

"Matt may have told you to become a patient here," Gray started, shocked at what he was about to do to try and save this man's life, "but clearly, you care about this woman. How could you not? She's Tessa." He shifted to the side and caught her eyes. "So, live for her." He stole one last look at Whit. "Let her be your reason the way she's mine."

* * *

"I'm, um." In the parking lot, Gray nervously turned to Tessa after Sydney unwrapped herself from him. Before he had a chance to apologize to Tessa, worrying she would get the wrong idea, Sydney grabbed hold of Tessa and hugged her too.

Gray swapped a look with Beckett, and Beckett shrugged. Sydney really was becoming more emotional ever since she'd met him.

"Shit, I'm a mess," Sydney confessed while swiping at her cheeks, laughing a little. "Just glad everyone is okay."

Gray wrapped an arm around Tessa and kissed the top of her head. Yeah, he was an emotional wreck himself after everything they'd just gone through. But Whit was cuffed, the bomb defused, and most importantly, Tessa was safe at his side. A place he never wanted her to leave for the rest of his life.

Sydney introduced Beckett to Tessa a moment later, making sure to use the words "my fiancé." When Gray overheard Tessa's name being shouted, they all turned to see who was trying to break through the crowd of officers.

"Naomi!" Tessa shrieked. She slid out from under Gray's arm, and since it was for a good reason, he let her go.

Beckett lifted his hand in the air and flicked two fingers, signaling to the police to let Naomi through.

Gray let go of a harsh breath of relief at the sight of Tessa hugging her best friend, then turned to the side, finding his family en route to get to them. *All* of them. Parents. Sister and brother-in-law. Both nieces.

"We'll give you some privacy," Sydney said.

Gray looked around at the police, media, and bystanders crowded out there. "Not exactly private."

"Grayson Chandler," his mom cried out. He could hear the half-scolding undertone she was using, more than likely for scaring her. With tears in her eyes, she pressed up on her toes and grabbed hold of him. She smashed her cheek to his chest, and Gray wrapped one arm around her, then another around Natasha, hugging them both. And he was crying again.

Gray lifted his chin from where it rested on his mom's head to find his father and Wyatt, side by side, studying them. Wyatt had Emory bundled in a blanket in the crook of his arm, and his other arm was slung protectively around Gwen.

"You did good, son," his father remarked with a nod.

"Pretty sure it was all Tessa," he replied. *Diffusing tension instead of defusing a bomb.* He let go of his mom and sister at the sound of Tessa's voice, but before he could snatch her back up again, his mom and Natasha beat him to it.

"Mom, you remember Tessa, right? From Walter Reed a million years ago?" Gray smiled, waving a semi-awkward hand between them once Tessa was free from the cage of his mom and sister's arms.

"I do. I always knew you were special," his mom said, drying her tears before Gray's dad hugged his mom to his side.

They exchanged a bit more small talk, and Tessa introduced Naomi to everyone. Gray turned at the feel of eyes on him and found Jack quietly standing at a distance, stroking his jaw. The sun had set a while ago, but with all the lights still on out there, he could clearly make out the distressed look on his best friend's face.

"Excuse me for a moment." Gray left everyone and went over to Jack, wondering why he was hanging back. "Hey, man."

Jack filled his cheeks with air before slowly exhaling. He leaned in and gave Gray a real hug. Not the manly one-arm shit they normally did. "You scared me," he said by his ear. "When I told you in Zurich you'd swap places for someone too . . . I didn't mean that as some foreshadowing crap."

Gray stepped back at his friend's choked-up words, and Jack dragged a hand down his face, trying to hide the emotions he was struggling to suppress.

"You have nine fucking lives, man." Jack nodded. "Let's not try and use up any more of them, though, okay?"

Gray tipped his head. "Yeah, okay." He pulled him back in for another hug, slapping his back harder that time.

Gray kept one arm wrapped around Jack's shoulders as they both made their way back to everyone.

Tessa motioned for Gray to join her off to the side. "There's something I didn't get to tell you in there." She wet her lips, and he snatched her cheeks between his palms, going a bit breathless with anticipation of what he hoped he'd hear. "You probably know it though."

His brows slanted as he leaned closer, drawing his face near hers. "Doesn't mean I still don't want to hear it." He brushed his lips over hers, not giving a damn they had an audience.

"I love you, Gray," she said when their mouths broke. "And I trust you. I need *you* to know that."

His heart swelled at both statements.

"I don't want you worrying what I'll think. I know you. I know your heart." She kissed him, urging his lips to part, and their tongues met. "I trust you with both my heart and my safety."

"Thank you," he whispered, his voice done for the night. "Can I take you home now?"

"Only if you stay with me."

He cocked a brow and chewed on his lip as he stared at her. "So damn bossy."

She smirked and, in a sexy tone, murmured back, "And you like it."

CHAPTER FORTY-TWO

A FEW WEEKS LATER - ARLINGTON, VIRGINIA

TESSA PEERED OUT THE FRONT WINDOW OF GRAY'S PARENTS' house with mixed feelings at the sight before her. Her father was gently cupping her mother's cheeks. Leaning in. Hesitant and unsure. "He's going to kiss her, isn't he?" Goose bumps peppered her skin, and she pulled down the sleeves of her sweater dress.

Gray strode up alongside her, peeked, then reached for the curtains to draw them closed. "I think so."

"And I should give them some privacy?" She smirked, and he slid his hands to her hips, turning her to face him.

He tossed a quick look over his shoulder, as if checking if they were still alone, before focusing back on her. "Want to steal a moment too?"

"Mmm." She set her forearms over his shoulders and linked her wrists behind his neck. "You'll never need to steal anything. I'll give you any and every moment you'll ever want. Freely."

"Damn, woman," he said with a light shake of the head, bringing his mouth closer to hers. "I fall more and more in love with you every day." He kissed her softly as she lifted one hand into his hair, teasing her fingers through his thick locks. He dragged his lips along her cheek, his facial hair tickling her skin, before bringing his mouth to her ear. "I've missed sleeping with you these last three nights." He stroked her back a few times before easing away to find her eyes. "I'm glad your dad is back, of course, but maybe if I get lucky, he'll wind up at your mom's apartment tonight so I can have my woman back."

They'd spent every single day together since the insanity of what happened with Whit at her practice, but when her father showed up single after his girlfriend dumped him to surprise her for Thanksgiving a few days ago, Gray had decided it'd be best for them to not all sleep under the same roof.

"Mmm. How much do you want me?" She teased her brows up and down, checked over her shoulder to ensure they were still alone, then focused back on her guy, arching into him, confirming he was harder than hard. He groaned and dipped down to slide his tongue along the seam of her lips. "Do you have a fetish for ChapStick like I do? You sure love to suck it free," she teased before he could answer her original question.

"I only like it when it's on your lips." He pulled back to look into her eyes. "I may have a thing for you in high heels too."

"Blue ones, if I remember correctly?"

"Shit, did I admit that at some point? Talk in my sleep?" He laughed.

"You may have said something on the yacht in Turkey.

That feels like a decade ago now." Had it really been less than a month since then? "So, tell me, how much do you want me?" she repeated in a sultry voice.

Bringing his hand up from her back, he fisted it in her hair, tugging just enough to angle her head while he stared down at her mouth. "You know I prefer showing to telling."

"Yeah, you certainly showed me how much you missed our sleepovers in my office yesterday." She thought back to the moment when he'd brought her lunch. When she'd asked where his meal was, he'd answered with his tongue between her legs. She'd never think about lunch the same way again.

Gray angled his head toward the window. "Maybe tonight."

Since her mom's last job in Peru with Doctors Without Borders had just wrapped up, and she was back in her D.C. apartment . . . maybe her dad would go there?

"You okay with them hooking up?"

She considered his question while listening to the rest of the guests Gray's parents had invited chat down the hall in the dining room.

Gray's mom had invited Curtis and Naomi as well, but they couldn't make it. Curtis was spending Thanksgiving with his mom in New York and Naomi was with her parents in Boston. It would've been nice to have them all together.

"Am I okay? Maybe. But they're so different. But I believe in second chances." She shifted in his arms so her back was now to his chest, her attention square on the room. He wrapped his arms around her in the position she could last a lifetime in. "We're evidence of that, right?"

His warm breath touched her ear as he replied, "Absolutely."

Before she could say more, she spotted Jack walking into

the room with Natasha and Gwen trailing behind him. He was holding Emory and looking comfortable and relaxed with her in his arms. He'd make a good dad if he ever found his "the one." From what Gray had told her, Jack had doubts that'd happen, which was sad. Jack was too good of a person to not find happiness.

"Is your dad still outside saying goodbye to your mom?" Gwen dropped onto the sofa and rested her head back as if she were stuffed from the huge meal they'd all devoured.

Jack walked over to the window and shifted the curtains to the side with his free hand. "Well, hot damn, the colonel is making out with your mom." He let the curtains fall back into place before Tessa snatched Emory from his arms. The way Gray stared at her as she held his niece . . . her heart was going to burst.

"It was hard to sit at the table tonight and not let your mom know your dad morphed into Bryan Mills not too long ago," Jack added with a laugh. "Is he going to tell her what really happened to you two?" He sat on the edge of the couch, and Gwen scooched over and made room for Natasha.

"Maybe he will? I don't know if she could handle the story though. I can barely believe it." Tessa tickled Emory, and she giggled. "You look exhausted," she cooed to her when Emory gave her a big yawn.

"Yeah, Wyatt and I should get her home before it's too late." But Natasha stayed on the couch as if she didn't have the energy to get up.

And as if on cue, Wyatt strode into the room and offered Natasha his forearm. "Come on, Mama. Let me get my girls to bed," he said as he helped Natasha up, then he leaned in and kissed the top of Gwen's head. "Stay out of trouble, will ya?"

"Me?" Gwen smirked. "Trouble? Never."

Wyatt rolled his eyes, then took Emory from Tessa, saying their goodbyes once Gray's parents were back in the room.

Wyatt opened the front door, and Tessa's father was standing there alone on the porch.

"I'm heading out as well," her dad announced once he'd stepped aside to let Wyatt and Natasha leave. "Thank you for the dinner," he said to Gray's mom. "Good to see you, Warren," he added to the admiral. Then he motioned for Tessa to come his way.

"Where are you going? Back to my place?" she asked him.

He cleared his throat and nodded toward the outside. "Your mom's place." He leaned closer and told her, "Your mom was always the love of my life, and I messed up. You and Gray have inspired me to go for my second chance."

Oh. My. God. She was going to melt.

"And tell Romeo he can return to your place tonight. You think I don't know he bailed when I showed up?" He kissed her cheek and squeezed her shoulder. "I'll come by to get my stuff tomorrow."

Wait . . . what?

He waved his hand in the air and said another goodbye to everyone. Just before he turned to leave, he whispered, "Oh, and tell Gray I thought about it, and my answer is yes."

Tessa turned back to the room, confused.

"He okay?" Gray asked with concern, reaching for her hand as the door closed between her and her father.

"Yeah, I guess. He's going to my mom's tonight."

Gray's eyes lit up. "Oh he is, huh?"

"He also told me to tell you yes to your question."

His lips broke into a broad smile. "Time for us to go too," he announced abruptly. Facing the room, he rushed out, "Thanks for dinner. It was great. But I'm full and exhausted. We're going to head out."

He let go of Tessa's hand and went over to his family to say his goodbyes, not giving anyone a chance to protest their sudden departure.

You must have really missed me.

Gray's mom shot him a knowing smile before hugging Tessa while whispering in her ear, "Thank you, my dear. Thank you for saving my son. Thirteen years ago. And now. You're who I'm most thankful for this Thanksgiving. Thank you . . ."

* * *

SITTING ON HER BED LATER THAT NIGHT, TESSA STARED AT her last message from Naomi as she waited for Gray. He'd disappeared into her office the second they'd arrived at her house, which was . . . weird, to say the least.

> Naomi: He's going to propose. He asked your dad for your hand, and he said yes. And he's got no patience. He wants you as his wife, now.

> > Tessa: Maybe that's not what he asked him. Maybe he asked him if he could do something else.

> Naomi: What? Permission to bang his only daughter? *crying-laughing emoji*

Her hands were sweaty just thinking about a proposal. Not because she didn't want to marry that man. Not because she felt it'd be too soon. But because she DID want it. Like yesterday. And if Naomi was wrong, she'd have to put on her big-girl panties and learn some patience. *But when you know, you know.* She'd known thirteen years ago he was the one, and she knew now. No question.

> Tessa: Just tell me how your night was. Distract me while I wait for him to do whatever he's doing in my office.

When the bubbles came and went, well . . . she knew something was off.

> Tessa: What is it you're not telling me?

> Naomi: I lied. *face-palm emoji*

> Tessa: What do you mean? About what?

> Naomi: I'm not with my parents. Hold on. Creating a group text.

A group text? With who? She popped up to her feet as she waited, confused yet again that evening.

> Curtis: Hey, sis. Um . . . I'm with Naomi.

Holy shit. "First my parents, and now you two?"

> Naomi: When he came to see you after the nightmare of what happened a few weeks ago, we wound up talking.

> Tessa: And by "talking" you mean having sex? *sly-smile emoji*

Curtis: . . .

Naomi: I didn't know how to tell you. We decided to escape for the holiday, just the two of us.

Tessa: I'm screaming with excitement on the inside. Seriously. THIS is a dream come true. My bestie and favorite brother together. SERIOUSLY, soooo happy for you two! Please get married. Make babies. Like now. I'm ready to be the cool auntie.

Curtis: *emoji cocking a brow* I'm your ONLY brother. But glad you approve.

Naomi: And also . . . slow down, silly. We're just getting to know each other.

Tessa: Yeah, in bed. *winking emoji*

Curtis: She knows. I told her. Just so you know.

Oh. Ohhhh. Wow. You told her you're CIA? No secrets between them. *That's huge.* And a relief. It'd been brutal keeping that secret from Naomi. *And I call BS on the "just getting to know you" stuff.*

Tessa looked up to see Gray standing in the doorway. She wasn't sure how long he'd been there, but he was casually leaning against the interior frame looking all hot and sexy, his hand on his belt buckle, his eyes set squarely on her.

Tessa: I have to go. He's back. Love you both. So happy.

She tossed her phone on the bed. "Naomi and my brother are having a secret hookup weekend." She tipped her shoulder. "Well, not a secret now that I know. But looks like this is a day of love, not just a day for saying thanks."

A slow smile spread across his lips, and he let go of the belt buckle that was undone.

"That's nice." He smiled. "Now, clothes off, sweetheart," he casually ordered.

She hastily removed and tossed her cashmere sweater dress, a slightly less sexy version of the one she'd worn in Zurich, to the floor. Boots next. She stripped out of her panties and bra a moment later, and she reveled in Gray's heated stare as he raked his eyes from her toes up to her breasts.

"What if I make use of those neon blue high heels I never thought I'd wear again? Maybe add a little more ChapStick to my lips too?" she teased.

Remaining rigid in the doorway, he quietly observed her, merely tipping his head yes. He was giving her that "grizzly" look, restraining himself the best he could. Keeping the sexy beast she wanted to come out to play locked up until just the right moment.

She went into her closet and slipped on the heels, then snatched her ChapStick from the dresser before striding as sexily as possible, without tripping, back to the center of her room. Every little movement she made seemed to command his attention, and it made her feel so freaking sexy and beautiful.

He always made her feel like she was the only woman in the world.

"I've been thinking about fucking you in just that for thirteen years," he rasped, his tone hoarse.

"Mmm." God, she was soaked at the thought alone. It wouldn't take much for her to get off. "What if we up the stakes a little?" After applying the ChapStick, she tossed it back onto the dresser. "Throw in one more thing you've yet to have of mine."

He cocked his head. "What's that?"

She swallowed back her nerves, her shyness, and her reservations knowing the size and thickness of his cock, and offered, "My third hole."

Gray stood straight, no longer leaning into the doorframe, and his shoulders slammed back as his spine went straight. His nostrils flared. "I'm pretty sure it'll hurt, unless you have some lube stashed in here somewhere."

Her eyes dipped to his belt buckle. "I could always bite into that to help get me through it."

He looked down at his belt, then back up at her as she cupped her breast, anxious for him to touch her instead. Then he unzipped his jeans, never removing his eyes from her face. "I've never done it that way before either, just so you know."

Ohh. A shiver rolled down her spine in slow motion, and she trembled from the chills that followed. "We can be *each other's onlys* again."

"I'd love nothing more than that." His brows slanted over his light green eyes. "But there's something else I'd like you to wear while I fuck your ass, my naughty girl." His gaze softened a moment later. "But maybe we should make love first the traditional way?" He sighed out a deep breath as he started her way. "I can't wait, Tessa. I need you to be my *only* forever. Under God. The law. All of it." He reached into his pocket for something, then unfurled his fingers and opened his palm. "I haven't had a chance to buy a ring, but with your dad saying yes tonight, I can't wait to ask. I'm not patient when it comes to you, so I improvised."

She covered her mouth with her hand when she saw the handmade metal ring in his palm. "You MacGyver'ed a paperclip into an engagement ring in my office?" She lifted her blurry eyes to his face. "That's what you were doing?"

"I'm no MacGyver, so it took like five tries. But until I can get you a ring, will you wear this?" When he attempted to get on one knee, which she knew was difficult with his prosthesis, she grabbed his forearms, stopping him from kneeling. He met her eyes and tipped his head. "Marry me, Contessa?"

She pushed the lump of emotion down her throat and nodded. "Yes, Grayson, I'll marry you."

A tear rolled down his cheek and fell onto their hands as he slid the ring on her finger. He pressed his mouth to hers, tasting her tongue. Kissing her gently before it turned into something fierce. Hot. Lovemaking with their mouths.

"You do realize I'll have to modify this proposal story, right?" she asked once they'd stopped kissing. "I can't tell anyone you proposed while I was naked, and we were about to do anal."

A deep, sexy rumble escaped his lips. God, she loved that man's laugh. "I should've thought about that. My bad."

"No." She slung her arms over his shoulders. "It's perfect. It's us." She smiled and gave him a close-mouthed kiss before pulling her hand back between them to look at her ring.

He frowned. "Sorry if it pokes or scrapes your skin."

She peered back up at him. "Mmm, a little pain can be good if it's for the right reason." She swiped at her happy tears, then snatched his hands and set them on her ass, arching into him.

"What are you saying?" He grinned.

"I'm also impatient, and I want us to skip straight to another shared first," she murmured.

He growled out a curse, confirming he understood the assignment, and tossed her onto the bed, then whipped his belt free from his jeans in one fast movement.

"Now be a good girl for me, sweetheart," he commanded while snapping the belt between his palms, "and bend over."

EPILOGUE

"THE WEDDING BAR HAS BEEN SET PRETTY HIGH NOW WITH this shindig," Jack said with a light laugh. He lifted his tumbler to his lips, his eyes set on the rolling green hills just beyond the castle's balcony where they stood.

Gray turned to the side and glanced at the ballroom. "It was McKenna's idea, you know that. She wanted her dad and Sydney to have a fairy-tale wedding, and well, Sydney's family has the money to rent a castle and make it happen." He spied Beckett's daughter dancing with her dad just inside the room, and he couldn't help but smile at the sight. *One day, I'll have kids. If I'm lucky, I'll have a daughter, and she'll take after Tessa.*

He focused back on the greenery, spotting Carter's dog, Dallas, and Chris and Rory's dog, Bear, chasing each other in circles. Both dogs had received an invite to the wedding, another idea of McKenna's that Gray had loved. Gray had assumed Dallas would've been Carter's plus-one, but he'd shocked everyone by bringing a date. And not just any date. *Zoey.*

"I was in town. He told me he was going solo. I offered an assist," Zoey had explained when everyone had stared at the "couple" in shock.

"An assist?" Jack had piped up. *"You think some bad guys might fast-rope in and ruin their wedding?"*

"This is us we're talking about. You never know," Oliver had joked.

"Why are you out here by yourself though?" Gray finally asked him.

It'd been a daytime wedding. Sun shining. Flowers in bloom. Pretty perfect. And no bad guys so far. So, why was his best friend so somber looking?

"I'm just getting some fresh air. Stuffy in there." Jack casually sipped his drink, and Gray folded his arms, studying him.

Gray frowned. "You sure that's all it is?" he couldn't help but press, and when Jack faced the ballroom and tossed a sharp look toward one particular couple dancing, well, he realized his answer. "You have feelings for her."

"Who?" Jack looked at him, cocking a brow.

"I have eyes, brother. I've seen the way you've been looking at her ever since Turkey. You can't hide that shit from me. You've been trying, and I kept my mouth shut, but—"

"Feelings and attraction are different." He grunted and tossed back the rest of his whiskey. "She's gorgeous. And I do have eyes. What do you expect from a single guy like me who hasn't been laid in too damn long?" He discarded his glass on one of the high-top tables on the balcony, then grasped the knot of his tie and loosened it. "But I'll never cross the line with her. I wouldn't even consider it."

Gray looked back toward the woman Jack had set his

sights on. "Mya brought Mason as her date because he's a friend."

"A friend with benefits," Jack barked out in a low, gruff tone.

"Tessa said they're *only* friends now. She gives me updates on everyone. Even when I don't want to know," he said with a laugh.

"Well then, what about Oliver? He's certainly one reason I should only ever admire her from afar." He let go of his tie and grabbed at the skin on his throat.

Gray's focus slipped away from him and back to the ballroom in search of Oliver. When he found him, Oliver wasn't looking at Mya and Mason dancing. Nope, he was standing by the bar and . . . if looks could kill . . . he appeared to want to murder the man dancing with Gwen.

Aw, shit. Do you have a death wish, man? Wyatt will kill you.

Gwen's date was in his twenties. She'd probably only brought him to appease her father and not give him a heart attack that weekend. But based on Oliver's face going a touch red, and how he was observing the two slow dancing, he might be the one to snap.

"I think Oliver and Mya have a more brother-sister relationship thing going these days," Gray admitted, which had become more and more obvious the last several months they'd worked together.

"Doesn't matter. I'm just attracted to her. That's it." He let go of his neck and twirled a finger in the air. "Boy Scout's honor I won't ever make a move on her."

"Just because we were in the Boy Scouts together doesn't make that oath worth anything now." Gray smiled.

"Go find your woman. Dance with her. I'm fine." Jack flicked his wrist, gesturing for him to scram.

Gray unlocked his arms from across his chest when he heard a change of music from inside the room. He looked over to see Beckett taking the microphone, dedicating a song to his wife. Beckett's brothers were gathering on stage to stand behind him with microphones as well. The Hawkins men all had damn good voices, and Sydney was going to swoon listening to her husband and his brothers sing. He was truly happy for her.

"And now Beckett is setting the wedding bar even higher by serenading his wife with backup singers," Jack said with a laugh, watching the scene unfold. "Yup, hopefully my future wife isn't in that room. I can't live up to all this."

That had Gray's attention. "So, you're thinking you will remarry one day?"

"Shit." Jack tossed his hand in the air. "Ignore me. I'm going to go inside and find a single woman to dance with so you can stop worrying about me for no good reason." He removed his suit jacket and tossed it over the railing before striding into the room.

Gray let go of a deep breath, then followed him in search of *his* wife. After his paperclip proposal, he'd woken up at zero five hundred and slipped away to take advantage of the post-Thanksgiving early store hours to buy her a ring. He was back by zero six hundred before she woke, and he set the ring box on her nightstand.

The look on her face had been everything. And then they'd made love again. And then a few more times. Basically, all over her house until her father had shown up to grab his things, nearly catching them mid-act. But the colonel had been happy to see the ring on her finger, and Gray had been thankful it'd been a real one instead of the paperclip for her dad to see.

They'd been impatient and had married in January. A

small church wedding with just their families, and best friends. It'd been perfect.

And his incredible wife really was perfect in every way. She'd even insisted on visiting Whit in prison, with Gray at her side, of course. And she wrote Whit letters of encouragement. She gave that man a reason to live despite what he'd done. And Gray had been relieved to report to him that soldiers had already been saved because of the program's "reboot" in January.

"Hey, you." Gray shook free from his thoughts at his wife's words, and he turned to face her on the dance floor. She draped her arms over his shoulders, and he wrapped his arms around her waist, and they joined in with the others to dance to the Cody Johnson song Beckett and his brothers were singing.

Gray spied Tessa's parents dancing not far away. Her mom was laughing at something the colonel was saying. They'd kept dating ever since Thanksgiving, and the colonel had decided to follow her wherever her job took her just as she'd once done for him.

"They look happy," Tessa mused. He thought she was referring to her parents, but when he followed her eyes, he found her focused on her best friend being twirled around the dance floor by her brother.

He wasn't sure if her parents would be the next to marry or if it'd be Naomi and Curtis. Like Tessa, Naomi had also become friends with Sydney and Mya in the last few months, resulting in Naomi receiving a wedding invite and bringing Curtis as her plus-one. It'd been damn good to see all the women in his life growing close and getting along. And it felt good that Tessa truly trusted him, particularly when he had to spin up with Sydney.

But leaving Tessa for work never got easier, and he doubted it ever would.

"What are you thinking about?" he asked, realizing her attention was now elsewhere. That time, when he followed her gaze, it was fixed on Griffin's wife, Savanna, cuddling Jesse and Ella's son in her arms. Savanna was six months pregnant and showing, and Gray had a feeling Griffin would soon slow down on operating with her entering her third trimester.

"I'm just thinking maybe I should ditch the IUD."

Gray stopped dancing and looked away from Remington Tucker McAdams, or Remi, as Jesse and Ella called their son . . . to focus on his gorgeous wife. Was she offering him the only thing he still wanted in life? A child with her?

"You serious?" He gulped and chills darted up his spine. Was it getting hot in there? Damn.

She teased her lip between her teeth and nodded. "What do you say?"

"How about I show you how I feel about it?"

She chuckled. "Now?"

He grinned and nodded. "You feeling adventurous?"

She lowered her arms from his shoulders. "What do you have in mind?"

"Come with me." He stepped back, took her hand, and they maneuvered through the crowd as they escaped the ballroom, one mission in mind. A few doors down the hall, he stopped at the sight of Dallas sitting in front of one of the rooms. "When did you come back inside?" he asked as if Dallas could respond.

Tessa crouched before Carter's dog, then peered at the room off to their right. "I think something's wrong. Someone's in pain," Tessa whispered as Dallas angled his head, peering at Gray.

On instinct, Gray reached for his back—and yeah, he had his 9mm on him, because "you just never know." He then motioned for Tessa to back away from the door.

She went to the other side of the hall and Dallas trotted over to her. She was a magnet for dogs, and he loved that about her. But if Dallas wasn't clawing at the door, he had to believe nothing serious was wrong on the other side.

He tested the handle, finding it unlocked, then slowly opened it and crept in. He peeked around the corner in what was an office, stopping in his tracks while lowering his firearm.

Carter was standing with his white dress shirt open, tie gone. Pants still on, he had Zoey on the desk in front of him, her dress bunched around her waist, ankles hooked around his back. He stopped moving, well *fucking* her . . . and casually looked Gray's way like he hadn't been caught in a hot moment. Carter kept his hand positioned on Zoey's stomach, pinning her in place, as his gaze cut to the 9mm in Gray's hand. "Is there a problem out there?"

Gray shook his head, blinking in shock. "Uh, nope. Sorry." He immediately left without another word and closed the door behind him. "You could've warned me, buddy. No door lock, I guess," he said as Dallas went to his hind legs and jumped on him as if laughing at the whole thing.

"Is everything okay?" Tessa asked as he tucked his weapon beneath his jacket.

"We're married, so that means you get to know everything, right?"

She smirked. "Of course."

He motioned for Dallas to get down, then hooked his arm with Tessa's. "Carter's banging Zoey in the office."

Tessa shot him a shocked look, quietly processing his words as he led her farther down the hallway.

He was still a man on a mission. Same mission as Carter, apparently.

"For two people who hate each other . . ." She smiled at him from over her shoulder, leaving him to finish the thought in his head.

Yeah, it's strange. They took the stairs, his mind made up to have their adventure outside. It was a mild sunny day. Plus, with Carter railing Zoey inside, he'd prefer to be farther away when he made love to his wife. "This whole wedding has been a bunch of curveballs. Jack having the hots for Mya. Oliver staring at my niece's date like he wants to kill him."

"Wait, slow down. You'll need to catch me up on what I missed," she said as they made their way to a trail that ran along a stream.

Gray filled her in on his observations from the balcony as they walked, stopping for a second to give her his suit jacket. It was only in the upper sixties, and she was in a sleeveless pale yellow bridesmaid dress—she'd been in Sydney's bridal party—and he didn't want her getting cold.

"Wait. Did you hear that?" Her gaze narrowed with alarm. "Is that yelping?" Before he could stop her, she started for the water, his jacket falling from her shoulders.

Oh hell no, he didn't need her falling into the stream and freezing.

"Oh my God. There's a puppy in the water." She stood at the edge as if preparing to jump in. At that point, the stream looked more like a fast-moving river, and he had no clue how deep it was. But there was a cute little brown dog hanging on a tree root that dangled just above the water's surface. His back end and hind legs were still under, but his front legs were clinging to the branch for dear life. "We have to help."

"I'll go in," he decided. But he didn't want to wear a sopping wet suit back into a castle.

"Hurry," she begged, then knelt by the water, keeping her eyes on the puppy.

He carefully set his weapon down, then stripped to his boxers, which had been his plan when they'd left the castle to begin with, but not to jump into the cold water.

He detached his prosthesis and, without another word, jumped into the water. The breath was knocked from his lungs. New York in the spring meant the water was still damn cold, and it'd been a long-ass time since he'd done any ops involving water. It only went to his waist, but without his prosthesis, he had to swim over instead of walk across. "It's okay. I won't hurt you," he told the soaked puppy, and the dog cried with what Gray assumed was relief once he was safe in his arms.

Tucking the puppy into the crook of his elbow, he swam back over to the ledge and handed the dog over to Tessa before hoisting himself back up onto the ground. While she began to wrap the dog up in his suit jacket, he dried off his leg with his pants and reattached his prosthesis. Then he slipped back into his pants.

"Oh my God, Gray."

At Tessa's concerned cry, he abandoned his efforts to put on his shirt and shifted alongside her, ignoring the cold biting into his back.

She opened the jacket up to show him something. "He's . . . missing a leg."

Gray hung his head, then reached for the little guy's stomach and scratched him, doing his best not to get choked up. He just rescued an animal that had lost a limb, and the symbolism was sure as hell not lost on him.

"If he doesn't have—"

"I don't think he has a home. He looks too young to even be out here. Abandoned." He was sick at the idea he'd been ditched somewhere, more than likely because of his leg, and . . . *Fuck. Now I just might cry.* "He can be ours, yes," he said, emotions pushing up inside him as he stroked the little guy's head.

"I know what we should call him." She peered over at Gray, and he knew exactly what she was going to say, God help him, he loved this woman.

"Lucky?" he asked.

She nodded. "He's lucky we saved him. But I feel lucky we found him." Tears streamed down her face, cutting through the makeup she didn't normally wear, but she'd had professionally done for the wedding.

"I like that." He leaned in and kissed his wife's forehead. "But we're still going to ditch the birth control, right?"

She laughed. "Without a doubt."

Gray snatched his shirt from where he'd tossed it and put it back on.

"What do you say, Lucky, do you want to be part of our family?" She leaned in and rubbed her nose against the puppy's.

He yelped and made a cute little whine for more attention that Tessa happily gave him.

"I think we should take that as a yes," Gray confirmed. He looked back toward the castle to see Bear flying their way as if he'd heard and sensed what was going on.

"Hey, boy," he said as Bear plowed into him, nearly knocking him to his back from excitement, sniffing and checking out their new friend. "I know, I know." Gray peered at Tessa cuddling Lucky, letting him lick and kiss her as she fell in love with him. "I'm a little jealous too."

ALSO BY BRITTNEY SAHIN

Find the latest news from my newsletter/website and/or Facebook group: Brittney's Book Babes

Other resources:

Bonus Scenes

Publication order for all books

Books by Series

Pinterest Muse/Inspiration Boards

Tiktoks

Spotify Music Playlists

* * *

Standalone Military Romance

Until You Can't

Let Me Love You

Falcon Falls Security

The Hunted One - book 1 - Griffin & Savanna

The Broken One - book 2 - Jesse & Ella

The Guarded One - book 3 - Sydney & Beckett

The Taken One - book 4 - Gray & Tessa

Stealth Ops Series: Bravo Team

Finding His Mark - Book 1 - Luke & Eva

Finding Justice - Book 2 - Owen & Samantha

Finding the Fight - Book 3 - Asher & Jessica

Finding Her Chance - Book 4 - Liam & Emily

Finding the Way Back - Book 5 -Knox & Adriana

Stealth Ops Series: Echo Team

Chasing the Knight - Book 6 -Wyatt & Natasha

Chasing Daylight - Book 7 - A.J. & Ana

Chasing Fortune - Book 8 - Chris & Rory

Chasing Shadows - Book 9 -Harper & Roman

Chasing the Storm - Book 10 - Finn & Julia

Becoming Us: *connection to the Stealth Ops Series (books take place between the prologue and chapter 1 of Finding His Mark)*

Someone Like You - A former Navy SEAL. A father. And off-limits. (Noah Dalton)

My Every Breath - A sizzling and suspenseful romance. Businessman Cade King has fallen for the wrong woman. She's the daughter of a hitman - and he's the target.

Dublin Nights

On the Edge - Adam & Anna

On the Line - follow-up wedding novella (Adam & Anna)

The Real Deal - Sebastian & Holly

The Inside Man - Cole & Alessia

The Final Hour - Sean and Emilia

Sports Romance (with a connection to *On the Edge*):

The Story of Us– Sports columnist Maggie Lane has 1 rule: never fall for a player. One mistaken kiss with Italian soccer star Marco Valenti changes everything…

Hidden Truths

The Safe Bet – Begin the series with the Man-of-Steel lookalike Michael Maddox.

Beyond the Chase - Fall for the sexy Irishman, Aiden O'Connor, in this romantic suspense.

The Hard Truth – Read Connor Matthews' story in this second-chance romantic suspense novel.

Surviving the Fall – Jake Summers loses the last 12 years of his life in this action-packed romantic thriller.

The Final Goodbye - Friends-to-lovers romantic mystery

FALCON FALLS CROSSOVER INFO

Where else have you seen some of these characters?

Gray Chandler was first introduced in *Chasing the Knight*, and he's also in the epilogue of *Chasing the Storm*.

Jack London was also in *Chasing the Knight*. (Dale was in chapter one marrying Clara).

Gwen Montgomery - Wyatt's daughter - introduced in Wyatt's book, *Chasing the Knight*.

Mya Vanzetti is a journalist in the contemporary romance, *My Every Breath*. And she is Julia Maddox's friend in *Chasing the Storm* (where she helps save Oliver's life). She joins Falcon Falls Security in Sydney's book - *The Guarded One*.

In *Chasing Daylight*, we first meet the Alabama crew (Jesse, Beckett, McKenna, etc). We also discover the tension between Ella & Jesse in this book, and that tension continues in *Chasing Fortune*, which is **Rory's (Jesse's sister's)** book.

Aside from the Falcon Falls Series - **Carter Dominick** was also in *Chasing Fortune* and *Chasing the Storm.*

Zoey was first introduced in *The Broken One.*

Oliver and **Griffin** are briefly in *Chasing the Storm* as well. But in *Chasing the Storm* - Griffin is only referred to as "Southern sniper guy."

Previous Falcon books

The Hunted One (Falcon Falls, book 1) is Savanna and Griffin's story

The Broken One (Falcon Falls, book 2) is Jesse and Ella's book

The Guarded One (Falcon Falls, book 3) - Sydney & Beckett's book

FAMILY TREE

Falcon Falls Team members:

Team leader: **Carter Dominick - Army Delta Force/CIA**

- A widower (lost his wife)
- Dog: Dallas

Team leader: **Gray Chandler - Army SF (Green Beret)**

- Now married to Tessa
- Dog: Lucky

Other family members:

- Admiral Chandler & Mrs. Chandler
- Natasha (sister)
- Wyatt (brother-in-law)
- Nieces: Emory Pierson & Gwen Montgomery

Jesse - Army Ranger / CIA (hitman)

Family / Friends:

- Wife: Ella Mae (son: Remington "Remi" Tucker McAdams)
- Sister: Rory
- Parents: Donna and Sean
- Brother-in-law: Chris
- Friends: AJ, Beckett, Caleb, and Shep Hawkins
- Beckett's daughter: McKenna (adopted son: Miles)
- AJ & Ana's son: Marcus (Mac)

Griffin Andrews - Delta Force

- Married to Savanna (pregnant)

Jack London - Army SF (Green Beret) / CIA (Ground Branch Division)

- Divorced (Jill London)

Oliver Lucas - Army Airborne

- Tucker Lucas - brother (deceased)
- Tucker was engaged to Julia Maddox before he passed away.

Sydney Archer - Army

- Married to Beckett / Son: Levi
- McKenna and Miles Hawkins (stepchildren)

* * *

Stealth Ops Team Members

Team leaders: Luke & Jessica Scott / Intelligence team member: Harper Brooks; Bear (canine)

Bravo Team:
Bravo One - Luke
Bravo Two - Owen
Bravo Three - Asher
Bravo Four - Liam
Bravo Five - Knox

Echo Team:
Echo One - Wyatt
Echo Two - A.J.
Echo Three - Chris
Echo Four - Roman
Echo Five - Finn

Made in United States
Cleveland, OH
13 June 2025

17700601R00277